Under Ground

UNDER GROUND

Megan Marsnik

Flexible Press

Minneapolis, Minnesota

2019

Enjoy reading about the roots of our family.

Susan Ely ♡

ISBN-13: 978-1-7339763-0-5

Flexible Press
Editor: Vicki Adang,
Mark My Words Editorial Services, LLC

For my father, Bernard "Fuzzy" Marsnik,
who always fought for the underdog.

And for Iron Range women everywhere.

The woman holds up three corners of the house.

Tell the truth and run.

—Slovenian proverbs

CHAPTER 1

THERE WAS PLENTY OF DUST, PLENTY OF WHISKEY, plenty of red earth, trees, and rock. There were not enough women. So they were sent for.

The women came from many countries. Italy, Norway, Sweden, Finland, Croatia, and Slovenia. They mostly traveled alone, but some dragged along small children or nursing babies. The lucky ones had been sent for by their husbands, who had been living in the iron mining community for a year, perhaps more. They had someone to greet them when they arrived.

The least lucky were sent for by the brothel owners. Their passages out of the old country were paid in exchange for a year of service. Most of these immigrant women thought they would be tending bar, serving pints to the exhausted miners and lumberjacks. When they arrived, they quickly learned that other services were expected. They had no money and could not turn back.

Sixteen-year-old Katka Kovich did not fall into any of the usual categories. Her parents died on March 30 and April 7, 1915, both from cholera. Five weeks later, a young man with an unruly mass of black curls and a thick mustache arrived on the doorstep of the tiny cottage where she lived, suddenly alone, at the foot of the mountains in the small village of Zirovnica, Slovenia. No one had visited in weeks, and Katka's long brown hair was shamefully unbraided. A few unwashed strands blew in wisps across her sunburned face, indicating an innate wildness about her. She was eating very little, and as the flesh-iness of youth and comfort disappeared, it was as if that wildness magnified. Her skinny body was covered with an old, torn frock that had belonged to her mother. The elders from town told her to burn all of her parents' clothing, but she had been wearing this garment for days and had not become remotely sick.

"Paul Schmidt," the young man said, bowing politely. "So sorry to hear about your ma and your *ata*. I had people, too, who caught the fever."

Katka stared at him. Paul Schmidt was clean and smart looking. She wished she had washed her face in the morning, the way her mother had always instructed her to do. The wildness had been speaking to her lately, drowning out the voice of her dead mother. Her hands were smudged with dirt and blackberries. Katka buried her hands in the pocket of her apron.

Paul Schmidt peered back at her, curiously. "Are you mute?" he asked.

"Not mute," she said, clearing her throat. Her voice felt scratchy from lack of use.

"Here," Paul said. He fumbled around in his coat pocket until he found what he was looking for. He thrust a letter into her hands. The same message was written twice, once in Slovenian and once in English.

> *Dear Niece,*
> *Words cannot express my sorrow. What a terrible accident. My wife and I are prepared to offer you a home in the town of Biwabik, in the state of Minnesota in America. I am sending passage and hope you will accept.*

Sincerely,
Your uncle, Mr. Anton Kovich
Biwabik, Minnesota, United States of America

Katka folded the letter and handed it back to Paul. "Why didn't he mention you?"

"If something happened to me, I would have given the letter to someone else to deliver. Your uncle and I had a tough crossing ten years ago, when I first went to America. It is better now."

"Why did you come back?"

"My mother died."

Katka said nothing but her eyes softened. "What was her name?" He told her, and she took his hand in hers, for just a moment. When she offered a blessing, he squeezed her hand once and let it go. In that instance, she felt a slight jolt. He had a bit of the wildness in him, too, she realized. Grief. It was love with no place to go. Too powerful to keep subdued underneath skin.

"My people live not far from here," Paul said. "Your uncle Anton and his wife begged me to look after you, persuade you to come back with me. They are good people, and Anton cared a great deal for your father."

"Why did he call their deaths an accident?"

"You may need that letter when you accompany me to the States. Cholera is not a word you should mention."

"It's not a word I *enjoy* to mention," she said. She looked around the rickety cottage where she and her grief had lived alone, feeding off each other for weeks. Although the place was relatively clean now, to her it would always smell of diarrhea, urine, and death. After the burial Masses, none of her distant family had offered to take her in because, she supposed, of the word she was not mentioning.

"I leave from Trieste on the vessel *Lapland* in two days," Paul said. "Will you accompany me?"

Katka's eyes widened. "Two days?"

"I know. It's not a lot of time to make a decision."

She beckoned him into the cottage. A skeletal mouse ran across the dirt floor and disappeared into a tiny hole near a mostly empty bag of dried food.

"Ugly critter," Paul said, shivering in queasy disgust. "I hate vermin."

"It's just a mouse."

The day after her mother's burial, the mouse had emerged from under the woodpile. He didn't run along the walls of the shack; he ran straight across the floor, quickly making his way toward the slowly diminishing bags of rice and grain. The first time she saw it, Katka picked up a book and threw it at the mouse. She missed. Over the next few days she threw more books. She also threw a clay bowl, a rock, the broom. The mouse eluded her every time. After more than a week of this, she gave up trying to kill it. "You again," she would say, watching. And her voice, surrounded by the unfamiliar silence that follows new death, sounded barbarically loud no matter how quietly she uttered the words.

"Do you want me to kill it?" Paul asked.

She smiled, ever so slightly. "It's not doing anything I wouldn't do."

"It's eating your food."

"What's a grain or two to me? I have half a sack."

"To last how long?"

Katka shrugged. "I'm sorry I have no coffee to offer you, Mr. Schmidt."

"Never cared for coffee," Paul said. "Gives me a gut ache."

"How about some water? I came from the well just a bit ago. And I did some picking. Please. Rest your weary feet."

They sat at the small wooden table. Katka poured water from a pitcher into two goblets and put a basket of blackberries between them. She popped a berry in her mouth. "Eat," she said. He grabbed a few berries.

"Who owns your land, girl?" Paul asked.

"I've never seen him," Katka said. "Can't remember his name. But the man who collects the lease, he will come in five days. He demands fifteen *krona*."

"How much do you have?"

"Seven."

"If you like, I'll give you the money. The money your uncle sent."

"How much is it?"

"Enough for three months' rent. Maybe four. Ah!" The mouse was on the loose again. Paul stood up, looked around for something to throw.

Katka laughed and gestured him to leave it alone. "I wish I were like that strange little mouse. Always, he knows where he's going. I'd run in a straight line and not stop until I got there."

Paul pointed to the letter from her uncle that she had placed on the table. "There's no straight line to get to your uncle's house. There are only crooked lines, but I know them well enough."

"Perhaps a crooked line is better than no line," Katka said softly.

"It is cold where your uncle lives. Colder than the coldest day of your life. Pack your valuables in warm clothes. Dress in many layers. Bring cookware and utensils. Books, if you have any. Lots of books. Your baptismal papers. Do you have any photographs?"

"I have one of all of us, when I was a baby. And the coffin pictures. Cost me twenty-two *hellers*."

"You won't be sorry. Most have no photographs at all. You will come?" He stood up to leave.

"What choice do I have?"

"You have many choices, Miss Katka." He bent down slightly and kissed her on her left cheek. "But I will send word to Anton today. I will purchase your passage directly. I will meet you at sunup at the train station in two days."

Katka thanked him, this stranger who had arrived like a ghost. She stood in the doorway and watched as he slowly walked down the mountain pass, his masculine silhouette growing smaller and smaller as he approached the bend in the soft road that was lined with violet crocus flowers. She watched as he stopped and picked something up off the road. A toad, she suspected. He held it up to his face, as if saying hello, before putting it down gently. His rambunctious locks escaped from the back of his hat. When she was alive, her mother used to joke about handsome men. "Best to find a plain one," she had told Katka. "They make better husbands."

A few hours later, after combing and braiding her tangled mane of hair, Katka walked three miles to the market square to buy provisions for her journey. She spent three *hellers* and filled her basket with dried meat, canned beans, walnuts, and rice. On the way home, she stopped at the church. She said goodbye to Father Leo. Of all the people left in the village, he would be the one she would miss. He was a kindly man with seventy-two years. She had worked for him as a cook and secretary since she was nine years old.

"Father Leo?" She peered into his private quarters and saw the old man crumpled in his chair, a blanket over his legs, his eyes closed.

When he heard her voice, he took to his feet and embraced her. "What is it, my child?" She told him the news, and he hugged her tight. He didn't speak for a long time. "It is to be expected, I suppose. Every day, another of God's children leaving the homeland. How I will miss you, my little pony! Now who will I talk to during the long days? Only God. He's a good listener, but not much of a conversationalist."

Father Leo gave her some books and a blessing. Finally, he stood on a chair and grabbed a simple clay chalice that was resting on top of a bookshelf. He got off the chair and told Katka to open her apron pocket. He emptied the chalice. As she walked back up the pass, the coins clinked optimistically.

The next day Father Leo arrived at her cottage with a wheelbarrow. "Father!" Katka bellowed when she saw the old man pushing such a lugubrious load. "Did you haul that all this way?"

"A present," he said, smiling his toothless smile. "To bring to America." Inside the wheelbarrow, draped in wool blankets, was Father Leo's typewriter; the one Katka had used to type his sermons.

CHAPTER 2

K ATKA'S STEAMER TRUNK WAS HEAVY. SHE HAD fastened a leather strap on one end, which enabled her to drag the burdensome chest when she could no longer manage to carry it. As for Paul, he carried no trunk to speak of. He had a small suitcase that seemed weightless under his large hands. At the station in the beautiful city of nearby Ljubljana, they boarded the train that took them to a seaport in Trieste.

They waited on the docks at the port for nearly three hours before the captain allowed passengers to board. A small man in a seaman's uniform yelled, "All aboard!" and the mad dash began. Paul grabbed Katka's trunk in addition to his own small suitcase.

"Hold on to me," he commanded. "Keep up and do not let go."

Paul bandied his way through the other passengers, as if he were playing a ball game. Katka held fast to the back of his coat. Paul joggled his way, with Katka at his back, to the staircase at the rear of the ship that led to the sleeping quarters for steerage passengers. Katka grimaced at the odor, which hit her like a slap in the face. Paul quickly found a berth not far from the staircase, where the air was less foul. He deposited Katka's trunk on the stained bed. "You will sleep here," Paul said. "Sit on your mattress and do not let anyone take it from you. If anyone asks, you are traveling alone."

"Why?"

"I can't explain. Not yet."

"But where will you be?" Katka asked, suddenly terrified.

She had been in her cabin for less than a minute, but her stomach was already churning. The berths had been quickly cleaned out, the straw on the mattresses replaced, but she swore she could smell the people who had been in here before. The air was thick with an aroma of rottenness. It was a like a torturous stew of feces and rotten eggs. She wanted to hold her nose. She wanted to run back, against the crowds, and leave this stranger who had promised to take care of her, but was now saying goodbye with no reasonable explanation.

"Katka?" Paul tenderly put his hand on her cheek. He smiled. "It's no palace, this I know. But you must remember it is also not a prison. We are at the start of a journey! Anything and everything can happen. We're like birds! Isn't that exhilarating?"

"Birds?"

Paul spread his arms like wings. "Eagles, we are. I will check on you every single day."

***

A Slovenian woman shared Katka's cramped sleeping quarters. She had four children. The baby, who was six months old, was surprisingly quiet, easily lulled by his mother's capable breasts. The next youngest boy, who looked to be about three, cried constantly on the first day and began vomiting on the second. The two older girls were in charge of cleaning up and washing out the soiled diapers.

Katka could have helped, but instead, she felt herself harden. She would not get attached to this boy, to this mother. She turned her skin into a wooden door that no one could open because she knew with certainty that the boy was going to die. Katka could smell it. An odd smell, death. It was nothing like sickness, and nothing like health. It was like bread, soaked in sour milk, but frozen solid in snow. You had to get close to detect the rottenness. For weeks she had done nothing but care for her parents, but when she smelled that undeniable stench, there was nothing left to do but watch. *Stay away*, she told herself. *You are a bird.* She imagined herself flying out of the cramped quarters and into a fresh blue sky.

Finally, after four days, the young boy had nothing left to spew. He lay down, rested his head on his mother's chest, and within an hour, he stopped breathing. Two hours later, the tiny body was thrown overboard. While the family was still on deck, Katka sat on her cot and gathered her knees to her chest. When her knees started to shake, she pulled the wool blanket over her head and sobbed uncontrollably.

Afterward, Katka's little berth was much quieter. The mother cried. When her tears were gone, she laid, stomach down, on the scratchy straw, and her shoulders convulsed quietly, as if struck with the fits. The baby remained calm as ever. The older girls, eight and six, began to look like old women who carried their sorrow in their dark black eyes.

One night, Katka awoke to find Alenka, the six-year-old girl, standing over her bunk.

"Do you think the sharks ate Franc?" she asked.

Katka rose to an upright position. "Your brother?"

"Yes. Franc."

Katka hesitated. "Did someone tell you that?"

"A boy on the deck. He said children, they have more juice. That's why sharks like them."

"What kind of boy said that?"

"Italia boy. With fat cheeks."

"That explains it. Italians do have more juice," Katka said slowly. "But sharks don't like Slovenians one bit. No fish do.

Slovenian kids are too skinny. They get whisked up to heaven straight away."

"Franc was very skinny," Alenka said, relieved.

Katka continued, her voice matter-of-fact. "My ma and my *ata*, they live in heaven and like it more than Christmas. They eat *Krofi* and custard every day. And they ride horses through purple fields. Does Franc like horses?"

"Franc loves horses."

"Did you know that in heaven there are ten horses for every child? Franc can ride a different one every day."

"Oh!" the little girl said. "Franc would like that. But what if the horse is too tall for him to get on? What if the horses in heaven are giant horses?"

"My *ata* would help him get on."

"Is your *ata* strong? My *ata*, he is very strong. He can lift two bales of hay at the same time."

"My *ata* can also lift two bales of hay."

"Then he *is* strong!" The little girl smiled. Then she yawned. "Can I sleep with you?"

Alenka crawled in before Katka could shoo her away. The little girl did not smell like death. She did not smell like vomit or decay. She smelled like damp earth. Clay. Katka opened her arms, and Alenka nestled next to her. She hummed a lullaby, and soon the child was breathing rhythmically. Katka could have let her go. She could have gently carried Alenka back to her own straw bed, next to her sister. Instead, she pulled her tight. The child shivered from the draftiness of the boat; then slowly, her body temperature rose as it seeped heat from Katka's chest, and her breath fell into a childlike, raspy rhythm.

Katka gently stroked the hair of the sleeping child. She remembered sleeping with her own mother. She'd done it well past the age of most little girls. Her mother would sit up in the short bed and talk for hours, her arms flailing to punctuate important points. Katka cherished those nights, even though her mother had been a terrible storyteller, always telling the end before the beginning. The smell of her mother's skin had been soothing. Lemongrass tea. Soap made of lavender picked from the spring hills. Cabbage. And childhood.

***

Each day, at no set time, Paul Schmidt found Katka Kovich. The day after Alenka's brother died, Katka was helping distribute soup into the bowls of the emigrants waiting restlessly and hungrily. There was no dining area on this ship for steerage passengers. The immigrants ate, crowded and standing up, on the small deck reserved for the poorest passengers, or they took their bowls back to their quarters. Katka always ate outside. The food was revolting, and sometimes the very smell of it made her gag. But it was worse down below, where there was no sea breeze to dissipate the stench of the overflowing toilets, the unwashed bodies, and the vomit. After all the food was distributed and the people in their many tongues began returning to their quarters, Katka remained on the deck, standing against the railings as the sun slowly descended.

She felt a gentle hand on her shoulder, and she jumped slightly. "Didn't mean to give you a start," Paul said apologetically. "How was your dinner?"

"Delicious," Katka said. "The eggs were so fresh today. The sausages, so spicy with just the perfect amount of mustard. And the strudel was sweet, and the custard thick." She smiled mischievously.

"Oh, how you torture me with your storytelling!" Paul said. "I would sell my heart for one good sausage. Pluck it right out of my chest. How is Mrs. Zalinsky?"

"As you would expect. She is a mother who used to have four children. Now she has three," Katka said.

"Is she showing signs of sickness? She ought not have brought the sick child on the boat. Not that I blame her, I suppose. How do you leave behind a child? If you see any signs, we will try to move you. Disease spreads quickly on a ship."

"I have a strong constitution," Katka said. "Surprisingly."

Paul reached into his coat, grabbed a round object, and presented it to her.

"An orange? Is it really an orange?" She jumped up and down, like a small child. "How on earth did you get this?" she exclaimed.

"It wasn't easy," he said. "Eat it before some bandit runs up and rips it out of your hand."

"They'd have to kill me first," Katka said. She peeled away the rind and bit greedily into the fruit, allowing the juices to run down her lip.

"Missed a bit," Paul said, wiping a smearing of pulp off her chin. He examined her for a moment and laughed. "You do have some child left in you after all."

"I am no child. I just love oranges."

Paul licked his sticky finger. "Me too," he said. "How old are you, Miss Katka?"

"Old enough not to be afraid of mice," she said.

Paul laughed. "Vermin disgust me. I admit it. I'd rather face a firing squad. Are there many rats in your bunk? I tell you, I woke up to one this morning. Size of a mountain lion! It was chomping on my hair, Kat, girl. My hair, I say!"

He called her Kat, like her mother used to do. "I will have seventeen years in the fall," she said. "And, to tell it true, I'd love to wait another seventeen years before I see another rat."

"I am twenty-five," Paul said. "But I feel much older. I have seen many things in America." He took off his hat, ran his fingers through his curls. "I like to feel the wind in my hair. It makes me feel invincible. Like nothing could hold me back, see. You should try it. The wind is fierce just now."

Katka threw the fragments of orange peel into the wind. Then she untied the dingy twine that held back her matted hair. The wind grabbed hold of her strands and made them dance, like the tails of a kite. She, too, liked the feel of it. She didn't feel invincible, but she did feel alive. And that was something.

**

Paul liked to talk. Every day he told her something new. If he ran out of tales from his own life, he told her stories from books. He always changed the names of the main characters. One evening he told her about a young man who fell hopelessly in love with a woman he was not supposed to love. She was resistant at first, but eventually she had no choice but to give in to his irresistible charms.

"What was his name?" Katka asked.

"Paul Schmidt, I believe. He was so handsome the women swooned."

She laughed. "And her name?"

"I don't remember. What do you think her name was?"

Katka, she thought. *Her name was Katka,* but she did not say it out loud. She willed the words to stay in her heart and not reach her tongue. She looked at his chocolaty eyes, and her stomach began to tingle, as if she had swallowed a firefly. Was this swooning? What a queer word. For a moment, she thought her feet might give out on her and her body would drift upward and float off the ship and into the sky. She reached for the railing.

"Everything all right?"

"Of course," she said, regaining composure. "A little seasick maybe."

"Drink this," Paul said, handing her his canteen. She took a long swig and handed it back to him.

"You are good at telling stories," Katka said.

"What is the name of the girl, Katka? In the story?"

"It's not my story."

"Isn't it?"

"Are you really who you say you are, Paul Schmidt?"

He smiled. "Your uncle sent me to find you. I have found you and will do my best to bring you to him. That is not a story." He leaned over and kissed her right cheek. "You are looking pale again, Kat-girl. Get some rest, and I'll look for you tomorrow."

***

The next day Katka stayed in her bunk all day, reading, or pretending to read, one of the books Father Leo had given her. The dizzy feeling abated as soon as she left Paul. She had never been seasick and would never be so, not on a single day of their long journey. A few times she saw men with Paul's coloring pass by her berth; each time the dizziness came back.

A few days later, Katka sat cross-legged on the deck, twisting her long strands of hair. A plum fell into her lap, and when she looked up, there was Paul, his eyes vivacious.

"How in Mary's name do you keep finding fruit?" she asked. She had skipped breakfast and lunch that day. The food was getting more and more rancid. She thought she would never be hungry again. But with the plum in her hand, she realized she was starving.

"Gambling," Paul said with a shrug. "You know how to play Smear?" Smear, pronounced "shmeer," was a Slovenian card game. She shook her head. "I will teach you," Paul said. "Then maybe you can win some fruit for me."

As she began to eat the plum, he sat down beside her and asked if she knew any English. "Yes. Father Leo gave me lessons every day in the summers. His mother was English."

"Father Leo?"

"I worked for him at the rectory since I was nine years old. At first I just helped with the cows. Later I helped with the making of the bread, and the last few years Father Leo taught me to type. He was writing a book. In English. He wrote longhand in English, and I typed for him. There are many words I cannot say the right way. But I know what they mean when I read them."

"Did he pay you decently?"

"Two loaves of bread every day. He paid wages whenever he could. And we needed the money. My father's plot had stopped yielding, and we were in danger of losing the lease. My mother helped him in the fields."

"Was the landlord rich?"

"All landlords are rich. Have you been in America so long that you do not know this?" She raised a mocking eyebrow.

"Some truths are universal," Paul said.

"You mean the streets are not really paved with gold in America?"

"They are for some. But there is hope for everyone in America. It is a suckling of a country and things will change. You will see."

***

On the tenth day of the journey, the winds were so loud that the passengers could not hear each other speak, even when shouting. The sky turned an ominous gray, and Katka and Paul watched the storm approach. They saw sheets of rain, like little black exclamation points, darken the gray canvass of sky. Whitecaps tossed the monstrous ship until even those with the strongest constitutions began to churn. Deckhands appeared out of nowhere, ordering everyone back to their berths. Katka and Paul ran toward steerage as soon as they were ordered to do so, but in less than a second, the rains were upon them, and they were both drenched to the spine.

The captain ordered that the door leading from the upper deck to steerage remain locked until the storms passed. The storm lasted more than a week. The bedpans filled to overflowing. The stench of vomit and feces was suffocating. Those who were not seasick, like Katka, helped take care of the other passengers. She read and reread her books. She sang songs to the Zalinsky children and began teaching them the English she knew.

She daydreamed. She thought of her parents and the lavender that every spring would sprinkle itself like purple snowflakes across the land they never owned. The purple would stretch up the Julian Alps like a pathway to God. She wondered if there were mountains in Minnesota, America. And goats. She wondered if there would be olives and walnuts. She knew nothing about Minnesota except what Paul had told her. It was extraordinarily cold in the winter, like Siberia. Yet it was hot in the summer. Her uncle and aunt lived there. There were mines where the men worked. She wondered if Paul worked in the mine. When she saw him next, she would ask him. When would she see him again?

Eleven days later when the storm finally abated and the door was opened, allowing sunshine and fresh air to seep into the cavernous alcove of their temporary homes, the steerage passengers rushed to the light with such speed that a riot ensued, prompting the deck hands to force everyone back into their berths. One of the deck hands shouted orders in English, and then another translated in Slovenian and Croatian, another in Dutch, another in Italian. "Clergymen first!" Katka translated for the Zalinskys, then peered out. She watched as a few religious men walked past her quarters.

The next call was louder and more chilling. "Dead bodies! Dead bodies only!" The quarters grew quiet. Katka watched with horror as seventeen bodies, eight of them children, were carried solemnly to the staircase and up toward the light. Short funeral rites were given to the dead before committing them to their watery graves. Twenty minutes later, they called for the sick, but no one came forward, fearing quarantine or deportation upon arrival in America. Women and children walked up to the air next, followed by the men.

Children ran, dodging their parents and playing catch with the newly distributed fruit. The men were unshaven, and the women, many of whom had given their diminished food rations to their children, looked even skinnier than they had before. Jawbones jutted like swords from their wan faces, but most were not unhappy. As they dumped soiled hay into the ocean, they could have cursed God for unleashing this storm upon them, pushing the boat off course, seriously delaying their arrival. But they did not. Instead, most of the emigrants gave thanks in dozens of languages. They interpreted the sunshine on their face as a sign of grace.

Later in the day, Katka saw Paul gazing across the tranquility of the turquoise sea. He stretched both of his arms high above his head and balanced on his tiptoes, as if trying to elongate his body after a week of being penned up. She wanted to run toward him, but she walked. She had missed him. She had missed the way he smelled of salt and wind. She had missed their conversations. She had missed how her skin sometimes pricked when his arm brushed against hers. "Been on holiday?" She stood right next to him, stood on her own tiptoes, and mimicked his pose.

He laughed heartily. "You look like a cat waking from a nap," he said.

"You look like a bear," she said, gesturing toward his thick beard. "And an ornery one at that."

"I was going for Tolstoy."

"You like the Russians?" she asked. "After all they did to our people?"

"Think what the Russians did to their own people." He offered her his arm, and she took it. They strolled around the deck.

"I try not to."

"Did they teach you anything about Lenin in school?"

"Father Leo taught me about Lenin."

Paul looked at her with surprise and intrigue. "Father Leo again," he said. "And what did Father Leo think of Lenin?"

"Father Leo thought the workers should find a way to improve their lot by more peaceful means."

"Sometimes a revolution is the only way."

"You sound like a pamphlet," she said.

"How romantic. I was trying to sound like a poet."

"Did you hear that our arrival will be delayed?"

"I did, Kat-girl. Looks like we're stuck with each other for a while. You'd better start telling me some stories." She told him every story she could think of.

***

After five weeks at sea, someone spotted a seagull. It was a Slovenian woman who could be trusted. It was a Jewish rabbi. It was a German child. The passengers—dirty, sick, and frightened—filled their hungry hearts with hope. Steerage passengers who hadn't spoken for days began to sing. Children stayed on the observation deck long after darkness fell, hoping to be the first to glimpse the new world or, at the very least, another bird.

Katka and Paul looked for birds too. They were doing exactly that, on a dark cloudy day, when a man with a camera approached them.

"Care for a photo of you and your wife, sir?" the man asked Paul in English.

"No," Paul said quickly. "We are not interested in photos."

"Why not?" Katka said. "I am interested in photos."

Paul looked at Katka with her hair hanging free and her face bronzed. He looked nervous. Then he looked back at the photographer. "If you take our photo, do you promise to give me the negative too?"

"What do you have? For currency?"

"Krona."

"For one American dollar I will give you the photo and the negative."

One dollar? That was an outrageous amount of money. But Paul nodded, and the man beckoned for them to follow him. Up on the deck, he led them to his brother, who had set up a tripod. The photographer told Katka and Paul to stand close together with their backs against the horizon.

"We want our photographs separate," Paul said. "We are not married."

"Of course you are married, sir," the photographer said. "For two American dollars I can give you a certificate that proves it. You know she will pass through more quickly with a photo of her husband." He gave Paul a knowing look.

"Even if she has a letter guaranteeing lodging and employment?"

"With a relative?"

"Her uncle."

"That will probably do. But can you be sure?"

They stood together. Close, but not touching. "Stay still," the photographer said. He adjusted his lens. "A storm is coming."

"Another one?" Katka asked.

"Not a big one. One day, two at most. But you will be my last customers today. Stay still."

Paul's elbow tapped Katka's forearm. A shiver went through her body. Thunder crackled in the distance. The photographer clicked his camera just as a jagged flash of light illuminated the sky behind them.

"That won't do," the photographer said. "Lightning in the background. Stay still now, and I will try another." When he finished taking the second photo of the two together, Paul asked him to take a still of each of them alone.

Three days later, Paul showed Katka the photo of herself. Katka looked stern and expressionless. Her hair, however, was blowing wildly in the wind. "Thank you for purchasing it, Paul. I love photographs. You do not?"

"It was risky. For reasons I can't explain. But you were right to insist. Photographs are important, Kat. One day, when you are an old woman, you will tell your children that when you were a girl, you boarded a ship with a stranger and sailed off to a foreign land. You will tell them what you saw on this trip. You will tell them about the rats that crawled in your berth. About the sickness on the boat, the dead bodies thrown overboard. The shoddy marriages conducted. The revolting food. And maybe they will believe you and maybe they won't. But you will have a photo. A photo of you, a beautiful poem of a woman, with the blush of youth still fresh on your body, standing at the ship deck, your hair blowing tempestuously about your face, a storm at your back."

He had called her beautiful.

***

The day of their arrival was marked with an equal combination of chaotic movement and waiting. The deckhands yelled, "Land ho!" and soon all the children and many of the adults were yelling those same two words with a mishmash of foreign accents. Steerage passengers, whose luggage had been packed since the first bird sightings, trudged up the ladders to the deck, moving as quickly as their burdens would allow. Katka lost track of Mrs. Zalinsky and her children, but she found Paul. When she first glimpsed the Statue of Liberty, Katka squeezed Paul's hand.

"Not in the clear yet," Paul said, pointing. "We must now navigate the Island of Tears." Katka thought he was joking, but his face was somber. He was uncharacteristically quiet.

The ship reached its port at Ellis Island. Katka, Paul, and the other steerage passengers waited for what seemed to be an eternity as immigration officials came on board and "inspected" all the first- and second-class passengers. Steerage passengers would endure a much longer process.

Once off the ship, they were shuffled into a large brick building on Ellis Island. Katka felt like an animal, being prodded along with words she did not understand. Katka and Paul waited in the baggage area with thousands of other emigrants. They passed the hours by playing cards and making up stories about the people they saw. On occasion, Paul wandered off, saying he recognized someone from the old country. Each time he left, Katka panicked. Would he return? What if he didn't? But he always did. Eventually, they were told to stand and wait in a line that stretched up the staircase to the great hall. They pushed their luggage to the line, which was crowded and stagnant.

"Kat-girl," Paul said, pointing. "Do you see that man in the dark uniform?"

She looked. "With the hat? Walking up the steps?"

"Yes. Do you see what is in his hand? Look now. He has stopped. He is marking that woman's coat." Katka saw him scribble an initial and circle it. "If someone tries to mark your coat, wipe the mark off as soon as he is out of sight. It is only chalk. If you cannot wipe it off, turn your coat inside out."

"What does the mark mean?" Katka asked.

"Doesn't matter. They are all bad. If you do not have a mark, you should get through quick." He gave her an encouraging half-smile.

"I will wipe it off." Her voice quivered. Would she get one? She patted down her tight braid. "Do I look...fit?"

"You look," Paul put his hand on her chin and locked his eyes with hers. "You look...*exquisite*." He used an English word. She didn't know what it meant, but she knew it was good. For a moment Katka thought he might kiss her. If he did, she would let him. But he didn't.

He reached for the inside pocket of his jacket and pulled out a thick, folded piece of parchment. "There is something else." Fumbling a bit, he undid the left pocket of Katka's gray wool coat. He slipped the parchment inside and patted the pocket gingerly. "Don't lose this. On this paper is the name of the train you are to board. It is written in English. Tucked inside is American money."

Katka stared into his face. Why was he telling her this? "You are coming with me, Paul Schmidt. You told me so." She heard the desperation in her voice; she didn't care if he heard it.

"I *hope* to come with you," Paul said. "That is my intent, Kat. But it is possible I will get delayed here."

"Are you ill?" Her voice was hard, almost angry.

"No."

"People who are sick always lie about it. My father lied to my mother. My mother lied to me. If you're sick, tell me, Paul."

"I'm not sick. And I have no desire to lie to you, ever. Sometimes I don't tell you everything, but that is not the same as lying. If I leave you, it is not by choice." He put both of his hands gently on her shoulders. "Katka. Do you know that? Tell me you know my heart. That I do not wish to leave you. Not here. Not..." His voice drifted off.

"Ever?"

He kissed her then. For a flicker of a moment. His lips were soft on hers. Soft like velvet. Soft like waking from a sugary dream.

"Not ever," he said. Then he took her right hand and moved it to her coat pocket. "Keep it buttoned," Paul said. "Do not open that pocket until after you see the doctor. They will send you to talk to some officials who will ask you questions. The same questions they asked on the ship. Don't mention me, but otherwise answer them truthfully. Show them the letter from your uncle, and when they ask if you have money, show them what is in your pocket."

"Will they let me through?" Katka asked. "What if they don't?" Her hands were shaking.

"You will get through. When you do, they will tell you how to find the train to Chicago. In Chicago you must change trains. Take the train to Duluth, Minnesota."

"Chicago. Duluth. Minnesota." She repeatedly the words slowly, memorizing the way Paul pronounced each syllable.

"Duluth is a town in Minnesota. Like Zirovnica is a town in Slovenia. After you get through the checkpoints, move slowly, and I will look for you. If more than an hour passes, you must go without me. Board the train. Buy some fruit and bread. Rest. Guard your money and your trunk. Your uncle will be waiting for you in Duluth. I have already sent word."

"Yes," she said quietly.

"Now there is just one more thing. When you are safe with your uncle, when he takes you to his home, he will ask you a question, and there is only one answer."

"There is never just one answer."

Paul smiled. "In this case, there is only one question and only one answer. It alludes to an old proverb. Your uncle will ask, 'What do you do after you tell the truth?'"

"Run," Katka said.

"I see you know it. It is a familiar saying. But the answer you must give is, 'Run to the fields.'"

"Run to the fields."

"Then you must ask him to fix the lock on your trunk. Can you do that? Promise you won't forget."

"My lock is not broken." An immigration officer beckoned the line to move forward.

Paul put both of his hands on her face and looked into her terrified eyes. "It is broken," Paul said. "But broken things can be fixed, just as lost things can be found. For now, we must separate."

He looked off in the distance, scanning the crowd. "When they ask you questions, just give them the letter from your uncle and show them your American dollars."

"I'm a little frightened."

"You are a tiger in the night."

"I only pretend to be. I'm a mouse, scurrying about in a ramshackle cottage."

"No. You are a tiger who knows what it is like to be a mouse." Paul looked behind him. He looked to the side. "I will see you again," he whispered. "I promise." He disappeared behind a mass of people and was gone.

CHAPTER 3

PAUL KNEW HE WAS IN TROUBLE. WHEN HE LEFT Katka, he went immediately to the designated place. Elizabeth Gurley Flynn was there, waiting, just as she said she would be. She wore a long black skirt and a white dress with plain long sleeves and ruffles up the front. She wore a wide-brimmed purple hat with a pink ribbon.

"You look fine as candy, Lizzy," Paul said.

"Wish I could say the same about you, lad. You look like last month's dinner. They know you are here," she said. "Someone tipped them off. Switch suitcases."

He put his suitcase down and picked up hers instead.

"Good luck. If you don't make it out, God will find another way. Or if he's busy, we will. Find the guard named Tommy O'Sullivan. He will know the code."

Paul nodded. "Watch that Anton's niece gets on the right train. She is going to Chicago, then Duluth, Minnesota. Her name is Katka Kovich."

"I will see to it. If I didn't, Lily would have my head on a platter. Give me your hat," she said, holding out her hand. "Your coat?" He handed it to her.

"What are my odds?" Paul asked.

"I'll be a-prayin' for you, lad. Now go." He walked into the crowd. When surrounded by people, he knelt down and opened the suitcase. He found a new coat and hat and quickly put them on. He closed the suitcase, put his hand in the inside pocket, and breathed a sigh of relief.

As he stood up, he felt a hand on his shoulder. He turned his head to see a man with a shock of yellow hair wearing a black suit with a white bow tie. "I do hope you'll come quietly this time, Mr. Schmidt. We'd hate for you to disappear." The man marked the left sleeve of his coat with the letter "A." Anarchist. Then he circled the letter.

"I am a citizen of this country. I have done nothing wrong."

"Of course you haven't," the agent said. "Everyone's an innocent."

Paul glanced around. Out of the corner of his eye, he spotted the wide-brimmed purple hat. Elizabeth was watching him. Should he run? As if reading his mind, Elizabeth Gurley Flynn shook her head no.

The immigration agent led Paul to a holding room just off the main hall. Inside, several men and a few women shifted uncomfortably on chairs. Many had been identified on their ships just as Paul had. Everyone had an "A." Paul looked around at the crowded room. Each person, he imagined, had a story to tell, but not all had a cause for which to fight. Although some were socialists, anarchists, revolutionaries, and political agitators, most of the people in the detainment room were naturalized citizens of the U.S., and some were even born in this country.

There had been several raids in New York in the last few weeks. The police had arrested numerous famous people, one of whom was the Russian immigrant Emma Goldman. Goldman, an anarchist married to a doctor who treated diseases related to poverty, was arrested for giving a speech in which she advocated access to birth control. Her speech violated the Comstock Act, which prevented the distribution of "lascivious" literature. She had waited in this same room only days prior. Goldman's arrest was lauded by newspapers across the nation.

Political writers urged that America weed out new immigrants, like Goldman, who were unhappy with the status quo.

Since the war with Germany had erupted, a new ideological movement had swept across the land, finding favor with several established members of high society and with Congress. This movement was well orchestrated, and its goal was to stir up nationalism and to create a common enemy, behind which the people in power could unite in their opposition. Books were published warning against what some referred to as the "mongrelization" of America. The new immigrants, they claimed, were nothing like the old immigrants, who had settled this country and made it what it was today. Their prejudice was particularly directed toward "Orientals," who were stealing jobs out West from regular Americans, and against people from Eastern Europe, like Katka and Paul, who were stealing jobs in the East and Middle West. According to data that was empirical rather than scientific, these new immigrants possessed a higher percentage of inborn socially deviant qualities. They were more likely to commit violent crimes, and the men were a threat to decent women everywhere.

New York's mayor read these articles. He listened to his wealthy benefactors. He ordered his police force to infiltrate union halls and arrest everyone inside. They also entered taverns in the warehouse districts and textile neighborhoods and arrested everyone who looked Slavic or Jewish. They loaded the captives and shipped them off to Ellis Island. Each day, a new group would be shuffled into this room, where an inspector would create a file before escorting them to their prison cells.

Paul took a seat in the back. "How long you been here?" Paul asked the man to his left. He was about fifty years old with a neck the size of an oak tree. The man had giant hands to match and a tanned face.

"In this room here? 'Bout four hours. They ain't in no hurry, I'll tell you that much."

"You don't look like you come off a boat."

"Came off my shift. I'm a dockworker. When I arrived this morning, there they was with their clubs. Told the whole lot of us to load up in the paddy wagon, else they'd kill us."

"What's the reason?"

"Said they heard we was organizing."

"Were you?"

"I weren't."

"You should have run."

The dockworker smiled a crooked smile. "Not exactly timely advice, wouldn't you say?"

Years ago the inhabitants of this room had their fates decided relatively quickly. They were imprisoned for a week, possibly two. Then they would go to trial, and a judge would deport them, release them to a charity family for observation, or absolve them.

In 1906, when Paul had first arrived in America, over a million immigrants had entered the country, and almost 900,000 of them had come through Ellis Island. The building had been overflowing, and the staff was insufficiently equipped. Immigrants with illnesses spilled over from the hospital wards into the detainment quarters. Those who did not have the necessary ten dollars in their pockets were also kept at Ellis Island, until money arrived by mail from relatives, friends, or contract labor companies under the guise of family members. Unmarried or unaccompanied women were also held there, often with their children, until marriage documents could be provided or a male relative arrived to pick them up. So many children had been detained that a playground was built and schools were formed. There were rumors that unspeakable things were sometimes done to unaccompanied women. Ungodly things. Paul tried not to think about that. He told himself that Katka would get through unscathed. That Elizabeth would intervene if she did not.

This was 1915, not 1906. War had erupted overseas and immigration was severely curtailed. The hospitals and detainment quarters were no longer overflowing. Fewer than 150,000 immigrants would come through Ellis Island this year, and over 90 percent would pass through the inspections within hours of arrival.

Those who did not pass inspections faced a new kind of destiny. Ellis Island was no longer simply a port of arrival for immigrants. It had become a jail for anyone who was suspected of anti-American activity. It also housed vagrants and New Yorkers with loathsome communicable diseases.

The war made it nearly impossible to deport anyone. Prisoners who in 1906 had been deported in three days found themselves living at Ellis Island for years. The lack of immediacy impacted the island's employees of Ellis Island. There was no rush to process anyone's paperwork. There was no rush to bring the cases to trial. No one was going anywhere.

Paul put his feet up, leaned back, and closed his eyes. He thought about Katka.

CHAPTER 4

THE IMMIGRATION OFFICIAL DID NOT PLACE A MARK on Katka's coat, and she was shuffled into the "lucky" lane, where she waited briefly to see the doctor. When she stood before him, she wondered if she looked as strong and healthy as an American woman should. The doctor did not see her as a woman, but instead maneuvered her body as if she were a horse in a barn. He looked at her hands, looked down her throat, and ran his fingers through her hair looking for bugs. Then he inverted her eyelids with a buttonhook, glanced briefly at each eye, and nodded. She had passed the medical exam.

"Language?" the doctor asked.

"Slovensko," she replied and was sent to an interpreter who spoke Slovenian. He found her name on the ship's manifest, asked her dozens of simple questions, glanced at her money, and read the note from her uncle. He issued her a new immigrant card and fastened a sign around her neck with her name and destination.

"Welcome to America," he said with absolutely no enthusiasm. "That way to the train."

She slipped the documents into her right pocket, grabbed the leather strap on her cedar trunk, and dragged it slowly, looking for Paul. When she stopped near the top of the staircase to look down on the immigrants below, a woman wearing a large purple hat bumped into her, dropping a small suitcase to the ground.

"Oh, sorry!" the woman said loudly in English. The clasp on the woman's suitcase had opened. Katka bent down to help the stranger retrieve the contents: socks, utensils, a few books, a man's shirt, a hat, a scarf, and a photograph.

The woman had a cloud of black hair and deep blue eyes. While their heads were near the floor as they shoved the clothing back inside, the stranger whispered, "Do you speak English?"

"Little bit."

"Your friend has been detained. Carry on." Before she left, the strange woman picked up the photo, glanced at it, and paused. Then she handed Katka the photograph. "I think this belongs to you."

***

Katka was desolate. After Elizabeth Gurley Flynn left her, Katka simply stood where she was. People swarmed past her and around her like bees. And her head was buzzing. "Detained?" What did that mean? "Carry on?" How could she?

Somehow she found the train. She boarded it and took her seat in a small compartment occupied by a man who looked to be her age. He nodded politely to her, and she nodded back. "No English," he said in a thick German accent. "Sorry."

She didn't feel like talking. When the locomotive lurched forward, her hands began to tremble. She took the photograph out of her pocket. She had glanced at it earlier. Now she had time to study it. There she was, just as Paul had described. Her dark hair blowing in the wind. Her face serene. And there he was. Paul Schmidt, with his locks as curly as a girl's. His hands were in his pockets. In contrast to her serious face, his showed just a hint of mischief. The photographer had told them to stay still, but he looked as if he were trying to suppress a smile. His lips were pursed together, but his dimples were showing. The pair looked relaxed, happy, and were completely oblivious to the fact that a large lightning bolt had cut its way through the sky. If the lightning bolt had been a millimeter longer, it would have cut the two in half. The way it was, the bolt stood just above them.

Katka's stomach hurt. It twisted around like an old tree root. But she wasn't in need of food. She ached with loss. She shouldn't have left Paul. She shouldn't have boarded the train. Surely there was something she could have done. But the woman—the woman who gave her the photo—had told her to go. Who was she? How did she know Paul?

She put the photo away, but her hands kept shaking. Finally, she rested them on her knees. Then her feet began to tap nervously. It was as if something inside her simply could not stay put. The energy came out of her like birds escaping a burning hut. She began to cry. She missed her mother. She missed her father. She missed Paul. She kept thinking about how his lips had felt on hers. Like a whisper. Ephemeral as a poem that was spoken, but not written. Her tears were soft at first, like a lady. She tried to stifle them, as a man would. Finally, she gave up, and the sobbing came out of her erratically, like a child who had been hurt but was unable to articulate how.

The man in her compartment handed her a handkerchief. "*Nicht weinen, Fraulein,*" he said, shaking his head kindly. "No cry." The man handed her a small flask of liquid. She waved it away.

"*Trinken,*" he said. She took the flask to her lips and swallowed. The liquid burned her throat and stomach. "*Ein weider,*" he said, gesturing for her to take another swig. She did.

Soon she was asleep. She dreamed of her mother, not in her last days when she had been bedridden, moaning and incoherent. But earlier. Picking berries in the sun, her bonnet hanging down her back. Her mother had loved the sun. She had visions of her father, who was a broken man in many ways. He always wanted to own his own land, but something always interfered. When she awoke, her thoughts returned to Paul. Did he own land in America? Was he still in America, or had they sent him back to Slovenia?

She distracted herself by looking out the window. There were no mountains here to contain the land. It simply stretched forward. Forest and farm, farm and forest. A house here and there. An occasional town. But when she looked up, never-ending sky. She longed to see the Alps, which had always connected the sky and land like a wedding. At home the mountains kept everything in place. Here things grew rogue. She didn't know exactly what she hoped to find, but it was not this.

It took two days to get to Chicago. How big was this country, America? It must be like Russia. She had heard stories of people coming to America, people who remembered every detail from the moment they arrived. People who noticed everything. But all she noticed was her own body and how it felt like the word "loneliness."

When she disembarked from the train, somehow she found her connection to Duluth. This time she sat in a compartment with a couple from Sweden, who offered her chocolate.

When she finally arrived at the train depot in Duluth, Minnesota, it was morning. A thick fog emanating from Lake Superior covered the ground, as if a cloud had fallen from the sky. The Swede in her compartment helped her with her trunk, dragging it to the door of the locomotive. Once there, an attendant grabbed it and set it on the ground. He took Katka's hand, and she walked, shakily, down the steps to the platform. Nervously, she looked around at the small throng of people waiting to greet the travelers. She saw another woman about her age disembark from a few cars down. A man approached the woman, took off his hat, and asked her a question. The woman shook her head, and the man moved on. As he approached Katka, she knew it was her uncle. He was average height for a Slovenian, nearly five feet, six inches. Although he was thirty-six, his sideburns were beginning to gray, as her father's had years ago. The uncle had a scar on his forehead where he had been kicked by a mule. Her father had been there when it happened and had spoken of the day often.

"Katka?" the man asked. "Katka Kovich?"

When she nodded, he hugged her. Then he kissed her on both cheeks. "Josef's little girl!" he said. "Last time I saw you, you were holding onto your ma's skirts. Goes without saying you changed some." He smiled good-naturedly. "Trip treat you all right?"

"Yes, Uncle."

"Good liar, you are. That trip don't treat nobody good. You are alone?" he asked.

"Yes."

Uncle Anton frowned and shook his head slightly. "You are a brave girl to come by your lonesome. Weren't too long ago that I made this trip myself. Ten years, actually. But no child was I, not alone, and still I was scared. This here your trunk? What you got in here, an accordion? Heavy son of a bitch."

"Not an accordion."

"Anything else?"

She shook her head and followed Uncle Anton to his buggy, which was hitched to two strong horses. The back of the cart was filled with crates of supplies: fabric, sugar, flour, soap, paper, salt, hops, barley, wheat, and beans in cans. The crates were secured, meticulously, by rope. "Done a bit of shopping," he said, placing her trunk inside.

"Uncle, Paul told me to..."

"Tell me later," her uncle said softly. "We got some forty-five miles of wretched trail to trek. Not to mention, you look like you ain't slept in a month." He helped her into the back seat of the buggy and handed her a basket of food and a blanket. She ate a slice of Slovenian bread, called *potica*, made by Anton's wife. Then she lay down with the blanket and slept.

When she awoke, the sun was high in the sky, and the horses had stopped. She was sweating under the blanket.

"Minnesota for you," Anton said. "Each morning and evening is the same, even in July. Cold as an old whore's heart. Afternoons? That's something else altogether. Can get right blistery."

"Are we here?" Katka asked, disoriented.

The buggy was parked on a dirt path next to a fast-flowing stream. Giant pine trees surrounded them. They were so tall that the skirts of their fragrant needles were over six feet off the earth. The trunks were exposed and resembled hairy legs. Looking at them, she imagined running into the forest, touching the trunks of the trees just as a small child would tap the legs of grown -folks as she ran through a crowd of people.

"Just stopping to rest. Don't want to bake the horses." He took the last swig out of his canteen and walked over to the stream to fill it. Then he came back, released the horses, and led them to the water.

Katka got out of the buggy. She walked around for a while, then washed her hands and face in the cool stream.

"So, Katka," Anton began. "When did you lose my dear friend Paul?"

"We separated at the medical checks."

"Did he look sick? Did they mark his coat?"

"Not sick. I didn't see them mark his coat. A woman told me he had been detained."

"Woman?"

Katka nodded.

"What she look like?"

"Pretty. Black curly hair. Blue eyes. Definitely not Slovenian. She spoke to me in English."

"Elizabeth Gurley Flynn. Are you sure she said 'detained'? Not 'delayed'?"

"I am sure."

"Damn," Anton said. He shook his head, muttered some more cuss words. He took a deep breath and let it out, slowly. "So, niece. What do you do after you tell the truth?"

"Run. To the fields," she said.

"A good girl, you are, Katka."

"Also, you need to fix the lock on my trunk."

"Has it been broken long?"

"Not that I have noticed."

"I'll be sure to do that."

CHAPTER 5

THIS TIME WHEN SHE GOT IN THE BUGGY, KATKA SAT in front with her uncle. They continued down the Vermilion Trail toward the village that would soon be her home, meandering around several lakes and waterways. The terrain was kindly with leisurely green hills and gentle slopes. They passed two encampments, one French and the other Ojibwe. Anton knew men in each, but did not stop at the French camp.

He made some quick trades at the Indian camp. Katka stared absently at the Ojibwe women, who strode about wearing a hodgepodge of clothing. Some wore white men's shirts, others in white women's blouses with long skirts. It was warm. Anton did not waste much time. He wanted to get Katka home before dark.

As they traveled farther north and west, the landscape changed slightly. "Why is the earth so rusty looking?" Katka asked.

"It will only get redder. This here, it is the richest land in the nation. Not a great climate for growing things, but the red iron runs deep. It's shipped all over the world. Made into roads, fancy automobiles, even weapons. All a man's got to do is take his shovel, dig out a scoop of grass, and there's the ore. Beautiful color, ain't it?"

"It is."

"Men have died for that color, I tell you. Some willing and some not." He explained a bit about the place where she would live.

The road they were on, the Vermilion Trail, was an important one. It connected the port town of Duluth to the vast stretch of mining towns that dotted the area. The region, from Ely to Grand Rapids, was called the Iron Range. The Range, as most people called it, consisted of three separate sections of iron. The town where Anton lived, Biwabik, was on the Mesabi Range. The purest, most valuable ore was found there, and the towns were booming as a result.

The sun was just setting when they approached their destination. The cerulean sky was streaked with brushstrokes of gold, and everything looked magical in the fading light. The temperature was dropping, and the wind had died down. Katka removed the handkerchief she had been using to keep the red dust off of her face. The Vermilion Trail had ended at a T. Anton stopped the buggy.

"This here is Blood Red Road. It connects all the mines and mining towns from Ely to Grand Rapids. It's over a hundred miles long. Our house is this way, to the east." He pointed to the right.

"Can we drive through the village?" Katka asked, curious. Would her new village be anything like the one she had left behind?

Anton hesitated. "Don't tell Lily." He turned left onto Blood Red Road, which bisected the town of Biwabik. "Lily don't think it's right for women folk to be in the town during candlelight time. It ain't nice, and it ain't quiet. Interesting, that it is. Things are brewing here. Things are changing."

The main strip was flanked by brick buildings, the windows lit with lanterns. When nightfall came in full force, the strip would be lit with electricity fueled by a generator donated ten years ago by the Oliver Mining Company. The lights would entice men from all over the Iron Range to enter the bars and brothels.

"See there," Anton said. The names on the storefronts were painted with words written in two, sometimes three, languages. "Workers come from all over the world. Over thirty languages spoken here."

Dozens of men went in and out of the buildings. Anton tipped his hat to a few and exchanged greetings with others. A woman locked the door to a building marked Cerkvenik's Mercantile.

"Evenin', Helen!" Anton called.

The woman turned. "Anton!" she cried. "That your niece?"

"Is there anything you don't know, Helen?"

"If I don't know it, it ain't worth knowing," she said with a smile. She waved to Katka. "Welcome, dear. Lily's been on pins and needles awaitin' on you. 'Spect she might have near exploded with excitement by now. You go straight home, Anton."

"Yes, sir." He saluted and whispered to Katka, "Biggest gossip in town, that one is. But she got a good heart."

Buggies, carts, single horses, and even a few automobiles lined the dirt road outside the shops and bars. Wooden sidewalks ran the length of town, and streetcar tracks went as far west as Katka could see. They passed Crooked Neck Pete's Scandinavian Saloon, Timo and Simo's Saloon and Sauna, Colvin Lumber Company, Jackson Hardware, and Gornik's General Store.

"School's up on the hill," Anton said. "Got over sixty kids now. When I got here, weren't no more than ten."

Rows of neatly arranged houses, identical in every way, were lined up behind the shops on either side of the street. "Company houses," her uncle said. "Leased by the mine for a king's ransom. May not look like much, but compared to the location shacks, each house is a czar's palace."

The town was surrounded on three sides by giant hills of red dirt. "Iron," Anton said. "This red dirt from the open pit and underground mines—that's why we all here. We poor "Fresh of the Boats" dig it up with our bloody hands, and the rich folk with no souls turn it into roads, weapons, and gold."

Anton turned his buggy around and headed back toward the Vermillion Trail, where they had come from. "Let's go home, gal."

As they drove through Biwabik the second time, two men ambled out of a tavern. One was screaming at the other in a language Katka did not recognize. Anton deftly maneuvered his buggy out of their way as one man tackled the other.

"Oh my!" Katka said. This village was nothing like Zirovnica.

"Ain't unusual to see a skirmish there. Vince Torelli runs the worst bucket-of-blood saloon in town. Best to avoid that place." Katka would remember that.

They drove east past the last building in town, Sherek's Butchery and Meat Market, and kept traveling for a little more than a mile and a half. The house was on the left side of Blood Red Road. To the right was a tree-lined lake, named for the Merritt brothers who had been among the first white men to find iron hibernating under the trees and rocks.

The horses stopped in front of a tall, imposingly beautiful log house. "This is it, Katka," Anton said. "Home sweet home." Out back were a barn, a chicken coop, a pigpen, a smokehouse, and a small fenced field where four cows were grazing. A dense forest of pine and cedar stood majestically to the north of the farmhouse.

"Big," Katka said, looking at the two-and-a-half stories.

"I married above me," Anton said, laughing. "And I tell you, Lily don't ever let me forget it neither. Her father made some money in the newspaper business in Minneapolis. He was a smart man with an education. Even got a paper that says his brains work. When he heard about all the prospectors coming up here, he sold his paper, rode up here with a team of sled dogs, and bought up as much land as he could afford.

"Had no interest in mining. No, he did not. But everyone who did, they had interest in him. He'd sell, on occasion. Bit by bit. Eventually he built this house and sent for the rest of the family. Wife never forgave him for it. I tell you, she hated it here. Said she'd rather live in the prisons in Siberia. But truth be told," he said with a wink, "her husband probably wished she did too. Before they went back to Ljubljana, they sold two thousand acres at top dollar to the Oliver Mining Company. Went back richer than before. Good for us, he left seven hundred acres and this house to me and Lily.

"This is the main entrance," Anton said, pointing. "Anton's Slovenski Dom" was hand-painted in elaborate script on the canvas awning above the door. "We have boarders and a bar. Helps us make a go of things. It's a safe and peaceful place, I tell you. Not to say we haven't had an exception or two. Most nights it's calm as church. Even so, Lily wants us using the back door. Can't say I agree, but it's never worth it to argue with Lily. Save it for the real fuss. That might be a good tip for you, Katka." Anton smiled. "Don't go ruffling her feathers. That's my job." He helped her descend from the dusty carriage, and then he grabbed her trunk and swung it to the ground. "Wait here. Lily will have heard the horses. If I know my wife, she'll be out before I get back from the barn."

Anton's wife emerged seconds later, from the "proper" door, wiping her hands on her apron and smiling. Her yellow-orange hair was pulled into a bun that was perhaps tight in the morning, but had yielded to gravity. The ringlets that escaped framed her youthful face like wildflowers. This aunt, whom Katka had never seen, was at least ten years younger than Anton. She wore a simple dress, light pink and faded, with a floor-length apron stained with flour and eggs tied high above her curvy belly. She looked to be about seven months with child.

"Follow me, niece." They walked into the house.

Looking at this aunt's wholesome girth made Katka feel even skinnier than she was. She was wearing her good dress from the old country, but she had been wearing it for days. It was filthy. She did not need a picture glass to know that her face was covered with bronze dust and grime. Seeing this ruddy-cheeked aunt made her miss her own mother. She bit her lip to keep her emotions in check.

"Katka?" The aunt raised one eyebrow.

"Yes, ma'am."

"You speak English! Impressive."

"Some."

"What a little thing you are! Like a little *matchka*! In English, the word is 'cat.' Like your name."

"My mother, she called me *matchka*," Katka said, smiling slightly.

"How could she not?" the aunt asked. "Well, my little *matchka*, I am Lilianna Kovich, your long-lost *teta*. You are a most welcome sight! You have no idea! I have been praying to the Virgin to send me some help. And what did she send? This!" Lily pointed to her stomach. "This little anarchist, rolling around all day long, kicking me in the back. But now my faith is restored, for here you are. I think we will be grand friends." She leaned over and kissed Katka's cheek, then grabbed her hand and started walking her toward the house. "We must get you some food. I made a cottage cheese strudel! And, I think, a good bath. I'm dying to hear your stories. You must have many to tell. I was born here, you know, so life for me holds no adventure. I envy those who do, even if it stems from tragedy." Lily hugged her close. "I am sorry about your folks. So sorry," she whispered.

"Enough, I tell you," said Anton, coming up behind them in the hallway. "Your constant chatter will scare the girl away, it will. You're a *gobec*." He put down Katka's trunk and wrapped his arms around Lily, patting her stomach and kissing her several times on the side of her neck. Like her own parents, her aunt and uncle were as affectionate inside the house as they were reserved outside of it. "Like a magpie, my wife."

"Shush, you." Lily said, laughing. "Now that Katka's here, you are outnumbered, Anton. Might as well wave the white flag."

"Never!" Anton said. "Besides, soon there will be two Kovich men in this house."

"It's a girl. Trust me. If it isn't, I'm leaving."

Anton carried Katka's trunk up the two flights of stairs and to the end of the hall. Then he pulled the rope that released the passageway to the attic. He lumbered up, struggling with the trunk. She followed him and looked around at her sleeping quarters. A pine bed, a small writing desk with a vase full of lilacs, and a lantern.

"Will this do?" Anton asked.

"It is good," Katka said. Her room was almost as big as her cottage in Slovenia. It smelled nothing like the ship, nothing like death. She breathed in the sweet aroma of the flowers and smiled. She did not know her aunt, but she loved her at once for putting lilacs in her room. "More than good."

"If you like, you can remove your things from the trunk now, and I will take it somewhere so I can repair the lock. And I have a good place to store it, if you do not mind."

Katka knew her lock was not broken. Another one of Paul's mysteries. She opened the cedar chest and removed the contents. She had her father's Bible. There were two dresses and some undergarments, a tin cup, silverware, and a plate she had needed on the voyage. The photograph of her with her brothers and parents when she was a baby, the coffin photos, a few letters, and a rock she had impulsively stashed in the trunk. The picture of her and Paul was carefully hidden in her coat pocket. She had one more possession.

Katka removed the typewriter from Father Leo, which she had wrapped in a wool blanket. It was heavy, but she had grown used to carrying it, and she placed it easily on the desk.

"You are a writer?"

"No," Katka said. "But perhaps one day."

Anton smiled. "I don't like to think about one day," he said. "If it is possible one day, it is possible today. Don't you think?"

"I suppose," Katka said. She liked this man. He had her father's same sunken coal-black eyes. But unlike her father, Anton's eyes were alive. Her father's eyes had always looked dull and weathered, even when he was laughing.

"I'll leave you to explore. Lily will come get you when your bath is ready."

She sat at the edge of the pine bed. The mattress was soft and covered by fresh linen and two quilts stuffed with goose feathers. "I'll just test the pillow," she thought. Within minutes she was dreaming of Paul.

CHAPTER 6

AT 5 A.M. THE NEXT DAY, MEN'S VOICES WOKE Katka. It was still dark outside. She put on her clothes and crept quietly partway down the stairs. In the dining room, she could see Uncle Anton and eight men dressed in coveralls seated at the long table eating a breakfast of hardrolls and jam, hard-boiled eggs, and bacon.

"*Teta* Lily!" one of the miners called, using the Slovenian term for "aunt" to show respect to Lily. "More *kave, prosim.*"

The boarder was young, only seventeen years old, tall and thin. Lily appeared with a carafe. "Milo Blatnik. You meathead. How many times do I have to tell you? English only at this table. We are in America."

"Where I come from, *Teta*," Milo said, choosing his English words carefully, "contempt for the mother tongue is same as contempt for your mother."

Lily smacked him lightly on the head. "What is it with you? Every morning, a different proverb! Didn't your parents ever teach you anything useful?"

"Poetry. Would you like to hear some poetry from the old country?"

"I got a poem," another miner said. "I hear it at work, I did. From a real cousin jack American. It go, 'I once knew a man from Nantucket—'" The men hooted.

"No proverbs," Lily said, putting her hands up like stop signs. "No poems. Just eat. You men are going to be the death of me."

As Lily topped off young Milo's cup, she saw Katka on the stairs and called to her. All of the miners stood. Anton introduced her as his niece, and the men told her their names, one by one. Old Joe, who sat at the head of the table opposite Anton, had a long gray beard and a slightly crooked back after nearly ten years of working stooped over underground. Most of the miners, however, were in their early twenties.

"A pleasure it is to meet you, Miss Kovich," Milo said, bowing slightly.

Katka responded in Slovenian.

"No, my love," Old Joe quickly corrected Katka. "Nice-to-meet-you-too," he said loudly and slowly, deliberately contaminating his own nearly perfect English. "We-English-only-here." Everyone laughed, including Lily.

"One day you will all thank me," she said. "What day? I can't say. Katka. Come with me. I could use some good companionship for a change." Lily beckoned, and Katka followed her into the kitchen.

The kitchen was the largest Katka had ever seen. Unlike at home, the cook stove was inside, not outside. There was a washbasin full of soapy water. A good-size icebox stood next to the door. A long table was pushed against one wall. On it were eight lunch boxes, each stuffed with a towel.

"We must get the pasties packed," she said. "Give me a hand?"

Lily removed crescent-shaped pies filled with meat, carrot, onion, rutabaga, and potato from the oven. Following Lily's lead, Katka wrapped them tightly to help them retain their heat. Lily explained that all miners ate pasties for lunch. They filled a belly good, and men could eat them with one hand. They closed the tin boxes, and each woman carried four, Lily balancing her load on her belly. "Follow me," she said. She led

Katka through the dining room, past the boarders who were finishing breakfast. When he saw them coming, Anton opened the strong oak doors that led to the tavern.

It used to be the front porch of the house, Lily explained, until Anton persuaded her they should renovate. "It will be like the pubs from back home, I tell you," he had said. "Who will want to come to a tavern with no gambling? No women? Good, decent men who want nothing more than to share a pint with some folks who speak his language, that's who, I tell you." Anton kept a running tab for the lodgers, and when they paid their rent, they also settled the bar tab. If a boarder could not pay, there was always a new immigrant worker waiting to take his place.

Katka and Lily lined up the lunch boxes on the bar. The boarders soon entered and laced their mud-caked work boots, which were arranged neatly along one wall. They donned their grimy coats and hats, which were on hooks above the boots, and grabbed their lunches. They left for the St. James mine, which was a little less than three miles away.

Once the men had gone, Katka and Lily washed the dishes. Then they sat down. Lily rolled a hard-boiled egg on the table, and when it was cracked, she offered it to Katka. Lily spoke to her in Slovenian, the language of her childhood. "You missed your bath. I went up to get you, but you were fast asleep."

"Yes," Katka said, peeling the egg. "I'm sorry. I smell worse than this egg, I know. But my eyes, they were so heavy."

"It's nothing," Lily said. "I took it. It was lovely. We will run you a new bath today. I noticed something, though, when I went to get you. I noticed you have a typewriter."

"My old priest gave it to me."

"Can you use it?"

"Yes."

"Will you teach me to use it?"

"Yes, ma'am."

"I will teach you to improve your English. You will teach me to type. It is agreed?"

Katka nodded.

"I've been wanting a typewriter for a long time," Lily said. "I begged my father for one, but he laughed. He said women can't write."

After breakfast, they went upstairs, passing Lily and Anton's bedroom and the two bedrooms that housed the boarders. There were four beds in each boarding room, double bunked. All were made up, sloppily. Down the hallway, they pulled the rope that opened the attic door.

"You first," Lily said. "I'm not as quick as I once was. This belly makes me all catawampus. Feel like a drunk circus performer, swinging on this rope ladder."

Once inside, Lily glanced at the keys of the typewriter. The Slovenian alphabet had no Q, no W, X, or Y.

"Oh, Katka," she said. "I'm pleased as a pup with two tails. We can't work here, though. It's too blasted hot."

"I'll carry it," Katka said.

She followed Lily back down to the pantry on the first floor, where Lily kept a few sacks of dried peas and carrots and her canned goods. Dried onions and garlic hung from a rope on the ceiling and emitted a pleasantly pungent odor. Gingerly, Lily rolled a rug to one side. A large, square space had been cut out of the wood under it—the opening to a hidden cellar. On her knees, Lily felt around for the indentation that opened the trap door. She found it and opened it. A sturdy oak ladder rested on some hooks, and Lily secured it.

"Don't breathe a word about this place," she said, crawling down. "It's where we store the liquor."

Katka followed, carrying the typewriter under one arm. In the cellar, Lily lit a lantern and pulled a cord attached to the rug above. If anyone entered the hallway overhead, they would see only the rug.

The cellar was much larger than Katka had expected. In fact, it was almost as big as the kitchen. On one side, Anton had stacked bottles of whiskey for the bar. Another side was covered with shelves that stored more provisions and some unmarked crates. The third wall also contained shelves, but these were filled with books. About a dozen Winchester rifles leaned against the bookshelves.

"A lot many guns," Katka said in English.

"Anton and I collect them." Lily smiled.

A small writing table with three chairs sat in the middle of the cellar. A large lamp, ink, quills, paper, and matches were neatly arranged at the edge of the table. A tin miner's cup was there too. A Slovenian dictionary served as a paperweight for some letters that had recently been written. Lily lit the lamp. "Place the typewriter there," she said, pointing to the table. The lantern's light gave everything in the cellar a slight red glow.

"You will teach me to type before the week is done. I have been working on a project for quite some time, but I have been doing it all in longhand. Your typewriter will be a godsend."

"What kind of project?"

Lily sat at the table and gestured for Katka to sit as well. "A women's paper," she said confidentially. "It will be the first here on the Iron Range. And it will change everything! You have no idea! You can help me write it. Surely you will! You can write the Slovenian version, and I'll write the English one.

"I barely recognize my own skin, *Teta* Lily. Everything is...I don't think..."

"You will make a positively grand reporter. I just know it. So? You are a new American. You will learn. And," Lily began, clapping her hands, unable to contain her excitement, "I already found someone who has agreed to print it and distribute it without saying a word about my identity."

Katka raised her eyebrows. Why the need for secrecy? America was a free country. "What do you plan to write about?"

"Recipes. Fashion. But mostly gossip."

"Sounds...dangerous?"

"Go ahead and laugh," Lily said. "But who will tell me secrets if they know I might print what they've said? Would you? You would not. We are positively desperate for this journal. Women hunger for distractions."

"Are you certain, *Teta*," Katka said, "you are not planning to write about something more?" There was a look in Lily's eyes. A look that said there was more.

"I knew you were smart. I am too. I finished the eighth grade, first in my class." Lily paused. Then she grabbed the water pitcher, poured a small amount into the miner's cup, and took a swig. "Life is so hard here for us. You have no idea. Outnumbered by men almost ten to one. And the work. You will see about the work."

"'Women hold up three corners of the house," Katka said. "That's what my mother used to say."

"My mother used to say that! And she didn't do a lick of work her whole life, unless you consider giving instructions to the maids work. It is true everywhere, though, to some extent. But some places are worse than others. I'd like to write about the women's struggles here. Let them know they are not alone. In time, I'll have a bigger readership than *The Company Chronicle*, I guarantee it."

"What is *The Company Chronicle?*"

"A newspaper. Owned by the Oliver Mining Company. They own nearly everything within seventy-five miles of Biwabik. After purchasing the land and the houses in the town, the Oliver bought the newspapers.

"Try as they might," Lily continued, "there are some papers the Oliver can't touch. The Finnish papers. A few South Slav rags. And, of course, the *Industrial Workers of the World* and socialist papers get smuggled in. But none of the papers are for women."

Katka's head was spinning. Lily kept lapsing from Slovenian into English, and although she tried to keep pace, Katka found herself feeling more and more lost. Her aunt spoke so quickly. She had been in this town for less than twenty-four hours and knew nothing about it. Yet somehow, by the end of the conversation, Katka had agreed to become a reporter for Lily's newspaper.

***

Katka slowly assimilated to life at the Kovich boardinghouse. She worked harder than she had ever worked in her life, but she was grateful for it. It kept her mind off of Paul. She and Lily woke early, built the fires, gathered eggs, and milked the cows. They prepared the pasties for the miners' lunch boxes. They set the table, served breakfast, cleaned up. They kept the fires going all day so they would have hot water. At eleven, Anton came home from the forest for a light lunch. They prepared it and cleaned up. Some days the two women walked to town to buy goods from Cerkvenik's Mercantile or Gornik's General Store. They washed the men's sheets and clothing. They tended the garden, picked flowers, and put them in vases.

After serving the evening meal, they often sat in the dining room and darned socks and knit sweaters for the upcoming winter. Katka loved the quiet of those evenings. She loved the sound of the needles. The rhythm of the clacking would transport her from this very real and tangible world to another place. She would float back to Slovenia and her parents, back to the boat, back to Paul. Paul, the only man who had ever called her beautiful.

Paul. Where was he? Every night after dinner, she asked Anton if he had heard from Paul. And every night Anton shook his head no.

"Do you think he is dead?" Katka asked Lily one night. "Paul Schmidt?"

"No, I do not," she replied. "That man's too stubborn to die. And he can talk his way out of most anything. He has a habit of disappearing and turning up. Don't worry, *Matchka*. One day, when you least expect it, he will come knocking on the door, asking me to make him a walnut *potica*."

They never discussed the women's paper at night when Anton and the boarders were within earshot. "I'd like to write about the sporting girls," Lily said one morning while rolling out the dough for a pasty.

"What is 'sporting girl'?"

Lily explained that they were women who did wifely things for money. "I know some personally. It's not what you think. Most of them, they didn't know what they were getting into. One day I'll take you down to the Mesabi Station, we'll watch the girls get off the train. Always there's a throng of men whose shift hasn't started yet. They watch the new girls, wondering who's going to the saloons, hoping to get a go at them. They yell and scream the crudest things. That's why Anton sent you to Duluth instead of sending you on a train directly here. He knew there was a chance you would be making the journey alone, and he did not want that for you."

"He knew that Paul would not make it?"

"He knew that it was possible. Paul knew too."

"*Teta,* why is Paul such a mystery? Why would they stop him at Ellis Island? Isn't Anton worried about Paul?"

Lily shrugged. "Worry early, worry twice. We have no facts."

"Will you tell me when you acquire some?"

"The very moment. Now about the sporting girls. We have plenty of facts where they are concerned. Women like me, we should help them, right? An injury to one is an injury to all. But we don't. The men help them more than we do. Sometimes the miners fall in love with the prostitutes. They buy them from the brothel owners and marry them."

"How often does that happen?"

"Often. Ain't that many of us here, remember? A used horse is better than none at all."

As Lily talked and talked and talked, Katka's thoughts drifted. Why did she come to this strange country? She would go back, back to Slovenia where she would marry the baker's homely son. He was a humorless boy who used to make fun of her skinny arms. He wasn't handsome like Paul. He didn't make up stories or drop fruit in her lap. But. The baker's son would not make her heart hurt. The baker's son would not make her miss him when he was gone.

A few times each week, Katka typed while Lily talked. "This article is called: *The Plight of Location Women*." She rambled on. "Women in the locations. Imagine: No running water in the shacks. Typhoid. Pneumonia. Women worked to death trying to keep the shacks warm."

Katka wondered if there was cholera.

"Tell me, Katka, how can a company that made over two million dollars in profit last year not be able to put running water in the houses?"

"Do you want me to type that?"

"Why not? When the revolution comes, we ladies have to be ready. My paper will mobilize us."

There it was again. That word. Paul had used it on the ship.

"The worker's time is coming. Every woman on the Range is a worker. When the revolution arrives, I'm going to make sure we ladies get a piece of the pie. The accident whistle blows at least once a month, and someone loses an arm or, worse, their life. When that happens, what happens to the women? How do they feed their children?"

Katka stopped typing. She longed for her mother's stories of fairies and magic. All Lily thought about was injustice. "You think a newspaper will make a difference? Maybe we should bring some rolls and jam to the locations, instead of writing about hunger."

"Good idea, *Matchka*! That is an immediate solution, and we will do that, this very day. It will make you feel important for a long time. And it may improve conditions for one hour, for one child. But the next day, while we are feeling charitable, the child will be hungry again, and the world will be no better. We need to think like the prophets and the saints. We need to think like Paul and Elizabeth and Emma Goldman. We need something bigger."

Katka gently pushed Lily away. She sat down at the desk and put her fingers on the typewriter. As she stabbed at the keys, she smiled when letters materialized magically on the page. The first word Lily wrote was *REVOLUCIJA*.

CHAPTER 7

MILO BLATNIK REMEMBERED THE FIRST DAY HE saw Katka. She was standing at the top of the stairwell looking bewildered, dirty, and so skinny that her dark brown eyes seemed two or three times their actual size. Her cheekbones jutted out like a skeleton. She reminded him of a starving deer. The gray dress she was wearing hung over her like a horse blanket.

Had he looked that ragged when he first arrived more than a year ago in Minnesota? Probably worse, he figured. Milo's parents had sent him to the New World because, as Milo's father had said, "No son of mine will become a soldier for the czar." Two weeks after Milo left for America, the Russian army arrested his mother, a poet, and his father, a famous cellist, for political agitation. They were taken to Siberia, and as far as Milo knew, they were still there.

On Milo's passage, a Slovenian named Leo Zalar befriended him on the ship. Leo had been offered work at the Belgrade mine in Biwabik, and he assured Milo he could get work there too. So Milo accompanied Leo, his wife, Ana, and their four-year-old son, Danko, to Biwabik. They moved into a company shanty in the Belgrade location, just outside of town, right next to the mine, offering to share their quarters with Milo for a piece of his paycheck.

The first night, as they sat down to a dinner of warmed beans and day-old bread from the company store, the ill-constructed shack of a house began to shake. The few belongings they had unpacked fell off the shelves and clattered to the ground. They heard a giant explosion, and dirt and debris fell from the ceiling. A chunk of wood that had served as a roof patch landed on a pink wood-fired plate Ana had brought from the old country. She had kept the set of plates safe throughout her long journey, thinking if she could keep the set together, she herself would remain intact.

They heard a low rumble. "Take cover!" Leo yelled, and the four of them scrambled under the flimsy pinewood table. The boy cried, and Ana held him close to her chest. The second blast was even louder than the first, but the impact was not as shattering. Nothing else fell from the ceiling. Then the rumbling stopped.

"What in the name of Mary was that?" Ana asked quietly. "An earthquake?"

"Dynamite blasting from the mine," Leo said. "I suspect we'll get used to it."

"I'll never get used to that," Ana said gravely.

But she did. As the months progressed the blasting became as much a part of her landscape as the giant oak and pine forest that she could see from her window. She'd hear the rumble and move with her boy to the corner of the small shack next to the shelves. She had packed away what was left of her mother's dishes and replaced them with tin cookware bought at the company store on credit. If a blast was powerful enough to knock a dish off the shelf, she'd catch it, replace it, listen intently for a possible encore, and if it didn't come, smoothly resume her tasks. It was like a dance between two partners, one of whom could anticipate the moves her partner was about to make.

On the morning of their first day of work, Leo and Milo put on overalls, boots, and cotton hats. They grabbed their lunch boxes. Each had a band tied around his hat to hold his candle.

In their pockets they carried matches. They exited the shack and fell into a steady stride, easily blending in with the other workers. When they reached the mine, Milo and the other miners headed for the cage. There were actually two cages attached by a pulley system. As one metal crate descended into the depths of the underground mine, the other ascended. The cage was aptly named; it looked more fit to carry livestock than men. The one at the Belgrade mine was standard size, perhaps four feet by three feet. Six miners could ride comfortably, but comfort was not efficient. The company required no fewer than eighteen men to ride per trip. The miners packed in like sardines, holding their lunch boxes atop their heads.

When the cage was loaded and on its way down, the darkness was all encompassing. Milo held his hand directly in front of his face. He could not see his fingers. He was disoriented and felt as if the men's bodies pressing against his skinny frame would surely suffocate him. When he got to the thirteenth floor underground, he and Leo exited the cage with a group. A miner who looked a hundred years old was waiting with a lantern. For a moment Milo was transported to his youth. He remembered his father, who loved to read, making him memorize passages from *Dante's Inferno*. The miner with the lantern was like Charon, waiting to deliver the shades of the dead to their eternal punishment. The Iron Range Charon swung his lantern to the left, and the miners shuffled in that direction. They loaded into rail cars, six men per cart. The rail cart operator yelled something in English, and the cars began to move away from the light and into the darkness until, once again, there was nothing.

Milo's head began to spin. He couldn't breathe. He couldn't see. Was he disappearing? He bit the inside of his cheek and felt reassured by the pain and the taste of blood. Then he felt himself falling again. Even on the darkest moonless night, his eyes had been able to adjust. This was something altogether different, surreal.

He reached into his pocket for a match. He needed to light his candle, regain his bearings. The man sitting across from him could not see Milo, but somehow he knew what he was doing. "Don't do it, son," he said. Milo replied in Slovenian that he did not understand. The miner responded in kind. "They deduct every match you use from your pay. Every candle. Even your dynamite. Everything. Don't waste your light here. Your workday doesn't even begin until you exit this cart and pick up the shovel."

Milo lit his candle anyway. With the light he could breathe again. Breathe the dusty, old air in this godforsaken underground tunnel. He heard the other miners laughing. He heard a few people mutter, in English, four words: "Fresh off the boat."

When the cart stopped, an old man pointed to him. "You, Bohunk, come with me." Milo followed. "And you, Wop." A young Italian immigrant did the same. When they got to the end of the vein, next to a huge pile of blasted ore, the old man handed them each a shovel, talking nonstop. "Careful with your shovels now, boys. You'll be paying for their use at the end of the month." They took the shovels.

"Ain't big talkers, I see. Probably can't understand a blasted word I say. I slept with your mother. Both of yourn. At the same time."

Milo and the Italian stared expressionless at the old man, who laughed. His voice echoed eerily throughout the tunnel, and Milo felt chills go up his back.

"Lucky for you, you don't need no English to be a mucker. Don't need no brains neither, which might work to your favor. This here's how you do it." The old man took his shovel and scooped the heavy rock into the tram cars. The "fresh-off-the-boats" did the same. "We get paid by the carload, not the hour. So, as the company men say, your workday starts now."

"Work," Milo said.

"Work," the Italian said.

And work they did. Sometimes the rocks were too big to shovel. They used a pick and hammer to break down the ore. To prevent their backs from giving out, they spent part of each hour on their knees working the larger boulders. By the time the whistle blew for lunch, Milo's knees were bloody. As he ate the pasty Ana had prepared for him, with the old man and Gino, the Italian, he felt the wounds starting to scab over. Then he went back to work for five more hours.

When the cage door opened into the breeze above ground at the end of his first day, Milo gasped for air. He felt as if he had swallowed a cat, and he coughed for a good ten minutes before locating Leo. His face and hands were grimy. His back hurt and his knees stung. Milo wanted to quit. One day in the mine was enough. But he could not quit. He owed the company store for his overalls, his hatband, the shovel, the ax, the hammer, the candles, and the matches. He owed the Zalars rent.

CHAPTER 8

S O MILO WENT BACK, MORNING AFTER MORNING. He worked six days a week for at least twelve hours a day. He went to work in the dark; he came home in the dark. He didn't see the sun until his first day off, Sunday, which he realized was the most aptly named day of the week.

His life fell into a pattern. Before the men's arrival home, Ana heated water on the stove and boiled strips of white cloth with eucalyptus leaves. "Can I help with your boots, *Ata*?" little Danko would say to his father.

"What a big boy you are!" Danko tugged at Leo's boots, falling to the ground when they finally came loose from his leg. Then Danko helped with Milo's boots. The two miners slipped out of their overalls and rolled their long underwear up to their thighs, revealing dark red patches of blood where their knobby knees had pressed against the sharp ore. Ana laid the warm cloths on their scabs and let the men sit with the poultices on their wounds until supper was served.

Some nights after dinner, Ana persuaded Milo to take out the guitar he had brought from the old country. He played familiar chords in unfamiliar patterns. He composed new melodies, tunes he made up at work while trying to stay mentally alive, but Ana had little patience for that. She was tired of new. "Play something from the old country," she would say. Milo did, and Ana sang along.

Milo worked first as a mucker, then a trammer, then a trackman, until he was finally assigned to a position where he was considered a real miner. He became a driller and received a slight raise in pay, at least in theory. There were four men on his crew, and only he spoke Slovenian. He learned how to say "run," "help," "look out," and "bossman coming" in Italian, Swedish, Finnish, and English. He could cuss in even more languages. The miners always knew when the bossman was about to walk through. They had worked out a simple system to communicate with each other about a slew of things. Four rhythmic shovel whacks followed by two short ones clearly told the miners on the level below that the bossman was coming down. If the miner spotted the supervisor on his own level, he moved his candle slightly off-center, to the left.

Milo learned how to do his job at just the right speed. He learned to take breaks, but not for so long that his back would stiffen. He learned to drill through only the rock the trammers and muckers would be able to load. If a crew loaded less than the quota, they received lower pay. If they loaded more, they received more pay, but then the foreman would raise their quota for the next month, and they'd have to break their backs just to receive the same pay they would have gotten for loading fewer cars the month before. He learned to drill the right amount of rock that he knew would result in an acceptable output and a fair day's wage. This scheme, which prevented the miners from ever getting ahead, was called the contract system, and the workers despised it. When his English was better, Milo would quietly listen to other miners discuss it.

"Only way to get rid of the contract system is to strike," he heard Gino say one day. Gino had come from Italy, where workers knew how to organize, he said.

"Who's going to organize us?" another worker said. "A wop like you?"

"Could happen," Gino said. "Don't forget it was an Italian mayor who got electricity on the streets and a school built."

"You know the mayor? What? He invite you to his parties? Let you date his daughter? Next time you sippin' whiskey with your Italian friend, you tell him this for me." The miner made a gesture, and the men laughed.

Milo listened to the men talk about politics. They talked about a man named Big Bill Haywood, one of the founders of a union called the Industrial Workers of the World, and another named Eugene Debs, who wanted to become the president of the United States. Milo listened intently, but every time he got lost in the English.

One night, after work, Gino asked Milo to stop off at one of the Italian taverns to grab a beer. "Can't," Milo said. "I saving my pay."

"For what? A woman? They ain't that expensive. Couple bucks will get you a decent one at Crooked Neck Pete's."

"Not a woman, no."

"What then? Got family back home to support?"

"No."

"Gambling debts?"

He wasn't sure he wanted to tell Gino because he was afraid he'd laugh at him. But Gino was already laughing, so what did he have to lose? "Last Sunday man came to the location with big cart. Ana, she wouldn't go to the door. Said she had no money and don't need the devil's temptation. So me, I go. And the man, he show me what in his truck."

"Women?" Gino said.

Milo shook his head, smiling. "Book."

"Bibles? You are saving your money to give to a Bible salesman? Listen, Milo, ain't nobody less Christian than a Bible salesman. Better to spend your money on moonshine."

"Not Bible. Cyclepedias."

"En-cyclo-pedias?"

"That what I say."

Milo explained to Gino how beautiful the volumes were, and that he figured by the time he got through all the volumes, he could consider himself a learned American man. Milo didn't tell Gino about his fear: that working in the mine was dulling his brain. He wanted desperately to stay sharp. His father had studied music for a brief time in Vienna and made his living playing the cello in a small orchestra in Ljubljana and giving music lessons to the sons and daughters of rich Austrians who lived there. His father had wanted Milo to attend university and had tried to reestablish a Slovenian language university in Ljubljana, where he had promised to teach music. Every time his father and his comrades had come close to fulfilling their dream, the Austro-Hungarian government shut them down.

"Salesman said be back in two month," Milo said to Gino. "That why I save."

Gino listened and did not laugh. "Tell you what. I'll buy you a beer. When you get your books, let me borrow them. I don't want no Bohunk thinking he smarter than me. In the meantime, I'll get you some things to read."

The following Sunday Gino showed up at the Belgrade location. When Milo opened the door, Gino reached into his inside coat pocket and pulled out some magazines. "As promised," he said. He handed Milo three publications: the *Industrial Worker*, the *International Socialist Review*, and *Solidarity*. Milo spent the next month sounding out the words in the magazines and reading out loud until the sentences actually made sense.

About six months into the job, when he could understand English adequately, he turned to one of his coworkers, a Finn named Johan Koski. "If the miners, we strike," Milo asked, "will you?"

"Tried that in 1907," Koski said.

"And?"

Koski paused. He leaned on his shovel. "Back then there were a lot more Finlanders like me working these here mines. Brave sons of bitches. They led the strike."

"It failed?"

"Yes. And my papa got the blacklist, which was better than some, who got killed. We were hungry. Many families, they left the Range. Those who stayed moved to the country, carved out homes in the land, tried to make a go of it there."

"But a strike would be different now," Milo said. "There's a war coming."

"We Finns are smart. I read. I go to the socialist hall and listen to the speakers. I know there's a war. I see no sense in it. I know there is talk of strike again. I think about that too. I don't know if I believe in a socialist takeover. I don't know if I believe that owners don't deserve more pay than we get. But I do know this: The poor will always stay poor if we do not get together. A rich boss is not going to give one man anything at all. You don't like your job? Go somewhere else. But a rich man cannot tell thousands of men to go away. If he does, he won't be rich anymore. He'll have no one to make his money."

"So you will support a strike?"

"Only if there is a plan," Johan said. Just then, they heard four shovel whacks followed by two short ones come from above. The entire crew picked up their equipment. Milo started drilling. They were all working in earnest when the foreman walked through. They did not take another break until lunch.

Milo and Johan Koski sat together at lunch. Another Finnish worker pointed to Milo and, his tone hostile, said something to Koski, who swore back at him in English.

"What I do?" Milo asked.

"We Finlanders, as a general rule, don't like your kind," he said to Milo.

"What kind?" Milo asked. "Nice-looking kind?"

"Slavs. Croats. Montenegrins. Bohunks. None of you Austrians."

"I never been Austrian."

"Well, you is to us. And the rest of the world too. On your papers, when you come to this country, do it say 'Slovenian'? No. It say, 'Austro-Hungarian Empire.' Am I right?"

He was right. Slovenians, or Slovenes as some called themselves, were one people with a separate language and beautiful culture. A culture that was maintained by his father, by his mother, and by the many artists whom Milo met in his youth. Although they had been under the control of Austria, they were not Austrian. Not to themselves. But here? They were all lumped together. They were called Bohunks. Eventually they called themselves Bohunks.

"As I was saying," Johan said, "we Finns don't usually talk to none of you Bohunks, except when we have to at work."

"Seems like you talking to me. Must be my charisma, no?" Milo had just learned that word: charisma. In Slovenian, it was almost the same: *Karizma*. Big Bill Haywood of the Industrial Workers of the World had charisma. Eugene Debs had charisma. Elizabeth Gurley Flynn had charisma. Milo read that in one of Gino's magazines.

"I don't know what charisma is," Johan Koski said. "But I do know that your people broke the strike in 1907." The whistle blew, indicating that the workers needed to return to work. "Lunch is over. But I want to warn you. Don't talk unions or strikes at work. Don't ask me questions. If the bossman heard us talking, he'd get some cousin jacks to roll giant boulders down the shaft and our whole damn crew'd be dead."

"You lie," Milo said, closing his lunch pail.

"Ask around. It's amazing what the Oliver dubs 'accident.' Keep your talk to the taverns and halls. There are spies everywhere in these mines. How do you know I am not a spy, ready to report you today?"

"Because you asked me that question," Milo said.

CHAPTER 9

"I DON'T THINK IT IS A GOOD PLACE FOR A BOY," Ana Zalar said to her husband, Leo, as Milo was leaving.

Milo had secured lodging at Vince Torelli's boardinghouse, one of the cheapest in town, with a notorious brothel and tavern. In the last year alone, nine men had been shot there, and four of them had died. Musicians played into the wee hours of the night, and men got so drunk they fell off their barstools or vomited into the spittoons. Milo had never seen a gunfight up close or, more importantly, a sporting girl. He couldn't wait to go.

"No place for a boy," Ana repeated.

"Ana," Leo said. "He is no more a boy. He is seventeen now."

"You are a stupid man," Ana said.

"Then you married one. What does that make you, aye?" Ana was due to deliver her second child in a month or two. The shack was small. It was time for Milo to move on.

Milo arrived at the boardinghouse on a Sunday, midafternoon. The tavern was about half full. He walked up to the long bar.

"Excuse me, ma'am," he said to a woman about fifty years old, dressed conservatively in black. She was pouring whiskey into a Mason jar for a customer.

"What will it be?"

Milo told her who he was.

"Eight dollars, up front," she said, tucking the money into her apron pocket. Then she looked at him closely. "How old are you, kid?"

"Twenty."

"Ever had a woman before?"

Milo hesitated. "Yes," he said. "Many women I have had."

She raised her eyebrow at him and watched as his face flushed. "I see how it is," she said. "I'm Edna, Vince's wife. We got a kitchen staff, and I ain't on it, so don't be asking me for food. Order from the bar wenches, and we'll bill you at the end of the month for anything over two meals a day." She poured him a small amount of whiskey, not more than a swallow or two. "Drink it. It's on the house."

Milo picked up the glass and drank it in one gulp. The liquor burned his throat, but he tried not to show it.

"Greek?" she asked him.

"No. Slovenian, I am."

"What do you think of her?" Edna asked, pointing toward a blonde who was delivering some drinks to a table full of gamblers in the back corner. The woman wore a long red dress with a low-cut bodice. She had a small waist. Her hair was curled in ringlets, and she had painted lips and cheeks.

"She beautiful," Milo said. And she was.

"I thought she'd be the one for you. Greek men always go for the blondes. Think they are exotic."

"I am Slovenian."

"Same thing. Tell you what, since you're new here, I'll give you half price on her. Just two dollars a row."

Two dollars? That was almost a day's wages at the mine. "Maybe tomorrow," Milo said.

"Deal's only good today." She poured him another glass of whiskey and watched him drink it. He started to feel slightly dizzy. "Get yourself settled. Your room's up the stairs." Milo picked up his rucksack and his guitar and carried them to his room.

The house accommodated over thirty miners who spoke nearly as many languages. Ten men were assigned to each room. At any given time, because there were two shifts at the mine, a miner could be found asleep on one of the foul-smelling beds. However, because it was Sunday, only a few men were sleeping off hangovers when Milo got to his room. Three men were lying on their bunks reading. One man with a mop of yellow hair and a scruffy beard was cleaning out his fingernails with his penknife.

"You the new man?" he said to Milo in a Swedish accent.

"Yep."

"That one." He pointed to the bed next to his and resumed his grooming ritual. "Fellow before you died. His name was Eric Gustafson. Upstanding guy. Got his self killed, right downstairs. Fighting over a woman, they say. Woman's husband walked in a few days ago, right into the tavern, and shot him in the back. He died a few days later. His last words were, 'Don't prosecute. I done what he said I done, and I deserve it.'"

"Sorry. About your friend."

"He were not my friend."

Milo unpacked his meager belongings. Ana had stuffed a linen sheet in his sack, and upon seeing it, he felt overcome with gratitude. The sheet that was on his bed was filthy. He replaced it with the cloth. He shook out the wool blanket. "The blankets, are they lousy?" he asked.

"Mine ain't. Guess you'll find out about yourn soon enough." The Swede introduced himself to Milo. His name was Lars. "We're not all named Lars," he said, "despite what they tell you. But me, I actually am. Lars Larson." He agreed to show

Milo around the place. "It's almost time for dinner anyways. Cook ain't that good, but the service is real pretty."

Milo thought about the blonde with the painted face. He felt an aching between his legs and hoped his longing was not visible to the Swede. He tried to think of something else. He thought about the encyclopedias he had been saving for. Maybe he could bargain with the traveling salesman, talk him down. "Take it or leave it," he would say. "Offer only good today."

Two dollars was an awful lot of money. But two dollars was half as much as four, which is what it would cost him tomorrow. And all he had was four dollars until next week's payday. He had it right in his pocket. He'd already had his first drink of whiskey. He was living on his own. What other firsts would this day hold for him? He couldn't wait to find out.

CHAPTER 10

S USAN FLETCHER WAS THE FIRST SPORTING GIRL TO
work at Vince Torelli's boardinghouse, arriving with the
"Original Seven" by train from Minneapolis nine years earlier.
The other six dispersed to various brothels. Susan had worked
at Torelli's ever since, and Vince had added four more girls.

Ina, Maria, Leppe, and Brina had been falsely lured by
Vince from their countries of origin to work as waitresses. Ina
and Leppe were both blondes from Sweden. They had lived in
Biwabik for more than three years and had hardened to their
fates. Maria, the Croatian, and Brina, the Russian, were both
dark-haired with olive skin. They had been working less than a
year. The bouncer, Moose Jackson, was aptly named. He was
huge. At the end of the night, he collected the money from the
sporting girls, gave Vince his share, the ladies their share, and
pocketed the rest.

Milo and Lars Larson sat down at a table near the bar.
Brina, the Russian, approached their table, but was called off
by Edna, who was still working behind the bar. She whispered
something to Brina, and a moment or two later, the blond,
blue-eyed Swede named Leppe came to their table. Without a
word she plopped a bowl of venison stew in front of each man.
Then she left, returning with a small loaf of bread, some utensils, and butter.

"What else?" she asked. "Whiskey, Lars?"

Lars said something to her in Swedish, and she laughed.

"You?" she said to Milo.

"Same ting."

By the time the two men finished their meal, Milo was so drunk he was talking to Lars in half English, half Slovenian. Lars responded in Swedish, and it was hilarious to both of them. After more than two hours had passed and many whiskeys were consumed, Edna was at the table, looking straight at Milo. "Deal is for one day only," she repeated.

"I have money," Milo said without hesitation.

"Good. She is waiting for you up the stairs. Past the boarder rooms, on the right. Last door. Think you can remember all that, Greek boy?"

"Slovenian."

"Right. What are you waiting for, then?"

"No ting."

Lars Larson patted Milo on the back, made a lewd gesture, and wished him luck. The first waitress who had waited on them, Brina, caught his eye. She quickly shook her head and mouthed, "no," but he paid no attention. Milo quickly made his way up the stairs, his head filled with visions of Leppe's breasts. He was thoroughly intoxicated, but he was young, and his body was eager.

Leppe was lying on the bed with her eyes closed, as if napping, when he opened the door. She stood up with a start. "Don't you have the decency to knock?"

"Sorry." Milo blushed. She was gorgeous. The most wonderful sight he had ever seen. "You are most beautiful girl in whole world," he said.

"How old are you?"

"Twenty," Milo said.

"Sure you are. And I'm a nun."

She began to undo the laces on her corset. Milo's eyes grew wide. She slipped out of her skirt and undergarments and stood before him, naked except for her hosiery and garters.

"Sweet Mary," Milo said. He thought he might faint and willed himself not to.

"It works better if you take your clothes off too," Leppe said dryly.

She watched as Milo loosened his suspenders, unbuttoned his trousers, and let them fall to his knees. Leppe looked at him. At the part no woman had ever looked at. She touched her breasts with her hands, slowly encircling her nipples. She licked her lips and held out her left hand. "Three dollars," she said.

Edna had said two dollars, hadn't she? Maybe he had heard wrong. Had she said three? His head was spinning, just a bit. He wished he hadn't drunk so much whiskey. "Two dollars."

He watched as Leppe's hand slowly started to wander down her body, to her navel, and then lower. "Three."

He bent down to the ground and reached into his trouser pockets and counted out three dollars, handing them to her quickly. She tucked them into a satchel on the floor. As she bent over, he pulled up behind her, reached around, and felt her breasts. "Please, no longer can I wait."

It was over quickly. He begged her to let him do it again, and it was clear he had the stamina to do it, but he didn't have three more dollars. He watched morosely as she put her clothes back on without making eye contact. "Please," he said. "I'll pay you tomorrow."

She slowly picked his clothes up off the floor. Her back was to him. Then she threw him his pants and walked out the door.

Milo found Lars sitting at the same table where they had shared dinner. A woman with dark hair was sitting on his lap, and he kept trying to put his hands between her legs. She pushed his hands away in disgust and walked away. When he saw Milo, Lars stood up and cheered drunkenly. He made the same lewd gesture he had made the last time he saw Milo. "Sweden is a great country, no?" He pointed toward Leppe, who was letting a man at the gambling table smell her breasts while she poured bourbon into their glasses.

"Lars. Borrow me two dollar. I pay you back on payday."

Lars chortled and shook his head. "Wash your pecker before you go to bed. I don't pay for no one's whore but my own."

Milo watched a man put his hands on Leppe's buttocks and squeeze. She slapped him, not hard. Milo stood up, infuriated. Lars pushed him back down. "Milo. Sit the hell down. Finish your drink like a man. Then go to bed. Don't start no trouble here. Not if you want to live. Don't confuse a whore with a lady."

"Okay," Milo said. He held up his drink, high. In the reflection of the glass, he could see the back of Leppe's head. Her hair was the golden color of wheat in the fall, but her curls had flattened and lost their bounce.

Later that night, as he changed for bed, Milo frantically searched his pockets. He had handed her three dollars as requested. But his other dollar was gone too. Leppe had robbed him.

CHAPTER 11

BEFORE WORK EVERY MORNING, MILO TOOK breakfast at the tavern, usually with the Swede. He ate half his meal, which was paid for by his rent money, and saved the rest to stuff into his lunch pail since he had no money for lunch. By dinnertime he was famished. He did not want to return to the tavern, to the place where he had been humiliated, but he had no choice.

Leppe did not serve his meal until four nights after their encounter. "Well," she said, "if it isn't my eager little Greek."

"Not Greek," Milo corrected. Now sober, Leppe's face did not look as beautiful to Milo as it had the first time he saw her. "Why did you do it?" he asked.

"Do what?" she retorted, placing a bowl of stew in front of him.

"Steal from me. I have no more dollar."

"Because you let me." Her voice held no apologies, but also no malice. "That is how it works here." Milo's face reddened as she walked away.

He wanted so very much to walk out the door. To return to a life filled with books and music and women who wouldn't let you hold their hand without a promise. He wanted to hate her, but he couldn't. She was doing a job, a job she probably despised. She was like the miners in that way. Debts to pay and nowhere to go.

In his first few weeks at the boardinghouse, Milo witnessed three knife fights and several fistfights. He had imagined that the fights would be big, brawling affairs involving many people, but they were not. All three knife fights had been between two men who had a score to settle. It was understood that men would have grievances, and they would necessarily be settled through violence. Only once did the sheriff come into the tavern, and it was to play Smear, a popular miner's card game that originated in Slovenia. Vince, the owner, was the sheriff's partner, and Milo heard that the two of them made forty dollars each in a tournament that lasted long into the night. There were a few brawls that night too, but Sheriff Turner did not intervene.

One night Milo heard Leppe arguing with Moose. "I don't need you," she said. "I'll collect the money myself. Why should you get a dime?"

Moose's right hand flew out of his pocket, and his fist, shaped like an iron heart, landed on Leppe's nose like a hammer. Leppe fell to the ground, covering her face. Blood seeped through her fingers. Milo stood up from where he was sitting. He walked toward Leppe, who was writhing on the ground; the big bouncer stood over her, wiping her blood from his hand.

"Why you do like that?" Milo said to Moose.

"What?" Moose said.

"Why you hit a lady?" Milo's voice was steady, but his eyes flickered with disbelief. "You so bigger than her."

The other customers grew quiet. At six feet, eight inches, Moose was a freak of nature. Rumor had it he had murdered two men in Minneapolis. He had done some time in Duluth too, before making his way to the Range. No one challenged Moose Jackson and expected to live.

"You're the Greek, aren't you? What's your name?"

"My name is Milo Blatnik. I am not Greek. I am from Ljubljana, in Slovenia."

"Nice to meet you," Moose said. Then, using both fists like a boxer, he pummeled Milo's face and kneed him in the stomach. Milo dropped like a ragdoll. For a moment he heard the other men in the bar cheering, but he didn't know if they were urging him to fight back or urging Moose to kill him.

CHAPTER 12

WHEN MILO CAME TO, THE SKY WAS BEGINNING TO lighten. He was leaning against the hard brick of Cerkvenik's Mercantile, where someone had dragged him. He had been awakened by the sound of buzzing. A small army of mosquitoes was swarming about him. They had been feasting on his bloody face for hours before he regained consciousness. The back of his head felt as if it had exploded, and his innards felt as if they had been reorganized by a jackhammer.

He felt something warm and wet on his face and reached for it.

"Don't touch," a soft voice said. He put his hand down. Milo tried to open his eyes. His left eye was completely swollen shut. He could open his right eye slightly. His vision was fuzzy. He could vaguely see a woman's face in front of his. Her hair was black. She was dabbing his wounds with a cloth.

"Do you have any people?"

"People?" He coughed blood and spit it out.

"To take care of you. You can't go back to Vince's place. Moose'll kill you."

Who was Vince? Who was Moose? Who was this woman? The words and images floated around him like ghosts. He tried to focus.

"Family. Friends," she said. "Anyone?"

"Leo and Ana Zalar. Belgrade location."

"Good," she said. "I will take you there, but we must hurry."

"Are you an angel?"

She hesitated. "No. I am Brina."

"Thank you. You save my life. Someday I return the favor."

"Can you stand?"

He could, but barely. He leaned on Brina, and slowly they stumbled their way to the Zalars' door. He slumped against it and fell to the dirt. Brina knocked hard three times and ran.

Ana Zalar opened the door. She was very pregnant. "Milo! My poor little boy," she cried. "Danko! Help me drag him to the bed!" Ana wondered what to do about Milo's smashed-in face and useless arm. "A lawless land, this is," she said. As Danko tugged at Milo's boots, Ana put water on to boil, added the eucalyptus leaves, and readied the white bandages.

Leo had heard all about the fight during his shift. When he came home from the mine, he was relieved to see Milo safe in his house. "My son," he said when Milo stirred, "how did you get here?"

"Woman," he said.

"What woman?"

"Her name was Brina."

"A woman like that," Leo said, "you should marry."

Milo tried to smile, but winced in pain.

"My arm, will it heal?"

Leo said nothing.

"Of course it will heal," Ana said loudly. "Good as new in no time."

Milo closed his eyes and drifted back into a fitful sleep. Leo looked doubtfully at his wife. "Good as new, ay?"

"In a land with no laws, faith is more important than anything."

CHAPTER 13

I T TOOK WEEKS TO RECOVER. MILO LOST HIS JOB AT the Belgrade mine. He lost his spot at the boardinghouse, not that he wanted it back. Ana Zalar, with Danko in tow, returned to Torelli's to retrieve Milo's possessions. A sporting girl directed her, with a bored gesture, upstairs to where Milo had slept. His bed was occupied by one of several snoring miners who were gearing up for the night shift. Milo's rucksack was lying empty in the corner. The other boarders had taken his canteen, his overalls, his candles, his knife. His guitar, however, was still there. Ana grabbed it and walked out of the tavern.

Moose Jackson had broken four of Milo's ribs in the one-sided bar fight. After two weeks, Milo could see out of both eyes, but he still had trouble breathing. He loathed the idea of going back to work underground. Nonetheless, he applied for and immediately got hired at the St. James mine a few miles away.

As he recovered, Milo read in *The Industrial Worker* that the United States would soon enter the mighty war raging in Europe. Never before had there been a greater need for the iron produced on the Mesabi Range, and never before had there been so few workers to dig it out of the ground. The government had enacted immigration quotas, which stopped the flow of unskilled workers to northern Minnesota. An injured man was preferable to no worker at all. The foreman who hired Milo even offered him an advance on his first month's wages to pay for his work clothes, candles, and matches. Two days later, he got word from Mr. Anton Kovich that there was an opening at his boardinghouse. It was outside of town and had a reputation for being peaceful.

But not long after his arrival, things would change. A girl would arrive from the old country. A skinny girl with big, dark eyes like a deer. Within months, trouble would barge through the door of the Slovenski Dom. Once again, Milo would not be able to walk away.

CHAPTER 14

"WHEN YOU GOING TO REPAIR THE SMOKEHOUSE roof?" Lily said to Anton one morning after the miners had left for work. "You promised that patchwork would be temporary. It looks low class."

"Lily, my precious flower, we got a nice house here. Bet Katka didn't even notice the patch on the roof, did you, niece?"

"What happened? A storm?"

"A right good one. Tree fell on it," Anton said. "It happened before your arrival. But Lily's right. I'll get a man to help me, and we'll make it right as rain."

"He will not," Lily said to Katka. "He always says he is going to do something, and then he runs off to the woods and hibernates."

"Do I?" Anton asked. He walked toward his wife, grabbed her hand tenderly, and pulled her toward him. He put his hands on her cheeks and kissed her. "Why don't you hibernate with me, you old nag?"

Katka liked to see her aunt and uncle so happy. Even when they argued, there was always an element of play in it. It made the long days shorter. She was exhausted. She and Lily rose at 4:30 a.m., prepared breakfast, and sent the miners off to work with a hot lunch. While they were cleaning up, Anton left for the woods to hunt or oversee the men who logged his land. When the women could no longer hear the hooves of his horse, they would grab a few hard-boiled eggs and a carafe of coffee and head to the cellar, where Katka continued to give Lily typing lessons. Lily was impatient and her work full of errors.

"You type," she said to Katka. "I'll dictate." They switched places and Katka's fingers moved like a musician's across a piano:

> *Chest Cold Remedy Cures What Ails You*
> *1. Gather a few armfuls of evergreen branches.*
> *2. Throw away all but the tips, which should be light green in color.*
> *3. Place the tips with half pound of sugar in a glass jar and cover (tight).*
> *4. Place the jar in sunlight for two or three weeks, until syrup forms.*
> *5. Serve a spoonful at a time to your man and children.*

In the three weeks since Katka's arrival, spring had gone and summer arrived. Apple trees bloomed and tulips blossomed and died. Wild lupine, which grew on both sides of Blood Red Road, exploded across the landscape in cheerful hues of purple and pink. The women picked the flowers and put them in vases throughout the house, even in the cellar where they worked on the women's paper. They had completed six articles and some sketches of women's swimwear that was now on sale at Cerkvenik's. Lily wrote about the ceremony for the first four graduates of Biwabik High School and what the mayor's wife was wearing. Lily also wrote a detailed article about the ten catalogue girls who had arrived from Finland a week earlier. Although she interviewed none of them, she included personal information on each bride. Most of this information came from her bosom buddy, Helen, who worked behind the counter at Cerkvenik's and lived for gossip. Nowhere in the pamphlet was there any reference to anything remotely controversial.

They christened their publication *The Iron Range Ladies Journal*. Lily tied a ribbon around the typed stack of articles and drawings, and put the manuscript in a small brown egg crate with a handwritten letter on top. She carried it to the chicken coop, put it next to the other crates, and covered the top with hay. The next morning when Katka went to gather eggs, the manuscript was gone, picked up by Lily's conspirator, who would typeset it and run off copies.

The following Saturday was hot and humid. Lily got word from Helen that the *Ladies Journal* had been delivered to both Cerkvenik's and Gornik's General Store and was selling like hotcakes. Lily and Katka decided to celebrate by doing nothing. "Besides," Lily said, "it's too damn hot to cook."

As evening approached, Katka and Lily laid out bread, meat, and cheese on the dining room table and let the men make their own sandwiches to eat at their leisure.

"It's fend-for-yourself night," Lily proclaimed to all the boarders. "We ladies need a rest."

Katka and Lily set up chairs in the backyard. "Anton always jokes about the weather here," Lily said to Katka. "He calls Minnesota the land with nine months of winter and three months of bad sledding. But wouldn't you know it? Because I'm carrying five pounds of warm coal on my ribcage, the *Farmer's Almanac* predicts it will stay hot until fall." Lily propped her swollen feet on a milk crate and rested a pint of cool ale on her protruding belly. "My feet hurt like a son of a bitch," she said to Katka.

Uncle Anton was in the Slovenski Dom. Some of the boarders were inside, but most chose to eat their dinner outside in the breeze. Soon after, several of the miners began playing horseshoes. Every now and then, a few miners would look their way and call out a greeting.

"Starved, you know," Lily said. "That's what they are."

"How could they be?" Katka asked. "All we do is feed them."

"Not that kind of starvation, you ninny. They're hungry for women. There aren't many single ones left, and this war in Europe is putting a stop to the catalogue brides. Don't you see the way they look at you?"

"At me?"

"Even Old Joe, who could be your grandfather." Katka and Lily glanced over at Joe, who nearly lost his balance while trying to swat a mosquito without spilling his beer. "Well, maybe not Old Joe." The women laughed loudly. When they did, the horseshoe players all looked their way. Milo Blatnik tipped his cap at them.

"You ladies want to throw?" Old Joe, his back hunched over from Crooks disease, yelled, gesturing toward the stake with a horseshoe. "Got to be better than Baby Milo here. He's a *cebula glava*, he is. Onionhead. I think you could take him, *Teta* Lily. Yes, I do!"

"'Course I could, Joe. Could take you too, probably faster. But if you haven't noticed, I'm in a bit of a predicament here," Lily said, pointing to her belly. "Trying to take advantage of my handicap?"

Milo walked toward the women. He was eighteen now, just turned. Although he was the newest boarder at the house, having arrived only a short time before Katka, he was well-liked and had made friends. He had grown four inches in the last year and was nearly six feet tall, a decided disadvantage for an underground miner. When he was standing in front of Lily, he stopped.

"Cigarette?" he asked.

"We don't," Lily said, amused.

Milo slowly took a prerolled cigarette out of his pocket and lit it. He took a puff, blew the smoke toward the sky, then looked at the ground.

"Something on your mind?" Lily asked.

"Yes," Milo said. "Miss Katka. I come to ask if you want to throw the shoe with me. This would be a great honor for me, and I think, more fun for you than sitting here. How about?"

Katka looked at her aunt with raised eyebrow. Her face communicated the unspoken question: What is the proper thing to do here?

Lily shrugged. "I'd play if I could."

As Katka got up, took Milo's arm, and walked to the horse-shoe pit, the miners clapped and yelled. "Onionhead got a girl," Old Joe bellowed.

The next morning Katka woke up tired. After two games of horseshoes, Milo, a kindly boarder named Dusca, and Old Joe somehow talked her into staying up late. They taught her to play Smear, and they took great pains to explain the game in terms a woman could understand. They didn't know that Paul had taught her to play on the ship. They also didn't know that he had told her to play dumb so she could hustle other players for fruit. She was shrewd. By the end of the second round, she was already keeping track of cards in her head, counting silently as cards from each suit were laid.

Milo was her partner. "Do you know what's out?" he asked her.

"Perhaps no," she said. "Perhaps yes." She laid the jack of diamonds and took the last trick.

"You should play for money," Old Joe said. "Reckon you'd make a hell of a lot more on cards than I make in the mine, that's for God sure, it is."

"We'll see," Katka said. "But before I make a fortune swindling miners out of their wages, I have to make you breakfast. In about six hours. Thank you for the lesson."

The men stood and tipped their hats to Katka.

"She looking real pretty," Dusca said when she left. "I think she wants to marry me." Old Joe punched Dusca playfully on the shoulder. "Ow! What you do that for, dumbass?"

"Ain't nobody going to marry you, knucklehead."

"Maybe she'll marry me," Milo said.

"You too skinny. And stupid. Deal the cards, Onionhead. We'll play three-man."

CHAPTER 15

A S KATKA PUT ON HER SHAWL TO GO OUT TO THE barn to gather the eggs for Sunday's breakfast, she was wishing she had said no to cards and turned in early instead. Her head ached slightly, and she knew it was from drinking beer. The ale was different here. She moved sluggishly. As she approached the door, she was startled to see Lily coming out of the barn, holding what looked to be an empty canvas coffee bag in her hand. She was smiling.

"What are doing here?" Katka asked. "To gather eggs is my job."

"I was gathering something else. But I can't tell you what it is until tomorrow after everyone leaves." Lily kissed Katka on the cheek. "It's so fun to have a secret!" she raved. "And perhaps you have a secret too? Anton tells me you were up late gambling with that rabble-rouser Milo."

"Rabble-rouser?"

"A man who makes trouble," Lily said. When Katka still didn't understand, she translated. Katka crinkled her forehead. "Milo, I don't think, is rouser of rabble." She thought about Paul Schmidt. Her Paul was a rouser of rabble. She knew this all along, perhaps. Maybe even from the day he and his curly locks had arrived at her cottage in Zirovnica. All those secrets on the ship. His hesitancy to be seen or photographed. His detainment. Neither Anton nor Lily spoke of him openly or often.

Lily had told her not to worry about him and also not to worry "for him." According to Lily, Paul wasn't a man who would make a reliable mate, as he had bigger doings afoot. "Forget about him," Lily had said. Katka stopped asking questions and turned to the next best thing: eavesdropping. One night she overheard Anton telling Old Joe that no one could endure prison as easily as Paul. When Katka asked him what he meant, Anton told her he was talking about someone else. But she knew he wasn't.

"Milo has a passion for you, I just know it," Lily said. "And you have a passion for him, too, no?" Lily made kissing noises as she tucked the canvas bag into her apron pocket. Then she stuck her tongue out at Katka, held the underside of her belly with both hands, and practically skipped back to the kitchen. She was the happiest pregnant woman Katka had ever seen.

On Monday morning, after Anton and the miners left, the two women crawled into the cellar. Lily took out a match and lit the lantern. The light cast its familiar soft red hue over the guns, the writing material, the covered crates, even their faces. Katka smiled when she looked at her aunt. Her strawberry hair looked alive, like the sky had on her passage over, just before the big storm.

They sat at the table, and Lily produced the canvas bag, which she promptly flipped over. Coins spilled out.

"Two dollars and twenty cents!" Lily said triumphantly. "Sold out in one day, can you believe it? My deliveryman left the printer a note with our earnings. It read, 'Next month print double, and we'll both be rich.'" She lifted her coffee cup in a toast. "To us!"

"To us!" Katka said, smiling.

"Oh my..." Lily said, suddenly gripping her stomach.

"What is it, *Teta*?"

Lily stood up slowly, holding her back with her right hand and her belly with her left. She winced in pain.

"Is it the baby?" Katka whispered, knowing full well that it was too early. "You stay here. I'll find help."

"No. I have to get out of this cellar." She was gasping now. "Help me." She pointed toward the wooden ladder resting securely on the hooks that led to the main floor.

"*Teta*, I don't think you should be climbing the ladder."

"Help me up. Do as I say, please." Katka yanked on the rope to unroll the rug above and climbed the ladder to release the floorboard. Then she turned back for Lily, who promptly vomited on the cellar floor. "Oh, no..."

Katka guided Lily toward the ladder and told her to put both hands on it. It was not a long way to go, perhaps six feet, but it felt like a mountain. She wrapped her own body around Lily's, and they spooned their way up to the first floor. Katka pretended not to notice the small spot of blood on the floor as she led her aunt to the upstairs bedroom she shared with her uncle. She whimpered with every step. Finally, in the bed, Lily lay down and started to cry.

"Go to the butcher's shop, down at the east edge of town," Lily said. "Tell Mr. Sherek I need his wife. Tell her to hurry. Then come back here quick as you can."

Katka ran as fast as her legs could take her. She had never been to the butcher shop. Anton always prepared his meats himself. As she ran toward town, she encountered a man standing next to his horse, who was watering at the stream. "Sir," she said in English, "you know Mrs. Sherek?"

"Baby coming?"

Katka nodded.

The man took her to the Sherek residence. Mrs. Adeline Sherek, a woman in her late forties, spoke to Katka briefly, then grabbed a bag.

"Has she lost much blood?" she asked.

"I don't know."

"We'll take the buggy. I'll tell my husband to locate Anton. Hunting in the woods, I suppose?"

"Said he'd be in the back forty today."

Mrs. Sherek disappeared for a second to find her husband, then the two women rode quickly to the boardinghouse. They found Lily right where Katka had left her, except she was no longer moaning. She was lying in a pool of blood. Her eyes were closed, and she was not moving.

CHAPTER 16

L ATER, KATKA TOLD LILY THE BABY HAD BEEN born dead, but that was a lie.

While the doctor worked on Lily, Adeline Sherek, the midwife, quickly handed the silent, blood-soaked child to Katka, who washed it and swaddled it in white linen. Katka was certain she saw the chest of the tiny infant rise and fall while in her arms. She saw the baby's miniature mouth pucker up, as if ready cry out. Then she watched the tiny blue lips go slack. Dead.

Sedated with ether, Lily slept until the next day. When she awoke early in the morning, the doctor was gone. Mrs. Sherek was gone. Katka was serving breakfast at the big table. She left, momentarily, to deliver tea to Lily.

Anton was at Lily's bedside. "Hey," he said softly to his wife. "You had everyone worried. But not me. I told 'em all, my Lily—she a feisty one." He told her what Dr. Payne had said. "Up and about in a couple of days. Almost bled to death, you did, but he said womenfolk recover from these things real good. Back to normal by the end of the week. That's what you'll be, I tell you."

"Anton?"

"Yes, my precious flower?"

"Where is our baby?"

Katka quietly slipped out of the room and returned to the big table to continue serving the men.

They all heard Lily's scream. It was a monstrous, guttural wail, more intimate than a whisper, more powerful than a dynamite blast. Katka dropped the plate of bacon she was distributing. It broke, and she clumsily picked it up, stuffing shards of porcelain and strips of pork fat into her apron pockets. All the miners put their utensils down. They waited until the screaming broke.

"Let us bow our heads and pray to the Virgin to take care of that baby," Old Joe said. "Just this once, let that baby girl into heaven, even without the baptism."

"What kind of God don't let a baby into heaven?" Milo asked quietly. He was seated opposite Old Joe. "That little thing ain't done no wrongs in the world. No wrongs! A God that cruel ain't worth praying to."

"Milo," Old Joe said, his face reddening with anger. "I suggest you take that back."

"I won't. It ain't never wrong to speak the truth."

"No blasphemy at this table. No blasphemy! Now take it back."

Milo stood up. He left the table, walked into the tavern, put on his work boots, and left for the mine.

Katka cleared the dishes while the men prayed to the Virgin.

CHAPTER 17

L ILY WAS NOT RECOVERED BY THE END OF THE week, but she pretended to be. There were chores to do, and Lily was convinced that working would be better for her than lying in bed. As she put on her shawl to gather the wood one morning, Katka stopped her.

"Why don't you write a bit? We have a deadline coming up. I cannot do it myself, and we can't miss an edition or we'll lose our readership. You write, and I'll get the wood. It will get your mind off things."

"I suppose I could take my pen and paper upstairs to the bedroom."

"Why don't you write about the need for a baby doctor up here?" Katka asked tenderly.

Dr. Payne was a good man. He knew how to set a broken leg, prepare ointment for a burn, stop a chopped-off finger from bleeding. But when it came to obstetrics, he was powerless. After Anton sent for him, the night the baby died, the doctor told Katka, "With woman problems, I'm mostly an observer. You were right to call Mrs. Sherek. Even a woman from the locations would be better than me." When his own wife, Agnes, was pregnant, he sent her to Duluth to pass her time. When she delivered, Dr. Payne was partridge hunting.

"I will try," Lily said.

Each day for the next two weeks, she worked upstairs, writing in longhand. She read the articles she composed to Katka, who offered suggestions and eventually typed them up in the cellar. Katka wrote too, first in Slovenian, then with Lily's help, she would translate each article into English. It was difficult, but she loved it. With Lily partially bedridden, Katka began to conduct interviews and write about things of her own choosing.

"What do you say, *Teta*," she asked one day, "if I write about that lady doctor Mrs. Sherek told me about?"

"Write whatever you like," Lily said. "You don't have to ask me for permission for everything you do. This is America."

Katka took the streetcar to Virginia, where she interviewed Dr. Andrea Hall. Dr. Hall was legendary on the Range. She had graduated from medical school in Minneapolis, but no one would hire a woman doctor there, so she traveled to find work in the boomtowns on the Range. She had very few patients in the beginning, mostly women and children. However, when the typhoid epidemic erupted, the hospitals overflowed. Dr. Hall opened up her own house and took in as many patients as she could. Unlike the hospitals, she quarantined her house, allowing no visitors. She worked with a few nurses and saved every last one of her patients. After that, Dr. Hall had a steady clientele. People repaid her in whatever ways they could.

Katka's article about Dr. Hall was published in the next edition of the *Journal*. The magazine's readership doubled. Lily was so excited that she vowed to stop taking naps. Although still struck with melancholy, she returned to the cellar and to her usual workload. Women, after all, lost babies every day. She was lucky she had not lost her life.

CHAPTER 18

MILO CONTINUED TO WORK IN THE MINE. HE despised every minute, but he stuck with it, putting money away a little bit at a time to buy his encyclopedias. He stored the money in an envelope that he kept hidden under the mattress in his room at the Kovich house.

Although he sometimes had an ale with the other boarders at the Slovenski Dom, he mostly stayed clear of the tavern. Instead, each night after dinner, he grabbed his guitar, walked across Blood Red Road to Merritt Lake, and sat by the shore, strumming out melodies.

He was propped at his usual spot, under a red pine near the rocky shore, guitar in hand, when he heard a voice. "Onion-head!"

Milo turned around quickly. In the distance he saw Old Joe with his stooped back walking slowly toward him.

"What you doin' out here?" Old Joe asked. He began to cough. It was a deep-throated miner's cough. He took off the handkerchief that was covering the bottom part of his face and blew his nose. Black mucus filled the cloth. He walked to the shore and dipped the handkerchief in the water, then wrung it out and tucked a corner into his pocket. He wiped his hands on his pants.

"Playing," Milo said. "I like to write songs here. To clear my mind."

Old Joe nodded. "Pretty out here." He pulled out some tobacco and stuck a wad in his lower lip.

"You wanting something from me?" Milo asked.

"Come to get you."

"Why for? I ain't done nothing. I just playing my songs to the frogs and the trees."

"Why do you come way out here to play? We got a whole lot a men who appreciate music."

Milo shrugged.

"Think you're too good for us?"

"No, old man." After a long day in the clamor of the mine, with his ears ringing from the drilling and the blasting, there was nothing Milo craved more than the quiet of the lake and forest.

"Come on up to the Slovenski Dom. There a grand mess of people up there."

"I prefer to stay here. I got into some trouble at the last place."

"I heard what happened to you at Torelli's. Brina told me. She said you were brave, and I believe her. I don't believe the talk. Anton don't believe it neither. Said it wouldn't make no sense for you to avoid the bar if it was true."

"If what was true?"

"You're a company spy."

"Spy?"

"They're everywhere you know," Old Joe said.

"I heard," Milo said, remembering his conversation with Johan Koski. "Just because I don't drink at the tavern every night, they think that?"

"The Slovenski Dom ain't just a bar. Even the Finlanders, they come in sometimes. Don't see that in this town, do you?"

"I don't see much in this town."

"I see the magazines you reading. From Gino and Koski. Them is Wob mags. They speak the truth. You know what our people did in '07?"

"I know some."

"Immigrant Slavs broke the strike. Finns were in charge. Never forgave us."

"I don't blame those Finns."

"Those Slavs that came over," Old Joe said quietly, "they were hungry just like you were. Didn't know what they were doing, taking those jobs. All they knew was what their bellies told 'em. Ain't no feeling stronger than hunger. Hunger changes a person."

"No excuse."

Old Joe looked thoughtfully at Milo. "There are no more workers coming in now, Milo. And the steel is more valuable than ever. If we strike now, there will be no scabs to break it. And we got word that the IWW will help us organize."

Milo didn't want any trouble, but he was intrigued. The Industrial Workers of the World, or the IWW, was the only labor union in America that welcomed everyone from all trades. It recruited blacks, Asians, and immigrants of all kinds. It even allowed women. Their goal was for every wage laborer to unite in one big union and support each other regardless of trade. They aimed to give a voice to the poorest workers in the country so they could fight to earn a decent living. Members of the IWW were called Wobblies. If his father ever escaped Siberia and moved to America, Milo was fairly certain he would join the IWW.

"You think you the only miner who hates his job?" Old Joe said quietly. "I used to be able to stand up straight. I sure weren't born this way. The time is ripe to make some changes."

"Is the Slovenski Dom a Wobbly tavern?"

"Who told you that?"

"No one."

"Well, I stand before you now and tell you it ain't. Anton ain't a miner, you know. He's a businessman. Just because there's a Wob or two in his tavern don't mean nothing." Old Joe slapped Milo on the shoulder, not hard. "Or do it? You better come see. Make up yourn own mind. Besides, they'll kick you out of the boarding house if you don't at least make an effort to educate yourself. You ain't missing Leppe, are you?"

"I sure ain't."

"Well, then. Giddyup."

The two men, one young and one old, walked steadily back to the Kovich land. Old Joe pointed to Milo's guitar. "You any good?"

"I am fair."

"Can you read music?"

"More than words."

"We might have a job for you."

***

A few people looked up when Old Joe and Milo entered the tavern through the main entrance, but not many. Someone had distributed three or four songbooks, and the men who could read English even a little bit were crouched around them, peering at the words.

"Read the words to me," Samo, one of the boarders, said.

"Long-haired preachers come out every night, / Try to tell you what's wrong and what's right," another miner read slowly.

"Okay, then," Samo said, and he began to sing, loudly "Long-haired preachers..." Samo was off-key, singing to the tune of "Twinkle, Twinkle, Little Star." The men laughed boisterously.

"Not even close," Toivo Eskola said. "I heard the mens at the lumber camps sing it. It a gospel mill song."

"Okay, then. What the words again?" Samo asked. The miner read them again, and Samo sang them, this time to the tune of "Amazing Grace."

During the laughter and singing, Old Joe managed to secure one of the small red booklets. On the cover it read, *Songs of the Workers, on the Road, in the Jungles, and in the Shops—Songs to Fan the Flames of Discontent*. It was the official collection of strike songs put together by the IWW. Old Joe handed it to Milo, who ignored the cover and paged through the contents.

"Page twenty," another boarder said. "It called 'The Preacher and the Slave.' Says the words are by some man named Joe Hill." The boarder nodded toward Milo's guitar, which was still slung over his shoulder. "Can you read music? The chords are listed."

Milo turned to the song they were singing. He pressed the booklet flat and propped a glass on the crease to keep it open. He started to strum. He played a few chords softly and adjusted his strings.

"Can you read English?" Milo asked Old Joe.

Old Joe nodded.

"Can you sing?"

"Like a pig."

"Grand. Help, I will need, with some words."

Milo began to play more loudly now. The men in the tavern turned toward him as he and Old Joe began to sing. Old Joe sang even more loudly than Samo had, watching Milo's face for cues. The lyrics were written to the tune of "Bye and Bye."

> *Long-haired preachers come out every night,*
> *Try to tell you what's wrong and what's right*

> *But when asked how 'bout something to eat?*
> *They will answer in voices so sweet*

As Old Joe and Milo reached the chorus, more and more workers recognized the melody.

> *You will eat, bye and bye,*
> *In that glorious land above the sky;*
> *Work and pray, live on hay,*
> *You'll get pie in the sky when you die*

"That's how it go!" Toivo Eskola yelled. "That just how it go!"

The miners in the tavern began to join in, singing if they could see the words in the pamphlet, or clapping if they could not see the booklet or read what was inside. When the song was over, they sang it again and again, until everyone in the bar knew the words to all four verses.

After a few rounds of singing, Old Joe left momentarily and came back with his own guitar. "I can play too," he said. "Just have to hear it first."

With two guitars playing, the music gained depth. More men joined Milo and Old Joe in singing the main verses as the words became familiar:

> *When the world and its wealth we have gained*
> *To the grafters we'll sing this refrain*
> *You will eat, bye and bye,*
> *When you've learned how to cook and how to fry;*
> *Chop some wood, 'twill do you good*
> *Then you'll eat, in the sweet, bye and bye*

As the men sang the chorus, a few men trickled out, knowing they had to get up early for the day shift. A few more men trickled in.

As they sang the chorus again, the main entrance of the tavern swung open. A Bulgarian man whom Milo had never seen before entered, carrying a rifle. He was out of breath and had obviously ridden his horse as quickly as he could to get to the Slovenski Dom.

"Shut your pieholes!" he yelled, gesticulating wildly.

Old Joe stopped playing at once. "What is it, Andre?"

Everyone stared at the Bulgarian man. It grew quiet.

"Turner's on his way." He spotted a songbook. "Get rid of those or he'll hang you all." The books disappeared.

As quickly as he had come, the Bulgarian was gone. He hopped on his horse and rode away. Some of the men started for the door. They didn't want to be anywhere near Sheriff Turner. Anton leaned across the bar to Old Joe. "Watch who tries to leave," he said. "Watch carefully."

Toivo Eskola made it to the entrance. He blocked the door with his arms. "Stay your body," he said to Luke Johnson, a welder. "Nobody's leaving."

"I ain't doing the blacklist, Toivo. Got a wife and four young'uns."

"Don't be such a bloody coward," Toivo said. "Nobody said nothing about no blacklist. Set!"

"But Sheriff Turner..."

Toivo pushed Luke, not hard, just enough to make a point. "Be a man. Set down. Drink an ale." Luke reluctantly went back to his table, avoiding all eye contact.

Toivo continued speaking. "All you, just stay calm. We ain't broke no laws. Anton, throw us a few decks of cards. Act natural."

Uneasy, the men who had not escaped went back to their barstools or tables. Milo started strumming again, an old Slovenian song he learned to play when he was six years old. Old Joe was scanning the room, committing every face to memory. Cards were dealt. Drinks downed and refilled. A few minutes later Sheriff Turner entered, accompanied by two deputies with guns drawn. The men stopped talking. They put their cards down. It was quiet. Very quiet.

"Howdy, Anton," the sheriff said, grinning.

"Sheriff Turner," Anton said without warmth. "Care for a spirit?"

Turner was a short, fat man with a precisely trimmed beard and mustache. It was no secret he made a lot of money as sheriff, not in salary, but in bribes and kickbacks. He lived in a nice house, and his wife had servants and a cook. Tonight, standing in the Slovenski Dom surrounded by grimy-faced miners, he looked practically glittery. He was impeccably dressed in a white suit and bow tie. The extra pounds around his waist and the puffiness in his face gave him a false image of softness. In contrast, his badge was pointy and rusty. He touched it for a moment, perhaps consciously, perhaps not. Milo wondered if he ever took it off or if he wore it on his undergarments when he crawled into bed, letting the prickly edges scratch his wife's chest, making her cry out.

"Wouldn't say no to a whiskey."

Anton poured him the drink and watched the sheriff down it in one swallow.

"Maybe you oughta tell your fellows to stand down," Anton said. He gestured to the deputies, who still had their guns drawn.

"Maybe I should, but I ain't gonna. Had some complaints tonight, Anton."

"Nearest house is more'n a mile away, Sheriff. Who complained? My wife?"

"*Serious* complaints. Don't think it warrants no explanation."

"Can't know what you mean," Anton said.

"You don't know what you're getting into." He said it so quietly that only Anton, who was standing behind the bar, and Old Joe and Milo, who were seated closest, could hear him. "Most things in this town, I don't give a blast about. Men want to shoot themselves up, I don't give a damn. But get mixed up in this Wob stuff, Anton, and I can't be responsible for what happens."

"I'm a businessman, Sheriff. Wouldn't do me no good to get mixed with politicals." Anton busied himself by washing the glass the sheriff had just emptied.

Sheriff Turner stared at Anton, his eyes beady and his skin flush with sweat. "I think you're lying."

"No disrespect, sir, but I ain't."

Sheriff Turner turned to one of his deputies. He said something Milo could not hear. Then, in a split second, one of the deputies flipped his gun, reached across the bar, and hit Anton solidly on the forehead with the butt of the gun. "Holy Mother of Christ!" Anton screamed. He put his right hand up to his forehead. Blood seeped through his fingers. With his left hand, he dipped the cloth in the hot water and applied pressure to the wound. "You're an ass, Turner."

Milo and Old Joe stood up, and within seconds, so did every other miner in the bar. Toivo Eskola sprang forward, pushing a chair out of his way. "Anton ain't done nothing to you!" Toivo had almost reached Turner when another man held him back.

Sheriff Turner reached for his Smith & Wesson. He pointed it calmly at Toivo's head. Toivo grew still. "What's your name, son?" His voice was flat, like an amused priest sitting in the confessional booth, waiting to hear a good story.

"Archibald Turner," Toivo said.

The two deputies lunged at Toivo, easily wrestling him to the ground. One held him down while the other delivered a direct blow to Toivo's left cheek, followed by a kick in his groin. Sheriff Turner kept the gun pointed at him.

"That'll do," Sheriff Turner said to the deputies. "Haul him out."

One of the deputies grabbed a rope from his pocket, wrestled Toivo's hands behind his back, and tied him up.

"You, son, despite your mother's excellent choice in names, are under arrest for disturbing the peace of our town."

The men in the bar protested loudly, but were quieted when the sheriff fired his revolver into the tavern ceiling. Debris crashed to the floor.

"Take that man outside." Before the deputy dragged Toivo out, the sheriff whispered something to him. Milo could not hear what he said.

The door that separated the boardinghouse from the tavern swung open, and Lily and Katka burst through. "What is going on?" Lily screamed. She saw the gaping hole in the roof. Then she saw Anton, nursing his head with a bloody rag.

"Go back in the house, Lily," Anton said. Lily froze. "Lily. Katka," Anton said again. "Back in the house. Lock the door. I'll be up soon."

The sheriff took a step toward the women. He put his gun in his holster. He bowed toward them, as if he were about to ask one of them to add his name to her dance card.

"Mrs. Kovich," Sheriff Turner said. "You are looking powerful pretty tonight. New dress? And who is this?" He gestured to Katka. "Aren't you a vision."

Katka was silent. She looked at the deputies. She looked at the guns. She looked at the ceiling. She began to tremble.

"Not a thank you from the lady?"

"Leave it," Lily said. "I loathe the sight of you, Archie Turner. You ain't fit for swine. Never were."

"Go in the house, Lily." Anton said. He gestured toward Katka.

Old Joe stood up. "I'll take them, Anton." He shuffled toward Lily and Katka, grabbed both of them by the upper arms, and walked them into the main room of the house. Katka kept her eyes on the ground, but Lily turned her head and did not take her eyes off the sheriff.

When the door slammed shut, the sheriff turned toward Anton. "Feisty girl you got. At least the young one is quiet. Tell you what I need from you, Anton. I need a list of every man who was in this bar tonight."

"Don't know half the people here," Anton said.

A single shot was fired from outside, and the men heard Toivo scream. Several miners ran through the tavern door and rushed to Toivo's side.

"That's what happens when you resist arrest," the sheriff said flatly. "There's one less name you'll have to remember. I need that list by morning. I think Mrs. Kovich should drop it off. I so enjoy her company."

Sheriff Turner and his remaining deputy walked out of the Slovenski Dom. Toivo muttered something before he died, but no one understood what he said. His last words were drowned out by the sound of the deputies howling as they mounted their horses and headed for Vince Torelli's brothel and boardinghouse. Seeing Lily gave the sheriff a craving for a woman. He hoped Leppe was working.

CHAPTER 19

BEFORE MARRYING LILY, ANTON WORKED AS A lumberjack. When the timber companies laid off workers, he would pick up shifts at the mine, but he hated it. He was a man of the forest and loved to be surrounded by pines and white oaks and all the creatures that lived beside or inside the trees. He had labored hard in the lumber camps and endured the cold, the lousy beds, the long hours, and the bad food. Then he met and married Lily, the daughter of a wealthy couple who despised him as much as Lily adored him. He wished he could say he'd earned his good fortune, not married into it, but that's not how it was. He had a wife he loved, and he worked for no man. His land belonged to him, and he was making a good income leasing a small portion of it to a logging company. He went out into the woods every day. There was something peaceful about riding his horse, Bruno, through the leaf-covered paths with the sun streaming through the canopy of branches. Sometimes as he rode through the noisy forest, he would be surprised by a voice. "Mine," the voice would say proudly. "All mine." The voice was his own.

Anton was also known throughout the area as a superior marksman. He was precise and rarely wasted a bullet. On off days, he shot rabbits, grouse, and squirrels, which he would bring home for Lily to make into stews for the boarders. On good days, he shot moose, elk, partridge, and deer. His boardinghouse was the envy of all because the men always had meat to eat, even when there was no pig to butcher. He and Lily smoked the venison and other meats in the shack in the backyard. What they couldn't eat, they sold to Sherek's Butchery and Meat Market.

In late September, Lily and Katka began to incorporate more controversial articles into their journal. Lily had wanted to write about Toivo's death and the injustices experienced at the Slovenski Dom, but they knew they couldn't risk it. Anton had deemed the place unsafe for meetings, at least for now. So the women continued to focus on women. In the fourth installment, Lily simply wrote, "Women in Finland and New Zealand have the same voting rights as men. Why don't we?" She had heard the news from Helen, who had heard about it from Avi Nurmi, who had just received a letter from her cousin back in Finland. Letters from the old country that did not report a death were a cause for celebration. Immigrants passed them around to all who could read. Avi Nurmi's cousin had actually voted in the last election.

"Perhaps our mayor and city council would push for running water in the mining locations if they knew that the women who washed the clothes and prepared the food had the power to vote them out of office if they ignored women," Katka said.

"Maybe," Lily replied. "But then there's always the issue of the husbands. Many husbands would not let their women vote."

"Nonsense. They'd tell their wives who to vote for and consider themselves as getting two votes instead of one."

In October, after reading some old copies of *The New York Times* that a traveling salesman had given her, Katka wrote about a woman named Margaret Sanger, who was teaching about ways to prevent pregnancies. This pamphlet created quite a stir. Copies of the article were floating around town, having been translated into Finnish, Latvian, Italian, and Serbian. The editor of the local paper, *The Company Chronicle,* wrote an editorial about Lily and Katka's pamphlet.

"Oh my stars!" Lily said to Katka one morning after breakfast. They were seated at the table in the cellar. She had a copy of *The Chronicle* in her hand and began to read out loud. "Not only is *The Iron Range Ladies Journal* not a legitimate journalistic publication, it is not journalism at all. The publisher of the pamphlet obviously has no regard for the basic tenets of the newspaper trade. There were no interviews, no direct quotations from legitimate sources. The cowardly author has refused to identify himself, thereby relinquishing responsibilities for its content. The most recent article about Mrs. Margaret Sanger's Clinic for Women failed to report the dangerous medical side effects associated with taking a tonic to prevent childbirth, not to mention the fact that the practice is abhorrent. No God-fearing man should allow his wife to read such drivel."

Lily was just about to cheer when she was jolted out of her chair by a shrill sound, forceful enough to be readily audible even in the relative obscurity of the cellar. It was the most horrific sound in the world. "Oh God," she said. "The accident whistle!" Lily shoved the article in her pocket, and the two women scrambled up the ladder.

When the whistle blew, all Iron Rangers within hearing distance froze, holding their breath for only as long as it took to recognize the deafening sound. Soon the church bells began to toll; their solemn chime carried fear and despair to the far reaches of town, past the mine locations to those who could not hear the whistle. The women ran to the mine, dragging small children behind them. The schoolteacher tried to keep the children inside, attempting to block the exit with her body, but she could not. The older children got through first, followed by the little ones. Finally, the teacher too walked slowly toward the mine. When she arrived, Katka and Lily were already there.

The townsfolk watched as the body of a Latvian miner was carried out and laid gingerly on the hard red ground. Next, the limp body of an Italian worker was brought up. Both were dead. Two other men, panting, muddy, and sopping wet, followed closely behind.

A murmur, like a ground vibration, flowed from the front of the crowd to the back. The names of the victims floated on the vibration. As the names were recognized, women sighed, unconsciously, with relief. "Not mine," they thought. "My husband, my brother, my cousin, my papa—he is safe."

The Latvian was unmarried, alone, with no family here to mourn his passing. The Italian had a brother who worked at the Sparta mine a few miles away.

The foreman appeared and glanced at the dead bodies. He addressed the two men who had surfaced alive. "Dead?" he asked.

"I told you that ceiling weren't safe!" one of the two survivors shouted. His entire body was covered with slick mud. A woman handed him a handkerchief, and he wiped his face.

The foreman tried to calm him down. "Nobody is more sorry about this than me," he said. "Horrible accident." And he did look sorry, Katka thought.

The other miners were slowly coming out of the mine. Some had come up in the cage; others had crawled up the tunnels via ladders.

"Accident, it weren't," the Finn said calmly. "Bloody murder, it is. I tell you and I tell you, the ceiling is leaking water. I tell you yesterday, I tell you this morning." He watched as the crowd gathered, holding a collective breath of anger and despair. The survivor began to scream. "I say, 'not safe, not safe, not safe!' Do he care? He don't give a damn!"

The men and women in the crowd encouraged him. "You tell him, Elmo!" somebody yelled.

"Now two good men are dead. And Sam and me, barely alive, we are. I told you there'd be a mud run, but you don't listen. There's blood on your hands."

The foreman's face went ashen. The men began to advance toward him. As they stepped forward, the miners began to chant, "Murder, murder, murder!"

Some of the miners were clutching their pickaxes. Others bent down, grabbed some rocks, and continued walking toward the foreman. "Murder, murder..."

"Oh, God," the schoolteacher said to Lily and Katka. "A lynching. We have to get the children out of here."

Katka made a move to help, but Lily clutched her arm.

"Let them watch," Lily said. "Let them see how brave their papas are."

"There's nothing brave about a mob! Are you mad?" The teacher tried to corral the children. She yelled for them to follow her back to the schoolhouse, but her voice was drowned out by the chanting. Many of the children had found their mothers among the crowd, and the mothers and children took up the chant. "Murder, murder, murder!"

Someone threw a rock at the foreman. It hit him hard on the forehead, and he lurched back but did not fall. "I didn't do nothing!" he yelled. "I was just following orders!"

"Murderer!"

Another rock landed squarely on his jaw and blood seeped slowly out of his mouth.

"We should stop this," Katka said. "That man didn't do anything."

"Exactly," Lily said. "He didn't do *anything*. Don't you fathom it, Katka? They care more about the dollar than the lives of those two men. It has to change."

A small child threw a rock and missed. Within seconds, rocks were being hurled from all directions. The miners were throwing rocks. The women. The children. The foreman fell to his knees just as rifle shots rang out.

Katka and Lily backed up. They saw eight men approaching on horseback. The man in front fired his rifle into the air. The rest galloped quickly to the foreman's side. One of the managers dismounted and hoisted the wounded foreman onto the horse. The rest of the managers spread out, pointing their rifles at the crowd. Following closely behind was Sheriff Turner.

When Sheriff Turner arrived, Mr. Augustine Stone walked out of the company office. He was one of three owners of the Oliver Mining Company. The miners rarely saw him in the flesh, but they saw his signature on their paltry paychecks every month. Some of the men in the back of the crowd began to boo Stone.

"Hush!" Mr. Stone said. "Who started this?" The foreman pointed at Elmo.

The men started screaming at him. They swore in thirty languages.

"Sheriff," Stone said. "Arrest this man for inciting a riot." He pointed to Elmo.

"Yes, sir," Sheriff Turner said. He pulled out his handcuffs.

"He ain't the murderer!" a miner yelled.

"And as for the rest of you, I suggest you get back to work. Accidents happen. It's unfortunate. Perhaps in the future you will exercise the safety precautions we have spelled out clearly for all of you. Safety first, that's our motto. Now go. You are not getting paid for standing out here."

"Murder, murder!" The crowd was more vocal now.

Stone looked up at the men on horseback and exchanged some words with the manager who was closest to him. The man took aim and fired into the chanting miners. A man fell to the ground screaming. He had been shot in the chest.

Avi Nurmi wailed and ran to her husband's side. "Oh, God! Oh, God!"

The crowd grew silent as Avi's cries rose. Her children were there now. Lily and Katka could clearly hear her sons speaking to their father in Finnish. "*Eivat die, Isa! Eivat die, Isa…*"

"Anyone else?" Stone asked.

Women gathered around Avi Nurmi. "Shh, now. The doctor will come, the doctor will come."

"He's dying," she said in Finnish. "Don't die, Hans." The Finnish women began to sing the Finnish prayer for the dead.

The men put down their rocks and took off their hats. Some of the men sang too, as if the calming rhythm of their voices could somehow make the bullet that had torn through Hans Nurmi's chest disappear.

In the midst of the song, the doctor arrived with the undertaker in a wagon. The doctor was directed to Hans Nurmi, whose blood had formed a small lake around his body. The doctor took his pulse, ripped away his clothing to reveal the wound, and shook his head.

"I'll do my best, ma'am," he said, then to some men standing nearby, "Load 'em all up."

Hans Nurmi was placed in the wagon with the two dead bodies. His wife, Avi, crawled in next to him. Her boys would have to run behind. The undertaker took the reins, while the doctor sat with Hans.

As the wagon pulled away, Mr. Stone picked up the megaphone. "Nothing to be done. Back to work."

The wind kicked up some red dust. It was October, and the breeze was cold.

"Back to work, I said. If you want a job tomorrow, you go back to work now."

A few miners picked up their shovels. Slowly, others followed suit. One by one, they headed for the cage. They descended from the despair of the day into the darkness of the mine.

They did as they always did after the whistle blew. They went back to work. Except, of course, for the two dead miners, who were hauled off to the coroner, and Elmo, who went to jail, and Hans Nurmi, who went to the doctor's office where he was treated unsuccessfully for a gunshot wound.

The Oliver Mining Company would pay for the funerals of the Latvian and the Italian man. Elmo was let go. The Italian's brother would receive a small settlement check. But Avi Nurmi and her sons were on their own. The company log recorded Hans's death as "Suicide on company grounds."

CHAPTER 20

F ROM THE IRON RANGE LADIES JOURNAL:

The men went back to work because that is what they always do. They went back to work because they worried about losing their jobs. They went back to work because they know the extreme importance of being able to support their wives and children, whether here or in their homeland. When they went back underground, after three men had died, the killing stopped. But for how long? Will the whistle blow again tomorrow? Will it blow again next week? To keep up with the war demand, the Oliver is willing to sacrifice safety for profit. What would happen if our men were to say, "We are not willing to sacrifice our safety for your profit?" I ask you, dear reader, what would happen then?

Once again, the editor of *The Chronicle* mentioned *The Iron Range Ladies Journal* in his editorial, stating, "The pamphlet is un-American. Its articles openly incite the wives of miners to support their husbands who refuse to do their jobs as required by their contract." The negative press from what many called

"The Company Man's Chronicle" fueled the need for more copies of *The Journal*. In November, they printed more than one hundred copies, and all of them sold.

The people of the Range enjoyed an Indian summer until they didn't. Winter arrived with a fury during the second week of November. Temperatures dropped into the teens, and Lake Superior froze. Because the ore boats couldn't get out until more icebreakers arrived at the port town of Duluth, production slowed at the mines. Men were furloughed. A few of the boarders left to work in the forests with the lumber companies. Those who remained hunted or worked odd jobs in town to make their rent until the mines took them back. Life became easier for the men and more difficult for the women.

With each week that passed, the temperature plummeted. The sky dropped white flakes as big as a newborn's hand until all the earth was covered in white. Some days Katka stood outside surrounded by the abyss of white and felt as if she were trapped in an eggshell. But never for longer than it took to complete her chores, for the wind hit hard, like a slap against her once-soft skin. Anton had told her that the northern air chilled a man to the bone. Although Katka had never heard that expression, she now knew what it felt like. The frigid blasts grabbed hold of her bones and sank their sharp teeth into the hardest, sturdiest parts. Many days she thought the wind would break her into tiny shards. Then she would rush inside, shake the snow off her wet clothes, and huddle by the woodstove, wondering if she would ever feel the tender warmth of the sun again.

Katka's chores intensified with the cold. She and Lily gathered more wood from the pile Anton had neatly stacked to keep the fires blazing. They had to let the wet wash freeze-dry outside so the clothing would not drip onto the floor indoors and create a skating rink. Then they would wring out the frozen fabric with their raw red hands and hang it again near the stove. When Anton emptied his traps, the women carefully sewed fur into hats and made liners for their coats and boots. They spent hours knitting warm mittens and socks for the boarders. They traipsed through several feet of snow to haul water from the pump. They milked the cows, gathered the eggs, and prepared the meals. Often exhausted, they had less time to work on the paper.

On occasion, Katka's thoughts drifted back to her homeland or to her trip to America. But compared to the reality of her chapped hands and constantly cold feet, her past seemed ephemeral. It was as if it had belonged to a different person. Her memories were fading, and if she hadn't brought the photograph of her parents from so long ago, she was certain she would have forgotten the shapes of their faces. She did, however, still retain a clear memory of Paul Schmidt. She stopped asking her uncle for news of Paul. When she was with him on the boat, she had been too excited to think. She just lived. And she was happy. And then he disappeared. If he was still in this country, surely he would have contacted her by now. If he was in this country and hadn't contacted her, well, that was a reality she didn't care to face. So she pictured him back in Slovenia in a field of wild lavender surrounded by the Julian Alps.

In December, she experienced the first of many blizzards. The storm dumped so much snow on the log house it was impossible to see out of the windows. Although there were twelve-foot drifts to shovel and flakes were still coming down, the miners could not risk being late to work.

"Lily. Kat," Anton said. "You will have to help me shovel."

Katka pulled on her galoshes and grabbed her coat and scarf, but Lily did not move.

"Lily," Anton said. "Get going, my precious flower. The dishes can wait."

"No. They can't."

Anticipating an argument, Katka put on her mittens, grabbed a shovel, and walked outside to begin clearing a path. A few minutes later, Anton emerged. He rested his shovel against a drift, looked up at the snowflakes, and smiled.

"What, Uncle?"

He ran to Katka and hugged her. "She's pregnant, Kat! Dr. Payne said she'd never have another child, but he was wrong, he was! I always knew that guy was a quack."

Katka's life became more difficult after Lily announced her pregnancy. She awakened every day at 4 a.m. and, covered with a thick wool shawl, hauled in the wood that Anton had chopped the day before. She started the cook stove and the fireplace in the dining room. Carrying a lantern in one hand and a basket in the other, she walked out to the barn and milked one of the four cows. She gathered the eggs needed for breakfast, boiled them, and laid them out to cool. She sliced the day-old bread for toast and began to fry the bacon. Finally, she placed the premade pasties in the oven so they would be piping hot when she packed them in the men's lunch boxes.

Lily awakened at 5 a.m., strolled into the kitchen, sat down, and started peeling eggs.

"Coffee for you, *Teta*," Kat said, setting a cup in front of her aunt.

"Thank you. Tomorrow I will let you sleep in. Tomorrow, Kat, I will haul the wood, make the breakfast, do the morning chores. It isn't fair to put all this on you."

"Isn't that why you sent for me?" Katka said, teasing. "Indentured servitude?"

Lily smiled. "I cannot tell you how glad I am that you came here. Truly. But I hate watching you work."

"Anton would have us both strung up if he saw you lifting a finger this time."

"I suppose." She drank from her coffee.

They had the same conversation every day since Lily announced her pregnancy. Last August's miscarriage had left Lily weak and depressed. The news of a second pregnancy within months of the first made Anton jubilant but protective. His wife was to do embroidery, cooking, and nothing more. She would rest until the day his son was born. The hidden cellar with the red light and the typewriter was definitely out of the question. Katka still worked down there, but more times than not she found herself nodding off and dreaming about Paul. She had the will to block him out of her mind during the day, but she was powerless in her slumber.

Although Katka's first winter on the Iron Range was brutal, there were always things to do. Helen Cerkvenik had introduced Katka to so many people. She received invitations to social gatherings almost every weekend. She attended bonfire parties on Merritt Lake, where she and the other residents roasted venison over the dying embers. Also, Lily gave Katka a pair of blades to attach to her boots, and Helen taught Katka how to skate.

One day she and Helen were on the lake, holding hands. Helen gracefully skated backwards, while Katka clumsily glided forward. When Helen let go of her hands, Katka couldn't stop. She barreled right into Milo, who sat unaware on the side of the clearing, attaching the blades to his shoes.

Soon after, Avi Nurmi's cousin Maiah asked Katka to accompany her to Laskiainen, the Finnish sliding festival. She was thrilled and wrote about it in the journal. Laskiainen was one of many traditions carried over from the old country. In addition to crowning a young Finnish girl "Miss Laskiainen," and demonstrating sewing and cooking techniques, there was also a great deal of sport. Katka and Maiah got dizzy as two young Finns hurled them about in the "whip sled." They also tried the toboggans. The men iced narrow luge tracks on a steep hill leading to the lake. Men, women, and children of all ages competed to see whose toboggan would travel the fastest and farthest. According to Finnish tradition, the farther the toboggan would fly across a frozen lake, the higher the flax would grow in the summer. As she sat on the toboggan at the top of the icy slope, with Maiah sitting behind and holding her waist, Katka felt happy. When a villager gave them a push and they went careening down the ice track, she felt invincible.

Afterward, they ate fish-eye stew and *lefsa*. Katka was beginning to love this land where people embraced the outdoors no matter what froze, burned, or fell from the sky.

Later that month there was another cave-in at the St. James. Katka helped lay out two dead miners on the dining room table and dress them for their funerals. They had been boarders in the house. She wrote letters to their families back home, then printed their obituaries in the journal. Replacement boarders arrived within a week.

One Saturday in early March, Katka was in the kitchen doing the morning dishes. Anton and Lily were seated at the kitchen table. Anton was scrubbing his boots, and Lily was reading aloud from *The Company Chronicle*, the Oliver Mining Company newspaper: "The war in Europe will increase the importance of the work we do. The workers who labor in our mines are true patriots," Lily read.

"If the workers are the patriots, why aren't they getting a raise? What does that company think these men are? Fucking slaves?"

"Watch your tongue, Anton!" Lily pointed at her belly. "Little ears."

"We immigrants do the work, and they get the money. No wonder the men talk strike when the winter breaks. The men have been asking for a raise for a year now, I tell you. With this war, there's no more workers coming in, but more demand for ore. They make men work twice as hard for the same pay. How could they not expect revolt?"

"They expect very little from immigrants," Katka ventured cautiously. "I haven't been here long, but it seems to me that in this country, the more languages a man speaks, the less respect he gets. In Slovenia, we were taught that a man who speaks many tongues is a wise man indeed."

"You were taught well, Kat," Anton said.

"And she speaks four languages," Lily said. "Slovenian, Croatian, Russian, and now English!"

From the hallway, someone cleared his throat. All three Koviches turned their heads to the doorway. Milo Blatnik was standing in the entrance, slouching slightly so his head would not touch the archway. Lily had indicated that Milo had a secret spot in his heart for Katka, but Katka didn't see it. They had played cards a few times in the summer. But he worked so much, picking up extra shifts every week. Said he was saving for something, but she didn't know what. His attentions were given too sporadically for her to take much notice. They were friends, but not close. So it was odd to see Milo in the kitchen, an area that was unofficially off limits to boarders.

"Excuse me, Anton. *Teta* Lily." He looked uncomfortable.

"Come in, Milo! Did you wish to discuss the state of the world with us?" Anton asked good-naturedly. "Katka seems to think the folks in this country have low expectations of us foreigners. What do you think of that theory?"

"She is, I think, right," Milo said.

"Go on," Lily said, intrigued.

"We foreign-borns have low expectations of ourselves in this country. If we wish to see our conditions change, we must be brave and make sacrifices for the good of all. What can one ant do? Carry more than fifty times his weight, until his back, it breaks. But many ants? They work together, create peaceful colonies thousands of miles long. The jobs they have, they are different. But everyone benefits from organization. Not just one ant."

"Are you a full-fledged Wob, now, Milo? Are you part of that?" Lily asked.

"The working class and the employing class have nothing in common," Milo said, as if reciting a poem. "There can be no peace so long as hunger and want are found among millions of working people and the few who make up the employing class have all the good things in life."

"Where did you hear that?" Lily asked.

"Read it. In the constitution of the Industrial Workers of the World." Milo responded. He smiled. "They sent me a card."

"So you are a Wobbly. I heard that those IWW men are atheists. Are you an atheist?"

"For the record," he said quietly, "not all anarchists are atheists."

"So you still pray like a good Catholic?"

"Matter of fact, I prayed last night, for at least thirty seconds."

"What did you pray for?" Anton asked.

Milo gestured toward Katka. "I prayed that your niece over there would say yes to my next question."

Anton and Lily laughed loudly, eagerly anticipating an amusing scene. Katka put the plate she was washing back in the sink. She wiped her hands on the dishtowel and looked at Milo expectantly.

"Miss Katka, I would like to teach you to shoot. Could you spare a few hours? I am a good teacher, and it is a *resplendent*, warm day."

"Shoot?" Anton yelled, laughing. "That's what you call a date? You were right, Milo. Foreign-borns do have low expectations!"

"Anton took me to the Socialist Opera House in Virginia on our first date," Lily said fondly. "*Carmen* was playing. It was the most wonderful night of my life."

"My precious flower says that every night," Anton teased. "Unlike you, Milo, I am a woman-pleaser. Before I got married, the ladies, they would line up just to get a glimpse of me and my burly lumberjack good looks."

"How much did you have to pay them?" Lily asked.

"They paid me. Don't you remember? As I recall, your first glimpse of me cost your *ata* an acre of land."

"I would love to go," Katka said, interrupting. "That is, if it is all right with you, Uncle."

"Do what tickles your fancy, Kat. You want to waste your first date with this onionhead, shooting the heads off small critters, that's your problem."

"Very well," Milo said. "How about in an hour?"

CHAPTER 21

THEY WALKED THROUGH THE BACKYARD TO A well-trodden path emerging from the forest. The pine trees were as tall and well-adorned as ever, but the giant oaks, the birches, and the maple trees were naked. The spring sun still lacked the strength to warm Katka's face, but it was certainly bright enough to shine through the leafless canopy and reflect light off the melting snow that lay at their feet like a carpet of white fox fur.

"Love this time of year," Milo said to Katka in Slovenian. Speaking and hearing his native tongue intensified his feelings of freedom. He walked blissfully along, breathing deeply, happy to trade the stale air of the underground mine for the fresh air of Anton's land. His rifle was slung over his right shoulder. "The time just before spring comes. It's like a song. Or a poem."

Katka looked around. "A sad poem, maybe. Look at the branches, so brittle. They look lonely, like they are waiting for a coat."

"Yes," Milo said. "But they know the coat is coming. They stored the memory of it, right in their trunks. They are filled with hope and visions. Visions of how beautiful that coat will be."

"I prefer summer. When the branches are covered with a hundred shades of green and flowers are bursting. When their fragrance is so strong you can practically taste it. That's the poem, Milo. When the waiting is over."

He stopped. "Look at this oak tree here. Must be two hundred years old. Its branches, like a grandma's gnarled fingers, reach out toward the light in the sky. In the absence of snow, leaves, or color, we look more closely. We see not only the tree, but also ourselves more clearly. In a naked tree, we see the hues of our own emotions. We see what is missing in our world, and we must look within to fill it."

Katka thought about that. She touched the tree. "Look there," she said. "Her arm was blown off in a storm."

"Yes. We wouldn't notice that in the summer. We wouldn't be able to see what she overcame; how strong she is. When the poets write about her like this, she will not be mistaken for another oak. And the poet will find himself worthy of her."

"Will you write about this oak? Are you a poet, Milo?"

"My mother was a poet. Always trying to make melodies out of letters." He shook his head and smiled. "Between me and you, it didn't usually work. It's easier if you add a violin, a cello, an accordion, or a guitar. People pay more attention to words when there's music."

They walked three miles into the woods before they stopped again in a flat area about five hundred yards long on the edge of a hill. It had been cleared. Several logs were stacked against the hill. This man-made barrier was approximately ten feet tall.

"Here we are," Milo said. "Anton's range. Rumor says his father-in-law built it and Lily learned to shoot when she was just a girl."

"*Teta* Lily?"

"Of course. She's Biwabik's Annie Oakley."

"Who's Annie Oakley?"

"A woman who can shoot better than most men."

"*Teta*?"

"Ask her if you don't believe me. You know Anton comes here most days. He practices. See that paper with the bull's-eye? You'll be hard pressed to find a hole in that paper that is not dead center. He's a hell of a shot, your uncle. He took us men out here, when we had the layoffs. Let us practice all we wanted, hunt his land. I got two deer and sold them at the meat market for cash. If I hadn't shot those, I might not have been able to pay my rent that month. 'Course, Anton knew that, I suppose."

"Does he treat you boarders good?" Katka asked.

"Best boardinghouse in town. And there are some bad ones. One joint kicked out the whole lot one day after rent was due. But none could pay, see, because the mine didn't pay them. They were punishing them because they heard a rumor they were trying to organize."

"Were they?"

"Of course. Foreman said, 'If you Bohunks, Finlanders, and dirty Wops don't like your pay, we'll keep it for ourselves.'"

"They can't do that," Katka said. "Not if you worked for it."

"What were we supposed to do? File a complaint? Not only that, Foreman said if we wanted our jobs back, we'd have to pay him five dollars cash. And people did it too. One guy—Lucky was his name—he didn't have no money, but he had a wife, real pretty. He let the foreman alone with his wife instead of paying the five dollars."

"How could he? You don't speak true."

"They had five kids, Kat. If he hadn't paid somehow, he would have been labeled a union agitator, put on the blacklist. How would they have fed those kids? Lucky said it was her idea."

"It wasn't."

"Happens more than you think, Kat. The things they make us do. I don't expect you to believe."

They stayed quiet for a bit. Then Milo said, "It's time to shoot, I think." Milo took the rifle off the sling.

"It's heavy," Katka said. "And very beautiful."

"A beauty, it is. This is how you load the chamber." Katka watched as Milo loaded first one, then another bullet. "Now you try."

Katka was surprised how quickly and smoothly the ammunition slipped in. After loading the remaining twelve bullets, she handed the gun back to Milo.

"See that tin can, propped up on the hay bale? That's our target." He raised the gun to his shoulder and pulled the trigger. He hit the can dead center, and it went flying. He ran and set the tin can back on the hay bale. "Now your turn. Before you take aim, you need to crank the lever out and down all the way, like I did. You'll do this each time you shoot. Spread your legs a little to get balanced and pull the butt in tight against your shoulder. Tighter. Yep. Just like that."

"Where do I put my cheek?"

"Against the wood. Put three fingers in the lever, with the other one sticking out until you're ready to go. When you squeeze the trigger, do it gently. If you jerk, you'll jerk the whole gun. You want each shot to feel like surprise."

"How do I line it up?"

"Use your dominant eye to look through the rear sight here. Some folk close the other one."

Katka closed her left eye and looked at the can. She pulled the gun into her shoulder and took a deep breath. Then, softly, as if she were tickling the cheek of a newborn, she pulled the trigger.

The noise was deafening, and she couldn't believe she had created it. There was very little kickback. Her shoulder did not hurt. The bullet did not hit the can, but Katka smiled. Shooting a rifle was not only easier than she had imagined, it was exhilarating.

"Can I try again?" she asked.

"Shoot as many times as you please. But before each shot, remember to rack the lever."

She lined up the gun as she had before, but this time she shot the rifle in rapid succession, each time racking the gun faster. The smell of smoke was intoxicating, and she felt a rush of adrenaline sweep through her body. Bullet casings flew in the air, landed in her hair, and bounced off her shoulders. She felt bigger and more powerful than she had ever felt before. Finally, on her eleventh shot, she hit the can and held the rifle above her head, whooping jubilantly.

"Lily's got competition," Milo said, laughing. "That's a deadly weapon you are celebrating with. There's one more bullet. Aim for Anton's bull's-eye paper. It's farther away, but worth a gamble."

She aimed the gun, lining up her target with precision. She pulled the trigger and watched as the bullet missed the bull's-eye by two inches, leaving a small hole in the paper.

"Blazes!" Milo said. "A natural, you are!"

Impulsively, she grabbed Milo's hand with her free hand, bent over, and kissed him on his knuckles. "Thank you, Milo. For the best day ever." Katka had one elemental emotion running through her body—joy. She loved shooting more than she had loved anything she could think of. She couldn't wait to shoot again.

He squeezed her hand in reply. "Next time we'll try to shoot some rabbits. Moving objects are more fun."

"Deal."

When they got back to the house, Lily called out for Katka to help her with chores in the barn. She thanked Milo, who went inside, and then headed for the chicken coop. First, she looked under the nest of Sasa, the fattest hen of all. She found a small pouch of coins, nearly five dollars. It was their proceeds from the latest edition of the *Iron Range Ladies Journal*.

"Well," Lily said, appearing in the doorway. "Did you fall in love with Milo over a dead squirrel?"

"I don't understand you," Katka said mischievously. "My English is not so good."

"Do you think you'll marry him?"

"Have you been drinking, *Teta*?"

"Did you feel tingly? Did you feel as if you couldn't breathe? Did you feel as if you wanted to stay just in that moment and be no place else in the whole world for the rest of time?"

Katka laughed. *Teta* Lily had too much life for one body. "Is that how you felt when you met Uncle Anton?"

"That is how I still feel about Anton. But we're talking about you here, not me. Did you feel it?"

She did actually. Katka felt all those things. But she knew it was not Milo who made her feel that way. It was love for something else—the 1873 Winchester. There was only one other time when she felt as if all of the physical parts of her body had turned to nerve endings, flushing her skin red. That was nearly a year ago, just before Paul left her. But she didn't say that to Lily. "Not exactly," she said.

"No details for me? None at all? You are an absolute bore. You don't entertain me in the least." Lily grabbed her skirt, pulled it up, and flashed Katka, exposing her knickers. Then she stuck out her tongue and went back to the house.

Katka jiggled the black bag of coins. Tomorrow she would buy some bullets.

CHAPTER 22

KATKA PRACTICED SHOOTING ALMOST EVERY DAY in March. Sometimes she went with Milo. He was a patient, strict teacher, and Katka obeyed his every instruction. Other days she went with Anton, who rarely spoke and never missed a shot. She memorized his stance, his posture, his timing. Then she tried to imitate it. It didn't work. When she asked him what she was doing wrong, his answer was simple. "Don't think. Just do. When your body feels right—everywhere—don't hesitate. If you do, you'll miss."

By the beginning of April, Katka was hitting the paper with nearly every shot. Anton encouraged her to leave the shooting range and move on.

On her first day hunting with Milo, Katka shot her first deer. She and Milo were walking back to the house, rifles slung over their shoulders, when Milo suddenly stopped. He put his finger to his lips. Then he pointed to the east. Katka heard the distinct sound of branches breaking. She looked over and saw it. A huge buck, staring right at her. He was grand. His eyes were the color of coffee beans. His coat was clean, and his ears stood majestically alert.

Milo raised his eyebrows toward Katka as if to say, "Take him."

Katka quickly racked the lever, then lifted the Winchester to her shoulder. She looked through the sight, pinpointed the deer's heart, and fired. At the sound of the shot, the deer jumped, but could not run. Katka's shot had been dead-on, and within seconds the legs crumpled under its body and the animal fell to the earth.

"Clean shot!" Milo yelled. "Don't even have to track him. That was magnificent, Katka!" Katka stood motionless for a moment. She watched as Milo ran toward the deer. "Eight points!"

Katka walked over to Milo and the deer. The animal had fallen over his wound, and his body was covering up most of the blood. He heaved up, then down. Katka watched. It was an odd sight. The deer was enormous; she was so small.

"How do you feel?"

Katka paused for a moment, trying to find just the right words. "Like a man."

She grabbed one of the antlers, tried to pull it. It wouldn't budge. Milo smiled. "We need to gut it first. Let it bleed out a bit. Do you want me to do it?"

"Yes," Katka said, and then changed her mind. "I think I should learn to do it, since it's my deer."

Milo showed Katka how to cut open the abdomen of the deer, how to reach her hands inside the warm body and pull out the organs. "Do you want to eat the heart?" Milo asked.

"Absolutely not." She grimaced slightly, holding the bloody entrails with both hands. "What do I do with this?"

"Throw it in the woods." She did. Then she walked down the path a ways to a spring, where she washed her hands. She wiped them on her skirt as she walked back to Milo.

Milo repositioned the deer so it would bleed faster. They sat on a log, listening to the chickadees. They did not talk, but both were smiling. Finally, they got up, grabbed the antlers, and pulled. Together they dragged the beast back to the house. With some help, they hung him in the smokehouse for Lily and all the men to admire.

After dinner Katka went back to the smokehouse to look at her deer. She pulled up a stool, sat on it, and watched it. To-morrow Anton would cut it up into steaks, chops, roasts. They would make sausages and jerky. They would sell the hide to the voyageurs when they came through town at the end of the week. She wanted to view the animal one last time while it still resembled itself in its most glorified form.

"Katka?" It was Milo's voice. He had followed her to the smokehouse. "Couldn't get enough, huh?"

"Hi, Milo."

"All the men. They keep saying, 'Milo, you got quite a woman. Got herself a heckuva a deer, with a clean kill.'"

"I had a good teacher."

Blood dripped from the dead deer's body. Not regularly, not constantly, but occasionally. Katka liked the smell.

"When they were saying that," Milo continued, "I started to wonder if it was true."

"You think it wasn't a clean kill?"

"No, it was a fine shot. You know that." Milo looked around for another chair. Not finding one, he finally settled on a metal bucket. He leaned forward. "I started to wonder if you was my lady, like the men think you are." He took her hand. "Can I kiss you, Katka? Not on the cheek, but on the lips?"

She said he could, so he did.

It was a brief kiss at first. Their faces separated quickly, as if they needed a moment to get used to the newness of it. Then they kissed again. This time it was a long kiss. Milo put his hands on her face, probed his tongue into her mouth. When they were done kissing, they both looked at the ground. The deer was still dripping blood, slowly.

"Did you feel anything?" Milo asked.

"What do you mean?" Katka asked.

"Poetry." She heard dripping, three drops in a row, then silence.

"It was nice," Katka said. "It was the longest kiss I ever had."

"But no poetry?"

She shook her head apologetically. "No, Milo." His tongue had felt like gravel in her mouth. "You?"

"No poems for me."

"I suppose that means something," Katka said.

He took her hand, brought it to his lips, and kissed it. Then he carefully placed it back in her lap. "Guess it means you ain't my lady, Katka." He stood up slowly to leave. "No hard feelings?"

Katka smiled with relief. "You will still teach me to shoot?"

He gestured toward the deer. "You can teach me." Milo tipped his hat. He left her alone in the smokehouse, gazing at her majestic buck, which had finally stopped dripping blood.

CHAPTER 23

K ATKA AND LILY WERE KNITTING BY THE FIRE. Milo and Old Joe strummed on their guitars, getting ready to play. Milo was humming bits and pieces of a Slovenian lullaby, as if trying to remember it.

"You sing so solemnly, Milo," Lily said. "I feel homesick for a place I've never been."

"You may not know Slovenia, Lily, but Slovenia knows you," Old Joe said, tuning his strings. He turned to Milo. "*Cebula glava*. Onionhead. You forget the tune?"

"Found it now," Milo said, playing quietly. When he came to the melody, which Lily remembered from her childhood, she sang along. When the words eluded her, she hummed.

Old Joe turned back to Lily. "You are the same as my wife when she was young. Stubborn as a goat but beautiful, with a voice like the Virgin."

"Didn't know the Virgin could sing," Milo said, smiling and strumming softly.

"'Course she can, you onionhead," Old Joe retorted. "She the Mother of Christ, for Christ sake. You, on the other hand, sing like a dying cow."

"Let's play, old man," Milo said.

Two other boarders, Samo and Dusca, were sprawled on the wood floor. Samo had a harmonica. Everyone sang. Soft songs, thick with remembrance. Flying carpet melodies, swooping listeners from the ground and transporting them beyond the mine pits, past the port towns, across the sea, and to the mountains or farmlands of childhood. Melodies like a gentle hand, rubbing out the knots in the backs of Samo, Dusca, Old Joe, and Milo, who worked for little pay, and also in the muscles of the two women who worked for no pay. They sang.

> *Tonight, oh tonight*
> *When the moon shines over the earth*
> *I will leave*
> *But don't cry my love*
> *I will be back in seven short years.*

All present in the room, except for Lily who had been born here, were back in the old country. The music transported them to a land where they had worked, not in the darkness of the underground mines, not in the extreme hot and cold of northern Minnesota, but under the soft breath of the golden Slovenian sun.

Old Joe thought of his wife with whom he had not communicated in over a decade. In Slovenia, they had lived a simple life. As the sixth child, Joe had nothing to inherit, and the couple farmed a small plot they leased. They were never prosperous. For years they tried without success to conceive a child. When their son finally entered the world, his face like an overripe tomato, everything changed. "You must make enough money for us to buy land," his wife told Joe. So, at the age of fifty-two, when his son was five, Joe set off for America to earn his fortune and secure a future for his son. After seven long years, he earned passage for his wife and child. He sent it to them. They never came. Still, he sang,

I will leave
But don't cry my love
I will be back in seven short years.

One of the miners in the tavern tried to open the door that separated the tavern from the house, attracted to the music.

"Stop him," Lily said to Milo. "Doesn't he realize this is my home? And tell Anton to get in here."

Milo stopped playing, grabbed his guitar, and walked through the door to the tavern, talking to the customer who had almost broken Lily's sacred separation of tavern and boardinghouse.

Anton appeared moments later. "You. Old Joe. In the tavern. Bring your guitar. You're stealing my customers, I tell you. I'll get my button box, and we'll play some happy music. Music that will make men want to drink, not cry like girls."

"Lock the door," Lily said. "I don't want any more of your blasted hoodlums sneaking into my house."

"Anything for you, my precious flower." Anton bowed low. He locked the door from the inside, grabbed his accordion, and went out the back door and around the house. He made a grand entrance through the main door of the tavern, playing a bawdy drinking song. The men applauded loudly and began to sing boisterously. Milo and Old Joe's guitars could barely be heard over Anton's accordion.

The women continued to sew until the men finished their second song, easily audible through the locked oak door.

"*Katka,*" Lily said conspiratorially, "I have it on good authority that something big is about to happen."

"The door's locked. Old Joe is keeping watch. No one is coming in, Lily."

"That's not what I'm talking about."

"What do you mean?"

"The whistle blew three times in the last three weeks. The workers are stretched so thin. With this war coming, the company started making the blasters work alone. There's no one to spot for them. Seven men injured and two dead at the St. James underground."

"Yes. I know. Maki and Hill. I brought food to the Maki household. He had three children. I thought he only had two."

"The Hill man had five children, all orphans now. His wife died last year of consumption. The company will give them a settlement, of course, but it won't feed those kids for a year. And Luka Vlasic, you know him. He comes into the tavern. They say he might lose his leg."

"What's going to happen?"

"If they strike, we must be prepared to help."

"We?"

"Especially you. I will have the baby to look after. You must manage the paper, which means you'll have less time for hunting. You must write about the strike. Give the miners' side. The company paper will only print lies, and the other papers, they will be no better. If there is a strike, the mining company will buy them off. I will do what I can to get information, but it will be harder when the baby comes."

"What makes you so certain something's going to happen now?"

"A little bird told me." Lily looked around the sitting room. No one was there except for them. The men were still singing loudly in the tavern. "Follow me."

When they got to the hallway near the back door, Lily gestured toward the rug that covered the secret entrance to the cellar.

"You can't go down there, Lily."

"I know. But you can. I need you to go down there. There's a letter I left there from my cousin that I would very much like to read again. I might have dropped it near the bookshelf."

"A letter? I will look."

Katka bent over and carefully pulled the rug aside, revealing the latch, while Lily kept watch. She opened the entrance and gingerly navigated the rope ladder, carrying an unlit lantern. She had done this enough times to be comfortable in the dark. When she landed with her feet on the ground, she put the lantern on the table and pulled the string, which replaced the rug up top.

In complete darkness, Lily lit the lamp on the table, and the tiny cellar became eerily illuminated as red shadows danced across the bookshelf, the guns, the crates of alcohol. The three chairs were still around the table, and the typewriter, paper, and dictionary laid just as she had left them earlier that morning.

But something was different. It was a smell. The smell of salt and wind. She heard slow breathing coming from behind her. She turned quickly and gasped.

There, seated against the back wall of the cellar, was a man. His clothes were dark. His hat was pulled down low, shielding most of his face. He wore a handkerchief around his neck. His right hand was bandaged, and his left hand was resting gingerly on it, as if to protect it.

"Hello?" she whispered tentatively.

The man snorted in his sleep.

"Wake up," Katka whispered. She gently shook the man, who woke with a start, his good hand reaching for the gun hidden in his coat.

"Don't shoot!" Katka said.

The man quickly put the pistol back in its holster. He stood up and pulled his handkerchief down. He looked at Katka's feet and his gaze slowly drifted up to her face, where it remained fixated. He took off his hat, and curly black locks tumbled down, partially covering his left eye.

He smiled broadly. "Kat-girl. My little tiger in the night," he said. "My cousin treating you all right? She talks a lot, but other than that, is she good to you?"

It was Paul.

CHAPTER 24

WHEN SHE WAS TOO LITTLE TO WORK BUT OLD enough to wander unattended, Katka used to stuff her pockets with bread and cheese and skip to the Creek of Lingering Love. She would stand on the north side of the rickety wooden bridge and throw a stick into the swirling water. Then she'd run across to the south side, watch it emerge from underneath her feet, and marvel as it disappeared into the current. The old ones warned against going there. "Bad luck," they said. And they told her the story of a man who loved a woman so much her name was like sweet caramel in his mouth. When she rejected him, he drowned himself in the creek.

During the time of high taxes and great strife, Joseph Rantich was known as a lucky man. Although he lived with his widowed mother and had no brothers to help him, the land they owned prospered every year. The animals in their barn were fruitful and healthy, which was considered a testament to his gentle nature. Joseph ran his mother's farm with the help of a cook and several hired men. The mothers on the mountainside who sent their sons to work for Joseph spoke highly of him. He was a kindly boss who fed the workers well and paid them on time. In addition, he was young in years and not unpleasant to look at.

One morning a woman who had faced great difficulties in her life walked to the Rantich farm to ask for food and money. She was accompanied by her two teenage daughters, Mara and

Melitza. It was clear they had walked a great distance, for when Mother Rantich offered them each a chair, they accepted without the customary three denials. Mother Rantich walked outside to the fire and put a pot of water on the grate to make peppermint tea. When she returned, the two mothers spoke in hushed tones.

As they were speaking, Joseph Rantich returned to the house to retrieve a scythe he had forgotten to take to the field. He noticed the water on the coals and poked his head into the house. It was then that he saw the two daughters. Mara, the younger of the two, was a quiet, orchid beauty. Her cheeks were high and fair, and her nose was delicate. Her lips were full as a red plum. Melitza, on the other hand, was not known for her appearance. Her eyes were huge, and her naturally brown hair was bleached from the sun in dramatic yellow steaks. Her nose was plastered with a hundred freckles. Her lips were slightly chapped, and she wore no gloves.

As the much revered Joseph Rantich peered inside at the girls, Mara immediately looked down, embarrassed to be asking for food and money. Melitza met his gaze, and he fell in love with her immediately.

"Mother," Joseph said. "What business is at hand?"

"It is not of your affair," his mother softly retorted, and the other mother sighed in relief.

"Is there something you wish of us?" Joseph asked.

"They have come to share a cup of tea with an old and lonely woman," Mother Rantich said.

"Ah. But you are not so old, and you are not lonely, Ma."

Melitza stood and faced Joseph. Her voice was strong, unapologetic. "We have come to ask for charity. We are beggars, no better, no worse. For if you give my mother what we ask, we will have nothing to give in return."

"Melitza, hold your tongue," Mara whispered quickly.

"Melitza." Joseph Rantich said it slowly. "That is your name?

"It is."

"Melitza," Joseph repeated, slowly digesting each letter. "Melitza. It sounds like sweet caramel in my mouth. Melitza."

"I didn't choose it, but I am quite used to it."

"Marry me, Melitza. Marry me, and I will give your mother all she asks and more. We will build a house on the hill where the cows like to graze. We will have sons to help me work the land. I love you."

The old ones attested that Joseph was afflicted with the truest and rarest form of love, the kind that blossoms faster than any flower, that runs more wildly than any river. He believed in his love, and because he knew it was pure, it did not occur to him that she would not feel the same about him.

"I do not love you," she said. Her mother and her sister gasped.

"Of course you do not love him," Mother Rantich said. "You do not know him." She smiled with pride at her son. "But you will."

"But he loves me. And he knows me not."

"Perhaps you will learn to love me," Joseph Rantich said.

"But *you* love *me* now."

"Yes."

"That must be quite a feeling. To love someone you do not know."

"More than exquisite. I cannot explain."

"I would like to feel that emotion. If I marry you, I never will."

So Melitza, the plain-looking daughter of the poor woman, refused to marry the most eligible bachelor in the countryside. Her sister, Mara, could not convince her to reconsider. Melitza's impoverished mother shook her head silently. Mother

Rantich said nothing more. Instead, she served her guests tea, and while her son rambled unintelligibly and desperately about his enduring love, Mother Rantich packed a basket of food for the family. Under the bread and fruit, she slipped two gold coins. From the open doorway, she watched the women, laden with gifts, walk home. Two days later Joseph Rantich drowned himself in Kupka Creek, which was never again called anything but the Creek of Lingering Love.

***

"Katka?" Paul said, raising his voice slightly to bring her back from her daydream. He had dragged himself to his feet and was standing in front of her. "Are you all right? You were staring at nothing for a moment. It was as if you disappeared. Are you not happy to see me?"

"I love you, Paul."

"Come again?"

"I love you."

He crooked his head to the side and smiled a big, dimply smile. "You do?"

"Your very name feels like sweet caramel in my mouth."

He smiled. "Sweet caramel, huh? Like the folk tale?" They were face to face, not touching. With his good hand, he grabbed hers. "For one year and five days, I have been thinking about your mouth, with or without caramel. I will never stop loving you, Kat. Not ever."

He brought her hand to his lips. He looked into her moistening eyes, kissed her palm, and then slowly, he kissed each of her fingers. She felt his desire, his love, his longing. How could someone feel so weak and so strong at the same time? She felt as if the bones in her body were turning to light, and all she was left with was skin: skin with crystallized nerve endings, like a perfect snowflake.

She kissed him then. A long, slow kiss that was as perfect as a poem written by the sun.

***

Paul and Katka stayed underground for hours. They stayed long after the last miner left the tavern, long after Anton had washed the last glass. They sat on the ground, Paul's good arm around her shoulder, with a tattered wool blanket covering them both. She opened a bottle of wine from one of the crates, and they drank it straight from the bottle.

"Where did they take you when you were detained?" she asked. "Were you imprisoned for a very long time? How did you get out? Why didn't you write to me?"

He put his fingers on her lips to stop her speech. It didn't work. So he kissed her quiet.

"Shh...my love."

But she had to know. "Who was the woman with the blue eyes? The one who told me you'd been detained? Was she your sweetheart? And if you're Lily's cousin, why are you hiding down here instead of being waited on in the living room?" He kissed her earlobes. She felt faint with pleasure.

"Kat, I will tell you everything I can tell you. But not here, not now."

"I know a perfect place."

"In the fields?"

She looked at him oddly. "The fields? No. Stay here. I'll be back in a little while. Rest while I'm gone." Paul closed his eyes. She kissed his lids softly, then Katka noiselessly climbed the ladder and exited the cellar. She put the rug that covered the underground space back into place. She looked around the cottage: It was dark and quiet; everyone had gone to bed. Then she walked out the back door past the barn with sleeping horses and then she followed the path past the smokehouse. The moon was out. An enormous, kindly orb that hung like an illuminated portrait of her grandmother's face. She took the tiny trail that led to the sauna, which a friend of Anton's had erected near the cold creek that ran to Merritt Lake. It was impossible to see the sauna from the main house, but anyone who was travelling would be able to see the smoke. But surely no one would be traveling at this hour. It was nearly 2 a.m.

The sauna was the cornerstone of Finnish life. On the Iron Range, Finnish immigrants who homesteaded usually constructed the sauna before they built their houses. They lived in the large, warm structures while they built their homes. It was more than simply a place to bathe. Women gave birth in the saunas. Children with croup or other respiratory problems were nursed to health in the saunas. Men signed land agreements in the sauna, and families used the steam bath as a spiritual place that enabled them to regenerate their *sisu*, or life force. Finnish saunas were ideally built next to a lake or river so bathers could run from the heat of the steam bath into the coolness of the water. In the winter, the bathers endured the steam for as long as possible and then ran outside and rolled naked in the snow. Experiencing two heat extremes in a matter of moments had healing powers. Because the sauna had no windows, it was also an exceedingly private place.

Anton was one of many non-Finns on the Iron Range who had embraced the tradition of the sauna. A Finnish friend had built it for Anton, according to his specifications. Iron Range saunas varied in size, but most included two rooms: the steam room and the changing room. Anton's sauna easily could accommodate eight men, four on each bench. He wanted to efficiently enable his boarders to bathe on a regular basis, for he had been convinced that cleanliness, above all else, prevented the spread of disease. He had first discovered this on his passage overseas, and later this theory had been confirmed as he spent many nights on filthy beds in the lumber camps.

As Katka approached the sauna, she noted with satisfaction that the previous bathers had indeed left the woodpile well stocked. She filled her apron with wood and opened the door. The changing room was stocked with clean towels and a shelf full of buckets. One of the buckets was filled with lye. Another held willow branches with leaves intact. Three buckets were stacked one on top of the other, and the long-handled spoon, or "dipper," hung from a nail next to the shelf.

The changing room was separated from the steam room by a windowless door. The walls of the steam room were also constructed of cedar, which smelled like heaven, if heaven were made of wood. Katka knelt down and started the fire in the small metal furnace. On top of the metal fire casing, flat rocks were arranged like buns in a bakery. They would heat up quickly and eventually provide the steam when water was drizzled on them. A two-tiered bench faced the stove. After lighting the fire, Katka took the two empty buckets down to the creek and filled them with ice-cold spring water. Then she dropped them off in the changing room and went back to find Paul.

"Where were you?" Paul asked quietly when Katka finally got back to the cellar. "I was starting to worry."

"Let's go for walk." She beckoned him to follow her up the ladder.

"Not safe," he said. "I promised Anton I'd stay here until the miners left for their shift in the morning. We're not sure where I will be staying. Where the best place is. Things will be less complicated when we figure out what my role will be in the uprising and if they plan to identify me or have me work underground."

"Your role? The uprising? Paul, I don't understand anything you're saying. But you'll be back before he arises. Anton won't wake until the cock crows."

"I could use some air."

"This way," Katka said.

He followed her up the ladder using his good hand. When they both were in the pantry, she took the necessary precautions to keep the cellar hidden, and they noiselessly walked into the backyard under the light of the moon. Neither spoke. Paul watched Katka for signs and followed her. They ran, first from the back door to the barn, where they stood and caught their breath. Then they ran from the barn to the smokehouse, and finally from the smokehouse to the safety of the woods. There was less moonlight in the forest, but their eyes adjusted rapidly. They walked down the trail in single file, Katka in the lead.

"Know where we're going, Pocahontas?" Paul asked.

"'Course I do." She beckoned up ahead, where smoke could be seen drifting near the treetops. Who was Pocahontas?

He stopped, and hearing no footsteps behind her, she stopped too and turned around.

"You ain't leading me into no trap here, are you, Kat?" His voice was playful, and at first she thought he was joking. Then she realized he was truly rattled.

"No traps, Paul." She walked back to him and took his hand. "Why would you ask that?"

"I've seen some things. Things that make you question everything, even the things that seem most good and pure. The things that you know, in your gut, have to be true or you couldn't go on living. I saw the smoke. Is anyone out here?"

"Just us."

"Where are you taking me?"

"To soap and water. You have a grand-looking face, but you smell something awful."

He smiled. "The sauna! I forgot it was back here. You are a clever one."

When they arrived at the sauna, Katka waited outside. Paul went inside the changing room, removed his clothing, grabbed the soap and one of the buckets of water, and entered the steam room. It was hot, but not sweltering yet. He splashed some of the cool water on his face, then knelt down by the fire. He added some wood, lining up the sticks like he was building a log house. A moment later, she entered.

Katka was carrying a bucket in one hand and the dipping stick in another. She dipped the spoon into the bucket and poured the water over the rocks. Steam immediately came up from the rocks, and the temperature increased.

Paul, who was sitting on the cedar bench, looked at her through the steam. "You're naked," he said. "Oh sweet Mary and Joseph. You are soo—"

"In a sauna," Katka said. "People are naked in saunas. That's how they work." She was nervous, and a little self-conscious, but she tried not to show it in her voice. She put the stick back in the bucket, stared at the rocks and the evaporating water that singed on contact. She could feel his eyes on her backbone. He came up behind her, wrapped his right arm around her waist. She took a breath in and held it, feeling his fingers on her soft belly. "Oh my," she said.

He filled the dipper with water, and leaning against her tender, flush body, he poured more water on the rocks. As the steamy heat emanated toward the ceiling, Paul kissed her in the small, tender spot between her neck and shoulder blade. She quivered. She could feel the sweat on his chest. She could feel her heart beating, beating in her own small chest. The feel of his erect nipples on her back was burning away the door she had built around her own heart. Everything, it seemed, was melting.

He filled the dipper again and raised it, not to the rocks, but above her head. He tipped it. Slowly the frigid water streamed through Katka's hair like rain, down her neck, in between her supple young breasts, to her navel. What was left of the water meandered down her inner thigh. She closed her eyes. Paul's fingers followed the stream of the water. Each part of her skin that he touched became electrified. Fingertips on hair. Fingertips on her clavicle. On her breasts, her soft belly. Fingertips, gently skimming the heart-shaped curls of hair on the space between her legs.

She moaned. Paul whispered into her ear, "Wait, my darling. One moment." He poured another dollop of water on the rocks. It was all steam.

He led her to the bench. "Lay on your belly," he said softly. "Please." She did. She heard the door to the changing room open, close, and open again.

He stood over her, in the steam, and massaged her shoulders and back with his wet hands. Then she felt the gentle whack of the leaves on her buttocks. "Oh!" she yelped quietly.

"Willow," Paul said. "Supposed to bring your emotions to the surface."

He rhythmically tapped her entire body with the soft leaves until she was all nerve endings. Then he gently rolled her over and lifted her into his arms, and she slid down until she was on his lap, straddling him. They were both glistening with sweat. She could feel the hardness of his manhood against her hot body.

"If you haven't noticed," Paul said, "my emotions are already at the surface."

"I'm noticing now," she said.

"I can wait, my love. I can."

She moaned again and kissed his words away.

"I will wait," he said. "We should wait. But I need to put a few inches between us."

Paul moved to the lower bench. Katka stood up and grabbed the bucket of water, the soap, and a washcloth. Then she sat directly behind him on the top bench. She spread her legs so her thighs and calves flanked him as they sat. She bent her head down, rubbed her hands down his sweaty chest, and kissed his neck until he whimpered. She dipped the cloth in the bucket, lathered, and began, very gently, to wash his hair. She dug her fingernails deep into his scalp, scratching away dirt and small stones. Then she lathered his shoulders, his back. She rinsed him with the cool water.

"Feeling better?" she asked.

"This is where dreams are made," he said. His eyes were closed. "If I die right now, I will have enough happiness to take me through many lifetimes."

"Lean on me," she said, and he did.

While he rested, she examined his body, noticing everything. The scars. The bruises. The bandage on his hand, coming undone. She washed his face with a delicateness that contrasted greatly with how she had washed his hair. She used the tips of her fingers only. She encircled his scar, washed his scruffy whiskers, and rinsed. Then, with the washcloth, she cleansed his chest, his arms, and his left hand and its fingers. When she got to the right hand, she carefully unwound the bandage. She dipped his hand into the bucket and stared at the wound.

"How'd you get it?" she said.

"Knife."

"Who did it?"

"Can't say as I got his name."

"Where were you?"

"Free speech rally in Ohio."

"You were as close as Ohio and you couldn't write?"

"I escaped from Ellis Island. I wasn't sure I'd been followed. I was trying to protect you. The union sent me to Cleveland right after they arranged my escape. But a day didn't go by when I didn't think of you, Kat-girl."

"And you could not write? Not one word?" She loved him, but she did not understand him. How could he have stayed away for so long?

He got up then, moved to the top bench where she was. She snuggled next to him, resting her head in his lap.

"I organize workers, Kat. That's what I do," he said, running his hands through her hair.

"You work for the Industrial Workers of the World? The IWW? You're a 'wobbly,' as Lily calls them?"

"Yes, a wobbly I am. Everybody's organizing. From New York to Cleveland to Leadville. Nobody's organized. That's why it's so dangerous. As Lily must have told you, I'm not exactly an easy man to be with. I start revolutions. There's not much that hasn't been done to get me to stop. They have been trying to find my weakness, my Achilles' heel. Do you know what I am saying?"

She thought she might.

"You are my weakness, Kat. My love for you. My love for your beautiful brain and sensational body." He moved his hands to her breasts again. He cupped them, gently, and encircled her nipples with his fingers. "If they knew about you, they might have... oh, I don't know. It makes my stomach churn to think about it."

She looked at his hand. "Does it hurt?" It was not bleeding and did not look infected.

"Nothing hurts, my little tiger. For the first time in a long time, nothing hurts."

As if to prove it, he lay down on his back and pulled her gently on top of his soapy chest. She could feel his manhood coming to the surface again. And feeling it again made her desire surface stronger than a thousand willow branches could have done.

"You are fearsome beautiful," he said. "You should always be naked."

"Mrs. Sherek told me men will say anything in moments like these."

"What kind of moment is this?"

"The moment before we make the love."

"Hmm..." he said. "Interesting." He kissed her again, slowly, and then turned his head. "For you, Kat-girl, I have waited a year and five days. I think we can wait a little longer. We should wait, no?" He pulled back. "A man is not a man for his power. A man is a man for his restraint."

That was the most ridiculous thing Katka had ever heard. Katka didn't want to wait. Not at all. Here he was, after all this time. She had not the patience for it.

"No," she said. "We are not waiting."

She moved her hand to his penis. It was rock hard, yet somehow soft, like a baby's skin. She began to caress it. To move her hand up and down. And then she touched the tip slowly, as if memorizing its shape. And she moved her body up.

"Are you sure?" he said.

She nodded.

He put his hands on her hips and slowly inserted himself, just a bit, inside of her secret part. She winced a little. But then everything was smooth. Velvety. She moved her body down on his. And up again. And down. They took it slow. So very slow. Until he started to whimper and pant. The steam was everywhere now. Outside of her skin. Inside of her skin. Enveloping her heart.

"Oh, God," he said. "Oh, dear God!"

Afterward, he washed her body tenderly. He thanked her. He loved her. And he cradled her in his arms, the two of them with their exhausted bodies lying on the hard cedar bench. He made a pillow out of a towel, and she rested her head on his chest.

As the fire began to die, Paul began to talk. Paul told her about the barracks in Ellis Island, how he had been jailed there for two months. Finally, he was able to find a guard named Tommy O'Sullivan who worked as a spy for the Wobblies. With Tommy's help, he was able to secure a suit of clothing belonging to an immigration officer. One day he simply got in line behind the other employees and walked out.

"Those months, were they terrible?" Katka asked.

"Been in worse prisons. But do you know what made me the most upset?"

"What?"

"That I'd lost your picture. The one of the two of us together on the boat with the lightning behind us. I loved that photograph. I never told you, but I bought it. I swear, Katka, so many nights in this last year, I would have given anything to have had that picture back. I wanted so much to see your face. I had to rely on my memories."

"Maybe one day you'll see it again," Katka said.

"I don't need to now. I have the real thing."

When they left the sauna, the moon was low in the sky, and the sun was nowhere to be seen. It was that mysterious time when it was neither day nor night, when history seemed beyond memory and the future had yet to be imagined.

They walked back to the main house via the smokehouse and barn. Paul climbed back into the cellar. Katka went into the dining room and fell asleep on the chair. The rooster would crow in less than an hour, and it would be time to gather the eggs and start breakfast.

CHAPTER 25

ABOUT A WEEK LATER, KATKA WAS STUFFING sausages in the smokehouse when she heard the alarm whistle. *Not again,* she thought. She shoved the last of the gelatinous meat and fat mixture into an intestine skin and then dipped her hands into the bowl of water on the upturned wooden crate they used for a table. She wiped her hands on her bloody apron and walked toward the house. She had to alert Lily, who was resting inside.

"Dear God," Lily said, lumbering out of the house as Katka approached. "Nothin' I hate more'n that goddamn whistle."

"Maybe it's a mistake," Katka said. "Once they blew it by mistake."

The Kovich cottage was surrounded by mines. There were mines to the east, toward Aurora. Mines to the north, near the Laurentian Divide. But this whistle was definitely coming from the west, close to the town center of Biwabik, which was surrounded by three mines. The two women started walking toward Biwabik, briskly at first. Then Lily touched Katka's arm and slowed the pace, a simple gesture to remind Katka that Lily's time was almost here.

"I don't think it was a mistake," Lily said when their steps had shortened. "I had a dream last night. I dreamed that I was running through the fields, and the fields, they were beautiful. The grass, it kept changing color, and every color was more beautiful than the last. It was blue, like the sky, and then yellow, but not the color of wheat, more like a yellow you'd see on fabric at Cerkvenik's, and then red, and finally it was purple. Light purple, like a lilac, followed by a deep purple, like the northern lights. And then the field *was* the northern lights, and I was running, trying to jump from beam to beam, so I wouldn't, you know, fall from the sky. And I wasn't scared at all, and it was like I was dancing almost. Or floating. Then all at once, I was scared. Terrified even. I started thinking, 'Don't look down,' but the more I thought about it, the more I wanted to look down. And I tried to keep my eyes up, but I didn't have the strength. I looked down—"

"And what happened?"

"The lights disappeared. I had nothing left to hold me up."

"You fell."

"I woke up. And the baby was kicking my ribs. Hard. It was as if the baby was scared too."

"I heard women can have dreams that are powerful strange when they are pregnant," Katka said. "Pay no mind."

"Yes. But one thing troubles me."

Katka looked at her questioningly.

"I've had this dream before, and I wasn't pregnant."

"When?"

"The night before Milo arrived."

They heard the sound of horses approaching slowly from behind them. They moved to the side of the road and turned to see who was coming. Adeline Sherek, the midwife, was at the reins. She waved broadly with one hand. She was pulling a cart full of men and women, all of them old, pregnant, or lame. The cart slowed to a stop.

"You heard the whistle?" Mrs. Sherek asked gravely.

The women nodded. "Lily, get in the buggy. Kat, sorry puddin' pie. You'll have to walk. I'm only carting around those who cannot run."

"Run?" Katka asked mortified. "Was it a cave-in?"

"Worse."

"What could be—?"

"Walkout."

"Walkout?"

"We got two more stops. Now help your *teta* get up here."

When Mrs. Sherek was gone, Katka ran toward the St. James mine. When she reached the creek, she turned off the main road and into company property. She ran through a field, hiking up her skirts to increase her speed.

When Katka arrived at the mine, overheated and out of breath, more than five hundred people had gathered outside the entrance. Everyone was talking at once, but even so, things seemed eerily quiet. She looked around, trying to decipher what was so different. Then it dawned on her. There were no tractors hauling, no ore carts creaking, no trains moving. There were no blasts, no dull thuds of ax hitting rock. The silence was unsettling. Although it was unseasonably warm, Katka shivered. Something terrible was about to happen.

Katka inched her way into the crowd. The men were at the front, and the women and children were behind them in the perimeter. Katka felt someone squeeze her shoulder. It was Helen Cerkvenik from the mercantile.

"Katka!" she said. "I couldn't get away from the store until just now. I had to lock everything up, and then I came quick as I could. What happened?"

"Just got here myself."

"Milo started it," another voice said. It was Ana Zalar from the Belgrade location. She had a six-year-old boy at her side and a little girl in her arms.

"Milo?" Katka repeated. "Is he...safe?"

Ana pointed toward the front of the crowd. "I tried to get to him, dress the wounds, you know? But they tell me he ain't hurt that bad. What that mean, 'ain't hurt that bad'? Here, everything is badder than people say. But what do I know? The mens, they formed a circle around him, see? To keep him protectioned, they say."

"What did he do, Ana?"

"Story goes, Milo takes one look at his paycheck, he does. And there ain't hardly nothing left, after supplies and whatnot. He curses the whole lot of them. Walks out all in a huff. As he walked out, he starts calling for the others to join him."

"And?" Katka asked impatiently.

"You got eyes," Ana said. "Look at 'em all."

A woman with dark hair joined the conversation. "How do you know this, Mrs. Zalar?"

"My husband. Forgot his lunch for second day in a row. Yesterday he went hungry and was mad as hell. Tells me, 'Ana, if your man forget his lunch, it your job to bring it.' I tell him it his job to remember it, mine to pack it. But he real particular. Not hisself. He talk to me like bringing his lunch is most important thing. 'Lunch is at 11:15 sharp,' Leo, he tells me. You be there at 11 and argue with the man in the front room until they agree to bring it to me. Raise Cain or they won't do nothing but eat it themselves. If the baby cries, no problem.'

"Sure enough. Today. He forgets his lunch again, like it was on purpose. I had the clothes to wash, the wood to chop. But I brung it to him anyway, and I did as he said. I argues with that foreman. Say I'm not going nowhere 'til my man gets his lunch. While we are arguing, another man, he come running in. Say a miner's making trouble. The foreman is annoyed, he is. 'Fire him,' he says. 'Can't,' the man said. 'He already quit. But he's causing a bloody stink.' Foreman says, 'Fine. Take Davenport's men. Take care of it and get back to work.' After that, the foreman made us leave. But I sensed something big. I tell Danko here, 'Let's just wait out here a spell.'

"Sure enough, not ten minutes later the first crew of 'em is coming out the door, singing those Wobbly songs. When Milo and his crew get up to the cage opening, a few mining guards were waiting for him. How many? I don't know. I heard the scuffle. There was yelling and punching. But the miners come out okay. Bloody, but all of 'ems, they walking. They singing something. What it is, 'Solidarity forever...the union make us strong.' The mens, they linked arms and walked out of the mine together. A little banged up, but like I say, walking."

"How did the rest of the men get out?" Katka asked.

"The next group of men exited from the cage, almost twenty-five crammed in like sardines. The Oliver men sent some more guards with guns, but they were outnumbered. A few of the miners got hit with the butts of rifles, but there were too many men to stop. They kept coming. My Leo was one of the first out. Not hurt a bit. They've been filing out ever since."

"Why didn't they shut the cage down?" Katka asked.

"They did. See? You can't hear it now. But a lot of men got out first. The rest of them, they are climbing out on foot. Up the ladders. See the doors? Men still coming out. Milo and his men are waiting for them. Then, I think, he will speak."

"Milo?"

"Like I say, he start it. His ma and *ata*, they were great leaders in our country. Made many sacrifices for the people. Tried to change things. Milo gots it in his blood whether he want it or not."

Behind them, Katka heard the sound of hooves. She looked back and saw Mrs. Sherek. Katka walked toward the cart and extended her hand to help the women get down. Everyone was asking questions, and Katka did her best to answer. Most of their questions were about their own loved ones.

"Did you see my husband?" Mrs. Kivela asked.

"Is my son safe?" old Mrs. Taborski wanted to know.

"My George is fine," Helmi Nelson said. "I would know if he not fine. When he lost that finger, I knew right then. And I was nowhere nears. My feelings is never wrong."

Finally, Katka helped Lily, who was rubbing her belly, out of the cart. "How's the baby?" Katka whispered.

"Excited to witness her first organized uprising," Lily said. She smiled wanly. "I knew this would happen soon, but Paul told me it would be after the baby was born."

"One thing he's good at," Katka said, "is keeping secrets." She hadn't seen Paul since she left him in the cellar. Anton told her he found "other accommodations" for the time being. No one was to let on that he and Lily were cousins. Anton expected word would get out eventually, and when it did, they'd adjust. But for now it was just another of many foggy truths Katka had begun to store under her skin.

"Lily Kovich! Lilianna!" A man's voice was heard, calling from the west side of the crowd.

The women looked left and saw Anton making his way through the swarm of women and children. He wore his riding boots, and his hunting rifle was swung over his shoulder. Katka could not tell if his face was flushed red from heat, anger, or a combination of both. She waved to him and called his name. When he saw them, he gruffly made his way toward them.

Katka could sense his tension. He looked for a moment as if he wanted to strike Lily, but then thought better of it.

"What are you doing here?"

"Mrs. Sherek brought me. I didn't walk."

He looked nervously toward the mass of miners at the mining gate. Then he looked at Lily's belly. "Look, Lily. You can't stay here. I don't know what's going to happen, but I promise you, it won't be safe. You must leave. Go home, I tell you. Katka will take you. If you walk slowly, you will be fine. But you must leave now."

"We're not leaving."

"Yes. You are."

"No."

Anton grabbed Lily's hand and squeezed it so tightly that Lily winced in pain. Then he leaned toward his wife and whispered something in her ear. Lily's face went white. Anton let go of her hand and walked to the front of the crowd to join the men.

Lily covered her left hand with her right hand. She was shaking. She watched as Anton disappeared into the sea of immigrants. "Let's go home, Katka."

Katka did not want to go. She needed to see this. She had been waiting for this moment almost since she had arrived. She had heard Milo speak of this day. She was not going to miss it. And surely Paul would be here.

"*Matchka*? Won't you walk me?"

"Of all the days you could choose to listen to your husband, you have to choose this one?"

Lily said nothing.

"We shouldn't have to miss this," Katka said. "It's not as if you're going to have that baby today. I need to find a notebook and something to write with. Stay right here, and I'll come back when I've got it."

Lily stayed silent. She looked pale and weak. She started to say something, but Katka interrupted. "Don't move from this spot," she said again.

She spotted the editor of *The Daily Chronicle* and boldly went up to him. She asked him for paper and a quill.

He looked at her curiously. "Can you write, missy?"

"Some," Katka said.

"Funny time to be penning a letter home."

"Yes, sir. 'Tis."

"What's your name, doll?"

"Maria," Katka said.

"You look fine as cream gravy, Miss Maria."

"Thank you, sir."

The editor reached into his vest and brought out a quill and some paper. He handed her two sheets. "Say hello to your mama."

With paper and writing instrument in hand, Katka ran back to where she had left her aunt, but Lily was nowhere to be seen. Katka called her name a few times and asked about her whereabouts. Finally, she spotted her. Lily had tried to walk toward home, but had stopped to sit on a boulder at the side of the road. Katka ran toward her. She saw that Lily was crying and wiping her face with her apron.

Katka wrapped her arms around her aunt, who sobbed into her shoulder for a moment, then stood up abruptly, pointing toward the top of the hill. "I have to get home."

"What did Uncle Anton say to you?"

"He said..."

"Yes?"

"If something happened to this baby, he would hold me and only me responsible for murdering his son."

"He didn't say that. He couldn't have," Katka said.

A tear ran down Lily's cheek.

"Nothing will happen, Lily," Katka said. "The uprising. It's got him acting strange."

"He looked so serious. Like he knew something."

"He didn't." Katka glanced back at the crowd. It was getting bigger.

"I need to go home."

"I will go with you."

"No," Lily said. "We only have two reporters. We can't both play hooky." She smiled half-heartedly. "This will be our biggest story yet. You better get it."

"I will, *Teta*, I promise. But first, I will walk you to the bend. The men are still coming up the ladders. I don't think anything will happen until they get them all up."

Lily nodded. "To the bend and not one step farther. I want a full report. Everything."

Katka put a hand on her aunt's back to give her support. When they got to the bend, Katka kissed her aunt on the cheek and raced back to the mine, once again lifting her skirts high above her knees as she ran.

CHAPTER 26

WHEN KATKA GOT BACK TO THE MINE PERSPIRA-
tion dripping down her face, the crowd had backed up,
and a miner had set up three crates. Katka wormed her way
through the crowd until she was almost to the front of the
women's section. Her view was adequate. Milo, who repre-
sented the miners, stood on the middle crate. Paul, represent-
ing the Industrial Workers of the World, stood to his left. To
his right was a man she had never seen before. Then, out of the
corner of her eye, she spotted Anton and slipped back a few
rows.

"Who's the man on the right?" Katka asked a woman standing next to her.

"His name is Andre Kristeva. They call him the Bulgarian."

"Never seen him," Katka said.

"Nor I. Until this very morning, he worked as an engineer
in the mine, they say."

"And they trust him to stand with him?"

"Wob spy, they say he is."

Before she had time to ask more questions, Katka heard
music. Someone had found a guitar for Milo. He started to
play, and the crowd grew quiet. Then he began to sing. It was a
song from *The Little Red Songbook*, a song she had heard the

miners singing in the tavern. The lyrics were set to the tune of the "Battle Hymn of the Republic:"

> *When the union's inspiration, through the work-*
> *ers' blood shall run,*
> *There can be no power greater anywhere be-*
> *neath the sun.*
> *Yet what force on earth is weaker*
> * than the feeble strength of one?*
> *But the union makes us strong.*

Milo's voice was loud and chillingly pure. Even workers who did not speak English—workers who had risked their jobs by following Milo—felt inspired by the courage of his actions and also by this melody, which rested on their tired shoulders like a firm paternal hand. As he sang the repetitive chorus, the voices of workers, their wives, and even their children could be heard clearly in the absence of drilling and blasting.

> *Solidarity forever! Solidarity forever! For the*
> *union makes us strong!*

It was peculiar to see Milo this way. Katka knew him well. Although he never became her beau, he had become her dearest friend, aside from Lily. Milo was steady and predictable. Smart, calculated, his innermost feelings known only to the trees and sometimes to her. But here, standing on that sugar crate, playing that guitar and singing, she saw him as others did. He was a man with his soul ablaze. The flames of discontent and injustice ignited in him a passion that seeped into his voice. He was no longer a philosopher, a man who studied labor pamphlets by candlelight on the cold back porch. His ideas had transformed into action, and he had become a man—a man people would follow.

Milo sang a few more verses. As each chorus grew in strength and volume, mine guards seemed to appear out of nowhere, materializing from the humid air like ominous spirits from beyond, each with a rifle slung against his shoulder. By the end of the song, the Oliver guards had almost surrounded the workers and their families. The crowd kept singing the chorus long after Milo had handed the guitar to the Bulgarian, who handed it to an elderly man in the crowd, who passed it back to its owner. The men linked arms and fanned out their bodies to become more of a presence. The women, children, merchants, and elderly men in the crowd followed suit. The Oliver guards took a step back.

Katka scanned the situation, counting heads. She jotted on her paper: "Oliver guards outnumbered at least ten to one, but every guard was armed." Katka noticed some movement in the crowd around her. Items were being passed from person to person, making their way up to the miners. A woman tapped Katka's shoulder and said something in a language she did not understand. She handed Katka a copper spike. Katka passed it forward.

There were not many weapons. Mostly pipes, crude knives, and arrowheads made by the Ojibwe, found by the new settlers. Not many guns. She counted. One, two, three... Katka looked back and saw Adeline Sherek poised like a drill sergeant on her buggy. She was back from another trip. More elderly and crippled people were being unloaded from the cart.

Katka noticed that all the passengers had blankets draped around their shoulders, even though the weather was steamy. She jotted a few notes on her notepad, then edged toward them to get a closer look. She watched as the passengers, despite their alleged infirmities, assimilated quickly into the crowd. Then she heard a clunk. One of the passengers, an old man with hair the color of a snow rabbit, had dropped something. It was a revolver. The person standing next to him nonchalantly picked it up and passed it forward. She kept counting. Nine, ten, eleven.

"Katka!" Mrs. Sherek yelled when she saw her. "Come up here. We will need some precious items stored in Anton's cellar. Do you know what I'm talking about?"

"I do." The rifles. "But I need to stay here, to cover the story. Lily is at the house."

"Why?"

"Anton sent her back. She will help you."

Adeline called to two boys, Andy the soda pop distributor's twin sons. They climbed up. Then Adeline grabbed the reins, gave the horses a slight prod, and took off toward the Slovenski Dom.

The miners stood behind Milo and Paul, their backs to the mine. They were arranged in makeshift rows, like ill-equipped soldiers. Their denim overalls had no protective armor, and their hats were tattered and grimy. They stood close to one another. The townspeople—business owners, women and children, and land toilers alike—gathered across from them, separated by the red dirt road that led from Biwabik to the mine. To Katka, the situation was unreal. It was as if the workers were on stage and the townspeople were about to either watch a much anticipated play or a hanging. To the east, the nine armed mine guards kept the crowd from entering the main office where the shift supervisor worked.

Katka positioned herself on the west side of the crowd, about fifty yards off, where she was slightly obscured by a giant piece of metal equipment that had been dumped outside the mine, waiting to be scrapped. She had a good view of Milo and Paul, and thought she might even be able to hear from where she was standing. She recorded a few observations in her notebook while she waited for the men to speak. "As the tension rose," she wrote in her notebook, "the temperature followed suit." It was downright hot, especially for the beginning of

June. She dabbed her forehead with the side of her long sleeve and undid the top button on her high-necked blouse.

Her gaze kept drifting back to the small opening next to the cage, where up to five minutes would pass between miners surfacing. She observed Milo, Paul, and the Bulgarian man, Andre Kristeva, watching the small opening too. Paul and Milo both held guns now, but Andre was empty-handed. She saw them whispering to each other. Every once in a while, they would point to someone in the crowd or gesture toward one of the men standing behind them. Furtively, they looked into the distance.

Katka heard hoofbeats from the west and looked behind her. Two men dressed in fine clothes approached the crowd. It grew quiet. Collectively, the gathering turned to stare at the new, and most unwelcome, arrivals. Katka stepped instinctively back toward the safety of the crowd. As she backed up, several people stepped forward.

Katka sensed the eeriness of this covert movement. Rifles, shotguns, pipes, and rocks were being shuffled from the front of the crowd, where Milo, Paul, and Andre stood, to the perimeter of the crowd where the fancy-clad men approached. "Twenty-one, twenty-two, twenty-three," Katka said to herself. Even some of the older boys, standing next to their mothers, had guns now. "Twenty-seven, twenty-eight, twenty-nine." Katka's vantage point was close to that of the men on horseback. From the west, it clearly looked as if the entire crowd was armed. Of course, that was not true, but she knew the men were surprised. Never would these men have imagined that the thirty or forty guns visible from the west were the only guns the miners had. They just kept shifting them around.

"I ain't afraid to shoot you!" a worker on the perimeter yelled. "Not one bit!"

The men on horses stopped. A short man, dressed in a fancy yellow suit, spoke. "Who the hell's in charge here? For your sake, it better not be you."

"Think I ain't good enough to kill the likes of you?" the miner asked. He cocked his rifle and pointed it at the man in yellow.

Milo, Paul, and Andre ran toward the fray. The crowd parted to let them pass. When they reached the miner with the rifle, Paul put his hand on the miner's shoulder. "We honor your courage. But you can put the gun down now."

Milo, Paul, and Andre turned until they were standing right in front of the men on horses.

"Afternoon, Sheriff Turner, Mr. Stone," Andre said, taking off his hat. "Bit warm for June, wouldn't you say, Stone? Your fine yellow suit is getting damp."

"You *turned*. Well, I'll be. You're one of them now, Andre?" said Augustine Stone, part owner of the Oliver Mining Company. "One of my foremen had doubts about you. Said you was immigrant filth and always would be. Told me and told me you was a fucking Wob spy."

"You know what we do to spies, Kristeva. Oh, you know very well," Sheriff Turner said. From atop his horse, he drew his gun. Augustine Stone did the same. The miners on the perimeter immediately showed their weapons.

"There are more of us than there are of you," Andre said. "For your own safety, gentlemen, I suggest you think about what you're doing. Don't make any rash decisions. Don't move too quickly."

"Or what? Your band of criminals will kill us?" Mr. Stone asked.

Milo Blatnik took an awkward step forward. He cleared his throat, then spoke boldly. "I think, sir, you are the criminal, no?"

"Me?" Mr. Stone laughed. "I am no criminal. This is my bloody land. Hell, this is practically my bloody town. I own everything you see. I probably own you!"

"Own me?" Milo asked. "You think?"

Mr. Stone stared back, meeting Milo's gaze. He raised his eyebrows.

"Who owns your boots?"

"You do, sir."

"Who owns your shovel?"

"You do, sir."

"Who owns your house?"

"Don't have no house. But you have my paycheck, and rent is due."

"So we agree," Stone said, looking satisfied. "I own your goddamn, fucking, bloody ass."

"So it appears," Milo said and smiled. "But last I checked, it is not legal to own another person, or even a part of another person, in the United States of America. Is that not true, Paul?"

"I didn't go to a university, like Mr. Stone here," Paul Schmidt said. "But I think that is true, Milo."

"That true!" someone in the crowd yelled. "I learn that in night school!"

Men within hearing distance laughed. The men on horseback pretended not to notice. "Got a point?" Mr. Stone asked.

Milo addressed the crowd again. "In that book of this country, the Constitution, do it say a man can own another man?"

"No!" the crowd screamed back.

"No, it don't," Milo said to Mr. Stone. "So. My point it being, you the criminal here, not us."

Mr. Stone laughed again. Sheriff Turner laughed too, but there was something unnatural about the way their laughter fell out of their mouths. It was almost as if they were coughing instead, and Katka could tell the big men were rattled. Mr. Stone looked at Milo anew, as if he were seeing him for the first time.

"If any of your dirty, son-of-a-bitch traitor-ass men want a job tomorrow, I suggest you tell them to get back to work."

"Or what?" Andre said. "Your men will shoot 'em? Like you did to Hans Nurmi?"

"Go back to work!" Stone yelled.

The miners stepped forward. Stone began to lose control. "Go back to work! Back to work! Go back to work this instant!"

The crowd did not flinch.

"If you stay out here, on my property, you will never work again. Mark me, not here, not at any mine owned by the Oliver Mining Company! Your children will starve! You will have no place to live!"

It was quiet. Not a sound. The silence unnerved Stone.

In her notebook, from her vantage point, Katka wrote, "Quiet as snow."

Then a man yelled, "Mine childrens—already they are starving!"

Mrs. Zalar yelled next. "The house you give is not a house. It is a shack not fit for dog! And you don't give. We pay!"

The voices multiplied. The volume increased. The languages melded until Katka could recognize few words. She continued taking notes. "If the workers and their families were afraid, they did not show it."

"Mr. Stone," Andre said. "You are correct. These workers will never work here again. At least not under the current conditions. Not under you."

"If you think you will organize these lawless foreign-borns, Andre, think again. It's been tried. They are easily broken."

"This is not 1907, Mr. Stone. There's a war on. We both know there are no workers coming in. There will be no scabs swimming off the ships in Duluth. These workers will not be broken. Are you sure you're not thinking of yourself? You are the one who will be broken."

The workers began to chant. "Strike! Strike! Strike!"

A child threw a rock that grazed the top of Turner's forehead. "Jesus fucking mother of Christ!" he yelled. "One of those fresh-off-the-boat immigrant slime tried to kill me!" He aimed his pistol at Andre's head. Andre held his breath.

At least fifteen men holding weapons stepped forward and quickly surrounded the men on horseback.

"I don't want these 'fresh-off-the-boat immigrant slime,' as you call them, to kill you," Andre said quietly. "If you value your life at all, I suggest you drop your weapons and hold your hands in the air."

Stone and Turner said nothing. Then Stone dropped his gun and held first one, then the other hand in the air.

"Both of you," Milo said.

When Turner also raised his hands, the workers chanted again: "Strike! Strike! Strike!"

Paul motioned for the crowd to be silent. Someone set a sugar crate in front of him. He stood on it. Before he spoke, Katka noticed that certain men were being called out from the crowd. They were interpreters. Paul waited until five men came forward. Then he began to speak in English. The speech was not long, but he paused after each sentence, allowing his words to be translated into Croatian, Slovenian, Swedish, Finnish, Italian, and Norwegian.

"This robber baron," he yelled, pointing to Mr. Stone, "whose company earned over two million dollars in profits last year, has treated you like animals, when in fact, you are men. He has let your children go days without food while you waited for that payday that only comes once a month. He has housed you in tin shacks with leaky roofs. He has forced you to work double shifts, with no extra pay, so he can keep up with demand for the ore."

Katka knew this was true. At the boardinghouse, it was not unusual for a miner to miss two, possibly three, meals and then come home to fall into bed, dog-tired. Some miners sought out the extra shifts. But if a miner refused, he was fired on the spot.

If he quit or was fired before payday, he was not compensated for previous days worked.

Paul continued. "Mr. Stone lines his pockets with gold. Mr. Stone lives in a fancy house. Mr. Stone has servants who wait on his wife and daughters. I ask you, who waits on *your* wife? Who waits on *your* daughters? He enjoys every luxury imaginable. Why? Because he works?"

"No!"

"In truth, he does work. But does he work harder than you? Why does he earn fifty times your salary? He profits from your labor. I ask you, do you profit from his?"

"Not me!" someone shouted. "I sure don't."

"He bought the mine. It is fair that he get back his investment. We are not disputing that. But he is filthy rich, while you, you are filthy and poor. It is not greed to ask to be paid fairly for the work you do. It is not greed to ask for two days off per week so your bloody knees can scab over and your back can get a rest. It is not greed to ask him to share more profits with those who do the work that makes him rich."

"Lynch him!" someone yelled.

"Shall we?" Paul yelled. The crowd roared in agreement.

Turner and Stone exchanged terrified glances.

"Let us go," Turner said.

Milo took a step toward the frightened men. "You look afraid. Like girls, I think," Milo said. "No need. We seek no violent activity. No one will harm you. We will not deprive you of your lives. Instead we will take from you the only leverage we have: our bodies. We will not work another day under these circumstances. You should stay. You have work to do. Who's going to earn your profits? Stone, you can be a mucker! Sheriff Turner, you can light the dynamite without a spotter. Stone's wife can pick up after the blind mules!"

"Strike! Strike! Strike!"

Andre gathered a small group of armed men around him and gave what appeared to Katka to be instructions. Then he stood up and yelled to the crowd. "We three will lead. The rest of you workers will follow. We will leave these cowards in peace. We wish no violence, for they are the violent ones, not us. Do not bring your weapons!"

"No weapons?" Doubt reverberated in the mutterings of the crowd.

"Show the courage they lack. Keep your hands in your pockets and shame the company!" This mantra was translated many times. Katka saw people in the crowd nodding, slowly understanding the logic behind it. Katka wrote it down and underlined it. "Keep your hands in your pockets and shame the company."

Andre, Paul, and Milo began to walk slowly. The other laborers, still dirty from working underground, fell in line behind them, loosely organized in rows of three or four. Those who had weapons passed them back to the crowd. As they walked by the Oliver men, one or two men spit at the ground, but all of them kept their hands at their sides.

Katka and the other townspeople lined the street. Because it was hot, some of the men discarded the long-sleeved shirts they were wearing under their overalls and handed them to their wives. The wives took them, along with candles, matches, and other items the men wanted held for safekeeping. The women also held the weapons. "It was a parade like no other," Katka wrote.

The last of the miners passed by. Katka recognized Samo, a boarder. "Where are you going?" she cried in Slovenian, breaking the solemnity of the moment.

"Come and see, Katka," he said.

Boldly, she stepped in line after the last of the workers. Many of the other wives, children, and relatives did the same. The parade of miners marched past the mine, through Biwabik, down Blood Red Road and kept going, up the road toward the Slovenski Dom. Word traveled quickly from the front of the line to the back. No one was going home. This walkout was bigger than the St. James mine. Milo, Paul, and Andre Kristeva, the Bulgarian, were leading the crowd to the Miller mine in Aurora, five miles away.

As they approached the Kovich farmhouse, Katka noticed that Mrs. Sherek's buggy was parked outside, her horses haphazardly tied to a tree. The two boys she had taken with her as gunrunners were playing marbles in the dirt next to the buggy. Bruno, Anton's horse, was standing aimlessly in the yard. Why hadn't Anton put him in the stable? She ran out of line.

"What's happening?" she yelled to the boys.

"Baby coming," one of the boys said.

Katka ran into the house "*Teta* Lily!" she screamed. "*Teta* Lily!"

CHAPTER 27

K ATKA RAN UP THE STAIRS TO THE BEDROOM LILY and Anton shared and thrust open the door. Mrs. Sherek was there. Anton was there. Lily was there. A baby suckled her right breast.

Katka was momentarily speechless. She looked from face to face. Mrs. Sherek was humming peacefully. Anton was grinning stupidly, looking at the baby, and Lily—Lily, of course, was talking: wildly, softly, a mile a minute to the child who had just entered the world.

"Healthy!" Katka uttered with relief.

"As a horse," Mrs. Sherek said.

"And as big as one," Lily said, laughing.

"Oh no, dear." Mrs. Sherek finished washing her hands in the basin. "Believe it or not, that's a little babe, it is. But they all feel like a watermelon."

"Funny, isn't it? No one bothered to mention that to me," Lily said, smiling.

"Of course not. If women told the truth about childbirth, the human race would end."

"Got that right."

"I should have been here with you." Katka peered at her cousin. "I am so sorry."

"No offense, dear, but you wouldn't have been much use. That baby's a determined one. Came barreling out like a bullet. Didn't have no ether, neither. Whole thing couldn't have taken more than fifteen minutes," said Mrs. Sherek. "Besides, Anton and I were here in plenty of time."

"Anton, will you ever forgive me?"

"It's a boy," Anton said, giddy. "We won't name him until the baptism, of course, but in my head, he already has a name."

"Don't I get a say?" Lily countered.

"Not if you still plan to name him some cousin jack American name like Clarence. This boy is all Slovenian."

"Yes. I can tell by his hairy back." Lily removed the baby from her breast, turned him over, and showed his backside to Anton.

"Not hairy," he said. "Manly."

"It's just baby fuzz. Be gone in a week." Mrs. Sherek took the baby from Lily and gently placed the sleeping infant in the top drawer of the bureau. "You two. Out. When the baby sleeps, Mama sleeps. That's the rule for at least three days. Lily is not to lift anything heavier than her baby."

Anton leaned over and kissed the new baby. He kissed Lily, too, before following Katka out of the bedroom and down the stairs.

When they reached the first level, Anton grabbed his hat. "Katka," he said quietly. How many dead?"

"None. They still walking. If you had looked out the window five minutes ago, you'd have seen them."

"Give it here. Your notebook. I gotta know."

Katka tossed it to him, and he glanced through.

"No violence? In truth?"

Rocks thrown. Nothing beyond that."

"Where they at now?"

"I suspect they're at the Miller by now."

"Yes. I'm sure you're right." Anton left the dining room for a minute and came back carrying his Winchester and a pistol, which he fastened with a strap to his leg.

"The Bulgarian said no weapons."

"Let me guess. 'Keep your hands in your pockets and shame the company'?"

"That's right."

"I like the sound of that." Anton smiled mockingly. Then he grew serious. "The Winchester's for you, Katka. I have to haul a few things into my cart. I'm going to leave the cellar door open for a stretch. Watch so as no one comes in," he said, tossing her the rifle. He hitched his cart to Bruno and led him to the back door. Anton went down to the cellar and brought up several heavy crates to load into the cart. "That'll do, Kat. Close up the cellar for me. When Mrs. Sherek leaves, bolt the door. Don't let anyone in unless they know the code. That includes regular boarders."

"Code?"

"Two long knocks, followed by three short. Like this." He rapped on the table. "And stay here. That walkout is no place for women. And it's no place for you either." He smiled.

Katka promised to stay put and wait on Lily until the miners came home. "You'll send word if anything happens?"

"I will. I don't plan to be gone long. But nothing is certain."

"Keep your eye on Paul, will you?"

"If you keep your eye on Lily. She did good, huh?"

"It's a grand baby."

"Sure is."

He mounted his horse and headed toward the Miller mine.

CHAPTER 28

NO ONE WAS MORE SURPRISED THAN MILO. IT worked just as Paul had said it would. He, Andre, Mrs. Sherek, and Paul had spent nearly every night in the last weeks planning at the underground field bunker, and it paid off. For here he was, on the second day in June, in his eighteenth year of life, leading a strike. "They will follow you," Paul had told him. "Trust me." Every single miner had walked out. How Paul had orchestrated it, Milo did not know. He would never ask. That was one thing he had learned from the men at the Slovenski Dom: You don't want to know too much.

Milo wondered if it would go as smoothly at the Miller. At the St. James he had Andre on the inside. Andre had known exactly how many mine guards would be on duty. He knew how many of the men were armed. He knew where the captains would be and had estimated how many men it would take to subdue them. Andre had been right.

"Is there someone at the Miller on the inside?" Milo had asked.

"Don't matter," Paul had told him. "One action leads to the next. If everything goes as planned at the St. James, the rest will fall in place. Don't pay to overthink. Would just get us in trouble."

"How so?" Milo asked.

"Spies," Andre had said with a crooked grin. "They're everywhere. Never know if you might tip off the wrong person."

Some of the miners had grabbed musical instruments. He heard a drum and a few trumpets. That helped them pick up the pace a bit. Dang, it sure was hot. Milo wanted to take off his shirt, like many of the men had done, and just wear his work pants and suspenders. But Paul and Andre still had their shirts and hats on. He was one of the leaders too, an official Wob now, just like them. He wanted to look the part. He kept walking, his head held high. Every once in a while, he'd look back. "Holy smokes," he'd think. The river of people stretched so far behind him. He knew his parents would be proud. When he got back to the boardinghouse, he'd ask Katka if she'd let him use her typewriter. He'd write them a letter. He wouldn't reveal any secrets, of course, but he'd tell them that he was a big man now, doing important things.

When they got to the Miller mine, they were almost five hundred strong. Three hundred were workers; the rest were wives, children, and strike sympathizers. The workers chanted the strike words raucously. When the first workers at the Miller mine emerged from the cage and held up their clenched fists in a show of solidarity, the crowd could hardly contain itself. Then they just kept coming. The workers began to sing.

As they reached the property line of the Miller mine, Milo's adrenaline soared. But there was no showdown at the Miller. The workers met no resistance from the captains and guards. This was a smaller mine, and management was outnumbered by a confident crowd. All the managers could do was watch as their operation was depleted of its workforce.

Someone with ambition was trying to form the men and women into tidy rows. "Heck," Milo thought. "Who said foreign-borns couldn't organize?"

"I think everybody's out of the shaft," Andre said.

"Time to carry on to the next mine," Paul said.

Milo saw Anton approach from the west, Bruno leading his cart. "Hold up," Milo said.

Anton pulled up next to them. "No violence?"

"None," Paul said.

"Glad to hear it," Anton said. "Got something for you, fellas." He swung off his horse, reached into the cart, and removed one of the three heavy crates.

Andre the Bulgarian tipped his hat. "We appreciate what you trying to do, Anton, but we don't want no guns. We're going bare-fisted."

"These ain't no guns." Anton grabbed the second crate and passed it to Milo. Then he lifted the third and put it down by the others. "And I ain't trying to do nothing for you. I'm a businessman. I'll send you a bill. I don't get mixed up in politicals." He got back on his horse and rode back to the Slovenski Dom.

Milo slowly opened one of the crates. "Well, I'll be," he said, shaking his head in wonder.

"What is it?"

He reached into the crate and pulled out a bottle. He held it high in the air. "Soda pop!"

The crowd was joyful. The temperature had risen above eighty-five degrees. The miners had already worked half a day and walked seven miles in the heat. The thought of a drink bolstered their already high spirits. Paul and Andre started emptying the crates, passing the bottles back into the crowd. When all the bottles were distributed, the strikers and townsfolk continued their march to the next mine.

CHAPTER 29

GOULASH:
1 pound venison or sausage
1 pound rabbit meat
3 tbsp. fat or lard
1 large onion
1 tsp. salt
1 tsp. paprika
1 cup chopped tomatoes
8 small peeled potatoes
Rice
Cut meat in cubes and sauté with onion in hot fat, stirring occasionally to brown evenly. Add seasonings and tomatoes. Simmer about one and a half hours or until meat is tender. Add potatoes and rice after one hour of cooking; add more tomatoes if necessary. Serve hot.

Anton went into the woods when he got back from delivering the soda pop. He returned an hour later with five rabbits.

"Make a goulash," he said to Katka. "The men, they will be hungry something terrible. Use the sausages you started this morning too, before they spoil in the heat. I'm going to Mountain Iron to find the priest to baptize the boy. I hear he's doing a funeral there. Don't know how long I'll be gone, and I might stay the night if he is not to be found. Where's the Winchester?"

"There," Katka said, pointing to the rifle resting against a shelf in the kitchen pantry.

"Keep it in your sights. I'm sure you won't need it, but..."

"I'll keep them safe."

He kissed her on the cheek and left.

Katka had never cooked goulash before. Luckily, Lily had published a recipe in the last edition of the journal. She grabbed a copy from the dining room and set it on the kitchen counter. She cooked the rice and fried the sausage and fresh rabbit with the onion and paprika. She was just about to add the tomatoes when she heard the baby cry. Katka spooned three dollops of hot rice onto a plate and walked up the stairs to Lily and Anton's room. The baby was wailing. She opened the door.

"Everything all right in here?"

Lily was in bed, holding her son in her lap. She had one hand on the baby's belly, the other supported his head. His screams escaped through the wide open door of his round little mouth. Lily was looking at her son and smiling.

"I gave birth to an angry goat," Lily said.

"Sounds just so. I brought you some food."

Lily looked at the plate of rice. "Where?"

"Here." Katka pointed at the plate. "Rice and lard. Mrs. Sherek said to keep your meals simple. Here, let me take the baby."

Katka set the plate on Lily's lap and took the squawking child. She made a fist and put her hand next to the baby's mouth. The baby immediately began to suck on her knuckle and quieted down.

"How'd you do that?"

"I don't know. There were lots of babies when I was growing up. Womenfolk were always handing them to me."

"I don't have any milk. I would give this baby anything in the world. And the only thing he wants, I don't have."

"You'll get it. It takes a while. How are you feeling?"

"I won't tell an untruth, Kat. Not in front of my son, for whom I must set a sterling example. So I'm gonna use the softest words I got. I hurt like a motherfucking son of a bitch."

"Lily!" Katka laughed and covered the baby's ears with one hand. The child bleated again, and Katka shifted him around. "You'll feel better if you eat."

"Make me some real food."

"No."

Lily picked up the fork and began to shovel spoonfuls in her mouth. "At least you used lots of salt." She ate the whole dish without stopping and handed the plate to Katka.

"You want the baby back?"

"I do. I reckon I'll keep putting him to my teat. Sooner or later I'll turn into a damn cow. In the meantime, why don't you cook me up a sausage with mustard seeds and cabbage? I wouldn't say no to bacon, neither. And can't you whip up some biscuits, for the love of Mary? Drizzle 'em with that honey Helen Cerkvenik left us?"

"You're impossible," Katka said.

She gave the baby back and made her way into the tavern, grabbed a glass, and pulled a beer. It was a dark, malty brew. Then she chopped up a sausage into small bits, fried it with a carrot and some cilantro, and mixed it with another plate of rice. She brought them both to Lily.

"Now that is closer to the tune!" Lily said. "I been craving a beer something awful. And some real food."

Katka wrapped the baby in a long cloth and affixed him to her back, the way the field workers did in the old country.

"Less than a day old and he'll already be working," Lily said between bites.

"He'll just be watching me work."

"Ain't that just like a man?"

Katka laughed. "Sleep, *Teta*. I got to finish the goulash. And who knows when all those men will be back here. Could get mighty loud."

"Goulash? Bring me some of that."

When Katka brought the baby back to Lily an hour later, a very thin milk had come in. The beer had done just what the old ones always said it would. She had also finished the plate of slightly less bland food and kept it down just fine. Katka handed the baby to Lily. He fed, and then mother and son slept for hours.

Katka worked on the dinner, stopping occasionally to look out the front window. When she finished the goulash, she rolled the dough for *potica*, pulling and stretching it until it was paper-thin. She fed the animals and chopped the wood. She did some of the wash and hung it on the line. She kept a lookout for Anton, for the men. When they did not come, she went back in the house, removed the goulash from the heat, and covered the pan. She checked on Lily and the baby. She fed Lily some of the goulash and gave her another beer. Everywhere she went, she dragged the Winchester with her.

Finally, just as the last light of the day faded into shadow, she saw the figures of men. There was no moon, and they did not carry torches. She grabbed the rifle and held fast to it. She blew out the lantern she had just lit, then bent down, trying not to be seen from the outside. She followed the shadows as they approached her door. No one had explicitly said this house was in danger, but Milo had led the walkout. By now Mr. Stone and his men would know where Milo lived. Paul served as the official IWW representative, sent from headquarters. Everyone in town would know who he was by now. Did they know he was

Lily's cousin? She was glad Anton had given her his Winchester. She was even gladder that she knew how to use it.

She saw shadows in the distance and thought she could make out voices. She held tighter to the gun. She pulled the lever and racked it, waiting. She loved to shoot. But right then, at that moment, it was not love for gunpowder that she felt. A quiet calm came over her. She envisioned Lily and the baby soundly sleeping upstairs. If anyone tried to hurt them, she would mutilate them.

She stood just to the left of the curtained window, watching the shadows approach. The men were obviously tired. She heard voices, laughter. "Slovenski Dom," one said pointing. "Let's sit for an ale." They went up to the tavern entrance and tried to open the door.

"Closed," another said. They kept walking, toward Biwabik, toward the location towns. They were miners.

Katka watched for fifteen or twenty minutes. A few others tried the door to the tavern. She recognized the voices and felt no fear. The men were coming back. They were unharmed, so far anyway. The voices were not filled with fear. She left the window, lit the fire, and heated the goulash, filling the room with the pungently sweet aroma of red paprika, cabbage, and sweet onions. Her boarders would be home any minute.

She was in the kitchen when she heard the code. Three long, two short. She ran to the door and opened it. Four boarders were followed by three more. Finally, Milo, Old Joe, and Samo entered. They were smiling. Laughing. Talking all at once.

"Sit! Sit! I'll serve you," Katka said.

The men sat, but the conversation continued. Using a metal cup, she splashed giant helpings of the goulash onto each plate, listening intently the whole while.

"Where's the beer, beautiful Katka?" Old Joe said. "A handful of 'do-nothing foreign-borns' stand up to the biggest company in America, practically change the world, and we don't get as much as an ounce of beer?"

"No beer in the house," Katka said. "Lily'd have your heads. And watch your language. If you want a drink, carry your plates into the tavern and eat there. I'll pull some pints."

From upstairs, the baby cried. At first, the cry was weak and muffled. Then it rose up, like a gust of wind on the prairie. Babies who have known hunger all their lives rarely cry loudly. They whimper, almost apologetically, expecting nothing. But this baby had been satiated earlier today. His cry became a roar as fierce as poverty and as strong as hope. The men stopped talking. They listened to the voice of the baby.

"The cry of a warrior, that is…" Old Joe said, "a boy?"

Katka nodded.

"Let us make him proud." Because he did not yet have a drink in his hand, Old Joe held his fist in the air instead. The other men followed suit, toasting the child of Lily and Anton with nothing more than their dirty, work-worn skin.

The next two days, the marches continued. By the end of the third day, various shifts of miners traversed Blood Red Road, shutting down every mine east of the St. James in Biwabik.

CHAPTER 30

THE FIFTH DAY OF JUNE WAS THE BABY'S FOURTH day of life, and it was the first day of rest for the miners. There was no work to do and no picketing planned. Katka thought perhaps the men would sleep in, but none did. They were all there at the breakfast table at 6 a.m., eating hard-boiled eggs, sausage, fresh rolls, and jam. Katka had been up since 4:30 a.m. and had found herself with a little extra time since she had no pasties to bake and wrap.

"Big plans for the day?" Katka asked, serving coffee.

"Think I'll do some fishing," Old Joe said, stretching his arms leisurely.

"In truth?"

Old Joe smiled. "I'd like to. Can't remember the last time I was off on a Monday."

"And how about you, Milo? Plannin' to do some fishing your own self?"

"Nah," Milo said. "Might head in to town. Visit some ladies I know."

"I heard that worked real swell for you last time," Katka said. "How about the rest of you? What's the plan?"

"You a reporter or something?" Old Joe said with a smile. "I'll give you a story that your lady readers will love: 'How to please Joe on his day off.'"

"No, thanks."

Samo planned to listen to birds. Dusca was going to go to church. Another wanted to catch up on some reading.

"Fine," Katka said. "If not a one of you is doing anything important, I reckon you can clean up after yourselves. I'm going to take a plate up to Lily, check on the baby, and head into town. Got to sell some eggs."

"You want us to do women's work?" Old Joe asked incredulously. "Now that's a story."

"I'm on strike too," she said.

"Women don't go on strike."

Katka delivered a plate for Lily, and when she got back downstairs, the men were gone. The dishes were left on the table. She cleared the plates and stacked the dirty dishes in the sink. Then she grabbed her shawl and basket and headed out to the barn.

"Morning, Sasa," she said to the hen.

"No one's ever called me that before."

Katka looked in the direction of the voice and smiled. Paul stepped out from behind a hay bale. She ran to his arms and kissed him.

"What are you doing here?"

"I stayed not too far from here last night."

"Slept in the barn?"

"Near the barn. I was on night duty. Wanted to see if anyone was coming for Milo."

"Then you haven't slept?"

"Well, my little tiger, I was just starting to drift into the most wonderful dream. You were there. And you were naked, of course. But then I heard something. Footsteps. And so I watched. I saw a man come in here. So I followed him, real quiet-like. With my gun, of course. And I watched him do the most peculiar thing. He went over to that big fat hen—"

"Sasa."

"Yes. And he looked underneath her body. I thought he was an egg thief. But then, finding nothing, he shook his head and walked away."

"I wonder what he was looking for," Katka said, her eyes fixed on a spider that was perched asleep on the corner of the doorway.

"Do you?"

She looked at him. Said nothing.

"Who was he?"

"I've never seen him in person, Paul. I don't know his name. Lily never told me. He helps us distribute *The Iron Range Ladies Journal*. The one I told you about."

"If he doesn't check out, Katka, you will have to get rid of him. We can't have strangers lurking around the farm. It's too dangerous."

"What do you mean, 'check out'?"

"When there's a strike, there are two sides of the table. No one gets to sit on the table. No one gets to sit under it. You're on one side or the other."

"What's going to happen today, Paul? The men all left early. I don't know where they were going."

"Different places."

"If I don't get it from you, I'll get it from Helen at the Mercantile. That's where I was headed anyway. But I'd rather get it from you. I'd like to be accurate."

"For your newspaper?"

"Yes."

"The men are meeting to make signs. The picketing won't start until tomorrow, at the earliest. There will be a big meeting at the Finnish Socialist Hall tonight. The Finns have agreed to let us use their hall as union headquarters."

"I missed most of the action. I wanted to get the perspective of the wives, the mothers. But I didn't, so I'll have to get it in town today. That man you saw, he was probably expecting a pamphlet. But I couldn't write it. Too busy."

He was silent for a moment. "Sounds like you need to go to Cerkvenik's Mercantile. I don't have a clue what the women think. But it is important to find out. Will you tell me what you hear?"

"Of course."

"Katka, how much do you know about the Wobblies?"

"I know that you went to prison because you are one."

"Yes. But I don't regret it. Are you sympathetic to the cause?"

"I'm a journalist. I just report the facts."

Paul laughed. "Never knowed a journalist like that. Don't reckon they exist, except maybe in your head. Which, by the way, looks a might pretty today. The humidity has curled your hair. I like how it falls." He kissed her neck, and she put her hands on his waist. She pulled him in. Even after a night of sleeping in a barn, he still smelled of wind and salt. His hand reached under her skirt, caressed her inner thigh, and moved upward. "Would you be interested in knowing a real Wobbly? From the inside out? For your paper, I mean?"

She moaned softly. "Not now. I'd like to, but I can't."

"You are soft, like a patch of velvet."

"I have to go to town, Paul. I need information. And I don't have much time. I didn't even get to the breakfast dishes, and in two hours I'll need to start lunch."

Paul reluctantly let go of her and took a step back. "I have information, Kat. More than you would ever find out in town. But there is something we may need from you in return."

"From me? What?"

"Meet me at Anton's stable around noon. Bring your notebook and pens. I will take you to a meeting. You can take notes for us. We will need a secretary who can speak languages. You speak Slovenian, Russian, and English."

"And Croatian. My mother was half Croatian."

"There are many who will be there who speak Finn. We will have to recruit a Swede, a Norwegian, others."

"I know many women from many countries."

"Kat, you will love working for the Industrial Workers of the World. It is a great union with the power to change lives."

"I work for *The Iron Range Ladies Journal*."

Paul laughed. He put his arms around her waist and pulled her close to him again. "I love Iron Range ladies."

"All of them?"

"Just one. The one who's about to become a Wob. If you're not recruited, you can use the information however you see fit."

"Noon?"

"That's right."

"I'll be here."

***

Paul was at the stable as promised. Katka entered and stopped. She waited for him to approach her. He kissed her mouth. "So many meetings I've been to in the past few years," he said. "But this—this—will be something different."

"We best not be late then," Katka said.

"We won't be. I lied to you about the time. Meeting's not for an hour and a half."

He slipped out of his trousers and smiled. She had changed out of her housedress. She was wearing a white shirt with ruffles down the front and a high collar. He tore at the buttons, then slipped his hand under her camisole. He placed her down gently on a blanket he had laid out on the ground. A horse flicked his tail at a black fly and snorted.

Katka laughed at the distraction. "One day we'll make love on a bed," she said.

"As long as I'm with you, Kat, it's like a fancy hotel every time." He raised her skirts up to her waist. "Ain't no heaven could smell as good as you. You're like lilacs. Lilacs and...milk."

They loved each other passionately. Only this time, it was faster, rougher, tinged with a danger and a sense of urgency that excited Katka.

Then it was over. They lay entwined. She could hear his heart beating. She put her hand on his chest, waiting for the rapid palpitations to return to a normal pace. What if that heart—that very real and tangible heart that she could feel now with the palm of her hand—started beating faster and faster until it exploded, leaving her with nothing but a handful of blood and collection of stories of a love remembered by no living thing other than herself?

"Your heart is beating so quick," Paul said.

"My heart?"

"Yes."

She realized that he too had placed his own hand on her heart. She reached for her chest. "It is not easy to hold so much music inside."

"Kat, when the strike is over, we will get married."

"We will? Says who?"

"Your heart. And mine."

Katka smiled.

"I love you," he said. "Just as the snowy earth, tired from months of frostbite, loves the spring sun that melts away the cold. I cherish you like a bird with a broken wing cherishes his other wing—the one that works. Before you, I was strong and broken at the same time. Now I just feel strong."

"I might marry you."

"As soon as this bloody strike is done. I tell you true, Kat. I want you to be my wife. And I ain't never wanted a wife. Not even a little bit. But now it's all I think about. You and me. Doing those things I never thought I wanted to do."

"Things?"

"Married things. I'd work a steady job. A less dangerous job. I'd come home, and we'd eat together. Something simple. A sausage. Some kraut. Then, after you cleaned up, we'd move to the sitting room, and we'd read until there weren't no light left. And maybe we'd be next to each other, my hand on your skirt, and maybe we wouldn't, but no matter. I'd hear you breathing across the room. I'd see you, your soft silhouette turning the pages, and I'd feel like the luckiest bloke alive."

"That sounds grand," Katka said. And it did. But she didn't want to dream about it. She wanted to make it happen. What was it that Anton had said to her when she first arrived in Biwabik? "I don't like to think about one day. If it's possible one day, it's possible today."

She got up and wiped the dust off her clothes. It was time to go to a meeting.

CHAPTER 31

K ATKA AND PAUL WALKED DOWN THE SAME PATH that she and Milo had walked almost a year before, toward the woods. When they were a quarter mile in, Katka saw a horse tied to one of the trees. She had never seen the horse before.

"Your carriage awaits." Paul helped her onto the horse's back, then mounted behind her. He gave the horse a swift kick.

"Where are we going?"

"To the fields."

They trotted through the forest to the rifle range. Anton was there, shooting. Three men from Biwabik were with him. When Anton recognized his niece and his wife's cousin, he put his rifle down.

"How's Lily? The baby?"

"Asleep."

"Is anyone else in the house?"

"No," Katka said. "The men have all gone to make signs."

"Old Joe is there," Paul said, contradicting her. Katka hadn't known this.

Anton gave a curt nod. "Anyone follow you?"

"Nope."

"You can leave your horse here. Come on, Copper," he said, taking the reins. "You'll have to walk back on your own. Copper belongs to my friend over there."

They continued walking. Katka followed Paul, down a narrow deer trail. Eventually they came to an oak tree that had been struck by lightning. It had fallen across the path and landed in the middle of another oak, splitting it in two, about four feet off the ground. Katka was trying to decide if she should climb over or under the tree when Paul stopped.

"We call this the slingshot tree. Follow the slingshot."

They turned in that direction until they came to three giant granite stones, positioned by nature in a triangle. Paul walked to them and stood directly in the middle. He picked up a stick and hit one of the stones in code. They heard the code returned from underground.

Paul brushed away some sticks and grass, revealing a wooden door. They opened it, and a man appeared, crawling up a ladder.

"Paul."

"Johan."

Katka climbed down with Paul close behind. The cellar was four times as large as the one beneath Anton's kitchen. It was loaded with crates holding guns and ammunition.

Seven men and one woman were assembled. Katka waved to Milo. Of course Milo was there. She was surprised to see Mrs. Sherek, the midwife, who greeted her warmly. There was a small table, a few cots, and five chairs. In the far corner, she saw a bedroll and a sleeping bag. This must be where Paul was staying. He never told her. Said he needed to keep his distance, to be on the safe side. No one knew he was Lily's cousin. Katka sat on a crate. Paul sat across the room next to Frank Little, who was part Ojibwe and also spoke French. The Bulgarian introduced himself as Andre Kristeva. She recognized him as the company man who helped lead the walkout.

"You're that engineer who switched sides," she said.

"Engineer I am, ma'am. But I never was on that side. I'm a card-carrying Wob. Just working from a different angle. We are the strike force. I think you know everyone here, most about. That there is Johan Koski. Next to him is William Jarvi from the Finnish Socialist Hall. They drew up the demands. You know Frank, he's 'Finndian.' 'Course you know Adeline," he continued, pointing at Mrs. Sherek. "She ran the women's auxiliary during the '07 strike, and she's sharp as a whip, she is. Today we will review the strike demands before presenting them to workers at the union hall tonight. Paul tells me you can read and write in four languages."

"Slovenian, Croatian, English, and Russian. I publish a newspaper. *The Iron Range Ladies Journal*."

He nodded. "We've all read it."

"If you want your strike to work, don't be forgetting the ladies," Adeline Sherek said. "Womenfolk must have a say. It ain't no picnic being a woman up here. While the men is working, the women is working too. We're slaving away, just like you, but we got to be watching the babies at the same time. We got to feed the boarders. When the paychecks stop coming, how are the womenfolk gonna buy eggs? When children get hungry, mothers will do anything to feed them. If that means convincing their husbands to cross a line, they'd do it before they see a child go without bread."

"I can't think of a single woman who would tell her husband to cross," Johan Koski said.

"That's because you're not a mother," Adeline said.

Andre turned to Katka. "Adeline says all the women read your paper. She also says everyone knows it's you and Lily who write it."

"In truth?"

"It's a small town, dearie," Adeline said, smiling. "What did you think?"

"The real question is," Andre continued, "will your paper convince the women to support their husbands through this strike, even if things get tough?"

"It might."

"The Iron Range Ladies Journal will be your cover. Being the primary reporter, now that Lily has the baby to care for, will give you journalist status and therefore access to the union meetings, even though you are not a union member. However, you are here because we need another publication too. The writer must remain anonymous. We want you to call it *The Official Strike Bulletin of the Mesabi Strikers*, and you will need to publish it as often as we need, sometimes in great haste."

"I suggest *Strike Bulletin.*"

He laughed. "I am nothing if not verbose."

Adeline spoke. "Katka has means of distribution established."

"Who is it?" Andre asked.

"I cannot tell you," Katka said, "because I do not know. Lily said the publisher wished to remain unknown. We drop off the papers, and he picks them up before dawn."

"I know him," Adeline Sherek said. "We can trust him."

"Consider yourself hired, Miss Kovich. Take out your notebook and pen. This is for your own education, but it's important." Katka did as she was told.

Andre gestured around the room. "All the folks you see here," he told Katka, "are old Wobblies, members of the Industrial Workers of the World. Except for Milo here. New, but—as you know—valuable. The IWW has already sent Paul Schmidt here, from headquarters." He gestured toward Paul. "We mighty glad you're here. They will be sending more of their best organizers today. They are set to arrive in Biwabik on the four o'clock train. They will send Carlo Tresca, an anarchist and labor organizer. He will take care of the Italians, but he also speaks perfect English and is a fiery speaker. Sam Scarlett and

Joseph Ettor will come. Probably more. Maybe they will even send Elizabeth Gurley Flynn. When this meeting is over, I will give you some literature. You will read up on these men and women."

Elizabeth Gurley Flynn. At Ellis Island, the woman with the black hair and blue eyes...her name was Elizabeth. Anton had told her that much. Katka recorded her name in her notebook. She would ask Paul about her later.

Katka wrote down the names and double-checked the spellings. Then she listened as Johan Koski and William Jarvi went over the demands the strikers would vote on. There was some discussion, some arguing, but by the end of the hour, Katka read her notes out loud to the group:

1. *Miners will earn $3.50 per day for work in wet places, deep underground. $3 per day for dry places in the underground mines. $2.75 per day for surface workers.*
2. *Eight hours constitutes a day's work.*
3. *A miner's workday begins when they arrive at the mine, not when they arrived at their mining location, which takes a long time.*
4. *Miners will be paid twice per month, not once.*
5. *The contract system will be abolished. Miners will be paid for the amount of time they work as opposed to how much ore they load each day.*
6. *Miners to be paid immediately after discharge.*
7. *Discontinuance of Saturday night work.*
8. *Abolition of private mine police.*
9. *Running water will be installed in all of the location houses.*
10. *If injured on mining property, married miners who have wives would be afforded the same access to hospital care as miners who are unmarried.*

11. *Miners who are injured at work will be paid their daily wage while they recover and will be able to resume work in the same mine when they return.*

The last three demands were not proposed by Koski and Jarvi. They were proposed by the midwife, Mrs. Sherek. "You want the women's support, you got to support the women," she said.

Two hours later they all left the field bunker in agreement. The big union meeting would take place that night at the Finnish Socialist Hall. Not all Finns on the Range were members of the Socialist Party, but all were welcome at the hall. The socialist hall was one of the largest buildings on the Mesabi Range. But would it be big enough to house the massive crowd of miners who would assemble that night to listen to the IWW organizers? They would soon find out.

CHAPTER 32

MILO AND HARRIS MAKI ARRIVED AT THE TRAIN station in Maki's buggy. Harris Maki was a big man, nearly five feet, ten inches, and a heavy equipment operator at the St. James mine. Milo had been instructed to take the soon-to-arrive IWW leaders to their hotel, feed them, and get them to the union hall for the 7 p.m. meeting. Three fellow miners were at the station to help them. Milo helped Maki tie up his horses, then shook hands with the other men. They stood on the east side of the depot and watched for the train to approach.

On the other side of the street stood Sheriff Turner, Mr. Augustine Stone in his yellow suit, and five armed mine guards. Mr. Stone called out to Milo and the men across the street. "Waiting for someone special?"

Maki called back, "Heard there might be some new ladies on the train." Milo winced.

"Heard the same thing," Mr. Stone said.

Each side stood and waited. Five miners on one side, seven company men on the other. Mr. Stone checked his watch. The four o'clock arrived and all the passengers disembarked. No Wobs.

The air was still unseasonably hot and humid. Mr. Stone had a chair delivered and he sat on it, smoking cigars while he and his men waited for the five o'clock. After a few minutes, some of the company guards sat on the ground.

The men on the east side sat on Harris Maki's buggy and chewed tobacco. Everyone was sweating, wiping foreheads with handkerchiefs, sighing. No one spoke much. It was strange now, Milo thought, how much could be heard now that the mines were no longer operating. Chickens in the distance, voices from Main Street, children playing chase in the mud.

The five o'clock train was late. Mr. Stone knew because his watch, which had been given to him by his father, told him so. Milo knew because his stomach told him so. Katka had made him a good, hot lunch, but it was obvious he was going to miss supper. He hoped the train wasn't terribly delayed. Milo hoped he'd have time to get the important men to their hotel before the meeting started. They were probably hungry too.

Some boys came skipping past. Harris Maki recognized them all. One of them, Benjamin, lived two doors down from him. Maki told him to run back to the location and tell his wife to bring him and his friends some food.

"Will you pay me a penny if I bring the food back, Mr. Maki?"

"Ain't got no penny, Benjamin," Maki said. "But I'll give you a knuckle sandwich if you don't. How that sound?"

"Ain't never had one of those."

"Always a first time, there is. Now run along." The boy and his friends ran out of sight.

Milo and his fellow miners took up a game of Smear on the buggy. They were three hands in when they heard the familiar chug and whistle of the engine.

"Train's coming," Maki said. "'Bout damn time."

They watched as the locomotive approached. The first passengers off the train were four women and six children. The men on either side of the street tipped their hats to them. Next, twelve scraggly-looking, dirty men lumbered off the train.

"You there!" Mr. Stone said, stopping one of the men. "Who are you, and what's your business?"

"Name's Peterson, sir. Came all the way from Minneapolis. We men heard there might be work here, opening up soon. Thought we'd beat the rush."

Mr. Stone smiled and put out his hand. "You are most welcome, Mr. Peterson. Take your boys to Vince Torelli's boardinghouse. They'll be good to you. Tell 'em Mr. Augustine Stone sent you, and your dinner's on me."

"Thank you, sir," one of the men said, tipping his hat. "We be sure to do that."

Most went straight away. A few lingered, lighting tobacco.

Stone called to Milo and the miners nearby, "Looks like you boys have been replaced!"

"Scabs!" one of the miners yelled. The men who had lingered said nothing.

After a minute or so had passed, four other passengers leisurely walked off the train. Sheriff Turner took a piece of paper out of his trouser pocket and stared at the drawings on it. He looked at the men and back to his paper.

The first man was tall and lanky with light brown hair carefully parted on the side. His suit was well made, but dirty. His name was Carlo Tresca. Behind him was Sam Scarlett, wearing a red suit, his mustache moist from the heat and his hair slicked back. Milo had seen his picture in the labor magazines his friend Gino gave him. Scarlett was known for the rousing speeches he delivered to recruit workers to join the IWW. Behind him were two others. Each carried a small suitcase.

The four men stood on the muddy street and looked at the two groups of men who were there to greet them. Sheriff Turner's badge was glinting in the sun. Mr. Augustine Stone rocked back and forth on his new white leather boots and smiled.

"Tresca, Gilday, Scarlett, Ettor," Stone said. "Welcome to the Iron Range."

The sheriff and the company guards raised their Lugers and pointed the guns at the newcomers. Then, as if he'd been practicing, Sheriff Turner said, "You are under arrest for threatening the life of a lawman."

"These men ain't done nothing, Sheriff Turner," Milo said. "They ain't even armed."

"I distinctly saw that one there, with the ungainly mustache, threaten to inflict bodily harm on Turner of the worst possible degree," Stone said. "You must have been looking the other way."

"He did no such thing! Stop your tale-telling," one of Maki's friends said.

Little Benjamin and his three friends emerged. They were running, playing a game of tag. They stopped when they saw the guns drawn.

"Hello, Sheriff," Benjamin said innocently. "Could I touch your badge? Is it powerful sharp like it looks?"

"It is. Too sharp to touch."

Benjamin was carrying a basket of food. "These fellows in the suits, are they bad guys, Sheriff?"

The sheriff looked annoyed. "Go home, boys," he said.

"I brought Mr. Maki some food," Benjamin said. He put the large basket on the ground in front of him. "There's a lot there. Maybe you all could share it." He looked around.

"What is your name, son?" Carlo Tresca asked. His voice was calm, as if he had failed to notice that several guns were aimed at his head.

"Folks call me Benny."

"We are not the bad guys. We're the good guys. You see, we haven't got any guns or weapons, right?"

Benjamin nodded.

"You and your friends are key witnesses here. Do you know what a witness is?"

"I sure do! How 'bout that boys? We are witnesses!" Their faces lit up with importance. "Witnesses to what?"

"An unlawful arrest. Now run along and tell everyone you know what you saw. These men, pointing guns at us. And us, with nothing but our integrity to protect ourselves. Go tell everyone. It's important."

"Yes, sir!" The boys ran quickly down the muddy road.

The sheriff motioned for the guards to restrain the men. "Those kids could've died. You four are under arrest for threatening a lawman and putting children's lives in danger."

Carlo Tresca stared straight into the sheriff's eyes. "Think you're a big man, huh? You ain't fit to lick my boot."

One of the company guards dropped his gun and lunged toward Tresca. He punched him in the stomach and kneed him in the groin. Tresca fell to his knees, and his face contorted in agony. He did not fight back, and his three friends did nothing but watch. When Tresca got back up, the company guard pulled his hands behind his back and tied them together with a rope.

"You are an even smaller man," Sam Scarlett said to the deputy. "Willing to do someone else's dirty work. For what? Certainly not the respect of the other men in this town, men who are willing to sacrifice for something worth more than themselves. Do you know what the real men of this town think of a man like you when you cross them on the street?"

"Shut up, Scarlett," Sheriff Turner said.

Scarlett ignored him and kept addressing the company guard. "Nothing. They don't think of you at all. You are that inconsequential."

"Shoot him, Sheriff," the guard said. He was still restraining Tresca. "Can't you just shoot the son of a bitch?"

"Go ahead," Scarlett said. "You think the men in this town are angry now? Imagine what they'll do if you kill me here, with no cause, in front of all these witnesses." He gestured toward Milo and his friends. "Imagine what they'd do to you. To your family. Got any kids? A wife?"

Silence.

Scarlett continued. "We are the IWW, the Industrial Workers of the World. We represent the working man and woman, and we strive for what is fair and just, something you folks don't spend a whole lot of time thinking about, I suspect." Scarlet gestured, with his chin toward Mr. Stone. "Contrary to what you may have heard, we do not condone or advocate the use of violence when other means are available. We tell our members to avoid violence whenever possible. In fact, that's what we're here to do tonight. But I got a feeling we might not get to that meeting. I suspect you got different plans for us."

"Got that right," Mr. Augustine Stone cried. "Get them to the jail."

Scarlett turned to Milo. "Have Paul Schmidt send a lawyer to the jail and money for bail. I'm afraid we will miss the meeting. Report what you have seen. It will infuriate your men further. It will fan the flames of discontent. Tell them to meet without us and we will join them as soon as we can."

Milo exchanged words with his friends, who nodded. They jumped in Maki's buggy and took off toward the Finnish Socialist Hall.

Milo picked up the basket of food, which had remained untouched. "I have been thinking, sir," he said to Sheriff Turner, "since I got myself some dinner, I'll accompany you folks to the jail." He picked up the basket Benjamin had left. "So as to witness the goings-on. The men will deliver your message at the meeting, Mr. Tresca."

The union organizers were roughly escorted to the city jail, where the sheriff put the four men in a cell that smelled like urine. Once inside, Milo passed venison jerky through the steel bars, which they eagerly accepted. Then Milo leaned against the corner of the jail and stood watch.

CHAPTER 33

B Y THE TIME THE MEETING STARTED, THE FINNISH Socialist Hall overflowed with workers. Men spilled into the street outside the main entrance like bubbles over the rim of a washbasin. Katka and Adeline Sherek had positioned themselves right in front. Katka had her notebook. Everyone was talking at once. Then Paul Schmidt and Frank Little put their arms high up in the air. Andre Kristeva, the Bulgarian who had spied for the Wobs, rapped three times on the table with his fists, and the hall was instantly quiet.

"We have organized this hall by language," Andre said. "I will be speaking English. If you don't speak English, go sit next to your translator." The translators were holding large signs with the name of their language painted on them. "Italiano, here!" a translator yelled. "Slovensko!" another yelled. "Norske!" "Deutsch!" Katka looked around. Most of the miners were already seated with the men who spoke their language, but the few who were not moved.

Andre waited until the movement had ceased. "The Finns have drawn up a list of demands. It has been once amended and approved by our strike council. Our task is to vote on this list, to come to an agreement. Then we will discuss our plans to get our demands met." He paused momentarily for the translators.

He listed the demands. In a little more than two hours, the miners agreed to the wording, and an appeal was sent to the local mine officials asking to meet and settle.

After the meeting, the miners filed out of the hall and walked to the city jail. They quickly surrounded the building and began chanting. Katka and Adeline joined them.

"Free the Wobs! Free the Wobs!"

Scarlett, Tresca, Gilday, and Ettor could hear it from behind bars. Each took off a shoe and banged it against the bars of their cell in time with the chant.

***

"Shut your fucking pie holes!" Sheriff Turner yelled. He was alone in the jail with his prisoners and Milo. The sheriff's deputy, Gene Baker, had gone to Vince Torelli's to get some dinner.

"Sounds like a good lot of men outside," Milo noted quietly. "Want me to see how many there is, Sheriff?"

The sheriff went to the window in the adjoining room. Milo followed.

"My guess is five hundred," Milo said. "More or less. How many bullets you got, Sheriff?"

Someone was pounding on the door. The sheriff did not answer it. The door opened. In walked Andre the Bulgarian, Paul Schmidt, and Frank Little.

"Evening, Sheriff. How much to spring these fellas?" Paul said.

"Ain't no bail."

"Why not?"

"Ain't no bail for threatening the life of a lawman."

"We got witnesses to say that did not happen."

"You mean Harris Maki and his boys? They're goddamn liars."

"We ain't talking about Harris."

"Can't use testimony from a little boy, if that be your argument."

"Don't intend to." Paul gestured outside to the crowd that stood chanting on the other side of the open door. In walked four men in fine suits.

"Evening again, Sheriff," one of the men said.

"What you mean 'again'?"

"Second time in a matter of hours that we could enjoy the pleasure of your company. You don't remember?"

"Can't say as I do."

"We were on the train. Twelve of us, actually. Please tell Mr. Stone that we had a splendid dinner at that boardinghouse. Vince's. It was right kind of Mr. Stone to foot the bill for us."

"You—you're the replacement workers?"

"We four are lawyers, actually. The others have different training. Reliable witnesses, though. Each one. So how much is bail?"

Outside the roar of the mob swelled. Men pounded on the windows with their fists, still yelling, "Free the Wobs! Free the Wobs!" The sheriff took a pull of whiskey from his flask.

"Five hundred dollars," the sheriff said. "For all four."

The lawyer smiled and lifted his brow. He gazed out the window at the workers. "They seem to be getting impatient." He let the cries of the workers fill the air like thunder approaching. "Should I tell them you have proposed that they pay five hundred dollars for the release of their leaders?"

"Four hundred," the sheriff said.

The lawyer reached in his pocket and withdrew one hundred dollars. He laid it on the desk in front of Sheriff Turner. The sheriff looked at it for a minute. Then he quickly put it in his pocket, walked over, and unlocked the cell door. The four organizers tipped their hats and walked out to the cheering crowd of workers. They marched slowly back to the Socialist Hall, where Sam Scarlett spoke briefly about plans for the next day.

Milo was one of the last out of the hall that night. He walked with the man who had persuaded the sheriff to free the men on bail.

"That was sure something," Milo said. "I never met a lawyer before. We're lucky to have you here."

"Just between me and you," the man said, "I ain't no lawyer. I'm a textile worker from Lawrence, Massachusetts, and a proud member of the IWW."

"Buy you a drink?" Milo said.

"Take me to the whiskey."

CHAPTER 34

I N A MINING TOWN, PEOPLE TELL TIME BY THE SUN and by the shift whistles. Social gatherings, where punctuality is not of the essence, often begin at sundown or high noon. Formal gatherings, like funerals and the secret meetings of the Knights of Columbus, commence with the shift whistles. Unlike the weather, the whistles never changed, and folks considered them more reliable.

Two days after the walkout, the shift whistles from the mine stopped blowing. Katka and some of the women in town overslept just a bit. They were more exhausted than ever. They had an extra meal to prepare and more bodies to clean up after. The meeting had run late. Katka hadn't arrived home until after 11 p.m., and when she got there, she spent almost an hour recapping the evening's events for Lily. When morning came, she slept until the baby's cries woke her at 5 a.m. She scrambled out of bed and rushed to finish the morning chores—milking the cow, gathering the eggs, setting the table, starting breakfast. As Katka scurried about the kitchen, she heard the boarders enter the dining room.

"Milo!" she yelled. "Milo!" His first response had been drowned out by the other voices, talking excitedly.

Milo poked his head in the kitchen door.

"Take this coffee pot," she said. "Tell the men to pour for themselves. I'm behind."

After he left, she finished heating the ham and carefully placed the hard-boiled eggs in a basket with the hard rolls and jam. Using her hip to open the door, she backed into the room holding a fry pan in one hand and the basket in the other.

The men, most of whom had taken saunas the day before, appeared at the breakfast table clean-shaven and dressed in Sunday shirts.

"What's this I see?" Katka said, looking around. She whistled. "Somebody getting married and forget to invite me to the service?" She walked around the table, plopping a slab of ham on each plate.

"If one of us was getting married, Miss Katka, you'd be sure to make the list," Dusca said. "Somebody got to cook the wedding feast."

"'Course," Old Joe added, "you might have other plans. Maybe you don't like the feminine jobs anymore. Gonna trade in your apron and become one of them rebel girls."

"Every girl's a rebel girl," Katka said. "Some just keep it on the inside." She walked back into the kitchen and heated water for the dishes. The dining room got quiet, and Katka knew mouths were being filled.

The men ate heartily, then filed out to the mine. They left without their candles, matches, and shovels. Today would be a different kind of work, and they were nervous and excited.

With the baby tied to her back, Lily came down and helped Katka clear the table. Then she nursed the baby while Katka did the dishes. "Anton left us his buggy. He said to bring the empty soda pop bottles to town and have Andy trade them for full ones. The strikers will be thirsty," she said. "Also, we should bring the rest of the jerky for those who didn't pack a lunch. We can follow the parade in the buggy, give people rides when they get tired."

When they got to the St. James mine around 7 a.m., things were just about to begin. The miners had already shut down all the mines east of Biwabik, but a daunting stretch of mines loomed to the west. The miners lined up in parade fashion on Blood Red Road. Milo and Andre were up front. They held a banner that read "Industrial Workers of the World." Paul stood behind them, holding a giant U.S. flag. Carlo Tresca, Sam Scarlett, and the other two Wobbly organizers who had been freed from jail the night before milled about behind Paul. The Biwabik Marching Band tuned up behind the IWW men. They had a bass drum, three snare drums, two tubas, a trombone, three trumpets, and seven accordions. Behind the leaders and the band, the miners lined up four abreast. They were followed by their wives and children and a few sympathetic townspeople. The buggies came last, carrying the elderly, the lame, small children, and pregnant women. Katka and Lily rode in one of the last buggies. Andy had loaded the soda pop and threw in two large blocks of ice for free.

"When you get to Mountain Iron," he said, "stop at L&M Distributors. They'll replenish you real good. Supposed to be griddle hot today."

"Heard it might hit ninety."

"For your sake, I hope it don't."

"Thanks, Andy."

When Lily was settled in the buggy, Katka took out her notebook and moved stealthily to the front of the line and stood briefly with Paul. Andre the Bulgarian was giving a speech, and she had already missed the beginning. She copied what she could salvage of his speech, writing frantically:

> *We are Americans now. We don't want to fight the flag. We don't want to fight anybody. What do we want? What we want is more pork chops. We will march and have a big, beautiful parade. Be peaceful, brothers, do not make much noise. Remember: Let the mining companies be the ones to incite disorder. We will put them to shame!*

The translators of many tongues went to work. Katka recognized "pork chops" being translated into Slovenian, Croatian, Italian, Finn, and Russian. When the men and women heard the translation, they nodded, smiling grimly. "I could use a pork chop right now," she heard a man say.

Katka ran back to her buggy and hopped in. The band started to play "Solidarity Forever," and the marchers moved swiftly. The townspeople walked from Biwabik to the McKinley location, three miles away. At the onset, the temperature was warm for an Iron Range morning but still comfortable. By the time they reached the location, the sun had risen, and so had the temperature.

The women and children who inhabited the impoverished location town flocked to the dusty street that separated one row of ramshackle abodes from another. The shacks were built of old found wood, gray, weathered, and rotting. "Did the wood ever have a glimmer of bright paint or varnish?" Katka wondered. The families shared thirteen houses and four privies. The stench of offal hung in the air. The water well was less than fifty meters from the privies. The women walked each day to fill their water buckets from the well. They were told the water was clean, but dysentery had killed too many to convince them. Yet, what choice did they have? Everyone needs water. After hauling the water, the women ritually boiled it before drinking.

There was no store, no restaurant or saloon. It was company land, and the Oliver Mining Company forbade business establishments in the locations. They didn't want to distract the men from their work or take business away from the company store.

The band played "America the Beautiful." Children jumped up and down, tugging on their mothers' skirts. "Look!" Katka heard a little boy yell in Slovenian. "A parade! Is it the Independence Day?"

The night-shift miners had not yet returned from work, and the day-shift miners were long gone. The wives were quickly apprised. They gathered provisions and babies, joining the procession. The entire stop took fifteen minutes.

The parade moved on, buoyed forward by music and hope. Their next stop was not an empty location town. It was the Rouchleau mine outside the town of Gilbert. It was a small mine with only forty workers and three bossmen on the shift. Even so, tensions were high. Milo and Andre led the march to the main entrance. The band stopped playing. The workers and unencumbered women fortified their positions, four people abreast. Women with babies clambered into the buggies and silenced the little ones with a breast. Toddlers were given sweets. Katka took out her notebook. She breathed in and held her breath. *This is what dawn feels like,* she wrote. *My world is about to change. June the 6th, in the year 1916.*

Paul and some of the other men walked the perimeter of the march, handing out leaflets with the words to a few IWW songs. Those who could read English took them. Those who could not passed on the leaflets. They began to sing the Wobbly anthem, "Solidarity Forever." By the fourth round, nearly everyone in the crowd could sing the chorus. It was, after all, a simple song: *Solidarity forever, solidarity forever, solidarity forever, the union makes us strong.*

Suddenly, a small man with beady eyes emerged from the office.

He spoke not a single word, this man with the pebble eyes, Katka wrote in her notebook. He simply gazed in wonder at the crowd. What was he thinking? He didn't look angry. He looked befuddled.

The crowd increased its volume. A Russian woman with a particularly strong accent, who had joined Katka and Lily in the buggy, tapped Katka on the shoulder.

"What is this word we sing? 'Vunion'? What it mean, the 'vunion make us strong'?"

"Union," Katka said. "The union makes us strong. It means that poor people are not like rich people. We have to work together. Like ants."

Two more men joined Pebble-eyes. They conversed among themselves, pointing to the crowd and gesturing back to the cage. *No weapons visible.* Katka heard the unmistakable sound of the cage being lifted. The clang when it landed above ground. Katka returned to her frantic scribbling. *Would they come? Would they join us? Will we fall?*

Twenty-one men emerged from the small cage. They had left their shovels behind to accommodate more men. All of them joined the strikers' parade. The cage was lowered again, and the remaining miners rose to the surface. The last man to join the procession was the cage operator. He was greeted with a hero's welcome. *Pebble-eyes and his friends were paralyzed by our numbers. They just stood and watched. This is what dawn feels like.*

The band began to play, and the march continued to the next mine, less than a mile away.

During the next two days, they walked to nineteen more mines and stopped at eight location towns. At each stop, they were greeted with the same response. Every worker at every mine walked off the job.

Katka wrote pages of notes, conducting countless interviews with men and women who rode for brief moments in her buggy.

> *The memory of a worker who has been oppressed is a long one. Here on this march, men who have forever been afraid of complaining about work for fear of losing their job found freedom of expression that was no doubt imagined by the founding fathers of this young nation. It was not until they walked off the job of their own*

free will that they found the courage to curse it.
For how can you curse a place where you choose
to work? That is like cursing yourself. They had
given their bodies to the company. They had lost
limbs and loved ones in the mines below. Their
backs were permanently bent, and pneumonia
had robbed them of their breath. Some will un-
doubtedly say that today they forfeited even
more; they willingly gave up their jobs. How-
ever, this is not how these brave workers think.
They think not of the position they have lost
(which will no doubt be temporary), but instead
they think of the dignity they have gained. "I am
not afraid to work hard," one man told me. "But
I want to be treated like a man, not a mule who
works in the dark until he topples over. It is not
until the mule is dead that they haul it out of the
mine into the sunshine."

One by one, the men spoke to Katka. They were tired, they said. Tired of working thirteen-hour days, six days a week. Tired of being paid by the cartload, not by the hour. Tired of wet feet, missing fingers, and being forced to work without partners because the oncoming war demanded more ore from the company. They were tired of going to the company store on payday, only to discover that they owed more than their paycheck was worth. They were tired of looking at the mine bosses' houses, sitting on the hills or on the shores of lakes, while their own families were holed up with leaky roofs in the location towns. They were tired of knowing that no matter how hard they toiled, they would never be able to save enough money to buy a patch of land. America was a land full of promise. For them, the promise had been broken long ago.

"What do you hope to accomplish today?" Katka asked an old Polish worker who spoke excellent English.

He paused. Then he beckoned for her to come closer to him, and he spoke in a tone barely above a whisper. "Don't repeat this," he said. "Do not write this down."

She closed her notebook.

He nodded. "Okay, then. What do I hope for? I hope for everything. But I am not a stupid man. I expect things will get worse for me, for my wife too, who has the rheumatism."

"Worse? How could they get worse? If no one works, they will have to give in to the demands of the union."

"You would think so. And I'm glad you do. It means you are young, and I love the young." He smiled.

"But..."

"But I am no longer young. I know this: He who makes sacrifices expecting change for himself is a foolish man. A revolutionary does not reap the rewards from the sacrifices he makes. The rewards are reaped by his sons, who never appreciate the blood spilled."

"Never?"

"Well, not my sons, but they have noodles for brains. Still, if their children attend a university or a teacher's college in this wonderful country, it will all be worth it."

"That seems like a long time to wait," Katka said.

"Change takes time. But shh. Don't tell them. If people knew how long it took to change the world, no one would bother trying." The Polish man gestured to the crowd. "They think their lives will be different in a week. If they knew the truth, they wouldn't be here. Revolution requires many things. One of them is stupid optimism." The old man hopped off the buggy. "Thanks for the ride, young lady. And the soda pop."

Katka wanted to write down his story the second he was out of sight, but another man hopped on the buggy and sat next to her. The interviews continued. The workers were unhappy with their jobs, but none she interviewed wanted to leave America. They simply wanted America to more closely resemble the

America that had been in their dreams when they came over on the big ships. They walked off the job not because they were unpatriotic, but because they *were* patriotic. You have to love something to fight for it. The time was ripe. It was time to strike. They were ready.

By high noon, it was blistering hot. At each stop, the miners who emerged were dirtier than the ones at the previous mine. Their faces were stained with red earth and black smoke. The above-ground miners were especially exhausted, working in the burdensome heat. They heard the band before they saw the procession, put their shovels down, wiped their brows with their handkerchiefs, and stood waiting when the march arrived. They quietly lined up in the parade, greeted with hearty pats on the backs, handshakes. At each mine, Katka reached into the back of the buggy and distributed soda pop bottles to the new additions. She continued her interviews while Lily drove the buggy. The baby lay next to her, sleeping and sweating in a wooden crate.

They marched all of June 6 and most of June 7. The parade stopped twenty-seven times, ending at the Hull-Rust mine in Hibbing, seventy-five miles from Biwabik, before turning back home. During the entire march, there had not been a single act of violence or aggression. Perhaps the old Polish man was wrong, Katka thought.

In the days that followed, marches and rallies continued on a smaller scale. Individual Range towns held protests and parades of their own. In Hibbing and some of the western Mesabi Range towns, strikers moved onto the Cuyuna Range. By the end of the first week, Katka published the first edition of *Striker's News*. The headline read: *Every Worker's a Striker: 20,000 Walk Off Job in Grand Show of Solidarity.* The paper was sold for five cents. Within two days her paper had raised $780: sixty dollars for printing expenses and the rest for the Strikers Relief Fund.

CHAPTER 35

KATKA KEPT CLOSE TABS ON THE GOINGS-ON IN town. If she couldn't be present to witness an event herself, she interviewed people who had. And Paul was a great source of information. There was no shortage of news.

In the second week of the walkout, the first trainload of forty replacement workers arrived from Duluth. They arrived not in Biwabik but in Virginia, a town twelve miles away, in the cover of darkness. They disembarked quietly and were greeted by Mr. Augustine Stone, several company bosses, the sheriff, and the deputies from eight different towns. Sheriff Turner kept his hand on his gun and looked around for strike leaders. He saw none. It was 2 a.m.

As the men, thin and hungry, walked off the platform and assembled, they were each given ten dollars in coins. "You will earn five dollars per day, paid at the end of the week," Mr. Stone said. "We have purchased work clothes for you, and they are waiting for you at Mrs. Johanson's boardinghouse. Her house is clean and less than a mile from the mine. She is a great cook, and all eats will be provided. We will escort you to the mine in motorcars each day so you will be safe. There will be no need for you to walk. You will work eight hours per day with twenty minutes for lunch." Mr. Stone looked around nervously. "We best be going."

"Mr. Stone," one of the men said. "We been talking on the train. We want to be paid daily, not weekly."

"Ain't gonna happen," Stone said. "Let's get a move on." They walked from the train depot to the boardinghouse. The armed deputies and mine bosses flanked the group, which arrived safely at the house. Mrs. Johanson, a large Scandinavian woman whose husband had forgotten to send for her when he went to find alternative work in Minneapolis, had laid out meat and cheeses on her kitchen table. The food had been paid for from the healthy stipend the mining company gave her. The men ate voraciously and were shown to their rooms. Deputy Baker, who lived near the boardinghouse, would keep watch outside. Mrs. Johanson gave him a thermos of hot coffee and some pastries.

The deputies and company bosses shook hands with the men and then went home to their various towns. Mr. Stone and Sheriff Turner, who both lived in Biwabik, took Turner's motorcar.

"Want to stop at Vince's for a tumble with Leppe?" Turner said.

"Not tonight," Stone said. "We may have avoided a ruckus tonight, but I expect we'll see something grand tomorrow when we bust those men through the picket line. I want to be rested."

***

At four o'clock in the morning, forty-eight bullets were fired into Mrs. Johanson's brick boardinghouse. She and her boarders awoke with a terrified start. None of the bullets hit a window, and no one was hurt, but the sound was deafening. The men scrambled to put their clothes on. There was chaotic yelling and stumbling about.

"Madness!" Mrs. Johanson screamed. "Madness!" She put on her bonnet and ran outside. The bullets stopped. She screamed for the deputy. "Deputy Baker! Get me out of here. They're trying to kill me!"

Deputy Baker called out to her. "My motorcar is around the bend. I'll take you to your cousin Ida's." They left.

Within minutes, four buggies pulled up. Armed miners, who had been hiding in the bushes and trees surrounding the boardinghouse, approached. One of the armed men was Paul Schmidt.

"Scabs!" he yelled to the men holed up inside. He crept forward until he was close to the window. Then he spoke loudly, but calmly.

"We could have fired in the windows. We didn't. We wish no harm to you. I know you. I have known you for years. You are hungry, yes? You are tired, yes? You have mouths to feed and no means. Your woman is disappointed in you, perhaps? You are pushed to the edge. I am right, yes?

"See these men surrounding this house? It is dark, so most likely not. There are fifty-two of us, in case you are wondering. They are hungry too. They want to be treated like men, and they are making sacrifices for that. They got babies too. Women they love. They are good men and don't wish you a lick of trouble. My men, see, they wouldn't start nothing. But once it's started, well, what kind of man would let another man take something away from him without fighting back? No man."

"You tell it true, Paul," one of the men yelled.

Paul continued to address the laborers hiding in Mrs. Johanson's boarding house. "That's precisely what you are doing, see? Taking something that ain't yours. Something that belongs to these men—their jobs. And we won't stand for that, will we, boys? We don't want to hurt you. We just want you to leave. What have you got to lose? You have coins in your pocket and food in your bellies," Paul said.

Silence.

"We will wait," Paul said. "We do not wish to harm men from the working class."

The door opened. The men filed out, heads down, and got into the buggies. The drivers passed the men some whiskey and left for the station. When they arrived at the depot, a train was waiting. Paul tipped his hat to the conductor as the laborers piled in.

The next day, when the motorcade arrived to take the laborers to the mine, they found Mrs. Johanson's boardinghouse deserted. Stone went immediately to Deputy Baker's house. After getting no response to his vigorous knocking, he kicked the door down. The house was a mess. It was clear that Deputy Baker's family had packed up as many belongings as possible and left in the middle of the night and fled.

CHAPTER 36

T HE STRIKE COMMITTEE WAS ASSEMBLED IN THE
underground bunker.

"We lost Deputy Baker," Andre announced. "Cleared out in the night without a trace. Took his family with him."

"What do you mean 'we' lost him?" Katka asked. "He was on our side?"

"As much as he could have been."

"I don't envy him his position," Paul said. "Let's hope he got far enough away that they'll never find him."

"He might have a chance," Sam Scarlett said. "Not much has happened here yet. It's only been sixteen days."

"Sixteen days seems like three years," Adeline said. "Isn't there anything else we can do?"

The Iron Range strike committee, with approval from the IWW, had sent and resent the strike demands, but the company would not respond, telling the newspapers it had no plans to negotiate.

"Is anyone wavering?" Sam Scarlett asked.

"No one I know of," Milo said.

"Send some spies," Scarlett insisted. "Feel it out. It is imperative that if any man is considering crossing the line, we stop him. Find a few guys from each nationality. Have them feel out their people. Find out if anyone is considering crossing."

"In the meantime, Mr. Scarlett," Adeline said, "I think we need to do something more than wait for your headquarter men to pay attention to us. Townsfolk, they all be starting to wonder if you know what you're doing. Don't take this the wrong way, but most of us here thought this strike be over by now and our mensfolk wouldn't miss no more than one paycheck."

"We're doing what we can, Mrs. Sherek."

"Ain't enough, sir."

"What do you propose we do?"

"When the president of the United States doesn't like something, he declares war. I suggest we follow his lead."

"You want us to declare war on U.S. Steel?"

"Yes, sir."

The rest of the group negotiated the wording of their declaration of war:

> *War has been declared against the Steel Trust and independent mining companies of Minnesota by the Industrial Workers of the World. The iron miners are mustering. Twenty thousand have left the mines and pits. The steam shovels are idle. The drills are silent ... these barehanded miners, driven to desperation, have declared industrial war against the United States Steel Corporation.*

Milo delivered the declaration to the home of Mr. Augustine Stone. It was June 18, 1916.

CHAPTER 37

KATKA CAME BARRELING INTO THE HOUSE WITH her empty egg basket. She had just come from town, where she sold all her eggs to Helen Cerkvenik from the mercantile.

"Lily, something terrible has happened," she said.

Lily was peeling potatoes while rocking baby Gregor's cradle with her foot. Anton sat across from her reading the latest edition of *Strikers News* and drinking coffee. When he saw her face, he put the paper down.

"What is it?" Anton said.

"The stores in town. They have been forbidden to extend credit to the striking miners."

"By who?"

"The town council. They told Helen they would revoke her license to sell dry goods if she extended a single more penny of credit to a striker."

"They are going to try to starve them back to work," Anton said. "The scab laborers they brought in were scared off by the parades and crowds. The company hasn't made a dime in three weeks."

"Neither have the workers! They're starving already!"

"Inhuman, I tell you," Anton said.

"So what are you going to do about it?" Lily asked.

"What am I going to do about it? Nothing. I don't get mixed up in politicals."

"Of course you don't," Lily said.

The next morning Anton was awake before sunup. Katka packed him a hearty lunch and filled his canteen. Lily, wrapped in a shawl, stood outside and watched as her husband hitched Bruno and another horse to his cart.

"All set," he said. "Back by nightfall tomorrow, I should be. If it doesn't rain. Don't be sneaking off with any lumberjacks while I'm away, you hear, my precious flower?"

"Oh, I hear you," Lily said. "Don't you fall in love with one of those trollop dock walkers. I hear they all have shriveled-up woman parts filled with worms. If you lay with one of them, you'll get syphilis, and your nose will fall off one clump at a time. Like this: Plop! Clunk. Plop. Within a week, you will have a hole in your face. From that hole, blood and pustules will seep down. Your own son won't be able to bear the sight of you, and I will be forced to marry a rich banker who is fit to please me in ways you only dreamed of."

"Good God, woman! Every time I go to Duluth, you mention that, Lily. Do you need to mention that every time? Every blasted time?"

She stepped up to the buggy and kissed her husband. "Be safe," she said. And he was off down the Vermilion Trail toward the big port.

When Anton came back the next day, his cart was loaded with crates of food. He stopped his horse next to the tavern door. Samo, Dusca, and Old Joe came out to help him unload.

"Where do you want these?" Samo asked.

"Load 'em up behind the bar, I say. Lily and Katka can get it all organized once it's there."

Katka and Lily were already behind the bar. In fact, they'd been there for about an hour, removing bottles and wiping down shelves. When the crates came in, they began to unload the wares: Sugar. Salt. Rice. Canned beans. Flour. Coffee. Yeast. They carefully organized the shelves, then replaced the bottles of spirits in front of the food items.

"Tomorrow we'll go into town, first thing in the morning," Lily said. "We'll go see Mrs. Sherek. She can find out who has the greatest need and take orders."

"What if the company discovers we are selling food on credit? Won't they shut down the Slovenski Dom?"

"They probably would if they found out, but they won't. I got it all worked out. I found us a delivery man who won't reveal our identity."

"Who?"

"Andy. The soda pop distributor. He travels all around the Range anyway. No one will think anything of it."

"You are grand, *Teta* Lily. Truly, you are."

***

Later that night, Anton asked Lily and Katka to join him outside. "Ten minutes, I think," he said. "Thereabouts. We'll have a beer and enjoy the night that is so lovely."

"But Gregor's asleep."

"Bring him in that old country contraption."

Lily gently put the sleeping infant in a cloth sling that swung from her neck. Then the two women put on their bonnets to protect their ears from mosquitoes, grabbed ales from the tavern, and walked toward the wooden table in the backyard. The night was dark and moonless. They stumbled a little in the dark until their eyes adjusted and they could see. Anton was already there, and when he heard them, he lit a small candle.

Katka could see that Anton was not alone. Paul was there too. He stood up, grabbed Katka's hand, and kissed it.

"Paul!" She jumped into his arms. He swung her around in a little circle and kissed her.

"You don't greet me like that," Anton said to Lily. "How come not?"

"Mostly it's your smell. Too many beans."

The air was soft and romantic. A slight breeze was rustling through the trees. Anton gestured for the ladies to sit.

"I have news."

"Are you with child?" Katka asked.

Anton laughed wanly. "I wish it were that. But this is no time for the jokes. I'll tell you what I know because I don't want you to be ignorant. Then Paul and I must move on and tell others."

Anton had seen something in Duluth when he had gone to get supplies. Something disturbing. He had already told Paul and most of the Wobbly men. The organizers planned to meet the next morning in the underground bunker. But in the meantime, they were telling as many people as possible, knowing that word would spread fast.

"Just tell us what you saw, for the love of Mary," Lily said. "This isn't a gothic romance novel."

"No. Ain't nothing romantic about it." Anton slapped a mosquito. "So on my way to get the supplies, see, I drove past the prison. Who you think I seen standing outside, talking to some man in a uniform?"

Neither woman wagered to guess.

"Sheriff Turner, that who."

"What was he doing there?" Lily asked.

"That was my question. I figure there weren't much chance in me finding out by asking him, being as we ain't exactly kissing cousins, see. So I looked around for the first saloon I could find. I went inside and ordered myself a pint. I started talking to the owner of the saloon. As I figured, the guards come in his place real regular. Saloonkeeper knew everything going on at the prison. He knew who Sheriff Turner was too. Said he and Mr. Stone had been by a few times in the past week or so, and they were making a deal with the warden."

"What kind of deal?" Katka asked.

"Mr. Stone bought himself some men. They should be arriving up here within the week."

"Men to work the mines? Scab laborers?"

"That's what I thought. But the saloon owner, he said no. They already got scabs coming in from Minneapolis. It's all arranged. Said he heard that Turner and Stone were not looking for miners. They were looking for deputies."

"Deputies?" Lily asked. "From the prisons? You must be plum outta your mind, Anton."

"They plan to release some of the prisoners—those who know how to wield a pistol—and hire them as company guards. The prisoners get a small stipend, and the warden gets a big one."

"They already got mine guards to watch the company property. They need more?"

Anton shot Paul a look. "Don't shield Katka, Paul. They need to be prepared. Tell her what you know."

"I've seen it before, Kat. Probably a brute force squad. The sheriff will deputize the criminals. They'll each get a badge and the powers that come with it. They'll be able to issue warrants, make arrests, God only knows what else."

No one spoke for a while. They could hear the frogs in the pond a ways off. The creatures sang to each other as they did most nights in the early summer. Baby Gregor began to fuss in his sling; Lily took a sip of her beer, then lifted him out of the sling and put the baby on her shoulder, patting his back and crooning.

"Give him to me," Anton said. He took the child from his wife and held him high in the air in front of him, arms out-stretched. "Look how alert he is. His eyes are wide open."

"Be careful," Lily said. "His head isn't strong enough for that."

"He's stronger than you think," Anton said. "See? He stopped the noisemaking."

"You terrified him into silence."

"Do you think they'll terrify us into silence?" Katka asked. "This brute force squad?"

Anton gave the baby back to Lily. "We have to be ready for them. Don't let anyone know about the food stash. If they find out what we've got, we'll be a target for certain. I've already talked to Andy. He won't tell a soul. He's a good man, he is."

"And a smart man," Lily said. "He told me what you're pay-ing him to deliver the food supplies."

"You expected him to do it for nothing, you did?"

"Nah. But I expect the strike committee to pay his delivery fees, not us. We're getting thin, Anton."

"Not compared to most, Lily."

"We have a family now. It's not just you and me living off the land anymore."

"At least you have land, cousin," Paul said. He spoke softly, addressing his words to Lily. "These miners ain't got nothing. And when these thugs arrive from Duluth, life here, it's going to get even worse. Even the strongest of men will be tempted to give it all up. The least we can do is put a biscuit in their stomachs."

"Yes, I suppose you are right."

"I am right. Do you understand what is happening here? This is big. Much bigger than your family and the families in Biwabik. This is the largest unified labor resistance in the his-tory of our country. And who is behind it? Immigrants like me and Katka and your husband. Like all your boarders. Men who know nothing about this country except that all things were supposed to be possible for all people. But that promise hasn't come true for any of them.

"They get here, and they are told that their skin is too dark. Their accents are too thick. That they can work like animals. That they are animals. But still, they don't stop believing; it makes them believe it more. That promise is all they have. And they will do whatever they can to make it come true. And five hundred armed thugs aren't going to stop them. There's nothing more dangerous, or more hopeful, than a man who has nothing to lose."

"What good is hope if you're dead?" Katka asked. "Armed prisoners wearing badges, running around our town? No. We have to stop this. Where are the lawmen? Are there not laws in this country? How can they make prisoners deputies? Who will protect *us*? The people who live here? Who will keep *us* safe?"

"There are laws in this country, but they are not always our friend. The same laws that protect the rich oppress the poor. If this strike is successful, we can change that. For ourselves, maybe, but for our children, definitely. Write about that in *Strikers News*. When these men come, we must be ready to protect ourselves. We must stand strong and stand together. There are hundreds of them, but there are thousands of us. Write about that."

"Your hothead cousin is correct," Anton said, gesturing toward Paul. "For once."

Paul whispered something in Katka's ear. They stood and walked from the table. Away from the candlelight, Paul pulled her toward him and kissed her.

"This is bad, Kat. Fearsome bad. All around us, the world, it is falling to pieces as I have seen in so many places, so many times. Mr. Stone, he is rotten to the core. And the sheriff. I think he is capable of unspeakable things. And these men coming. Worse, I tell you. Bad, bad, bad."

"Oh, Paul," Kat said.

"Shh...let me finish. There are hurtful things everywhere. Injustice. Hunger. Pain. I have seen this for years. But I see these things more clearly because you are in my life. I look at the world, and I am inspired in ways I never was before. I want to fix the world so you, when you open your eyes, you will see the world you deserve.

"At the same time—now this is the fanciful part—I see things less clearly because you are in my life. Some days all I can think of is how, on hot days, your hair curls up in these little damp ringlets around your neck. Or how soft the skin is on the inside of your wrist. In spite of all the bad and everything that might happen tomorrow, that probably will happen, the world is a wonder. It is hopeful and somehow good. I am full of contradictions, and I do not care."

He kissed her. They barely noticed the mosquitoes.

"I love you," Katka said. "When you arrived on my doorstep, I knew my life had changed forever. I would have followed you anywhere."

"I won't let anything happen to you."

"The worst thing that could happen to me would be for something to happen to you," Katka said. She fingered the scar on his cheek. "Be careful. You and danger seem to find each other even on the calmest of nights."

"The mark you have left on me, Katka, is deeper than any scar. I will be careful for you."

"But now you must go?"

He nodded. She looked toward the house and saw Lily and the baby. Lily was holding the candle, waiting for Katka to walk back to the house with her. "My chaperone awaits."

Paul left with Anton to warn others about the "deputies" who would be arriving soon. At each stop, they assured the men to whom they spoke that the Wobblies would come up with a plan during their meeting the following afternoon.

But it was too late. As Paul kissed Katka, the first trainload of criminals was unloading at Mesabi station. The men were ordered to walk straight to the boardinghouses where they were being lodged. Most, however, got lost along the way and ended up at Vince Torelli's boardinghouse.

As the men entered the tavern, Leppe, Brina, and the other sporting girls knew immediately that their lives had just turned from grim to worse. Brina walked straight to Vince, who was pouring vodka into a glass behind the bar.

"You best call the law, Vince. I ain't never seen a sort looking this unwholesome before. Call the law, or I'm out. Maria, too."

Vince laughed. "Call the law? Got news for you, doll face. The law hath arrived. And you ain't going nowhere but where I tell you to go." He handed her the vodka he had just poured. "I suggest you drink up. Gonna be a long night."

CHAPTER 38

TWO DAYS PASSED. IN THOSE FORTY-EIGHT HOURS, the recruited company guards had made their presence known in town. They stayed up late into the night drinking whiskey and occasionally getting into fights with each other. They wandered the streets of town, popping in and out of taverns. A few of them walked up to Merritt Lake, past the Slovenski Dom, to swim. They could perform no legal duties until they were deputized, so their first few days were like a paid vacation.

The strikers walked the picket lines in shifts from 6 a.m. until 9 p.m. Each mine had its own revolving circle of men holding protest signs. The women came to deliver lunches and refreshments. Sometimes the women with older children stayed and sang or chanted slogans with their husbands. But the wives with young children had too many chores to finish, and most only lingered long enough to exchange food and quick greetings. Because the company deputies were still not authorized to work, the strikers outnumbered the guards by at least thirty to one at every mine. There had been no violence.

At night, the strikers met secretly to plan. The groups that could not speak English met at boardinghouses in the middle of the night. Other larger gatherings assembled in the forest.

The deputizing ceremony was slated to begin at 8 a.m. on June 21 in Biwabik. Katka was there on time, but she noted that

only a handful of the new arrivals showed up. The rest meandered over to the courthouse closer to 10 a.m. Some obviously
hadn't slept yet. Many were still drunk from the night before.
They laid about the grass of the courthouse lawn, some snoring
loudly. None seemed in a hurry to start the job they'd been
hired to do, especially since they knew so little about it.

Finally, at 10:30 a.m., Mr. Augustine Stone, owner of the
Oliver, and Sheriff Turner came out onto the lawn. The sheriff
handed each man a shiny five-point badge. He looked at his
new deputies with disdain. They were a mangy lot. How many
of these men had he arrested previously?

The sheriff looked about at the crowd, as if taking inventory
of which labor leaders and strikers had shown up. Andre the
Bulgarian was not there. Milo was nowhere to be seen. Sam
Scarlett was there, standing by himself near the regal steps
leading to the front door. Paul was there too, holding his Luger,
standing protectively next to Katka, who was vigilantly taking
notes. Adeline Sherek and Helen Cerkvenik stood across the
street with a group of women outside the mercantile. A few
businessmen were there with their wives, and several children
hung in the perimeter. Harris Maki was present, his buggy
parked on Main Street. Andy, the soda pop distributor, had
been there since early morning. It was the hottest summer anyone could remember, and Andy was doing well. He had already sold more than five hundred bottles to the new deputies.

The sheriff motioned for the men to rise. Katka watched as
the recruited men raised their right hands and swore to be
stewards of justice. More than a few men laughed as they did
so; the irony was lost on no one. After they had received their
badges and had taken their oath, the men came up, one by one,
and were issued weapons. A few men fired shots into the air.

"Stop!" the sheriff yelled. "None of that. We can send you
back where you came from and don't you forget it! Do not fire
without cause. Do not discharge your weapons unless

provoked. This is a town. There are children living here! Which one of you hoodlums wants to go back to jail?"

No one spoke.

"Do as I say. I assure you, you'll have plenty of action if you're patient. You can fire your weapon anytime you see a striker committing a crime. As for crime..." The sheriff took a document out of his pocket and read from it. "'It is hereby declared a crime for union miners to gather in groups of four or more.' Did you all hear that? It is against the law for union miners to gather in groups of four or more!" The deputies looked around at the miners and townspeople who had assembled. There were groups of women, but no men in groups greater than three, except in Harris Maki's cart. But they were old men, not union miners.

"You were right about that," Katka whispered to Paul.

"They make that rule during every major strike," Paul said. "It's good we were prepared. I've seen men gunned down within seconds of the declaration." The deputies scanned the crowd again, some registering obvious disappointment at the lack of disregard for the new law.

Sam Scarlett stepped forward and addressed the sheriff loudly. "None of us here would be stupid enough to violate the decree made by a lawman like yourself, Sheriff Turner," he said sarcastically. "But what about the townsfolk who are not present? Been my experience that the law needs to be made known before a man can knowingly break it, ain't that right? Just how do you plan to make that law known, Sheriff?"

The sheriff held the document high in the air. "Law's written out plain as my face. Before high noon, fliers with the new law will be everywhere across the Range. There'll be no excuses. Ignorance of the law is no excuse for breaking it."

"When does this law restricting the right to assemble take effect?" Scarlett asked. He spoke deliberately, loud enough for even the women at the mercantile to hear.

"The minute a man hears my voice describing the decree or reads the flier, I reckon."

"When do you suspect the miners in Virginia will see this flier?"

"As soon as this ceremony is over, we'll be dispatching some of the deputies west and some to the east. Our own Moose Jackson will be leading a team on horseback to Virginia."

Katka looked over at Moose Jackson. Of course they had recruited him. She wondered who had taken over as bouncer at Vince Torelli's.

The sheriff continued, "They should be there within a few hours. The law will take effect when they distribute the fliers."

Paul took his watch out of his pocket and glanced at it. "They should be safe," he whispered to Katka.

"Let's hope."

The sheriff continued speaking to his new deputies. "There are other crimes committed by the miners here. The strikers have officially declared war on the Oliver Mining Company, a subsidiary of U.S. Steel. As you all know, there's a war going on overseas. Even if we ain't officially in it, there's a lot of weapons to be made and sold. Miners and steel workers are considered 'essential workers.' Gov. Burnquist has authorized us to do everything in our power to get these men to return to work and help get American steel overseas. 'Men who refuse to help America in these turbulent times will be considered traitors and can receive sentences of up to twenty years in prison.'"

Everyone began talking at once. Seeing what a stir the declaration caused, the sheriff read it again. Katka wrote furiously in her notebook. English speakers translated as best they could to the non-English speakers.

"We can arrest men who don't go back to work?" one of the new deputies asked.

"You can, but we'd rather you *convince* them than arrest them," Stone said. "Your job is to help them make the right decision. We wish to give all the workers a chance to return to their jobs. We do not wish for any of our workers to go to jail. We want no person harmed. We will give them three days. Although America is not currently at war, we are supporting the British in any way we can. Steel has never been more valuable or necessary. Helping the war effort is patriotic."

People in the crowd began to yell. Many had come here to escape war. No one wanted to get involved in a war if they didn't understand the reasons.

"It is our duty as human beings to avoid war when we can," Adeline Sherek yelled. "Why fight the Germans? The British threatened our merchant ships too. This war is about money. Money for the master class. We don't want money for the master class. We want to fill our children's stomachs! We want chicken in our soup!"

"Chicken in our soup! Chicken in our soup!" The crowd started chanting in several languages. As the fervor gained momentum, the people instinctively drew closer to each other.

"Stand back!" Paul yelled in Slovenian as he saw two older men walk toward two younger men. "No groups of four or more men. Do not give them reason to fire!"

The men moved back. The crowd kept its distance, but kept shouting.

Mr. Augustine Stone held up his hand and addressed the midwife directly. "Let me remind you, Mrs. Sherek, that we have jails for womenfolk too. You are lucky we are kind enough to give you three days to learn the new law of the land."

"I do not thank you," she said. "I spit on your laws."

"Arrest her!" Stone said. Three deputies quickly pounced on her. Helen Cerkvenik and Ava Nurmi held fast to her.

"Stop this! Release her!" Sam Scarlett screamed as townsfolk ran to her defense. "Do you wish to have violence within moments of your decree? Do you think you will persuade the workers to return to your slave caves if you arrest this woman here and now?"

"Arrest me!" Mrs. Sherek cried. "I would rather spend twenty years in prison than a lifetime with no hope for my children!"

Katka moved toward the steps, notebook in hand. "Mr. Stone," she said. "I am recording everything that happens here. Within twenty-four hours, every word I write will be translated into thirty languages. Show some mercy, and I will record that as well. I only write the truth."

Stone stared at her. "Who are you?"

"My name is Maria. I write for *The Iron Range Ladies Journal*."

"No one takes seriously a women's magazine. Who would read the writings of a girl, except silly girls like yourself, who cannot even vote? You are made to give men pleasure and babies milk."

"It's possible that *you* will not read what I write, sir. But you will be the only one who doesn't." Katka's voice was even, strong. Her gaze was steadfast. Although Stone was twice her size and armed, she was not afraid.

Stone laughed loudly, as if he found Katka's words hilarious.

"Let Mrs. Sherek go," Katka said. "If not out of common decency, then for the sake of your own reputation."

Stone considered her words for a moment, then gestured wildly. "Fine. Free the midwife. She's hardly worth our energy!" The deputies took their hands off Adeline Sherek. "This ceremony is ended. Deputies, pick up your fliers. No arrests for three days. You will travel from town to town putting up fliers announcing the ban on assemblies, parades, protests, and the consequences of disobeying the governor's edict to return to work. Sheriff Turner and his First Council will take care of everything."

Mr. Stone stormed off to his motorcar. The townspeople stayed glued to their spots. They watched as the sheriff summoned his "First Council." They were not from the prisons. They were from Biwabik and the neighboring towns. Katka recognized a few of the men, all of them large in stature. The tallest man appointed to the First Council was former bouncer Moose Jackson. Katka had never spoken to him, but she knew who he was. He was the man who had beaten Milo to a bloody pulp before he had come to live with Anton and Lily. Now this man would be in charge of the deputies who would patrol Biwabik and the mining towns surrounding it. She drew a quick sketch of him. As she drew, Moose Jackson caught her looking at him and smiled. Then he grabbed his crotch and squeezed it, raising his eyebrows up and down.

It began to rain, a fast downpour of giant droplets. Katka's clothes were soaked in moments. People scattered across the street and took shelter under the building awnings.

Then, as quickly as it came, the rain stopped. Katka shivered. Even when Paul put his arm around her, she could not shake the chill. She knew with absolute certainty that her life was about to change.

CHAPTER 39

WHILE THE HUNG-OVER CRIMINALS WERE BEING deputized in Biwabik, approximately two thousand workers were lining up in Virginia for a rally and strike parade. It had not rained a drop there, although it was humid and overcast. Milo, Andre, Carlo Tresca, and Johan Koski spoke. Each organizer did his best to convince the strikers that the union understood their needs and had a plan for meeting them.

Johan Koski, using a bullhorn supplied by the Wobbly organizers, spoke first in English, then in Finnish. "We know the businesses around here, they been told not extend credit to strikers. We know that you are hungry. The Finns in my community have set up co-operative grocery stores. You can exchange food and services there to get you by. If you have nothing to exchange, tell someone at the co-op, and other arrangements will be made."

Milo spoke in Slovenian and English. "We must keep our numbers high at the picket line. I know. It is not easy to see our old friends cross the line and get a paycheck that is two times higher than what it would be if we weren't striking. They are benefitting from our sacrifice, and that is not fair. But so it goes. When workers unite, when they form under the big union, the companies all a sudden find gold coins in their pockets. All a sudden they can pay the wages they said they couldn't afford. When ordinary workers like us band together, workers everywhere, even workers not in a union, reap the rewards. I hear our strike is in the newspaper all the way in the East, in Michigan, in Ohio, in West Virginia. The companies there are giving in to worker demands because they are afeard their workers will form unions and strike like we are doing. We are hungry, yes. Now. Here. But we are heroes everywhere."

Carlo Tresca spoke in Italian and English. He explained what he imagined was going on in Biwabik with the deputizing of criminals. He explained that this was common practice and the thugs would be used to terrorize the workers. "We will form our own force," he said, "to police your neighborhoods and protect our workers from harm. We do not have enough guns, but we expect to get some sent here in the next weeks. Big Bill Haywood himself from the IWW promised, and he is a man of his word. We have already set up a network who are informing us of company plans. If you hear anything, you must tell a strike leader immediately. It is possible that the brute deputies will arrive today to disrupt this rally. If they try to give you a flier, do not take it. If they speak to you, you cannot understand them. Understood?"

Andre spoke last. He explained how the company planned to make the workers look unpatriotic. "By fighting for our own equality and justice and dignity, we are honoring the spirit of America," he said. "We do not want to fight the flag; we don't want to fight anyone. Be peaceful, brothers. Do not make much noise. Let the mining companies be the ones to incite disorder. Keep your hands in your pockets and shame the company!"

They lined up, four abreast. Men took turns carrying a banner that read "One Big Union." Some of the men carried red flags. Although most of the socialist miners were in the union, not all union members were socialists. For them, the red banners were a symbol of the blood they had spilled in the mines. Blood they hoped to never spill again. The band played "Solidarity Forever." They marched through the streets of Virginia to the Alpena mine. The men walking the picket line cheered. The parade marched back into town down Second Avenue. When they got to Seventh Street, they discovered they could not cross. They stopped and stood in silence looking at what lay before them. Forty-four newly deputized lawmen wearing shiny badges and dirty clothes sat atop their horses, smiling smugly. Each deputy held a stack of fliers.

Paul and Katka had left Biwabik for Virginia at the same time as the deputies. Because they had taken the train, they arrived first. They stood under the awning of Oleson's Bar with several other patrons.

Moose Jackson was positioned in the middle of the deputies, his gigantic frame perched on a strong gelding. He looked incredibly pleased with his new position of power. He began to yell. "My men will be distributing a pamphlet that you all must read!" The criminals-turned-deputies approached the men, shoving fliers toward their faces. Moose began to read the same document that the sheriff had read earlier regarding the governor's edict. He stumbled over the word "insubordination." He skipped it and moved on to "disloyalty, mutiny (which he pronounced as mutt-in-nye)...or refusal of duty in the military...or shall willfully ob...obstruct...shall face up to twenty years in prison." He was so intent on trying to read and pronounce the words on his pamphlet that he paid no attention to the assembly before him.

"Moose!" one of the deputies yelled. "These son of a bitches are all fresh off the boat. Not a one will take a flier. They can't read or speak a lick of English. Look at this." He pushed a flier toward Milo. Milo put his hands in his pocket and kept his eyes on his shoes.

Moose Jackson looked at Milo, as if trying to place him. His forehead crinkled and then eased as he recognized Milo as someone he had once punched. He responded to the deputy. "They're faking it. Force the immigrant slime to take 'em." Each striker stood his ground. The fliers flittered off the men's chests onto the street. It was still humid, and the air was stagnant.

"How about this?" Moose said. "I got a new law to deliver. It ain't okay for you men to have your little parades anymore. As of this morning, they is against the law. This law be different from the other one, the one that says we can arrest you for not working. That one don't take effect for three days. But this one, it takes effect right now. Sheriff Turner decreed it this morning. No more than three union men can assemble together in a group on public property. And what do I see here? One, two, three, four. Four, right there in the front row. Four more behind them. And four across as far back as I can see. Now, do we need to arrest you boys, or are you going to split up and go back home?"

Milo took a step forward. "Vidmar!" he hollered to the conductor of the band. "Start playing!" The band began to play, and the men sang "Pie in the Sky." As they sang, they inched forward and surrounded the riderless horses. The deputies on the ground were befuddled.

"What do we do now, Big Man?" one of the deputies asked.

"This." Moose Jackson, who was still perched on his horse, grabbed his rifle, which had been slung casually over his shoulder.

He fired one shot into the air, and all the strikers stopped. It was silent. Then Milo, in the strong voice he inherited from his father the musician, broke the tension with his song. "Solidarity forever...solidarity forever...solidarity forever, the union makes us strong!"

Moose Jackson aimed his gun directly at Milo's head. He fired, slightly off his target, and a bullet grazed Milo's jaw. Milo fell to the ground, hand on face.

"Disperse! Disperse!" Carlo Tresca yelled.

"Get out of here!" Andre screamed to the strikers. "Do not fight back! Do not retaliate!"

The deputies were excited now. They fired over thirty shots, mostly into the air, some into the crowd. The miners ran, and all but three, including Milo, escaped on foot.

Paul and Katka rushed over to Milo, who was being held up by Johan Koski.

"You okay, Milo?" Carlo Tresca asked.

"Looks like a surface wound," Koski said. "Check the others."

Tresca and Andre moved over to help the other men.

Katka stooped down. "Oh, Milo. Are you all right, really?" She looked at his jaw, where he had been shot. It was not bad. But Milo had a gruesome expression on his face. She turned to Paul. "Go find Dr. Andrea Hall. Tell her three miners have been shot."

"I need..." Milo coughed. Blood came out of his mouth and mixed with the blood on his jaw. Katka took her scarf off her head and dabbed at his mouth.

"A doctor? Paul just went to get one. You'll be right as rain in no time."

"No..." Milo said. "No doctor. I need a...priest." He gestured toward his abdomen.

Katka and Johan Koski exchanged glances. Katka opened Milo's jacket. Blood spilled out like wine. He had been shot not once, but twice.

"Get a priest, Johan," Katka said.

Johan took off running.

She removed her apron, squeezed it into a ball, and pressed it into Milo's abdomen. "Shall I pray for you Milo?"

He nodded.

"In English or Slovenian?"

"Both," Milo said.

"Our Father who art in heaven," she began, "hallowed be thy name, *pridi k nam tvoje kraljestvo, zgodi se tvoja volja kakor v nebesih tako na zemlji.*"

"Katka," Milo interrupted. "Under the mattress in my room..." His voice was faltering. "I have money. Give it to...." He whispered a woman's name in her ear.

The other men who had been shot were not injured critically, although one of the victims could not walk. Andre stayed with him.

Carlo Tresca ran back to Milo. "I sent for the doctor," he said.

"Dr. Foley?" Katka asked.

"Yeah."

"He won't come. He's on contract for the Oliver Mining Company. I sent Paul to find Dr. Hall. She'll come."

"Priest..." Milo said again.

"Don't worry. Johan went to get him. Our Lady of Peace is one block away." Katka continued to pray and hold his wound with her hand while Tresca looked on.

"Here's the father now," Tresca said.

The priest was running. Clumsily, nervously, his robe flapping awkwardly about his fat body. Johan Koski was running too, directly behind the priest. His hand was on the priest's back, as if pushing him forward. When they arrived, the priest bent over, wheezing asthmatically.

"Say the words," Johan Koski said. "This man was shot in cold blood. Give him the last words."

"Last rites," Katka corrected. The priest began to shake. "Soon, please, father."

"Father, forgive me..." Milo said.

"No," the priest said. His voice was as quiet as a child's and more timid.

It was then that Katka saw it. The gun. Johan Koski had not placed his hand on the priest's back. He had placed a gun on it. The priest had been forced here against his will.

"Father, please. We haven't much time," Katka begged.

"I'd like to help, but the company...our main benefactor. They said if I helped the strikers..." His voice evaporated. "I lose...everything."

"You are a man of God!" Tresca yelled. "He is a Catholic. Give this poor man the last rites!"

The priest said nothing.

"Shoot him," Tresca said.

"No." The voice came from Milo.

"You sure, Milo?" Johan asked. "I ain't Catholic."

"Neither is he," Katka said, gesturing to the priest. "Get out of here. And run like the coward you are."

The priest ran.

Milo coughed up more blood. "Sing."

"Sing? I'll sing anything, Milo. What shall I sing?"

"Sing about promise."

Katka began to sing in English. "My country 'tis of thee...sweet land of liberty..." The men joined in softly.

By the time the song was over, Paul had arrived with Dr. Hall. She pronounced Milo dead.

CHAPTER 40

LILY AND KATKA LAID OUT MILO'S BODY ON THE dining room table. They washed his wounds and dressed him in fresh white linen. As they worked, women came and went, bringing baskets of food. The men came and stayed, drinking in Anton's Slovenski Dom. The men were silent at first. Then they were boisterous, and songs filled the air long into the night. By 2 a.m. the fistfights began, and *Teta* Lily had had enough. She burst into the tavern and told the men to get the hell out.

"You heard her," Anton said. The men filed out of the bar.

When the last boarders had gone upstairs, Katka and Lily sat at the bar next to Paul.

"Serve us up," Lily said to Anton. "Vodka."

He poured four shots. They drank to Milo.

"Again."

They drank until the wee hours of the morning. When the sun came up, they were all sobbing.

CHAPTER 41

ALTHOUGH MILO HAD BEEN GUNNED DOWN IN broad daylight in front of thousands of eyewitnesses, no one was arrested. The armed deputies paraded through each town on the Iron Range, bragging about the murder and egging on strikers to confront them. No one did.

The next day, a Friday, there were no assemblies, no parades. Small groups of strikers turned up quietly at each mine. They picketed silently in shifts of three. No one dared to violate the anti-assembly law, not after what happened to Milo. The women came sporadically to deliver food and coffee at mealtimes. They, too, were eerily silent, exchanging nothing more than a nod or gesture with their men.

But at night in their homes, in their meeting places, or in the forests where the townspeople felt untouchable, their anger and sorrow over Milo's murder exploded like dynamite. Up until the moment Milo had been shot in cold blood, the townsfolk had mostly supported the strike, even if they did not necessarily trust the outsiders who helped organize the workers. But now, with the grim cruelty staring them in the face, the townspeople became more united than ever. It was clear that the company would use any means necessary to get them back to the slave caves. And they were not going back without a victory. Milo's death would not be in vain. The complacency displayed at the picket lines was just a stall tactic until they could come up with a plan.

In the field bunker, Katka and the strike force—now consisting of six members, not seven—met to plan Milo's funeral. A few of the Wobbly leaders from headquarters joined the local leaders, and the space was physically cramped and hot. The overwhelming sadness took up even more space than the bodies, making the field bunker seem all the more claustrophobic.

"Any luck?" Adeline asked Sam Scarlett.

"'Fraid not, ma'am. I sent men to every church from Ely to Grand Rapids. No priest is willing to risk offending the company by performing the Mass."

Katka wished Father Leo were here. He would have done it. "We can't wait any longer," Katka said. "With this heat...his body won't do well." And so they planned the funeral themselves. It would take place four days after the murder, on Monday, June 26, at the Socialist Opera Hall in Virginia.

By Saturday, the first throng of reporters arrived in Biwabik and the neighboring towns. It seemed to Katka that every newspaper in the country was now covering the story. Across the nation, thousands of ironworkers went on strike in a show of solidarity. Sentiments were changing worldwide in favor of the strikers.

Sheriff Turner and Mr. Augustine Stone decided to change the image of his deputized thugs. He made all of his newly sworn-in deputies get a shave. He instructed them to be on their best behavior. "Arrest no one. If anyone asks, remember to tell them that Milo Blatnik was a socialist anarchist who fired on U.S. deputies."

Katka expected a large crowd, but she never imagined that Milo's funeral would draw as many as it did. When she arrived early with Lily, baby Gregor, Anton, and the other boarders, the hall was already packed. They moved expediently to the front of the hall and slipped into the second row, which was reserved for immediate family. The Zalars were already there with their children. Paul was seated on the other side with Andre the Bulgarian, Carlo Tresca, and a few other organizers.

Katka caught his attention and gave him a stilted wave. He put his hand on his heart. She wished she could sit next to him. She wished he could hold her hand through this, keep her strong. But Paul insisted they keep their distance now, more than ever. Nothing was safe anymore.

Although the funeral was not set to begin for another forty-five minutes, Ana Zalar was crying. Leo had his arm around her. "There, there," he said. "Milo's in the good place now. He's with the Virgin. Don't let the children see you cry."

An hour later, the funeral began. Not only was the opera hall packed, but the streets surrounding the hall were filled. Katka heard later that more than three thousand people from all across the Range and the state had assembled to pay respects to Milo. There were the locals, of course, and the workers from the neighboring towns. But there were also union representatives and labor sympathizers from all across America. An entire shift of textile workers from Minneapolis had taken the train up north to attend the funeral.

Finally, Sam Scarlett rose to speak. The hall grew dead silent. Eventually that silence seeped into the streets. The heat had finally broken, and the sun was more forgiving to those who stood underneath her rays, unable to hear the funeral speeches. A breeze blew steadily through the crowd. Inside, Sam Scarlett's words ebbed and flowed like the tide.

"It was this simple, intelligent man," Katka heard him say, "Milo Blatnik, who began this strike. This one man united us all. An immigrant with an accent. Never forget that the efforts of one man with a yearning for justice can change the world. This one man, Milo Blatnik, had the courage to inspire thousands. He knew he deserved better, he knew you deserved better, and he was willing to do anything it took to make that happen. He gave his all to ensure the right to a decent wage with safe working conditions. What did he get in return? Two bullets. One in his jaw, the other in his gut."

Katka listened until Scarlett's words became background noise. Her mind drifted to other things. She remembered the little mouse that had lived in her cottage back in Slovenia. Did it starve to death when she left? Scarlett was a good man, but he didn't know Milo. He didn't know that Milo saw poetry in the woods or that he wrote songs in his head as means of coping with a job he hated. She thought about how Milo had taught her to shoot and how he had almost been her beau. She knew Milo hadn't come to this country to change the world. He had hoped that men would follow him when he walked out of the mine that day, but he didn't plan on being a revolutionary, not really. He had not considered that his actions would change the lives of twenty thousand men. She wondered how he would feel about becoming a martyr.

After the service, thousands of people joined the procession to Calvary Cemetery. Anna and Leo Zalar, who had been like parents to Milo when he first arrived, led the procession on foot. Behind them, Sam Scarlett carried the American flag. Two men carried a black banner with large white lettering: "Murdered by Oliver gunmen." Behind the banner, Anton, Katka, Lily, and baby Gregor walked with the boarders. Two beautiful stallions pulled the hearse with Milo's body. The Wob organizers and strike leaders blended in with the masses and walked behind the hearse. It was a clamorous parade of mourning.

At the cemetery, Carlo Tresca asked all present to take a solemn oath. "I ask you to swear before God and everyone here today that if any Oliver guards shoot or wound any miner, we will take a tooth for a tooth, an eye for an eye, a life for a life."

Katka looked around. Everyone, as far as she could see, had raised their hand. Everyone was repeating the words. Except for her. Except for Lily. Except for Anton.

Her eyes scanned the crowd. Moose Jackson was there, rifle slung across his shoulder, standing watch with the other company guards. She wanted to kill him. If she had seen him a moment earlier, she too might have raised her hand and taken the oath.

She kept scanning the crowd. She saw a woman, dressed in black, whom she had never seen before. The woman was silent, nearly motionless except for her fingers, which traveled slowly up and down her rosary beads. "Who is that, *Teta*?"

Lily turned and stared at the woman. "Her name is Brina. She's a sporting girl at Vince Torelli's."

So that's Brina, Katka thought. Brina, the name Milo had whispered into her ear only moments before he died. Brina, who saved Milo's life when he was left for dead after the pummeling by Moose Jackson. Katka had something to give her.

Later that night Katka went up to the room Milo had shared with three other boarders. She found the wad of cash that Milo had told her about, wrapped in parchment and stuffed in a book under his mattress. On the parchment, Milo had carefully written: "money for encyclopedias."

The next day Katka asked Samo, one of the boarders, to take the money to Vince Torelli's saloon and buy out Brina's contract with Milo's savings.

Two hours later Brina was on a train to Minneapolis to start a new life.

CHAPTER 42

THE DEPUTIZED FORCE OF CRIMINALS SHOWED restraint just long enough for the last out-of-town newspaperman to leave town.

Although they had all the rights of a U.S. deputy, their salaries and lodging were paid for by the Oliver Mining Company. Johan Koski tried to organize the businesses in town. "Do not sell anything to the Oliver guards," he said, and the business owners agreed. On the first day of the boycott, Timo from Timo and Simo's Bar and Sauna refused to serve two deputies. One took out his Luger and proceeded to shoot every bottle of alcohol in sight. With continued violence, eventually even the co-op buckled under the threats of the deputies and guards.

Two days after Milo's funeral, a group of strikers organized a parade in defiance of the group assembly law. They marched down the Main Street of Hibbing until the deputies fired shots, wounding but not killing protestors.

By the beginning of July, shootings, threats, and beatings were commonplace. People tried to walk in groups. If the deputies found a miner walking alone, they would confront him: "Go back to work, commie." If the miner replied, he was shot, usually in the foot. If he said nothing, he was beaten senseless.

Dr. Andrea Hall was one of the only doctors on the Range who openly treated injured miners. But her services were in such demand she couldn't keep up. She began a nurses training program and taught women how to tend to wounded strikers and townsfolk.

With no paychecks or credit, families relied more heavily on Anton's food supply. Mothers had no acceptable answer for children holding their stomachs and asking, "Mama, where's the food?"

Eventually a few miners began to cross the lines. Because the picketers could only assemble in groups of three or risk going to jail in violation of the anti-assembly law, it was easy, physically at least, to cross. Psychologically, it was much more difficult. The taunts endured by workers who crossed the line were fierce. And there were rumors that men who crossed would be rounded up by the strikers and humiliated. Some managed to work only a single day as scabs. For others, their guilt at betraying their fellow workers was assuaged by the coins in their pockets. Most of the men who crossed were not monsters. They were desperate. They had families. They had dying children. They had debts. The mining company now was paying replacement laborers triple normal wages to cross. And they paid them daily.

On July 3, the organizers met once again in the underground field bunker. Everyone was there, including Anton, who had taken over for Milo. "When will the guns arrive?" Johan Koski asked Carlo Tresca. "You said they'd be here two weeks ago."

"I told you. They got confiscated. We had a rat. But don't worry. He'll be taken care of all right."

"When are the guns coming?"

"Given the latest developments, I'm not at liberty to say how, where, or when. But soon."

"Better be soon," Paul said. "Morale is beyond low. It's a bloodbath out there, and the strikers police force we established is barely armed. The deputies and guards have rapid-fire pistols. We don't stand a chance."

"The guns are coming. Times are tough. The union is experiencing some internal struggle, and although Bill Haywood wants to fortify you one hundred percent, there are others who need convincing."

"I don't give a damn about Big Bill Haywood or whatever is going on at headquarters," Adeline Sherek said. "We are the union. We, the people who live here. I'm not about to wait for them. We're smart people. We need to figure something out now."

"Paul, how many injuries have there been so far, according to your count?" Scarlett asked.

"Hundreds? All they count is deaths, not near-deaths. Not torture. It would be impossible to count the beatings. Goes without saying there hasn't been a single prosecution. Folks are starting to think this ain't worth it. Life is worse now than it ever was before. There's talk about going back to the mines. Not one or two men, but a lot of men."

"I know. It's difficult to boost morale when we can't rally. Whenever someone tries to rally, someone gets maimed."

Adeline Sherek stood up. "Katka and I have a proposal."

"Yes, we do," Katka chimed in. "Tell them, Adeline."

"The law specifically states that no more than three union members can assemble together on public property."

"Yes, Adeline. We know."

"Well, Katka and I are not union members. Lily is not a union member. Helen Cerkvenik is not a union member."

"What are you saying?" Anton said. "If you are suggesting that the women take over this strike, you've gone plum loco."

"That's exactly what we are suggesting, Uncle," Katka said. "The company has paralyzed you. You said so yourself. But the women are exempt from this law. We can walk the parades. We can carry on the strike."

"We appreciate the idea," Johan Koski said, "but no, no, and no. This is not women's work."

Adeline laughed, so loudly that everyone present felt immediately uncomfortable. "Do you think walking in a parade carrying a banner is harder than the work we already do? We get up before you men. We chop the wood. We start the fires. We cook the breakfast and clean up. We heat the water to wash your miner clothes, sometimes when it is forty degrees below zero. Our hands are open sores. You men, you complain about your unfair working conditions, as you should. But we have unfair working conditions too. You complain about shift work. We work every shift. When the babies cry at night, it's our shift. We have the day shift, the night shift, and the evening shift. My mother always said, 'Women, we hold up three corners of the house.' Well, now that you men are on strike, we hold up four. And somehow, at the end of the night, you still expect us to find the energy to love you."

The men looked at her, open-mouthed.

Katka continued. "Who is explaining to the babies why their stomachs hurt from hunger? Are you? Who is giving up your own portions at dinner to feed the children? Are you? The women in the locations especially, you should see their bones jutting out. They can barely walk. Women have as much reason as you men for wanting this strike to end and for your wages to increase. You think you're tired? Your workload has lessened since this strike began. Ours has increased."

It was quiet for a while. "Do you doubt our words?" Adeline asked.

"It's not that," Johan Koski said tentatively. "It's just that it ain't right. Women taking over the lines is dangerous. And how do you think us men would feel if something happened to our women?"

"We are not afraid," Adeline said.

"It's been done before," Sam Scarlett said. "The women near the border, the Mexican women. They took over the strike and won."

"And don't forget the garment workers," Tresca said. "The International Ladies Garment Workers Union in New York put up a hell of a fight. It's in the IWW bylaws. Everyone is equal in the Industrial Workers of the World. Even womenfolk."

"Something don't feel right about this," Johan said.

"Paul, what do you think?" Katka asked.

He looked around the bunker. He looked at every face before fixing his gaze on Katka's. "I say if the women want to give it a try, we should let them. But if anyone gets hurt, I will never forgive myself."

Katka smiled. Adeline nodded. "So it's settled. The women will take over the lines."

"I wish to go on record as saying I disapprove. I do not support this, not one bit," Johan said. "The world is backward. Backward, I say."

"I will record your opposition in the minutes," Katka said.

They discussed the logistics of the rally. Katka and Adeline would set the network in motion. Women from each ethnic church would spread the word. Seven towns across the Range would hold women's rallies. The strikers police force would monitor from a distance. The first rally would be held that Saturday in Biwabik.

CHAPTER 43

E VERYONE WAS NERVOUS. AT FIRST THERE WERE
only a handful of women on the street.

"No one's coming," Katka said to Adeline.

"They'll come," Adeline said. "Trust me."

And they did. Moments before the rally was set to begin, the women converged from all directions on Blood Red Road in front of Cerkvenik's Mercantile. They had been given the usual banner to carry: "One Big Union, One Big Enemy." But they had made other signs as well: "Sanitation!" "We Want Running Water!" "Medical Care for All." Those who didn't carry signs carried children.

"I tried to get my husband to take the baby," Georgia Smith said, "but he said he wouldn't know what to do with it."

Adeline Sherek had a whistle in her pocket. She blew it, and women tried to hush the babies. "Line up four abreast. When I blow the whistle again, Madeline LeForte will beat the drum, and we will march to her rhythm. We will walk to the Biwabik mine and back. You will be home in time to serve lunch."

Katka, Lily, Helen Cerkvenik, and Ava Nurmi, the widow, were in the first row. Anton had agreed, reluctantly, to watch Gregor. Helen's son carried the American flag. Andy Lamppi's two children, about ten years old, carried a banner with the words "Industrial Workers of the World."

Katka looked around, up at the hills surrounding town, and spied members of the IWW and the strikers police force. They were assembled in twos, armed and prepared to protect the women. The deputies were not obscured. They stood in plain sight on the boardwalks.

Mr. Augustine Stone had come out to witness the occasion. He brought along his wife and three children. They stood outside Torelli's Saloon. Vince Torelli had set up a chair for Mrs. Stone. The Stone children sat on the wooden boardwalk, playing jacks.

Adeline blew the whistle. As Madeline beat the drum, the women protestors moved forward. As they walked past Vince's place, some of the deputies made obscene gestures and shouted remarks usually reserved for prostitutes.

Protester Georgia Smith pointed her finger at Mrs. Stone. "Shame!" she yelled. "Shame on you and your husband who let men talk to ladies like this. He's an animal!" Mrs. Stone stood up, her face red, and walked away.

"Where you going, dumpling?" asked Mr. Stone.

"Home. Come on, children."

The women's march was loud and boisterous. They chanted slogans written on the signs. With each block, they gathered more courage, and their volume increased. The company guards watched with amusement as they walked past the city limits toward the mine. When they had made it through town incident free, they began to sing union songs. They were less than a mile away from the mine. They kept walking. The deputies followed.

When they arrived at the Biwabik mine, they saw the picketing strikers. There were only three of them together, walking in the line, pacing back and forth. About ten feet away were three more men, making another circle, abiding by the law. When the parade of women got there, they took over the picket lines. They chanted for workers' rights and for women's rights.

Katka was poised for violence. She had a feeling that something terrible was going to happen. Nothing did. After an hour had passed, they marched back to town, disassembled, and went home to fix lunch for their husbands, children, and boarders.

The next day they did it again. The usual male strikers were there in groups of three. But off to the side, several onlookers had arrived. A few had cameras around their necks.

This time as the women picketed, four motorcars carrying replacement laborers approached the mine entrance. Adeline Sherek blew the whistle.

Sheriff Turner was driving the first car. He stopped the car about fifty feet away from the women, who were still assembled in a large circle.

"I suggest, ladies, that you move your picnic elsewhere. I'd hate for something bad to happen to such fine ladies."

"Four lines!" Adeline said. "Form four lines." The women formed four separate lines blocking the entrance.

"I'm warning you," Sheriff Turner said. "I will step on the gas!"

"Try it," Lily said.

Sheriff Turner stepped on the gas pedal and charged the line with his car. Three women went flying. They hit the dashboard and rolled onto the ground. The strikers who had been watching from a short distance came forward. Old Joe was one.

"Disperse! Disperse!" he yelled.

"No!" Katka yelled. "Hold the line! And you men, stay back. Don't give them reason to fire."

The women quickly reformed the lines, yelling, "Strike! Strike! Strike!"

Sheriff Turner had broken through, but the other three cars had not.

The sheriff stopped. "What are you waiting for?" He yelled to the next driver. "Charge!"

The driver looked at the women and back at the sheriff. He was still trying to make up his mind when the man with the camera approached.

"Greetings, sir. Allow me to introduce myself. I'm Quincy Johnson, reporter for the *Duluth Labor News*. Am I to understand that you intend to maim and possibly kill a bunch of defenseless women and children?"

"Well, no, sir. That ain't my intent. Sheriff gave me twenty bucks to give these boys a lift. That's all I signed up for."

"Mind if I take your picture?" He put the camera to his face, looked through the lens, and snapped.

"Yes! I mind. I mind very much!"

"Stay still now. It will turn out much clearer."

Stop that! There must be a law against taking a guy's picture when he don't want it taken."

"There isn't," the reporter said. "But there is a law against assault and murder."

The driver looked back at the sheriff. Then he put the car in reverse. Careful not to hit the third car, he turned the car around and left the mine. The women cheered. When the reporter started taking photos of the drivers of the third and fourth cars, they did the same thing. Six replacement workers made it into the mine that day, but eighteen did not. The women went back the next day and the next during different shifts at the mine.

The Oliver Mining Company was losing millions of dollars. Their operations were barely running. Katka wrote in *Strikers News* about the numerous reasons the company had to be worried. She believed that they were, but apparently not enough to negotiate. The strike committee kept sending and resending their list of demands. They had them published in every newspaper from Biwabik to Duluth to Minneapolis.

Finally, a representative from the Duluth office of Oliver Mining Company came to meet with Mr. Stone. "Perhaps you should negotiate with the miners," he suggested. "They're not asking for much."

"Never," Stone said. "We cannot give a bunch of immigrants the idea that they can make the rules. This is a white man's country and always will be. These foreigner-borns are here to work the jobs we regular Americans will not do at the wages we dictate. We cannot let them become us. What's next? Colored men giving orders? Indians? By not negotiating, we are protecting more than our business. We are protecting the business of America."

"Is it true your business is losing money every day?"

"Not for long. I have a new plan that will break the women's picket lines. Then we'll be able to get the replacement workers in from Minneapolis. I got a hundred or so men lined up to arrive next Tuesday. I guarantee we'll get them in. I got a man making a list of every woman walking the line on every shift in each of the seven Oliver mines. I got another man making a list of every union organizer in town. Something big is about to happen."

CHAPTER 44

DURING THE SECOND WEEK IN JULY 1916, KATKA walked into town as she did every morning to sell eggs and gather news. Her first stop was the mercantile.

"Katka, thank heavens you're here," Helen Cerkvenik said, ushering her into the shop.

"Helen, I only have eleven eggs today. Sasa's not producing, and the other hens can't seem to make up for..."

"I do not care about your damn eggs, Katka. Have you not heard?"

"What is happened?"

"Anton didn't tell you?"

"He did not come home last night."

"Who's with Lily and the baby?"

"Samo. Dusca. Old Joe. Probably more. What happened?"

"They arrested Johan Koski and three others last night. Accused them each of union agitation. They're in the jailhouse right now."

"Heavens no!"

"But, Katka, it gets *worse*."

Katka immediately thought of Paul. God, let him be all right. Let him have escaped trouble, just this once.

"They did something. To Johan Koski's wife, Esther." Helen began to cry. Her whole body shook, and Katka put her arms around her.

"What is it? Helen? Tell me."

Helen spoke in a whisper. "They *raped* her, Katka. *In front of her children.* Before they took Johan to the jail."

Three customers came into the mercantile, their deputy badges not quite as shiny as they were a month ago. They ordered chewing tobacco, and Helen coldly filled their order. In a daze, Katka nodded to Helen and left the mercantile. She stopped at several other businesses before walking back home. Everyone had a story. The deputies had begun systematic home raids to intimidate workers into returning to the mines. They were given the go-ahead by Sheriff Turner to use "any means necessary" to get the workers to join a shift. A few were taken by gunpoint. They were there now, prisoners working in the mines against their will.

When Katka got home, Paul and Anton were sitting at the kitchen table, and Lily was serving them coffee. They spoke in hushed tones. After hearing them promise to get the men out of jail, Katka went immediately down to the cellar where she wrote up the story. It was printed and distributed within forty-eight hours. People began locking their doors at night, and men spent less time in the taverns and more time at home protecting their families.

CHAPTER 45

IN MID-JULY, THE DAYS WERE GETTING SHORTER, but not by much. Light still clung to the night sky like a tired child who refused to shut his eyes for fear of missing something. When the light was finally gone, the temperature dropped ten degrees, sometimes more. After Katka's chores were done and her articles written for *Strikers News*, she walked almost every night, alone, to the secret meeting place in the field bunker to see Paul.

This particular night they had a task to accomplish. The cache of guns had arrived from Wobbly headquarters, wrapped in gunnysacks and hidden in the costume crates of the traveling opera that had come to sing at the Opera Hall in Virginia. They would be performing *The Magic Flute* on Saturday night, and Katka and Paul planned to attend. Two stagehands had transported the weapons from Virginia to the bunker in Biwabik without being detected.

"Here they are," Paul said, unlocking the crate.

Katka looked inside. "That it?" she asked. "Can't be more than twenty guns in that box."

"Twenty exactly," Paul said. "Not much, I agree, but at least it's a start. Means they finally found a way to get them through undetected. We'll start distributing them tonight. You can take two back tonight to the Slovenski Dom. Give them to Anton. He'll know who to give them to."

"On one condition," Katka said. She pointed to a silver-plated Colt Frontier Peacemaker revolver. It had engraved mother-of-pearl grips. To Katka, it looked more beautiful than any piece of jewelry she could imagine. "I want to shoot that one."

"How did that get in there?" Paul asked. He picked it up gently and handed it to her. "Know how to load it?"

"Better'n you, probably," she said.

Paul gave her some ammunition, and they walked out to the shooting range together. Their inventory could wait. Katka wanted to shoot the revolver in the moonlight.

***

By 10 p.m., Katka was still not back. Luckily, Anton thought, the moon was bright as a lantern. He didn't like the thought of Katka walking in the dark while the deputized thugs were in town. Anton was tending bar at the Slovenski Dom. Most of the boarders had taken their beer out back or gone into town. He had only two customers.

"Beauty of a night we got here," Anton said as he put a pint of ale in front of Andy, the soda pop distributor. "Bet it still be seventy-five degrees. Why you ain't outside, smoking in the moonlight?"

"A man gets sick a bein' in the out'o doors," Andy said. "This heat been good on my business, shore 'nuff. But all day, every day, I'm out there in the thick of it selling the root beer. Them deputies got money to burn. Some of 'em buy three or four bottles at once. By the end of these hot days, I'm plum tired. Just want to set down on this stool and drink 'til I fall asleep."

"I think it feel real good to be out'o doors so much," Old Joe said. "That's one good thing about being on strike. Got me a sunburn today."

The front door to the Slovenski Dom opened, and two boarders—Samo and Dusca—came in carrying their empty glasses.

"Your wife, Lily, done kicked us out of the yard," Samo said to Anton. "Said we keeping up the baby."

"You tell her to shut the window?"

"*Teta* Lily? I don't tell her *nothing*. Last time I gave her a suggestion—just a little one. I say, 'Add a touch more paprika to the *sarma'*—she don't give me no breakfast the next day."

"Sound like my Lily. It's cooler in here now anyway. And I was getting sick of talking to Old Joe, I tell you."

They heard horses approaching, and instinctively, everyone in the saloon looked toward the door. Deputy Moose Jackson entered, followed by four new deputies. Anton recognized two of them, Eli Sandinski and John Logan. They were a mangy lot with scraggly beards, dirty clothes, and unwashed faces. Their badges were prominently displayed. All four were armed. Moose Jackson was smiling.

"Whiskey, Anton," he said. "All 'round."

"Dollar each," Anton said, not moving.

"Dollar? For a glass of whiskey?"

"Times is tough, I tell ya, Moose. That the going rate."

The newly deputized Moose Jackson shook his head. "That ain't why we're here, anyway, you stupid Bohunk."

"Then why is you here?"

"We're here to shut you down."

"On what grounds?"

"Sheriff Turner says what you got here is a blind pig. Operating this fine establishment without a license."

"Sheriff Turner is wrong. We got a license, and we pay taxes like every other business owner in town." He pointed to the liquor license that was framed and hanging behind the bar. "There it be. Right there."

Moose Jackson took out his Luger, aimed for the frame, and shot it. Glass splayed. Anton barely flinched.

"Get out of my saloon." His voice was steady. "You folks is trespassing. You got a beef with me, you come in here with a proper warrant, and we'll take this up in the court of law. And you can pay for the damages too."

Moose laughed. "You forget. We are the law. And you are under arrest."

In one fluid motion, Anton bent down and pulled a knife from his boot. He didn't aim the knife at anyone; he just held it in his hand, almost leisurely, as if he were about to cut a bit of salami. He spoke slowly. "I ain't done nothing illegal. I don't aim to cause no harm or make no trouble. But I am a man. And where I come from, see, a man don't let another man take something that is rightfully his. This bar is mine. My body is mine. You got rights to neither."

"Drop the knife," Deputy Logan said.

"Or what?"

"In the name of the law, Deputy Jackson will blow your brains out."

"Deputy?" Anton spit. "Moose ain't no more the law than I am!" Anton said. "He's a criminal. Just like you!"

Moose reached across the bar and grabbed Anton's hand. He slammed it down on the bar until Anton dropped his knife. Then he lifted Anton up as if he were a cornhusk doll and threw him to the ground on the other side of the bar. Anton's head hit the wooden floor with a thunk, and blood spilled from his temple. Logan grabbed the knife. Anton mumbled something unintelligible.

Andy and Old Joe ran to Anton's side.

"Reckon you boys ought to help us drag old Anton out. You'll do that, won't you?" Moose said.

"Sure we will," Old Joe said. "Right after we cut off your pecker and feed it to the pigs. That is, if you even got a pecker."

Moose aimed his Luger and shot Old Joe once in the leg.

Old Joe screamed. "You dirty bastards! Company thugs! Have you no decency? Shooting an old man? What's next?"

Restraint, exercised as a survival tactic by the miners during the whole of the strike, evaporated. Samo and Dusca ran toward Moose and tackled him. Their fists became weapons fueled by the injustice of unearned power. Old Joe dragged himself along the floor, tracking blood along the way. He grabbed hold of a barstool and managed to swing it across the back of one of the "deputies," just as the thug was about to shoot Samo. Anton lay silently on the floor.

Lily entered the room from the dining room. She said nothing, staring in disbelief. But baby Gregor, who was attached to her body with a sling cloth, began to wail. The child's cry had an unusual impact on both the miners and the deputies. Perhaps they were simply surprised. Movement stopped, and everyone stared at the mother and child who did not seem, even remotely, to belong in this turbulent setting.

Moose Jackson, who had been pummeling Andy, the soda pop distributor, dropped him to the ground. He walked toward Lily.

"Well," he said, "if it ain't the lovely Mrs. Kovich. How nice to see you."

Lily frantically glanced at Anton, his body lying in a distorted mess on the floor. Old Joe caught her eye, shook his head, and mouthed in Slovenian, "He'll be okay."

"Get out of my house, Moose."

"Put your baby down," Moose said.

"Why?"

"Because if you don't, Sandinski here is going to shoot your husband." Deputy Sandinski pointed his gun at Anton. The other deputies pointed their guns at Dusca, Andy, and Samo. "And there's something I want from you, Mrs. Kovich.

Something sweeter than that screaming runt. Are you going to put your baby down?"

Lily held Gregor to her chest even tighter, watching Anton and Sandinski out of the corner of her eye.

With one swift movement, Moose yanked baby Gregor out of Lily's arms, breaking the cloth sling. He threw the bundle across the room, as if lobbing a horseshoe. The swaddled baby slid into the corner of the room with an ominous thud.

"No!" Lily screamed.

As she moved toward her baby, Moose grabbed her and punched her in the nose. He did not hit her hard, at least not for him. Even so, she staggered, covering her face as she veered. Samo rushed forward and caught her, steadying her. Her face was bleeding, but she didn't seem to notice. She looked dizzy, as if she were trying to get her bearings.

Old Joe dragged his body toward the baby.

Moose Jackson motioned for Samo to back off from Lily.

"I won't!" Samo yelled.

"Then I'll kill her."

"Do as he says," Lily said. One hand was still covering her face, but the bright red blood seeped through her fingers and dripped onto her dress. "Do as he says."

"But *Teta*..."

"Do it."

Samo took a step away, and Lily looked furtively back toward the corner. She saw Old Joe, his back to her, cradling the baby, who had stopped crying altogether. Blood flowed from the bullet wound on his lower calf.

"I have no business with you," Lily said to Moose Jackson. "Let me take care of the baby. I leave you men to your brawls."

"Tell you what," Moose Jackson said, his gun still pointed her way. "I'll make you a deal. You can have your baby." He lowered his voice. "But I get you."

"Never!" Lily yelled.

Samo, Dusca, and Andy charged Moose. They shouted in English and Slovenian, trying to get close enough to Lily to create a buffer around her.

The deputies fired their weapons in the air, then began shooting at the miners. As the men dodged bullets, Moose grabbed Lily in a chokehold. He picked her up by the neck and slammed her down on a bar table. She could hear her ribs crack. Moose forced his tongue into her mouth. She bit it and drew blood.

"So that's how it's going to be?" Moose punched Lily in the stomach, and she yelped in pain.

Samo, Dusca, and Andy tried to get to her, but they were stopped.

"Want us to tie these men up?" John Logan asked Moose. "We ain't got no cuffs, but Sandinski's got rope."

"You're an animal!" Samo yelled to Moose as one of the deputies tied his hands together. He and the other miners struggled to no avail.

"Moose," Sandinski said as he finished tying Dusca's hands to a chair, "think about this a spell. We got our man. Hell, we got all of them. Maybe that's enough. We'll leave here, drop these boys off at the jail, and stop by Vince's for a romp with Leppe."

Moose looked at Sandinski. "You gone soft?"

"I ain't got much in terms of morality, but it takes a pretty yellow man to hit a lady, not to mention a mother. We all got mothers. They different than whores."

Deputy Logan spoke up. "This don't feel right, Moose. Not a bit. Let her be."

Moose loosened his hold on Lily's throat. She gasped for air.

"That was mighty eloquent of you," Moose said. "But I don't have a liking for speechmaking. Question me again and I'll shoot you."

He tightened his grip on Lily and she wriggled like an insect on a pin. "You," Moose said, pointing to a deputy, "wake up Anton. I don't want him to miss this. This'll be something to write home about." He pushed her back on the table. Lily screamed cuss words until Moose slapped her again. He yanked open her blouse and pushed it down to her waist, revealing her simple white corset with the strings loosely tied.

"Is Anton awake yet?" he yelled.

"Just coming to."

"Bring him over. He's going to get a front-row seat."

"You'll burn in hell if you touch her, you will," Dusca said. He fumbled with the rope that secured his hands behind his back.

Moose lifted Lily's skirt to her waist. She kicked and flailed. Samo was saying the Lord's Prayer in Slovenian.

Anton opened his eyes. "Where...Where am I?"

"Ti si v peklu!" someone shouted. And he was. He was in hell.

CHAPTER 46

"**S**URE IT AIN'T AN IMPOSITION FOR YOU TO WALK home alone?" Paul asked. "I can be a little late with the deliveries, I can."

"Already you are late," Katka said. She kissed him happily on his left ear. "Thanks for letting me shoot. I love pistols. They're so light, yet so powerful. Besides, the moon is so full tonight it's like daytime. I know my way back."

"All right, little tiger. Give me a real kiss. And when I'm done delivering these weapons, I'll stop back. I might throw a rock at your window, so pay attention. Remember to give both extra guns to Anton. Is your own rifle loaded? In case you come across a bear?"

"Fully. Are you sure I can't trade it in for the Colt?"

Paul was sure. They said their goodbyes, and with the rest of the guns, he took the heavily wooded back trail, west of the bunker, traveling south for the Belgrade location. Leo Zalar had been told to expect him one night this week. He hoped Leo would be awake and ready to distribute the weapons.

Katka took the worn path to Anton and Lily's house, her rifle slung nonchalantly over her right shoulder. She had a lantern but did not light it. The blue moon was enormous, bigger and rounder than any she could recall seeing. At the end of the trail, she heard noises. At first she thought it was a cat crying in the night. Then she realized it was not. Something was happening at the Slovenski Dom.

She put the lantern down and picked up her pace. Instinct told her to move quickly but quietly. The yelling grew louder as she approached the house from the back. The voices were obviously coming from the tavern, but she knew better than to walk around and peek in the windows.

She silently let herself in the back door into the kitchen. She leaned the two extra rifles against the pantry wall and positioned her Winchester. She cocked it. She walked, her back against the wall, through the dining room to the door separating the living quarters from the tavern. She stood on her tiptoes and looked through the window.

Teta Lily was being held down on a table; her face was bloody. She was exposed, and an extremely tall man with his back to Katka was pulling off his suspenders. Men were tied up, helpless, yet shouting in protest. Two Oliver gunmen, both carrying weapons, physically held Anton. One of his arms hung limply at his side. Blood poured from the wound on his head. He kicked ferociously, trying to break free.

"Touch her and I kill you!" Anton hollered at Moose Jackson, who responded by smashing his fist into Lily's face a third time. Then he let his pants drop to his knees. His back was to Katka.

Katka opened the door silently but swiftly, lifted the Winchester and took aim. "*Don't think. Just do.*" She remembered Anton's voice, when he was teaching her to shoot. *When your body feels right—everywhere—don't hesitate. If you do, you'll miss.*" Through her scope, she stared at the tall man's hairy buttocks. In a millisecond, she figured out the height of the table where *Teta* Lily was positioned. She stood on her tiptoes so she could shoot from more of an upward angle. She fired and shot Moose Jackson in the ass.

"Motherfucker!" He yelled. "Holy fucking shit!" His pants fell from his knees to the ground as blood spurted downward. "Help me!" he yelled. He doubled over, clutching his groin.

"Bullet went right through to your cock, Moose!" Samo yelled. "It's just dangling there, you son of a bitch!"

Moose tried to lift his pistol to shoot Samo, but he had no strength. He moaned. All the color was draining from his face.

"Are you all right, *Teta*?" Katka called.

Sandinski, who had been holding onto Anton, let go of him. He ran to help Moose, who had been castrated. Lily sat up and, in a daze, pulled her bloody clothes back over her body. Katka's bullet had missed her completely.

"Where's my baby?" she said in a voice so small it sounded as if it belonged to someone else, someone who lived a long ways from here.

Samo jerked his head toward the back. "Old Joe slipped him out."

Lily limped out of the tavern as quickly as she could, holding her broken nose.

Moose moaned like a bull. "Am I going to die?" he asked Deputy Sandinski.

"I ain't no doctor, Moose, but I 'spect you'll live. 'Course, you'll be a eunuch for the rest of your life." Moose moaned again. "Men," Sandinski said, "get some more law in here. And get Doc Payne so Moose don't bleed out."

One of the Oliver gunmen left. Deputy Logan stationed himself next to the door, his pistol drawn.

"Don't worry, Moose. She'll pay for what she done," Sandinski said.

"Listen," Moose said, his voice raspy, "I don't want no one knowing."

"Knowing what?"

"That I got shot by a woman."

"But you did get shot by a bitch," Sandinski said. "We all saw that little thing of woman blow through your asshole like she was shooting a pop can. It was marvelous. Perhaps the most goddamn amazing thing I ever saw."

"No. No! You didn't *none* of you see that. I will not have people saying some immigrant bitch shot me. I won't have nothing if people think that. Won't be able to show my face. Anton did it, understand? Tell 'em Anton did it." He removed a bloody hand from his genital area, and wiped it on his trousers that had fallen to the floor. Then, he reached into his coat pocket and pulled out several bills, waving them toward Eli Sandinski. "Promise me you will tell everyone it was Anton."

Sandinski counted the money. It was over four hundred dollars. He tucked the stained bills into his own pocket, and turned to Anton.

"Apparently you shot a deputy, Kovich. Paddy wagon'll be here before you know it. If your girl give us her weapon, we won't tell no one she had a part. And we'll leave your wife alone, too. Sorry about that part, Anton. I ain't a fan of that, I ain't."

"We are not going anywhere," Katka said. "There are witnesses. Everything done here was in self-defense. It will hold up in the court system. And I didn't kill him. I could have, but I didn't."

"You're saying you missed killing him on purpose?"

"Of course I did."

Sandinski laughed. Katka did not waver. He looked at her, and suddenly he knew she was telling the truth. He gestured toward Deputy Logan stationed at the door. "Disarm her."

"Drop your gun, miss," Logan said.

"No."

Logan fired his pistol at Katka. Katka ducked.

A man's voice rang out. "I've been shot! I've been shot!"

It was Moose Jackson. He had been shot in the back.

"Bullet must have ricocheted off something," Sandinski said. He walked over to Moose and turned him over. "That's a life stopper," he said. "Looks like you're going to die after all."

As Moose's blood ran steadily from his body, Katka untied Andy, who helped untie the others. Then they heard the siren and the roar of the police wagon. Reinforcements had arrived.

Lily, limping and her face still bleeding, burst in the door. "Fight, men! Don't let them take you to jail!" she yelled.

Anton was mostly useless. With his good arm, he held himself up by leaning against a barstool. He armed himself with a small piece of glass. As the police wagon unloaded and entered the saloon, Samo and Dusca fought the company thugs with their fists and anything else they could lay hands on. Andy, the soda-pop delivery man, armed himself behind the bar with two bottles of malt liquor. Katka grabbed Lily and tried to persuade her to get back inside the house.

Then it happened. A shot was fired at Anton. Anton ducked, and the shot hit Andy, who was still behind the bar defending himself with two small bottles of whiskey. He collapsed immediately. The fighting stopped.

Samo vaulted the bar and knelt by his side. "Shot in the heart," Samo said.

Anton walked over to Moose Jackson, who lay dead on the floor. "So that how it is? I come to this country to see my friend killed in my house? To see cowards watch as this bastard tries to have his way with my wife? This ain't no land of the free. This is hell." He grabbed Moose's pistol, which had fallen to the floor, and pointed it at Moose's body.

"No." Lily stopped him. "There's nothing to be done, Anton. He's dead anyway."

Anton didn't care. He fired the pistol into Moose Jackson's bloody corpse. Then he fired again and again and again. He started hollering. He cursed at Moose. "I may not have killed you," he said, "but I wish I had! I wish I had killed you! And you and you! All you good-for-nothing thugs!"

He cursed the Wobblies too. He cursed the United States of America. Lily tried to calm him. Finally he crumpled to the ground himself, and Lily wrapped him in her arms like a little boy.

"I couldn't protect you, Lily," he whispered. "I couldn't protect you."

CHAPTER 47

NO ONE WAS ARRESTED FOR THE MURDER OF ANDY, the soda pop deliveryman. Samo, Dusca, and Anton were put in chains. When Lily protested, explaining what had really happened, they arrested her too.

"No!" Anton cried out at Mr. Augustine Stone and Sheriff Turner. "She has done nothing! Nothing but be abused by your men! They are the ones who should be imprisoned. Your company thugs are not deputies. They are devils!" But it was useless.

The only two witnesses who were not arrested were Katka, whom Eli Sandinski insisted had "only walked in a second before and had no part whatsoever in the affair," and Old Joe, who had taken the baby to the barn and passed out from the pain of the bullet in his calf. The deputies had forgotten about him.

"Get my baby," Lily said quietly to Katka. "If I'm going to jail, so is my baby. I am no more guilty than he is." Lily got the baby from the barn.

Sheriff Turner wanted Lily and the baby to be taken immediately to the women's jail in Biwabik, but Dr. Payne insisted that Lily go to the hospital first. Her eye was nearly swollen shut from where Moose Jackson had punched her, and her nose was obviously broken. The baby was also in need of medical attention.

"All of these men should be taken to the hospital first," the doctor said. "Look at this man," he said, pointing to Anton. "I need to set his shoulder."

The sheriff told the doctor to set his shoulder here and now, and the doctor did.

Next, Dr. Payne examined Samo and Dusca. "Both of these men require stitches," he said.

"Stitches ain't life threatening," Mr. Stone said. "Fix 'em best you can. That's all they're getting." The doctor gently dressed their surface wounds. He took his time, as if he were trying to delay the trip to the jail as much as possible.

Four deputies carried the body of Moose Jackson to the wagon. Andy's body remained untouched.

Finally, the men were loaded into the police wagon with Moose Jackson's corpse. Lily and the baby were taken in the doctor's buggy to the hospital, a deputy accompanying them. Lily was given thirteen stitches, and both she and the baby had broken ribs, which were wrapped. Mercifully, the doctor gave Lily a small amount of ether. She nursed the baby, and they both fell asleep.

Katka stood alone in the Slovenski Dom, dazed. Mechanically, she walked to the kitchen, added wood to the fire, and put the kettle on. She brewed a cup of tea and sat at the dining room table. Her hands were shaking so badly that she dropped the cup, the hot liquid spilling onto the table.

She heard footsteps and closed her eyes. The footsteps got louder, and she heard her name.

"They gone, Katka?"

"Paul!"

"You gone loco, child? It's me. Old Joe."

She opened her eyes. Old Joe's leg was bandaged with kitchen towels and a thin rope. He was resting his weight on one foot. "Got the bullet out," he said. "With my pocket knife."

"They took them all, Joe," she said. "Took them to jail. Even *Teta* and the baby."

Old Joe shook his head. He paused for a long time. "Guess we all that's left. We'll get 'em out though. We'll spring 'em if we have to."

"Yes," Katka said. She looked toward the tavern. "But first we got to clean up Andy."

"Andy?"

"He's dead."

Slowly they dragged Andy's body from the tavern to the house. Like so many men before him, they laid him out on the dining room table. They gently cleaned off the blood that had splattered onto his face and hair. Old Joe took out his pocket-knife and cut off Andy's crimson-stained shirt.

"Poor Andy," he said. "Who'd want to kill a fellow whose only purpose in life was to offer a man a cool drink on a hot day?"

They dressed him in Anton's best suit and then waited until the news traveled through the town, through the locations, until it reached the ears of Andy's wife. She gathered her twin boys to her chest, borrowed a neighbor's wagon, and went to the Slovenski Dom to claim the body of another casualty of the strike of 1916.

***

Katka and Old Joe left for the hospital after Andy's body was gone. They were told that Lily and the baby had been treated and transferred to the women's cell at the city jail.

"I wouldn't go nowhere near there if I was you, Katka," a nurse told her. "Word is, they're arresting every miner they see. We treated more wounds in this one night than in all of the strike. They pulling out all the stops, I say, Katka. All of 'em.

Go on home. The doc gave Lily a real strong sedative before they took her away. She'll be good at least until the morning."

Katka and Old Joe went back home. They waited for a sign. Surely someone would come and tell them what to do. Paul would come, throw rocks at Katka's window, and tell her everyone had been let go. Or Mrs. Sherek would come by in her buggy, bringing Lily and the baby home to safety. But none of that happened.

Although the bullet that killed Moose had obviously come from one of the deputies' guns, Deputies Sandinski and Logan told the sheriff that they weren't sure who had killed Moose. It might have been Anton. But perhaps it was Samo or Dusca. "Happened real fast," Sandinski had said.

Sheriff Turner determined that Anton Kovich and those present at his tavern were not the only ones responsible for Deputy Moose Jackson's death. At 3 a.m., Turner and his men found IWW leaders Sam Scarlett, Carlo Tresca, Frank Little, and Arthur Boose. They were dragged from their hotel, shackled, and put in the Virginia jail, twelve miles from Biwabik. None of the three men was within twelve miles of the Kovich home when Moose Jackson was killed. They were arrested for "murder due to their speeches."

During the next two days, mass arrests followed. Local and international strike leaders were rounded up and thrown in jails across the Range. One of them was Paul Schmidt.

CHAPTER 48

JAILS ACROSS THE RANGE WERE FULL.

Sheriff Turner and Mr. Stone were delighted. The incident at the Kovich house had given them an excuse to break the leadership of the strike. More than fifty strike organizers had been found and arrested. Outside the jails that dotted Blood Red Road, crowds formed. The men, women, and children—together with the business owners—rallied to free the prisoners. In Biwabik, Katka tried unsuccessfully to get inside to see Lily, Anton, and Paul. Like scores of other women, she left food with the names of the people she loved at the entrance to the prison.

Fearing mutiny, Sheriff Turner finally decided to let most of the men and women go. The remaining, he moved to the county jail in Duluth, loading them up in cars that came like locusts in the middle of the night. Ten prisoners in all were transported. Paul, Anton, Lily, Samo, and Dusca were among them. Katka never got to say goodbye. None was officially charged with the death of Moose Jackson, yet the Steel Trust was still assembling a grand jury to indict them, and it had stumbled across a few roadblocks.

The coroner who examined Moose Jackson's body had been problematic for the company. He stated, on the record, that it was impossible to accurately determine who was responsible for the deputy's death. But he did report that Moose Jackson had been killed by a weapon owned by one of the company deputies. He refused to recant or amend his statement. In addition, Dr. Payne, the only medical man on the scene, agreed to testify on the condition that he also testify about the death of Andy Lamppi, whose young boys played baseball with his own sons, and about the wounds inflicted on the miners and Mrs. Kovich. As a possible witness, he was determined unreliable and was dismissed.

The imprisonment of the IWW leaders and the miners received international attention. U.S. Steel sought to portray the miners and their organizers as violent men who refused to respect the law of the land. They hired the greatest legal team they could find, led by prosecuting attorney Warren H. Greene. The steel company took great pains to "purchase" a grand jury. Each member chosen for the grand jury was to be given significant monetary compensation in exchange for a guilty verdict.

In the meantime, Anton, Samo, Dusca and Lily—who all witnessed the shooting—sat in jail in Duluth. They were allowed no visitors, no information. Although Frank Little and Arthur Boose had been released, Wobbly organizers Carlo Tresca, Sam Scarlett, and Paul Schmidt were not. Local organizer Adeline Sherek, who had been delivering a baby at the time of the incident, had also been arrested. She shared a jail cell with Lily and baby Gregor.

Protesters arrived every day and picketed the prison. The protestors consisted of Iron Rangers and union members from Duluth to Minneapolis. The Dockworkers Union had a large presence. The Longshoremen came. The garment workers. The lumberjacks from across the northland. Socialists, labor activists, and IWW members appeared in Duluth to support the imprisoned strikers. Newspapers from all over the world covered the arrests and subsequent protests.

To appease the protesters, Adeline Sherek was released. Lily Kovich and her nursing baby remained in prison.

The IWW assembled a team of defense lawyers, but they were denied access to any official reports, eyewitness accounts, or testimony. Because no charges had been officially filed, the IWW lawyers found it impossible to prepare a case. Finally, several weeks after they were arrested, Anton, Lily, Samo, and Dusca were indicted in the killing of a deputy sheriff with a dangerous weapon. Carlo Tresca, Sam Scarlett, and Paul Schmidt were charged with inciting murder by their speeches. The trial date was not yet determined.

Meanwhile, baby Gregor, skinny and dirty, had learned how to smile in a six-by-eight-foot prison cell.

CHAPTER 49

THE MINES STAYED CLOSED. THE PRISONERS remained jailed. Anton's food supply was no longer available or distributed since he was in jail and Andy was dead in the ground. No credit was extended at the company store, and no paychecks were coming in. The gnawing face of hunger deprived the strikers of the one thing that had consistently nourished them up to this point—hope. Families started moving away. Men began to cross the line, men who had been strong supporters in the beginning. Considering the Mesabi strike a lost cause, the IWW stopped funding it so they could focus their energy elsewhere. Without the aid of its central leadership, the union of immigrants began to crumble.

Katka kept the livestock alive. She and Old Joe hunted in Anton's woods. She shot rabbits, squirrels, even a skunk. The other boarders fished with cane poles and brought the scaly creatures home to Katka. She cooked huge stews every single day, tasteless because she had run out of salt. Hungry families stopped by every night at dinnertime anyway. They got just enough to eat to want more.

In the evening, she wrote for *Strikers News*, doing everything she could to combat the company-owned presses that depicted Anton, Lily, Samo, and Dusca as vigilantes. When she finished her third edition of the paper since the attacks, Katka grabbed her lantern and took the typed paper to the usual place. No one had picked up the last two, but she thought she'd give it another try. She looked around in the candlelight, remembering how Paul used to wait for her. It was here, in this barn, that he told her he wanted to marry her. She ached for him. She put the ribboned manuscript in the box and hid it under Sasa's nest. The next day when she went to collect eggs, the manuscript was still there.

"Your distributor is dead," a voice said. "But we found you a new one. It'll be about a week."

Katka turned away from the hen. A woman was standing in the doorway of the barn. She had dark, curly hair and pale blue eyes. She was not from here, yet she was strangely familiar.

"Who are you?"

"Elizabeth Gurley Flynn. We met briefly at Ellis Island. You don't remember?"

Slowly the memory floated back. Elizabeth was Paul's friend. She had worn that wide-brimmed purple hat. She dropped her suitcase after Katka and Paul had been separated at Ellis Island, giving Katka the photo of her and Paul in the lightning storm. And Andre the Bulgarian had spoken about her. Told Katka to read up on "the rebel girl."

"Last time I saw you," Katka said, "you told me Paul had been detained. He is once again detained."

"I'm here to help, Katka. Do you have any coffee?"

"Only rose hip tea."

Katka and Elizabeth walked from the barn to the house. When the tea was ready, Katka sat at the kitchen table across from Paul's friend. The IWW had sent Elizabeth to the Range to help raise money for the defense team and to increase morale in the deflated strikers. Elizabeth was a famous Wob organizer, beloved by laborers and newspapers. She had mass appeal, and her speeches were uplifting. She had been up to Minnesota's Iron Range once before, during the failed 1907 strike. Joe Hill, the man who wrote most of the Wobbly songs in *The Little Red Song Book*, had even written a song about her called "Rebel Girl." Katka had sung it when the women were on the lines.

"Andy Lamppi, the soda pop peddler. He was the one who distributed your newspaper," Elizabeth told her.

Katka thought of Andy, sweet Andy, who always had a free bottle of root beer for a penniless child on a hot day.

"Our Andy?"

"He was a good Wobbly. Even his wife didn't know." But Lily knew. She had known all along and had never told Katka.

"What do you plan to do about Lily? Her baby's in there. Did you know that? Her baby! And Anton? He didn't kill that deputy. He didn't kill anyone, much as he wishes he had."

Elizabeth took Katka into her arms. And Katka cried and cried. "And what about Paul?" she sobbed. She needed him. She needed Paul to help her get Anton and Lily out of jail.

"You care for him a great deal, don't you Katka?"

Katka nodded, but said nothing. With him, she felt like a tiger in the night. Without him, she was a frightened mouse in a ramshackle cottage.

"Listen to my plan."

Elizabeth Gurley Flynn's plan was twofold. She had been sent here to raise money and to breathe life into the movement. Every day for several weeks, she traveled up and down Blood Red Road, giving rousing speeches to raise the spirits of strikers and their wives. Everywhere she went, crowds followed. Soon the picket lines were stronger and more populated than ever before.

At night the strikers posted signs bearing the names of all business owners in town that had sold out to the mining company by agreeing to stop issuing credit to strikers. Strikers stood outside these businesses recording the names of every person who purchased as much as a nail. Their names were posted all over town. Mass boycotts continued until the business owners caved and began to extend credit again to the strikers. It was a small victory, but did not go unnoticed.

All the businesses were suffering. There was no one to spend money on a pint of ale, on flour, on cloth, or on newspapers. The attitudes of company-funded newspaper editors and of local politicians of each mining town began to change. Initially, they had vehemently taken the side of the Steel Trust and Oliver Mining Company throughout the strike, asserting that the Wobblies promoted violence. However, after the incident at the Slovenski Dom, several of the local politicians began to rethink their positions. It was clear that the often drunk, trigger-happy company gunmen deputized by the U.S. government at the request of the steel magnates had created far more chaos and violence than any Wobbly striker. They had brought lawlessness to a new level, and the citizens lived a life of terror. It was also clear that if a politician hoped to serve another elected term, he would have to start listening to the strikers. A band of Iron Range mayors agreed to form a committee to listen to the grievances of the miners and citizens with the hope that that negotiations would end the strike.

Elizabeth and Katka sat in the Kovich backyard drinking well water.

"Part of the plan is working," Elizabeth acknowledged. "Momentum has shifted."

"Yes," Katka said.

"But we are raising almost no money. Everyone here is starving. If they had a dollar, they'd give it. But they simply don't."

"Can't bleed a rock."

"Then we must get it elsewhere. I'll tap into some networks. Better yet, I'll get Eugene Debs."

Katka had read about Eugene Debs. He had run for president on the Socialist ticket countless times and lost every time. But he was famous. More famous than Elizabeth.

"Debs will come here?"

"Yes. I'll get Debs. In the meantime, you work with Johan Koski. I'll tell you what to do."

Katka assembled the Ladies Auxiliary in Lily and Anton's house. They aided Johan Koski, who was the treasurer of the Relief and Defense Committee of the Mesabi Iron Range Strikers, in his mission to keep the strikers from going hungry and to make sure the Kovich story was in the forefront of America's conscience. The women and girls spent hours each day writing to unions across the nation, urging them to support the defendants with monetary contributions and to start their own letter-writing campaigns. It worked.

Contributions from unions and socialist organizations came pouring in. The ladies took great enjoyment in reading the communications from around the world. They received an envelope, full of mostly small bills, from the Brooklyn Local of Amalgamated Clothing Workers. They received letters of support and contributions from Oklahoma, Illinois, the Carolinas, Colorado, and Montana. Ladies auxiliaries in labor communities across the nation began letter-writing campaigns of their own, appealing for the release of the Mesabi prisoners. In Scranton, Pennsylvania, thousands of members of the United Mine Workers went on strike in sympathy with the Mesabi miners and "to show that the legal murder" of laborers by corporations "must cease." Across the ocean, labor organizers from as far as Liverpool, England, and Italy took up their cause, referring to the arrests as a "labor frame-up." The overseas unions vowed to make it known all over Europe that workers emigrating to the United States faced little or no legal or human rights protections.

Major corporations—steel companies, manufacturers, and shipping companies—took notice. They did not want their own companies to lose the kind of money that the Mesabi strike had cost U.S. Steel. To avoid it, they granted their workers small concessions. The Iron Range workers continued to suffer, but workers across the state and nation began to know better conditions, however meager, because of their suffering.

In a month's time, while the prisoners sat in jail, the auxiliary had raised enough money to hire a new and better defense team. Elizabeth had been true to her word as well. About a week before the trial was set, Eugene Debs arrived in Duluth. There, before ten thousand people, he would deliver a speech in the warehouse district by the shores of Lake Superior.

***

Elizabeth offered Katka and Old Joe a ride to Duluth in a borrowed motorcar. Although the summer of the strike on the Iron Range had been the most suffocatingly hot that anyone could remember, the weather in Duluth was different, foggy and comfortably cool, as if Lake Superior had exhaled a refreshing, breezy mist on the port town.

Katka and Old Joe wandered around for a spell, poking into a shop here or there, and gazing into the vast span of water.

"Pretty town," Old Joe said. "This was your first view of Minnesota, ay?"

"I barely remember it," Katka said. "I had left everything familiar behind. When I got on that buggy with Anton, he was a stranger, and everything around was new. I saw everything and nothing all at once. It was like I was blind." So much had changed. She was no longer the timid, skinny orphan who had arrived with her name fastened around neck.

They walked down the hilly streets of Duluth to listen to Eugene Debs. The crowd looked like ants, Katka thought. The men dressed in shabby brown suits or faded overalls, the women in tattered shawls. Elizabeth, on the other hand, wore a sharp, ruffled, button-up blouse the color of pearls. Her skirt was long and practical, but she was wearing her telltale wide-brimmed purple hat. She looked beautiful, and several news-papermen took her picture as they waited for Debs. Finally, Elizabeth took her place up front on the stage. Katka and Old Joe stationed themselves about fifty feet back. Katka wanted to hear everything.

The wind was blowing as Eugene Debs took to the podium, and the crowd applauded loudly. Debs was a smallish man whose bald head glimmered in the sunlight. Debs was one of the founders of the IWW, and he had been to Minnesota often. He waved to people he recognized in the crowd. Although he had recently left the Wobblies over some disagreements with current leader Bill Haywood, he was an ardent supporter of the Mesabi prisoners. He took a sip of water and then hushed the crowd with a hand gesture.

Debs began by giving a brief background of the plight of the miners on the Range and of the abuses the Steel Trust inflicted on them in their quest to exterminate laborers who tried to organize.

> *If they dared complain, they were discharged. Spies among them kept them under suspicion of each other. Petty bosses ruled over them like despots, and if they would hold their jobs, they must be bootlicking sycophants and slaves.*
> *Finally these insulted, outraged peons could endure it no longer, and a whirlwind of revolt swept them into a strike.*

"He's a good speaker for such a little man," Old Joe whispered to Katka. "And he tell it true, too." They listened as the speech progressed. Debs recounted the specifics of the case, particularly calling into question the deputizing of the company gunmen, almost all of whom had criminal backgrounds. Debs focused on the fact that the men had entered Anton's tavern without a warrant and precipitated a fight. When Anton and the miners tried to defend themselves, they were considered criminals.

> *The Steel Trust is itself the arch-criminal in the case, and its clutches are red with the blood of the innocent, but no grand jury will find an indictment for these multimillionaire murderers. It is only the poor who are indicted for being the victims of crime and only the rich who go free in spite of their guilt.*

Katka took notes as quickly as she could, hoping that the Ladies Auxiliary would help her translate the speech into as many languages as possible. But there were two moments in the speech when Katka's quill simply would not move:

> *...there is not a shadow of doubt that the trust has them all marked for execution...*
> *...These comrades, though as innocent as babies, will be murdered by the Steel Trust as certain as the coming day unless the working class is aroused and stands between the brutal trust and its intended victims...*

Debs's words reverberated in her head as the crowd burst into applause at the end of the speech. Even as she saw Elizabeth gesturing her forward to the stage where she had sat, Katka could not get three phrases out of her mind: *innocent as babes*. She thought of Lily, pregnant and making jokes with the men who were throwing horseshoes. *Marked for execution.* She thought of Anton, perched on his buggy blankets covering goods he smuggled for the strikers. She could hear his voice: "I don't get mixed up in politicals." *Murdered by the Steel Trust*. She thought of Paul. His curly hair falling crazily on his forehead when he arrived at her door in Slovenia. The scars that dotted his naked back when she had first glimpsed his body in the sauna. "You are a tiger in the night," he had told her. She wasn't. But because he believed she was, she tried to become one.

Katka felt herself being led by Old Joe through the few rows of people that separated them from the front.

"Katka!" Elizabeth cried, grabbing her hand as she navigated the stairs. "Wasn't it a grand speech? I told you he was marvelous, and now you know how right I was. And here's the good news. Eugene has an engagement later tonight in Minneapolis. But before he goes, he would like to invite all of us to luncheon with him. At the Fitger's restaurant."

"Me too?" Old Joe said.

"Of course, you!"

They scurried toward Elizabeth's borrowed motorcar, Mr. Debs shaking hands along the way.

"Bully for us, Katka," Old Joe whispered. "Never ate at a fancy restaurant. Think they'll let me in?"

They let him in. But he never got to eat.

CHAPTER 50

THEY DRANK WATER OUT OF FANCY GOBLETS AND looked at the menu. Old Joe, dressed in denim coveralls, was excited. Elizabeth and Mr. Debs talked with great animation. Katka was preoccupied. Debs had given her the speech he delivered. She was cross-checking it with her notes.

A waiter approached carrying a silver platter. He lifted the lid and revealed a note card with the monogram of the hotel on the outside.

"A message for you, ma'am," he said to Elizabeth.

"For me?"

"We have a telephone. I was told to find a blue-eyed woman with a wide-brimmed hat. Are you Mrs. Flynn?"

"I am."

"I do apologize for interrupting your luncheon."

Elizabeth Gurley Flynn turned the notecard over and read the brief message to herself.

"It's from the defense team. The state has approached them with a settlement. They want me there as an advisor. We must go at once."

They dropped Debs off at the train station. "Give 'em hell!" he yelled as they drove away. Then they rushed to the court-house, Elizabeth honking her horn and passing buggies on the road. When they arrived, Elizabeth stopped the car. "Can you park it?"

By the time Katka and Old Joe entered the courthouse, Elizabeth was nowhere to be seen. They walked into a foyer, and a scholarly-looking man with a monocle and a thin tie stopped them. When Katka told him they were with Mrs. Flynn, the man told them she was engaged in an urgent private meeting. He took them to a waiting room. "The negotiation room is down a hallway just beyond. I will tell her you are waiting for her here."

Katka and Old Joe sat. A parade of men in suits filed through the waiting room and into the hallway. Katka recognized Warren H. Greene, the chief prosecutor. His picture had been in all the papers. Then nothing happened for a long time.

"Should have brought a deck of cards," Old Joe said.

"I'm too nervous to do anything but be nervous," Katka said. "I can't think straight."

"Don't need to think straight to play gin rummy. Maybe I'll ask that skinny man with the eyeglass. Even learn'd men play cards."

Just as Old Joe was getting up, Elizabeth emerged from beyond the door. As usual, she was a blizzard of energy, and her words came out like a windstorm.

"I think we have something that will work, but it is not our decision to make. Lily and the men are en route from the county jail. Ultimately, it will be their decision."

"Is it a good deal, Elizabeth? Will they be freed?" Katka asked.

"I hope so. Either way, you'll be able to see them. They should arrive shortly."

Katka's heart was beating so loudly she was certain that Old Joe could see it from under her clothes. She felt warm all over. Her brain began to spin. She was excited. She was terrified. Paul was coming. And he might be freed.

She heard the outside door in the foyer open and close. She held her breath and strained to listen. At first she thought she was imagining things. She heard something. A giggle. Followed by a high-pitched screech. The doors to the waiting room opened, and in walked a smartly dressed woman, a secretary perhaps, carrying an infant. The baby reached his arms toward Old Joe. "You family?" the woman asked. When Old Joe nodded, she handed baby Gregor to him.

A moment later Lily came in, her arms chained, her copper hair a mangled nest. There was a deep abrasion on her cheek. Her nose was misshapen. She walked in a shuffle, her legs enjoined by manacles. She was escorted by a police officer.

"Lily!" Katka cried. She ran toward her *teta* and threw her arms around her neck.

Lily turned her head and kissed Katka's cheek. "How's my little *matchka*?" she whispered.

"Stand down, ma'am!" the police officer cried. "Do not touch the prisoner! No physical contact!"

Katka held on tightly. "I love you, Lily. I absolutely love you." By the time the officer pried Katka's hands off Lily, Katka was sobbing. "Are you all right?"

Lily smiled wanly. "Seen better days. But I guess I've seen worse too." She glanced over at baby Gregor, who was content with Old Joe. She lowered her voice. "They fixing to kill me today?"

"No, Lily, that's not it."

Gregor squealed. Old Joe was tickling him.

"See my boy?" Lily said. "He's a strong one, he is. Going to win a popularity contest one day. Makes friends with everyone, even the rats. They don't make me wear these chains in the cell. Today's a different day. They don't tell me anything. I don't know what's happening. If they kill me, Katka, you have to take care of Gregor."

"They're not going to kill you."

"You're the godmother, that's your job. Didn't know what you signed up for, did you? Gregor's old enough now. He can go on the cow milk and do just fine. Ask Adeline if you have any questions."

"Come along now, Mrs. Kovich," the guard said. He gestured toward the wood door.

"What's happening, Katka? No one tells me a damn thing." The guard pushed Lily inside before Katka could respond. "Watch my boy," Lily yelled, disappearing behind the door leading to the negotiation room.

Katka and Old Joe heard more clanking sounds and men's voices from the foyer. Two guards entered, followed by Sam Scarlett and Carlo Tresca. They were manacled too.

Then she saw him. Paul. She took a deep breath and instinctively patted down her hair, as if she were getting ready for a photograph. He had grown a beard, and his face was grimy. But to Katka he looked like the most handsome man in the world. As beautiful as he had the day she met him. She wanted desperately to put her head on his scruffy neck and breathe in his scent, that smell of wind and salt. She wanted to bottle it up so when she missed him, she could inhale it. As long as she could recall his scent, he would always be with her. But the guard cautioned her to be still.

When Paul's eyes caught hers, he smiled. "You are a sight," he said to her. "I have been dreaming of your face for eight weeks."

"Please," Katka appealed to the guards, "can't we have just one minute together?" One of the guards hesitated, considering her words.

"Let me kiss her," Paul said quietly. His voice was different. Needy.

"No contact with the prisoners. Those are the rules." The guard shuffled Paul forward, and like Lily, Tresca, and Scarlett, he vanished behind the big door.

Next came Anton, Samo, and Dusca, all with glazed, fearful looks on their scruffy faces.

When Anton saw Katka, his eyes moistened. "Where is my Lily?" he asked.

"Right inside, Uncle. She is safe."

Elizabeth Gurley Flynn followed them as the last of the guests were escorted to the sequestered room. She waved meekly.

Once again, Katka and Old Joe were alone. Or almost alone. Little Gregor was nestled on Old Joe's lap, tugging on his white beard. They waited.

CHAPTER 51

"**L**OOK AT THIS ONE," OLD JOE SAID. HE WAS HOLDing the baby upright on his lap. "Three months old and he can already bear weight on his skinny little legs. I remember when my boy was this little. Sure do miss that little fella."

Katka leaned over and kissed baby Gregor. She couldn't believe how much he had changed in three months.

They sat with the boy for an hour. Then several men whom Katka had never seen before and some she recognized as lawyers for the prosecution came out of the negotiation room and into the foyer. They were smoking and talking about going to get a sandwich. Katka studied their faces for signs, but all she saw was fatigue.

Elizabeth entered the foyer. She motioned them inside.

"You can come now," she said. "I told them you were family. Now that the details have been hashed out and the deal's on the table, they say you can come in. The lawyers have given them some time to make up their minds."

Old Joe picked up baby Gregor who had been lying on his tummy on the floor. They walked into the room.

No one was shackled anymore. Two guards stood at the door, looking bored. These prisoners were too engrossed in conversation to think about escaping.

Lily and Anton sat together. She held both of his hands.

"Do not do it, Anton. Do not do this," she pleaded.

Samo and Dusca sat nearby. They were talking to defense attorney Arthur Le Sueur.

"You are sure, one year?" Samo asked.

"If you trust what they say," Le Sueur said. "It is a leap of faith."

"It is not," Elizabeth said. "I would trust them. Attorney Greene gave me his word. You will not serve more than one year."

Carlo Tresca and Sam Scarlett were the only ones who looked calm. They were joking with one another. Tresca passed Scarlett a flask of whiskey that Mr. Le Sueur had given them. "Ah, I missed that," Tresca said.

Katka went directly to Paul. She hugged him. When he squeezed her with his strong arms, she felt safe for the first time in months.

"Paul," Katka asked, "are they going to let you go?"

"Most likely. Monday at the earliest."

Katka kissed his lips. "That's positively grand!" she whispered.

Paul's face was troubled. "It's a fair deal for me, for Scarlett, for Tresca. I don't think it is for the others. I tried to tell them. Anton will not be persuaded. For the first time in his life, he won't listen to a lick of logic."

"What do you mean?"

"The prosecution said if they don't take the deal, they will seek the death penalty. I think they are bluffing. But I don't know. We hear so little about the outside. But once they brought up Lily, Anton made up his mind."

"To do what?"

The lawyers for the prosecution entered.

"We are ready for your decision," Greene said.

"We are ready to give it, I tell you," Anton said. He waited for the lawyers to take their seats. Then he proceeded in a calm, metered voice. "We agree to your terms, absurd as they are. Tresca, Scarlett, and Schmidt will be set free, as they should be. Charges will be dropped on Monday, as you say, and they will be freed. But my wife and my son, both innocent as babes, will be let go at once. Not Monday. Today. Never again will she wear your chains of shame. My son will spend all of his remaining days in the sun. They get to go home with Katka and Old Joe. If not, there will be no deal."

The prosecuting attorneys looked at each other. They exchanged words Katka could not hear.

"Go on," Greene said to Anton.

"My wife will be free, all charges dropped. In exchange, Samo, Dusca, and I will plead guilty to murder in the first degree."

Katka and Old Joe gasped. Lily sobbed openly.

"With the agreement," Elizabeth Gurley Flynn stated emphatically, looking at Lily, "that none of the three men will serve more than a year in jail. Correct, Attorney Greene?"

"That is our agreement, yes, Mrs. Flynn."

Defense Attorney Le Sueur spoke up. "Samo, Dusca. You are sure? Anton speaks for all three of you? I have told you my opinion. I think you should bring it to a jury. There's a good chance you will win. And any imprisonment for a crime you did not commit is unjust."

"A year in prison is better than twenty," Samo said.

"Anton speaks for all of us," Dusca said. "*Teta* Lily, she been through enough."

As the men in suits wrote in their notebooks, Lily said goodbye to Anton. He held the wriggling Gregor close.

Katka and Paul made their way toward the corner of the room, farthest from the guards. They sat on two chairs, their knees touching.

"On Monday, in just two days, when court resumes, they are to set you free. We will be together."

Paul nodded. "I don't know what the judge will do, Katka. I've been to these hearings before. When you're a Wobbly, they make some funny stipulations. I'm not saying it will happen, but it might."

"What do you mean?"

"Listen. I don't know how much time we have. It's important that you do something for me. Don't tell a soul. Do you remember the proverb I asked you to deliver to Anton when we were at Ellis Island? What do you do after you tell the truth?"

"Run. To the fields."

"And do you remember the message?"

"About the broken lock on my trunk?"

Paul nodded. Then he gave her some specific instructions.

Additional guards came in to haul the prisoners away. Before they manacled Paul, he thrust a tiny slip of paper into Katka's hand.

"See you, Monday, my little tiger," he whispered.

CHAPTER 52

THE TRIP BACK IN ELIZABETH GURLEY FLYNN'S motorcar was a quiet one. Lily and the baby sat in front. At first Gregor laughed at the feel of the air blowing in his face as the motorcar sped along. When they approached Island Lake, three eagles flew overhead.

"Should we stop so the baby can see them?" Elizabeth asked. "Eagles are good luck."

Lily was despondent. She shrugged, so Elizabeth kept driving, humming a familiar Wobbly tune.

Katka unfolded the paper Paul had given to her. The script was messy, written quickly. "Come with me," it read.

When they arrived home, it was dark, and most of the boarders were asleep. Katka hauled the water and heated it for Lily's bath. While Lily and the baby soaked, Katka cooked a pot of rice and added chopped tomatoes. She and Lily sat in the kitchen eating.

"Needs paprika," Lily said, smiling slightly. "You'd think you'd be a better cook by now."

"My teacher has been away."

Lily looked like a new person. Her hair was neatly braided, her face was clean, and she moved with ease in her dressing gown. Gregor was asleep in her bedroom, nestled between two pillows. "Do you want to talk?" Katka asked.

"My heart is too full."

"No hurry."

When Lily finally went to bed, it was past midnight. It was quiet. Now would be the best time to go. If she waited until tomorrow, when it was light, she could be discovered. She put on a light coat and stockings to combat the mosquitoes and slipped out the kitchen pantry door. She grabbed a lantern, but did not light it. She waited for a moment until her eyes grew accustomed to the dark and then began walking, past the barn, past the sauna, down the trail to the fields.

She walked about a mile until she came to the place where the underground field bunker was hidden. Moving away the brush and opening the trap door, she slipped down the ladder into the familiar space. This was where the strike committee had met. This was where she had first become a Wobbly.

Katka lit her lantern and did as Paul had instructed. Crates were lined up on the walls, covered with wool blankets. She removed the blankets until she found the large crate stamped "Peterson's dry goods." With a great deal of effort, she managed to get it down to the floor. When she opened the crate, she saw her old trunk, the one she had brought from Slovenia. It looked just as she remembered. The lid compartment had a hatbox, a shirt compartment, a coin box, and a document box. The body of the trunk, where she had stored her typewriter, looked empty.

She reached inside and felt along the left side. One slat of wood was slightly rougher than the others. The grain was cut a different way. She pushed on the slat, just as Paul had told her to do. When she did, it gave way, revealing a secret compartment.

Inside were two small books. On the cover of each was written "Passport of Russia" in Russian. She opened the first one. Paul's name appeared with the surname "Ivanski." On the bottom right was a photograph of Paul taken on the ship. Under "comment" it listed his status as married. She quickly looked at the second passport. In the bottom right-hand corner was the photo of her taken on the ship. She looked younger and thinner. Although she was not smiling, her eyes were happy. The name on the passport was Katka Ivanski, married to Paul Ivanski. She put the two booklets in her corset, replaced the crate, climbed up the ladder, and walked slowly back to the big house. Katka Ivanski. That would take some getting used to.

The next morning was Sunday. News traveled quickly. Soon most of Biwabik had heard about Lily's release. Before 10 a.m., the house was full. Women came hauling baskets of bread and eggs to welcome her home. Men came too. They mostly spoke to Old Joe, who recounted all he had witnessed the day before in Duluth.

Adeline Sherek came too. She embraced Lily long and hard. They had shared a cell for those first few weeks and cemented a bond.

"I know you don't want visitors," Adeline whispered to Lily, looking around at the full house. "I didn't either. But it won't last. And it's important for them to see you home and free. It gives them hope. And a year is not so long as it sounds. Anton will be home before you know it."

Before leaving, Adeline gestured to Katka. "Walk with me?"

When they were out of view, Adeline stopped. "I've heard from some people. I'll sum up. It sounds as if they plan to honor the deal struck. But Johan Koski told me to tell you that Tresca, Scarlett, and your Paul are in great danger. It is important that they get out of town as soon as they are released. They should not return here. I don't know if Elizabeth understands this. You have got to get those men out of Duluth as soon as possible. There's a price on their heads. Paul alone is worth five hundred dollars. And if you can, don't bring Lily to the sentencing. She's seen enough." She whispered some instructions to Katka and put a handful of bills for incidentals in her apron pocket. Then Adeline left.

But the next morning, Lily was up and dressed before Katka. Helen Cerkvenik was sitting with Lily at the dining room table. Baby Gregor was lying on a blanket on the floor.

"I know how to take care of a child, Lily," Helen said. "I've had five, you know."

No amount of persuasion would keep Lily from going to the sentencing. When Elizabeth pulled up in her borrowed motorcar, Lily and Katka got in. Lily had assembled bundles of clothing, food, and books for the three prisoners who were not expected to be released. She included paper and quills so she could keep in touch with Anton. Katka had brought a few bundles herself.

The courthouse was packed with reporters. Nonetheless, when Lily arrived, she was immediately recognized, and the men in front made room so she, Katka, and Elizabeth would be seated near the prisoners. They were carrying the baskets of food and clothing they had brought. When they sat down, Katka noticed that Elizabeth's car key was placed in one of the baskets. She moved it into her own basket, the one she had prepared for Paul.

The men entered the courthouse right on schedule. They were seated next to their legal team. When Anton saw Lily clean and taken care of, he smiled. He tapped his heart. Lily did the same.

Soon after the judge called the courtroom to order, he asked Sam Scarlett, Paul Schmidt, and Carlo Tresca to stand.

"You have been charged with inciting murder by your speeches. I believe you have done exactly that. However, this court requires proof. At the recommendation of the prosecution, I hereby drop the charges against you and order your release."

Approximately half of the crowd erupted into applause. Lily and Elizabeth clapped furiously.

Katka held her breath. The judge was not finished talking. He looked harshly at the three men he had just released, who were embracing each other and shaking hands.

"Just a second there," the judge said. "I don't like your sort, and I'm not afraid to say it. This is a conditional release. You and your agitating kind are not welcome here. You must never return to St. Louis County. You have three days to get out. Leave the state. That goes for you too, missy," he said, pointing at the front row. "Mrs. Flynn must leave too."

"I am not on trial here, sir!" Elizabeth said indignantly. "And you certainly do not have jurisdiction over the entire state."

"Don't be so sure about that," the judge said. "Would you like to be held in contempt of court?" Katka pulled Elizabeth to her seat, where she sat mute.

The judge ordered Paul, Sam Scarlett, and Carlo Tresca to sit. He asked Anton, Samo, and Dusca to stand. The judge shuffled some papers. He put on his glasses and read a prepared statement.

"Mr. Anton Kovich, Mr. Samo Zupitz, and Mr. Dusca Kalsich," the judge said. "I have followed your case with great curiosity since your arrest on July the seventeenth. I have spent the better part of last night and this morning reviewing the sentencing agreement recommended by the prosecution and the defense. You are aware of the terms of this agreement, are you not?"

"We are," Anton said.

"Then you are aware, no doubt, that in this agreement, all three of you men have confessed to the murder of Deputy Jackson. You are guilty of manslaughter. Your signatures all appear on the document. I feel compelled to apprise you that unlike the team of lawyers with whom you met, I do not take lightly to the crime of killing an officer of the law. I think you are cold-blooded killers."

"This can't be happening," Lily whispered to Katka. "What is he saying?"

"Therefore," the judge continued, "I reject the recommendation of the prosecution and the defense. Based on this signed confession, I hereby sentence Mr. Anton Kovich, Mr. Samo Zupitz, and Mr. Dusca Kalsich to twenty years of hard labor to be served at the St. Louis County Jail. You have the right to appeal, but do not expect to win."

As he adjourned the court, Lily fainted. She never got to say goodbye to Anton.

CHAPTER 53

As KATKA FANNED LILY, TRYING TO ROUSE HER, Katka looked toward Paul.

"You have to help her," Katka said to Elizabeth.

"I will," Elizabeth said. "I'll take care of everything."

"You have to," Katka said. "It was your deal."

Elizabeth went white. "Attorney Greene gave me his word, Katka. Honest. I would never have sold your men out to save ours. Never. You must believe me. They'll release them in a year, tops."

Katka walked quickly toward Paul, who was still at the front of the courtroom, surrounded by reporters. She carried a large basket covered with a blanket. He raised his eyebrows at her. She nodded. Slowly he inched his way toward her until they were together.

"Unbelievable," Paul said. "Do you still want to go through with it?"

"Adeline will take care of Lily. And Helen." She pulled Paul forward, grabbing his hand. "We don't have much time," she said. "I've got the key to Elizabeth's car."

The courtroom was chaotic. People were yelling, screaming, celebrating, mourning. Katka and Paul took advantage of the commotion. They dodged their way between people and finally made it outside.

"I'll drive," she said.

When they were both inside the vehicle, Paul wrapped his arms around Katka and kissed her. "You got the passports?" he asked.

"In the basket," Katka said. She drove while Paul talked.

"Twenty years," Paul said. "I can't believe it. I should not be surprised, after everything I've seen. But I am. Surprised. How can that be? Jail must have scrambled my brain finally."

"Says something about your nature. No matter how many injustices you see, you keep thinking that right is just around the corner. Makes you an optimist in spite of yourself." Katka sped up, driving frantically. "We must get to the train station before they start to look for you. Adeline told me there is a price on your head."

"I figured."

"It's a handsome head."

"If you think so, you really must love me. I've been dirtier and smellier, but I can't say when."

By the time they reached the station, they had discussed their plan. They would take the next train out. They would go to the biggest city on the schedule and eventually find their way to New York, where they would board a ship to Russia. They would use their Russian passports to enter the country.

"And when we get there," Paul said, "We'll find a priest to marry us. And we'll have ten little girls who all look exactly like their mother. We'll name them all Katka. What else do you have in that basket? I'm starved."

Katka reached in and gave him a roast beef sandwich and a beer.

When they got to the station, Katka checked the schedule. She used the money Adeline gave her to purchase two tickets to New York City, with a transfer in Chicago. It was as if they would be retracing her steps, the steps that had led her to the Iron Range in the first place.

"We're in luck," Katka said to Paul. "They are boarding now. The train leaves in ten minutes."

They took their seats on the train. The whistle blew to signify that the train was about to depart.

"One moment," Katka said. She kissed Paul on the cheek. "Ladies' room."

She slipped out, leaving her basket on her seat. She strode down the aisle of the train. She hesitated briefly at the exit. The whistle blew a final time. Katka took a deep breath, opened the door, and left the train and Paul behind.

A moment later she stood on the platform, holding nothing but Elizabeth's car key. The train lurched forward, and Katka felt as if she had swallowed her heart. She tried to make out Paul's head through the windows, his curly locks, but saw nothing. When the last car whisked by, she simply stood in place, staring at nothing. A moment later she was shaking. Then she sobbed. At some point—it might have been a minute, it might have been an hour—a train station attendant gently escorted her off the platform.

She found Elizabeth's motorcar and drove back to the courthouse to find her aunt.

"Stop your tears," she told herself. "Be strong for Lily."

***

It took Paul fifteen minutes to realize Katka had left him. He walked up and down the aisle of the train. He asked another female passenger to check the ladies' room. Finally, back in the compartment, he opened the basket. Inside, just under the linen towel, he found a photograph. It was of him and Katka on the ship. Her hair blowing wildly in the onset of a storm. He was smiling, just a little, and bolt of lightning divided the sky behind them. How he had longed for that picture when he was imprisoned at Ellis Island. He wondered how Katka had come upon it. Under the photo, he found a flower. He had no idea what kind. It was familiar and unfamiliar at the same time. It looked like a daisy, but it was pink. He also found an envelope and opened it. Katka had placed the Russian passport with his picture in it. Fifty dollars was tucked neatly inside. There was also a note:

Dearest Paul,

I love you. I love everything about you, and I would love to be your wife. But I cannot live a life on the run. When you met me, I had no home, no purpose. I was soft as clay, impressionable as a child. But I am no longer a child. Anton and Lily gave me a home. The newspaper gave me a sense of worth, and the injustice suffered by the people of the Range, the people who are now my people, gave me a purpose. I want to continue to fight for the rights and dignity of these people, who are like family to me. If I have learned one thing since this dreadful strike began, it is this: You cannot change a situation by leaving it.

It pains me more than I can express to know that we will be separated by an ocean, but you will be alive. Your life will no longer be in danger. That will be enough for me. My days will be long without you. I will never forget you. I urge you to find happiness in your new life and not let memories of me impede on your future days. I write this with a heavy heart.

Your Katka

EPILOGUE

I T WAS 1924. EIGHT YEARS HAD PASSED SINCE THE brutal strike of 1916.

The weather was perfect for July: cool air and bright sun. Lily and Katka were decorating five wooden tables in the backyard of the Slovenski Dom. They laid out tablecloths and, careful not to prick their fingers, put small bundles of wild roses in the vases. They carted dishes outside and carefully arranged them on the placemats.

"How's the pig coming, Joe?" Lily called out. She could smell it cooking over the fire pit.

Old Joe emerged from near the smokehouse. "He's dead," Old Joe said, walking toward them.

Lily laughed. "I suppose that's a good thing. They're easier to eat that way."

"I still don't know why you're making me cook for my own party," Old Joe said. "I'm an old man."

"Seventy years is a long time. Sit a spell, Joe," Lily said. "Half the town is coming to wish you happy birthday. You best be rested."

"They're only coming because they can't believe I lived this long. Want to witness a miracle."

So much had changed since the strike. Fashions had changed. Politics had shifted. The town of Biwabik was different. Except for Old Joe, all the old boarders had gotten married or moved. Even though it was 1924, Iron Rangers still used 1916 as a way to measure time. They would begin a story by saying, "A few years after the strike..." or "Not long before the strike..."

For those who stayed on the Range, the years before and the years after blended together, but that summer stuck in their minds as if it had happened yesterday. After the sentencing of Anton and the miners in Duluth, Elizabeth Gurley Flynn had remained on the Range for two more months, refusing to obey the judge's order to leave the state. She and the local strike force tried to keep the strike alive, but they were defeated by hunger and despair. By September, the workers were near starvation, and they knew they would never survive a Minnesota winter without an income.

Despite demands from the Department of Labor, the Oliver Mining Company never negotiated with the union. The workers went back to the mines, vowing that when winter was over, they would strike again. U.S. Steel declared victory; they had broken the strike, and the workers had lost.

It wasn't until some time passed that people who lived and worked on the Range began to realize that, although their losses were easy to count, they had made gains too. In the four months of the strike, the steel company had lost millions of dollars. Although they appeared to never flinch when faced with the miners' concerns, they were actually terrified of another strike. To prevent the Mesabi miners from walking off the job again come spring, the company granted many of the miners' demands. It did not happen all at once. But for the first time in the history of mining in Minnesota, a company feared the consequences of ignoring its workers' concerns enough to make minor changes in safety and wages. In October, the Oliver increased wages by twenty percent. The following year, they increased them by another ten percent.

Across the nation, large companies learned lessons from the Mesabi strike. They, too, increased wages and improved conditions to prevent their own workers from going on strike.

"I wonder what time it is," Katka said, looking up at the sun. "People will be arriving soon." They were expecting at least fifty people to join them for the party.

"Oh my stars," Lily said. "I forgot to cut the watermelon. Did we forget anything else?"

"Not that I can think of."

While Lily was inside, a car pulled up. It was a bright blue, four-passenger sedan with shiny white tires. At the sound of the vehicle, four children came running from the barn. The oldest, a boy, was eight. The younger three were all girls.

"Who's here, *Teta* Katka?" Gregor asked.

"Who is it, Mama?" one of the little girls echoed. "Who has come in such a fancy motorcar?"

"Perhaps someone for your *ata*," Katka said. "Go get your father. He's taking a sauna." The little girls scurried off to get him. Gregor stayed by Katka.

The driver's side door of the car opened, and out stepped a man. He helped the backseat passengers get out of the car. All three were clean-shaven and dressed in suits and hats. Katka was shocked speechless.

"I don't believe my eyes," Old Joe said. He hobbled forward to greet the men.

"Who are they, *Teta* Katka?" Gregor asked. "Mafia men?"

Katka laughed. "Not Mafia men. The older one, his name is Mr. Le Sueur." He was the Wobbly lawyer who had defended Anton, Samo, and Dusca in one unsuccessful appeal after another, over the course of several years. The prosecuting attorney, Warren Greene, who had made the deal with Elizabeth Gurley Flynn, had been drafted into the Great War and was never heard from again. His promise that the men would serve no more than a year in jail was never kept.

"That one is Samo," Katka said, pointing. "The really tall one is Dusca, and that one there, the really handsome one coming out of the passenger side door, is..."

Lily came barreling out of the house. "Anton!" she cried.

"Come here, my precious flower!" He held out his arms, and she ran to him. She kissed his head, his forehead, his nose, and finally his mouth. She almost knocked him down.

Then she began talking nonstop as usual. "How did you get here?" Lily asked. "And why didn't you tell me you had another appeal? Are you free, really free?"

"I'm home to stay, Lily."

"Then you better get to know your son. Come on over here, Gregor. Meet your *ata*."

Gregor walked over to Anton, smiling shyly. Anton bent to his knees and looked into the boy's eyes.

"Look how grown you are. Guess we can't call you baby Gregor anymores. You're practically a man. You been a good boy, Gregor?"

"Yes, sir."

"You listen to your ma?"

"Yes, sir. Everybody listen to Ma. Don't nobody have a choice."

Anton laughed. He hugged Gregor tightly, then put his arm around Lily's waist.

"You did a good job raising him, Lily." Then in a lower voice, he whispered, "What you say we run off to the sauna and make another one?"

They looked toward the sauna and saw Paul jogging toward them with two of his daughters in tow. The other he carried on his shoulders. When he recognized Anton, Samo, and Dusca, he put his youngest down and embraced each man for a long time. He shook Le Sueur's hand.

"I'd heard you came back here, Paul," Le Sueur said. "That took guts."

"I tried to leave," Paul said. "But there are some places ain't meant to be left. I made it as far as Chicago before I turned around and came back to marry the most beautiful woman in the world." Paul kissed his wife on the forehead. Katka smiled.

"They give you a rough time?"

Paul shrugged. "Water under the bridge."

"It's good to be back," Anton said. "So good." He looked at his son, then looked around at the yard and the forest of pine that surrounded it. "This is the most beautiful place in the world." He took a deep breath.

They heard an accordion off in the distance. A few moments later they began to decipher voices.

"We're having a party, *Ata*," Gregor said. "For Old Joe's birthday!"

The townsfolk were coming up to the house from Biwabik. They were dressed in their party clothes and good shoes. As they walked, they kicked up the red dust from the road, but they didn't cough or care. Their children orbited around them. Their hearts were joyful, like new suns.

A NOTE ON THE HISTORICAL ACCURACY
OF THIS NOVEL

"Under Ground" is a work of fiction based on actual events that occurred in northern Minnesota during the tumultuous iron mining strike of 1916.

Some locations on the Iron Range were altered to make the story easier to follow; events in Biwabik in the novel sometimes actually occurred in neighboring towns. Also, the Range is peppered with mines, both open pit and underground. Milo's experience in the underground mine was based on my research not on a mine in Biwabik, but on an underground mine in Soudan, Minnesota, where my grandfather, father, and most of my uncles worked at some point in their lives.

Although characters were inspired by actual Iron Range natives, their lives and words as portrayed in this novel are imagined, placed in historical context of the times. For example, fictional character Milo Blatnik was inspired by two miners: Joe Greeni and John Alar. On June 2, 1916, Greeni led the strike walkout at the St. James mine and was followed by more than 20,000 men. On June 22, Alar, a husband and father of three, was fatally shot in the yard of his Hibbing home as picketers marched nearby. Alar's funeral procession followed a black banner that read "Murdered by Oliver Gunmen," photographs of which are available at the Discovery Center in Chisholm, Minnesota. Thousands attended, and his death marked a turning point in the uprising. The character of Lily Kovich was also an amalgamation of two real people: my grandmother, Mary Kalsich Kuzma Marsnik, whose family ran a boarding house for miners in Ely, Minnesota; and by Melitza Masonovitch of Biwabik. More on Melitza later.

The "What We Want Is More Pork Chops" speech delivered in the novel by fictional character Andre Kristeva was a real speech delivered June 22, 1916, by mining clerical worker and IWW activist George Andreytchine, who was friends with Margaret Sanger and Leon Trotsky.

The real names of national and state figures are used in this novel with their words and actions captured as closely as a work of fiction would allow.

Strike organizers did declare war on U.S. Steel. Frank Little, Sam Scarlett, Carlo Tresca, Arthur Boose, Elizabeth Gurley Flynn, Big Bill Haywood, and other Industrial Workers of the World (IWW) labor organizers played a key part in the 1916 strike, although their roles are fictionalized in this novel. Minnesota Gov. Joseph Burnquist and his actions during the strike are accurately presented within the context of a fictional story.

Socialist presidential candidate Eugene Debs did not speak in Duluth, but wrote extensively about the Mesabi strike and was a major advocate for the miners. The speech he gives in this novel is excerpted from an article written by Debs, titled "Murder in the First Degree."

Dr. Andrea Hall was an Iron Range doctor remembered as a great friend to miners and lumberjacks, but the events in which she is portrayed are fictional.

The Oliver Mining Company did hire its own guards to patrol the mining towns, and hundreds were deputized during the strike. The altercation with one such deputy at the tavern of fictional characters Anton and Lily Kovich was inspired by an actual incident at a Biwabik boardinghouse owned by Philip and Melitza Masonovich. Deputy John Myron and bystander John Ladvala were killed during the raid. Melitza Masonovich was badly abused and beaten. She was placed in a jail cell with her 9 month old baby. Philip Masonovitch and his boarders were also arrested for the alleged murder of a lawman. No charges were filed for the death of Ladvala, who was a sodapop delivery man.

Prosecutor Warren Greene did make an agreement with IWW leader Elizabeth Gurley Flynn that the men who agreed to guilty pleas would serve no more than one year of their twenty-year term. But Greene went off to war, and it took several years of appeals before Masonovich and his boarders were released.

When people think about strikes, particularly an iron miners' strike, most think of the men involved. But in every desperate situation, there are women working too. Women who must explain to the children why there is no food. Women who, like the women on the Range, took to the dangerous picket lines when the men were forbidden. Women who were willing to sacrifice nearly anything to ensure that their children would have a better future. These women were real. They still exist. As my grandmother Mary used to say, they hold up "three corners of the house."

—Megan Marsnik

ACKNOWLEDGEMENTS

Thank you to all my teachers.

My mother, Jayne Marsnik; my father, Fuzzy Marsnik; and my grandmother, Mary Kalsich Kuzma Marsnik taught me to be proud of where I come from. Thank you.

Marvin G. Lamppa's book, "Minnesota's Iron Country: Rich Ore, Rich Lives" was paramount in providing historical, geographical, and cultural context for the novel. Neil Betton's essay, *Riot, Revolution, Repression in the Iron Range Strike of 1916* was also a golden source. Kathy Bergan of The Iron Range Historical Society in Gilbert, Minnesota provided crucial historical documents in the early stages of my research. Although all mistakes are mine alone, John Zakelj of the Twin Cities Slovenians selflessly agreed to review the Slovenian words used in the book. Karel Winkelaar, retired miner and Soudan Underground Mine tour guide, provided valuable feedback on the scenes that took place underground.

This book was drafted at The Loft Literary Center in Minneapolis, where I met my writers' group. William Burleson and Stephen Wilbers provided careful critiques and much-needed encouragement during all stages of the writing process. I am extremely grateful to my early readers: Katy Gorman, Shannan Marsnik, Peggy Wilson, Mary Stachovich, Colleen Gorman, Susan Marsnik, Neva Simmonsen, Kathy Hill Gray, Marissa Bertram, Paul Winkelaar, and Jessica Winkelaar. Thank you to Tyeastia Green, David Setnicker, and Ross Phernetton who provided inexplicable support in the writing and marketing of the final version. Thank you to Liz Otremba, for her brilliant cover design and for her friendship.

I am indebted to *Star Tribune* books editor Laurie Hertzel and to assistant managing editor Kate Parry for selecting "Under Ground" as its serialized novel for 2015. Kate Parry meticulously edited the first version of this novel. Thank you to Vicki Adang, who edited this version. Thank you, William Burleson of Flexible Press for Publishing "Under Ground." I feel honored to be published by a press with such an amazing mission statement.

Finally, thank you to my son Quincy and to my daughters Maddy and Georgia who inspire me daily. This history is your history.

59057605R00200

Made in the USA
Columbia, SC
31 May 2019